'What are you in

again.

'Oh, I'm the doc

She peered up at

she had contact len

'Yes.'

'A proper doctor?'

'I think so. I mean yes. You know. The ship's doctor . . . What do you do?'

'Teacher. Didn't you guess?'

'No.'

'Been here before?'

'No.'

'Like it?'

'Hardly seen it.'

'A weekend's about right. Are you really a doctor?'

'Yea . . . Why do you keep asking?'

She lowered her voice and said, 'A friend of mine met a chap from a nuclear submarine. Said he was a gynaecologist. She should have known.'

Colin Douglas

Wellies from the Queen

ARROW BOOKS

Arrow Books Limited
17–21 Conway Street, London W1P 6JD

An imprint of the Hutchinson Publishing Group

London Melbourne Sydney Auckland
Johannesburg and agencies
throughout the world

First published by Hutchinson 1981

Arrow edition 1982

Made and printed in Great Britain
by The Anchor Press Ltd
Tiptree, Essex

ISBN 0 09 927590 2

PART ONE

'Sorry, Campbell, but someone's got to do it.'

'Thank you, sir.'

'I don't think you understand, Cameron. I said someone's got to go. Someone's got to do it.'

'Fine, sir. Thank you.'

'Can you hear me all right, Campbell? Terrible line.'

'Loud and clear, sir.'

'Good. Anyway. Sorry about all this. And sorry about the short notice. What I'm saying is that someone's got to do it and you're the only chap we've got spare just now, so you're the one who's going to have to go.'

'Thank you, sir.'

'Can you hear what I'm saying . . . um . . . Campbell?'

'Yessir.'

'So you'll go. Like a good chap.'

'Happy to, sir.'

'Sorry and all that. Especially with Christmas coming on. Going away up there . . . Far from England, home and beauty.'

'It's all right, sir.'

'Of course. You're from Scotland.'

'Yessir.'

'And I'm told Christmas isn't such a big thing up there.'

'No, sir.'

'But you'll be away for New Year as well, you know. And Hog-whatever-it-is.'

'Hogmanay, sir.'

'That's more important, isn't it?'

'Yessir, but . . .'

'I'm sorry, Campbell. Someone's got to do it.'

'That's all right, sir.'

'What?'

'I said it's all right, sir. I expected to be away.'

'On leave? Yes. People generally get away for Christmas. But this business up there makes it all different.'

'No, sir. I mean I expected . . .'

The surgeon captain, or perhaps even surgeon rear admiral, on the other end of the line was in no mood for explanations. He was out to pass on bad news, regardless of how it was being received. 'You're going, Campbell. And that's that.'

'Yessir.'

'That's the spirit. Good of you to take it that way and not moan. Thank you . . . Have a good trip . . . and . . . Merry Christmas.'

'Thank you, sir. Same to you . . . Sir?'

'What now, Campbell?'

'What ship, sir?'

The line crackled and Campbell asked him to repeat what he had just said. This time the line was clear but the speech indistinct.

'Say again, please, sir.'

'Oh, God. I spell. Whisky India November Charlie Hotel Echo Sierra Tango Echo Romeo.'

Campbell, to whom the standard NATO phonetic alphabet was not yet second nature, had got lost after 'Whisky'. 'Say again, please, sir.' The crackling had died down.

'*Winchester*!' the appointer bawled. 'Bloody *Winchester*! Like the school and the jail. *Win-chester*.'

'Thank you, sir . . . And where . . . ?'

'I suppose you'll want to know where she is?'

'Yes, please, sir.'

'Hmm . . . That's difficult. She's somewhere I'm not supposed to talk about on the phone.'

'Oh . . .'

'By rights I should get my chap to signal Ops Room down your way. Or your ship, I suppose. But he might have sloped off. Where are you?'

'Portsmouth, sir. On a ship.' Campbell was immediately conscious of a small lapse. Naval personnel were not 'on' ships, but 'in' them.

'What ship are you in?'

'*Cerberus*, sir.'

'Of course . . . That's where my chap tracked you down. So if I can find him again I'll get him to wop off a quick signal to you in *Cerberus* saying where *Winchester* is.'

'Thank you, sir.'

'Oh, God. Look, I'll . . . sort of tell you . . . now. Can you think of somewhere . . . up your way . . . that makes you think of sheep?'

Campbell could not. 'Not immediately, sir.'

'Oh. That makes it difficult.' Campbell was beginning to get cold. 'It's a loch, actually.'

'Yessir.'

'That makes *you* think of sheep.'

'Oh. I get it, sir. You mean Loch . . .'

'Careful, Campbell.'

'Yessir. I know where you mean.'

'Good. So get yourself up there by tomorrow.'

'Yessir . . . Should I take anything special?'

'Well . . . I shouldn't bother with your tropical kit. Merry Christmas, Campbell. Glad I caught you.'

'Thank you, sir. Merry . . .' The line had gone dead. Campbell put the phone down, reflecting that leaving his tropical kit behind posed no problems. He didn't have any, a fact that troubled him slightly. It was another aspect of his not quite belonging.

He turned from the phone and started to walk across the quarterdeck to the door which led down to warmth and the wardroom. Able Seaman Gudgeon, the bosun's mate, caught his eye and smiled. In a long dark blue overcoat with its collar turned up, Gudgeon was warm enough. He leaned on the top of his tall desk, a varnished wooden affair like a lectern, with a yellowish light directed down on to the various lists and orders perpetually enshrined under its perspex surface. He peered across at Campbell in the gathering dusk, his face lit from below, grinning like a gargoyle that had specially descended from the eaves to read the lesson at evensong below in some surrealist cathedral. 'A little draft, sir?'

'Sounds like it.'

'Sounded more like a pierhead jump.'

'Well, you know what they say,' said Campbell. 'That's life in a blue suit.' The bosun's mate grinned even more fiercely, and Campbell felt slightly fraudulent, having learned only a matter of days before that that was what they said.

''sright, sir. If you can't take a joke . . .'

'. . . shouldn't have joined the service,' said Campbell, completing the quasi-liturgical exchange, another acquisition of the last fortnight.

The sailor leaned back and made an expansive gesture with both gloved hands. For an absurd moment Campbell thought that this demonic celebrant – in his ammo boots, white gaiters, greatcoat with white webbing belt, whistle and chain, and cap (sailor's, round, white, with cap-tally reading HMS CERBERUS) – was about to pronounce a benediction. He may have looked puzzled. The bosun's mate leaned forward again. 'Leaving us tonight, sir?'

'Looks like it.'

'You'll want a taxi then?'

'I suppose so.'

'And the times of trains to *Nemesis*.'

'*Nemesis*?'

'Yessir. HMS *Nemesis*. Shore establishment. On Loch Ewe. Where you're going. To join *Winchester*.'

The bosun's mate seemed to know a lot. 'Know anything about *Winchester*?'

'An 'ell-ship, sir.'

'What?'

'My mate from *Raleigh*'s on 'er.' The rules of naval diction were observed less strictly on the lower deck. 'An absolute 'ell-ship, 'e says. Still. Can't be helped. Someone's got to go.'

'So he kept saying.'

'I 'eard 'im. Now let's get you the trains for *Nemesis* . . . Glasgow for starters.' He opened the top of his pulpit. 'Then

Mallaig.' The desk contained a large box of cigarettes, several railway timetables, a racing newspaper and a form book, a handful of foil-wrapped contraceptives and a selection of the most explicit pornography that Campbell, being a hitherto untravelled man, had ever seen.

'Let's see,' said the bosun's mate, riffling through the grubby pages of the appropriate timetable. The ship moved slightly, responding to the passage of some larger vessel in the main channel outside. The gangway creaked. The woven cane fenders between the ship's side and the wall squealed and sighed. A necklace of bare bulbs, rigged above the gangway to light drunken sailors safely to their bunks, danced in slow time, unsettling the shadows on the quarter-deck. 'Let's see,' he said again. 'You'd be lucky to get a sleeper up first night of Christmas leave. But you'll get there sitting. Or standing, sir, if your luck's out. And the 0943 from Glasgow Queen Street. You'll be there in time for your dinner tomorrow on the 'ell-ship.'

'Thanks, Gudgeon.'

The bosun's mate looked at Campbell again and furrowed his brows. 'Don't mention it, sir . . . Sir . . . am I right in thinking you . . . wanted to go?'

'Up there?'

'Yes.'

'Well, yes. I mean I was expecting to. With *Cerberus*. I mean in *Cerberus*. And in my last ship.'

'We was lucky. Very lucky. Nobody fancied it. Highly fortuitous, that condenser trouble.'

'Well, I don't mind going.'

It was clear that the bosun's mate considered that such irresponsible enthusiasm on the part of officers was the cause of at least half the trouble in the Navy. He shook his head and ceremoniously lowered the lid of his desk, slowly, between outstretched gloved palms, resuming the blank, eyes-front demeanour of a junior rating who would not dream of eavesdropping on officers' telephone calls, especially those concerned with sensitive postings. Campbell went below to his cabin to pack, for the fourth or fifth time since taking the Queen's shilling.

HMS *Winchester*, if ever he found her, would be his third

ship in three weeks. This was not Campbell's fault, or indeed that of the probably drunk appointer who had just put the phone down. It was simply a hazard of naval posting, and part of the larger, richer tapestry of life. His first ship, HMS *Lachesis*, had been standing by to go north at four hours' notice. Tension had eased, and she had been withdrawn to her home port to wait a week at forty-eight hours' notice, before coming off the standby list to resume her previous programme. His second ship, the *Cerberus*, naturally at the other end of the country, had actually put to sea in response to renewed crisis shortly after he had joined her. One day out from Rosyth she had succumbed to the condenser trouble alluded to by the bosun's mate. The engineers had nursed her all the way back to Portsmouth, judging it nicely for Christmas, and most of the ship's company were now off on unexpected but universally acceptable Christmas leave.

Campbell, having twice expected to go up to the scene of the action, and having twice been stood down, found his attitude changing from one of resignation to one of thwarted ambition, and had phoned the appointer's office several times in the previous twenty-four hours to ask if any of the ships now being ordered north still needed a doctor. Various clerks and secretaries had taken messages, and nothing had happened; then the appointer himself, no doubt clearing his desk between the office party and his own Christmas leave, had rung up to bully him into something he now wanted to do anyway, presumably because he needed to find a medical officer for a ship, and no one had passed Campbell's message on to him. That, plus the after-effects of the postulated office party, would go a long way to explaining the confusion of the phone call.

In the train north Campbell had time, if not comfort, in which to contemplate his varying fortunes of the previous weeks. Only a month before, his six-month appointment in the casualty department of his teaching hospital almost complete, he had found himself without a job to go to, but not too worried about it. No obvious career presented itself, and he had no particular reason for staying in Edinburgh. He was twenty-six. He had a medical degree and, perhaps more importantly, he had had some practical experience. Eighteen months of lowly clinical toil, divided equally between medicine, surgery and casualty, was enough to convert his innocent parchment into a useful passport. Even his six-month stint in research was not the complete waste of time it had once seemed. It had permanently averted his ambitions from the *longueurs* and posturings of academic medicine and appeared now in retrospect to constitute another vivifying and liberating experience. If he didn't want to be a proper physician in a teaching hospital, there were a thousand-and-one related inane pursuits which he no longer even had to pretend to be interested in.

Casualty had proved, as Mr Gillon had predicted, an ideal job for someone who hadn't made up his mind. Campbell had emerged from it tired, but considerably extended, capable now of basic bonesetting, of cobbling up most lacerations, of a little amateur psychiatry and of sorting out the various commoner medical emergencies, whose victims seemed to have no regard for the proprieties of the textbooks, but played things along individually, which was irritating at first, but fine when you eventually got used to it. Haltingly, diffidently and only some two years after graduating, he had felt early stirrings of something approximating to professional responsibility – which, on closer examination, amounted only to a feeling that, at a moderately severe street accident, he would be of more use than a Boy Scout or a St John's Ambulance lady with smelling salts.

He was grateful and had said as much at the customary fatherly farewell with Mr Gillon, who had thanked him in turn and said, as is usual on these occasions, that he would be glad to help his departing junior in any way possible. ('The usual stuff. References. A quiet word here or there. That sort of thing . . .') Then their conversation had taken a curious turn, and ten minutes later Campbell found himself walking out of Casualty, with a year to kill but the firm assurance of a job as senior house officer on Mr Gillon's general surgical unit at the end of it.

Life had been quite pleasant since then. Perhaps for the first time in his career, Campbell was the object of the professional envy of his contemporaries. Even Bones had been grudgingly impressed, as Gillon's SHO post was much sought after. Various surgically oriented oafs, who had started cutting each others' throats for it as early as fourth year, spending absurdly long hours on the unit and crawling to everyone from the senior registrar to the tea lady, made scathing remarks which Campbell graciously chose to ignore. There were only two problems, or perhaps one-and-a-half: the first was that of the year between, now providentially being solved by a reserve commission in Her Majesty's Navy; the second, upon which Campbell had spent less time and even less thought, was that he was not sure in his heart of hearts that he wanted to be a surgeon.

The station at Mallaig was dark and rainswept. Just beyond the ticket barrier a man in a nondescript, slightly naval uniform and a peaked cap was waiting. He saw Campbell looking round, stepped forward and said, '*Nemesis*, sir?' Campbell followed him to a waiting car, wondering how transport had been booked and what had prompted the driver to pick him out as its appropriate passenger. The latter point was more easily settled: of the dozen or so weary survivors still on the train at Mallaig, Campbell, though not particularly naval-looking ('anchor-faced', sailors called it), was the only male of service age whose hair did not touch his shoulders, and hence the only possible client for service transport. The former point, how anyone had known to organize it, remained obscure, but that seemed to be the sort of thing that happened in the Navy. You were propelled randomly across and around the country in the service of obscure higher purposes and, just when you were beginning to have doubts about it all, some gesture like this, ordained by a kind of benign institutional telepathy, rescued you and allayed your suspicions.

Campbell settled into the car while the driver put his case in the back. Deliberately and enjoyably, he began to forget the crowds, discomfort, sleeplessness and aching boredom of the journey now almost over. 'Durty night,' said the driver, in a soft Highland voice. Campbell agreed, and nothing more was said for the forty miles of black glens and torrential rain between Mallaig and whatever came next.

The main gate of HMS *Nemesis* was very impressive, even in the dark and the rain, and much more imposing than the entrance to any other naval shore establishment that Campbell had ever seen. They had already passed several off-putting signs warning successively that there was no through road, that it was inadvisable to proceed further unless on duty, that police dogs patrolled the area regularly and that all baggage was liable to thorough search.

The gate itself stood at the end of a long alley of high wire-mesh fences, and was closed. A red and white barrier was in place in front of it, and in front of that stood a Ministry of Defence policeman in a drenched cape, his head lowered in the rain. Under the high floodlights which lit the whole area, he had a dark, wet-metal sheen, and looked for all the world like a figure on a village war memorial, stone-still even when the driver had rolled the car forward to within inches of him and wound down the window.

The monument moved and shook itself, then leaned down towards the open window, water running from the peak of its cap.

'Oh, it's yourself, Donny. And who is the chentleman in the back?'

'It's the new doctor for HMS *Winchester*,' said the driver.

'I don't think I was expecting him . . . I wonder if the sarchant will know . . .'

'Where is she, Ian?'

'Oh, I'm afraid HMS *Winchester* is in the purple area, Donny . . . So I can't chust let you in as if it was the Broomielaw.' Rain ran, in a thinner but still steady stream, from the policeman's hat. 'And I don't suppose the doctor has a purple pass.'

'I wouldn't know,' said the driver. Campbell wound down the rear window and leaned towards the enquirer. A small monsoon caught him square in the face.

'Ah, doctor. Have you such a thing as a purple pass?'

'No,' said Campbell. 'I've got a . . .'

'Sorry, sir. I'm afraid we must insist on a purple pass. With all these nuclear deterrents about it's only sensible.'

'Of course,' said Campbell, who was beginning to find all this leisurely West Highland officiousness more trying than the ordinary kind. 'I've got an ID card.'

'Ah, an identity card. Now that would be a help, at least in establishing your identity, while we enquire into the whole question of allowing you access to the purple area . . . Thank you, doctor.' He took the proffered card, and held it just inside the stream of rain running from his cap. 'It's not a . . . not an ordinary ID card, is it, sir?'

'No,' said Campbell. 'It's . . .'

'So I'll just go now and show it to the sarchant, before we go into the question of letting you in amongst all the nuclear deterrents . . . If you don't mind waiting a moment, doctor . . .' He stomped away through the rain towards the lit windows of a low building on the right in front of the gate.

The driver turned round to Campbell. 'It's very difficult if you don't have a purple-area pass or a proper ID card. I expect they'll be making a few phone calls.'

After a while the policeman came across again. 'The sarchant is chust making a few phone calls, and would appreciate it very much if you could stay where you are, doctor, perhaps for chust a few minutes more. All right, Donny?' He resumed his memorial pose in front of the red and white barrier.

Rather more than a few minutes passed, then a voice summoned the policeman to the hut. He returned and beckoned to Campbell to follow him across. Campbell ran through the rain to a covered veranda.

'There's no hurry, doctor. No hurry at all. The important thing is to get it right. And the sarchant would like a few words to sort things out. So if you don't mind waiting . . . in the waiting room.' Campbell took a seat and familiarized himself with the various risks of rabies, the penalties for smuggling, a few points from the Official Secrets Act, the previous season's programme of the Loch Ewe and District Bowling Federation, the identification features of the Colorado beetle and the uniforms of Russian armoured corps and naval infantry, both winter and summer, from a selection of posters provided for the purpose.

He was just nodding off, to an agreeable reverie of the as

yet unseen sergeant being summoned, like Drake from a game of bowls, to deal with a Warsaw Pact amphibious assault, when the policeman came and took him to an inner room, where the sergeant sat at a desk.

'Sorry about all this, sir,' he said, in a brisk, businesslike accent from somewhere south of Watford. 'Just been checking up. Your ship's expecting you, but she's in a sensitive part of the establishment . . . and we haven't seen one of these for a while.' He held out Campbell's ID card, lightly by its corner, as though it were a very hot piece of toast.

Proper members of the Royal Navy carried a little plastic card with a colour photograph of themselves. Campbell's portrait, in black and white, mounted on the corner of a larger piece of buff cardboard, had a do-it-yourself look about it that had aroused the proper suspicions of the guardians of a base so secret that even surgeon rear admirals knew not to talk about it on the phone. Campbell took it from the sergeant and put it back in his wallet.

'Reservist, eh, sir?'

'Yes.'

'Used to meet 'em when I was in the mob meself. Gentlemen pretending to be sailors, we used to say. You up for your two weeks' training?'

'Sort of.'

In general Campbell tried to avoid casual conversations about his exact status. Most reservist doctors, having done a couple of weeks at Dartmouth learning the difference between a chief and a commodore, and the elements of naval vocabulary, such as calling your bedroom your cabin, were summoned to the colours for a couple of weeks every year, to further their training and eventually to fill slots while their regular colleagues went off on leave. Not many did what Campbell was doing, which was sufficiently unusual to come under suspicion of not being quite respectable. He had made enquiries and found out that not only was it possible to serve for longer periods, but that the medical branch of the Navy was so short of doctors as positively to welcome the services of reservists for more or less any time they were available.

'What do you mean "sort of"?' said the sergeant. Campbell wished he had simply said 'yes'.

'Well, I'm in for a bit longer than a fortnight.'

'Really?'

'Yes. Until I start a civvy job I've got lined up for next year.'

'I see,' said the sergeant. 'Thought you'd have a nice long holiday?' He smiled. Campbell wondered what paragon of naval medical idleness or incompetence the sergeant had come across in his service life. Campbell smiled back at him. 'Well, there we are,' he continued. 'Bad luck you got *Winchester* . . . Your driver'll take you down to her now.' He handed Campbell another piece of card, diagonally striped in buff and purple. 'This is a purple area temporary pass. Sign it on the front now. And sign it on the back when you hand it in to an authorized officer . . . Have a good trip.'

'Thanks, sergeant.'

'There are fixed penalties for being in unlawful possession of purple area temporary passes. Goodnight.'

Campbell went back to the car, which stood now between the red and white barrier and the gate. The policeman was chatting with the driver. The gate was not yet open but Campbell had a distinct feeling that progress had been made. Before he could get into the car and out of the rain, the policeman stopped him.

'Now, sir. If I might chust glance at your temporary purple card we can all be getting on with things . . .' Campbell took out his wallet, and eventually found the buff and purple card in a pocket along with his driving licence and banker's card. 'Perfect, sir. You see it's all perfectly easy. Chust a question of getting it right . . . With all these . . .'

'Thank you, constable . . .'

'Goodnight, sir. Goodnight, Donny.' He cast an unfavourable glance at Campbell and added darkly and softly a phrase probably Gaelic and definitely disparaging. While Campbell stumbled thankfully into the shelter of the car, the policeman walked over to a little glass sentry box at the side of the gate, opened it with a key on a chain and pressed a lever on a control panel, which caused the tall grey gate to slide silently open. The driver accelerated into the darkness, switching his headlights on moments later to reveal nothing but a shiny black ribbon of road curving on into the night.

Eventually, after about half a mile, signs of naval habitation began to appear. On the left was a single-storey brick guardroom, with a brass ship's bell hung in a well-lit veranda, and a block of cells stretching out behind. Once more the car stopped. Nothing happened. On the right was a large Nissen hut with an inn sign swinging above its door which read 'The Shaggy Sheep. HMS *Nemesis* Junior Rates Club'. The driver sounded his horn and very shortly afterwards a sailor in a long greatcoat and white belt, with the whistle and chain of office denoting a quartermaster, dashed out of the Nissen hut, round the back of the car and on to the veranda of the guardroom, where he stood for a moment before stepping gravely towards Campbell's car and saying to the driver, 'Halt. Who goes there? Oh. Hullo, Donny.'

'Doctor for *Winchester*.'

The quartermaster stooped and peered into the back. In the expectation of considerable delay and parleying, Campbell wound down his window. 'Hullo, sir,' said the quartermaster. 'Got your purple area pass from the coppers?' Campbell started to dig for his wallet again. 'Fine, sir,' said the sailor, waving the car on. 'Have a nice trip.'

They drove on. Buildings were thick on both sides of the road: miscellaneous accommodation blocks and workshops, mainly of wartime construction from the look of them, but patched up and painted for a fourth decade of temporary service, in the manner of most naval shore establishments Campbell had seen. The car turned right, down a drenched redbrick canyon between two high buildings and stopped before a barrier and gate rather like the first one, except that the policeman was standing in his glass sentry box out of the rain and there was a large white notice with purple lettering saying VETTED PERSONNEL AND PURPLE PASSHOLDERS ONLY in emphatic capitals.

Campbell had his pass ready for inspection. The policeman waved at the driver, and barrier and gate opened simultaneously. The car proceeded down the redbrick alley and turned right again, along a well-lit waterfront. Campbell shifted in the back to see as much as he could. What he saw somewhat puzzled him. Clusters of lights of the kind normally found at motorway roundabouts, but in this instance suspended from the towers of a forest of dockside cranes, lit a large, oblong tidal basin whose sole exit was from the middle of the opposite side. A launch, marked MOD POLICE puttered around in the oily rain-spattered water. In one of the further corners lay a small, slightly old-fashioned-looking frigate. There was no sign of the nuclear deterrent that had so preoccupied the first policeman: no submarine, aircraft carrier or other major warship could be seen, though there was room for several of each. The frigate, reduced by the scale of its surroundings to a status approaching that of a plastic duck in the bath, was, apart from the police launch, the sole floating occupant of the purple area basin. In large black characters on its side was its pennant number, F.126. With any luck, it would be HMS *Winchester*.

He knew a little about her already. She was one of a class that was no longer the Navy's pride, if indeed it ever had been. Designed originally to operate as part of a forward screen ahead of a carrier group, she had a big radar on top and a couple of heavy guns on front. Aft, on the quarterdeck where the gangway was, a smaller anti-aircraft gun was shrouded in a canvas hood. Her paintwork, even to the inexpert eye, was not perfect, but the name WINCHESTER picked out in red metal letters on her quarter gave Campbell infinite reassurance and a very welcome feeling of having got somewhere at last.

The car drew up at the foot of the gangway. The quarterdeck was lit and a grey-painted screen door opened off it into a covered space containing a standard quartermaster's desk. On the front of the desk hung an ornamental white lifebelt with the ship's crest in the middle and HMS WINCHESTER painted round it in blue letters. That added to the feeling of arriving. The driver unpacked Campbell's bags and waited while he got out, then drove off, turning tightly on the quay and receding off round the basin.

There was no sign of life on board. A quartermaster did not appear as expected, summoned from warmth and comfort by the noise of the car outside. It was still raining, so Campbell took the smaller of his bags and walked up the gangway, saluting the quarterdeck as he stepped on to it, as was the rule and custom, to be kept even in the absence of witnesses. He went back for the other bag, saluting the quarterdeck again, and feeling more self-conscious about it. There was still no one around.

The quartermaster's hideaway was empty, so Campbell proceeded forward and found a more promising screen door in the starboard waist. He opened it, negotiating its heavy steel clips with some difficulty and grazing a finger as he did so, and got out of the rain into the warmth and friendly whirring noise of the ship's interior. A short ladder led down one deck to the main passageway. There was still no sign of anyone. A door on the right was labelled 'Sickbay', and carried a little notice saying 'Emergencies seen at all times. Pipe for LMA. Other Cases 0830.' Campbell put down his bags and tried the door. It was locked.

There was a disturbance behind him. A sailor in a long greatcoat and a white belt came running up the passageway. He was wet all over, very drunk and clearly distressed by what Campbell was doing.

'Ye canny go in there. It's the bay. If ye're ill ye should get the LMA. He's doon his mess. But ye canny go in there.'

Campbell was about to explain himself, when a lieutenant appeared from the other direction, immaculate in mess undress of bow tie, stiff shirt, short black jacket and trousers cut far tighter than the regulations encouraged. He addressed the rating.

'Down, boy. Really. There's a good chap, McGuffy. We've been expecting Surgeon Lieutenant Campbell. Surprised you didn't meet him at the gangway.' He broke off and opened a door on the other side of the passageway and called, 'Reggy!' A voice replied, 'Sah!' and an enormous sailor appeared, clad only in flip-flops and blue Y-fronts. He stood to attention in front of the lieutenant. Campbell, in a civilian lounge suit, felt suddenly out of place. The drunk McGuffy quailed to attention.

'Get your hat, McGuffy,' said the lieutenant.

'Ah've goat it oan, sur,' said the sailor.

'You know perfectly well what I mean, McGuffy. You're in trouble again.' He turned to the man in underpants. 'Take charge, Reggy. The usual things plus being absent from place of duty, I expect. Thanks.' Finally he turned to

Campbell. 'My dear doctor, what you must think! What a welcome.'

The large man murmured, 'Come on, Sambo,' and led the man in the greatcoat away.

'He was probably doing what he thought was best,' said Campbell. 'I'm someone he's never seen, trying to get into the sickbay.'

'His best maybe.' The lieutenant smiled blandly. 'Too drunk, too late and in the wrong place. Come and meet the wardroom. We can sort out McGuffy later. Come and meet the chaps. Really. What you must think of us.' He paused, then said, 'Roddy Ayres. Navigator,' and stuck out a hand, which Campbell shook.

'David Campbell.'

'Yes. We were actually expecting you for dinner. But we'll get a cook to throw something together. Cheesy hammy eggy topside suit you?'

'Sounds fine. Thanks.'

'Trouble finding us?'

'The purple business at the end was a bit trying. Otherwise fine.' Campbell had no reason to believe that the navigator would be interested in a routine British Rail horror story.

'Yes, the MOD plod on the gate rang us up and asked if we knew about you.'

'It all seems very hush-hush.'

'Oh, that's nothing to do with us. We're very dull. We're just in here because it's cosy and handy for the phone and so on. Anyway, come and meet the rabble. Shall we pop your bags in the bay meantime?' He opened the door opposite again and said, 'LMA?' A voice within said, 'Coming,' and another voice laughed obscenely. A tall thin sailor, neatly dressed and wearing blue-tinted spectacles, came out into the passageway and said, 'Evening, sir.' He had a red cross on the sleeve of his shirt.

'LMA Smith. Surgeon Lieutenant Campbell RNR.'

'Evening, sir. Would you like to put your kit in the bay for now?'

'Thanks, LMA.'

Smith opened the sickbay door with a key on a chain and he and Campbell took one bag each. 'You shan't want showing round till the morning, I expect, sir. But here's your key to the bay for your things.'

'Thank you,' said Campbell.

'Goodnight, sir.'

'Goodnight.'

'Thank you, Smith,' said the navigator. Smith locked the bay and disappeared whence he had come. 'Come and have a drink.' The navigator waved airily in the direction from which he had first appeared. 'The wardroom's up here somewhere.'

Campbell followed him forward along the passageway, up a ladder, through a space marked 'Secret' and filled with large boxes that hummed and glowed, and down another ladder. 'You'll keep getting lost for the first month or so. Everyone does,' remarked his guide, as they arrived outside a door marked 'Wardroom'. 'David, isn't it?'

'Yes.'

They went in to a large room with a neat bar in one corner. A dozen or so officers, all dressed in the same uniform as the navigator, stood around. Most had glasses in their hands. Once more Campbell felt improperly dressed. It was a scene of elegance and civilization, of conversation and cigar smoke. 'We've just had a little mess dinner,' the navigator explained. 'On an opportunity basis. In case we don't get another chance for a while. What would you like to drink?'

Most people seemed to be drinking spirits, many of them liqueur brandies. Campbell hesitated. 'A beer?' said his host.

'Lovely.'

Ayres leaned over the bar and found a red can and poured it for Campbell. 'I'll take you round the chaps in a minute.'

The initial impression that all naval officers looked the same did not last long. There were some very young ones, and some were quite old, or at least middle aged. There was a tall one, and a short tubby one with a greyish-ginger beard, who looked the most senior present, and appeared to be the only lieutenant-commander. He detached himself from a group and came over, sticking out a hand.

'Hallo, doc. Ben Bowers. First lieutenant.'

'Evening, sir.'

'Gotta drink? Good. We can talk business tomorrow. Take

you up to see the old man when he comes back in the afternoon. Meantime look round. Sling your hammock and all that. Any problems, see me. You had dinner?'

'Fixing it, sir,' said the navigator. He went over to a hatch and opened it, calling through 'Tak!'

'Sah!' said a strange, high-pitched voice.

'Cheesy hammy eggy topside for the new doctor. Can fix?'

'Sah!' said the strange voice.

Another officer, also a lieutenant, came up, glass in hand, as the first lieutenant departed. He was in his middle twenties, like the navigator, but was thin and had a faintly old-fashioned set of black whiskers. His moustache tended to the flowing, and there was a slight curl at the point of his beard. His face was pale and languid with a hint of the invalid. He would not have looked out of place, Campbell thought, in one of Queen Victoria's vast sepia hen-and-chickens family portrait photographs, as a weedy and perhaps even haemophiliac princeling mournfully holding a pony. He too stuck out a hand.

'Ken Muir. Security.'

Most naval officers, on shaking hands, did the warm-hearted, firm-of-purpose business school bit. Lieutenant Muir did not. 'Good trip up?' He finished the question with a nervous laugh.

'Not too bad, thanks.'

'I'm security. Any problems in that department, I'll do what I can.'

'Thanks. What do you actually . . .'

'Oh, intelligence and general cleverness. Death rays. Ciphers. False moustaches.' He tugged at his right handlebar and said, 'Sod it. Must have put too much glue on,' and giggled. Campbell smiled politely. 'Seriously. Anything I can do to help . . .'

'I don't think there's anything yet. All this purple stuff was a bit of a pain in the neck . . . What's the . . .'

'Oh. *Très secrète*. Very 'oosh-'oosh. Second line port for the nukes. But that's need to know.'

Campbell was familiar with the phrase. Any sensitive information was spread through the Navy on a 'need to know' basis, which meant in general that people minded their own business and in particular that doctors rarely got involved with anything complicated with ciphers or megatons in it. 'I see. Oh, there is one thing you might be able to help me with.'

'What's that?' said Lieutenant Muir, looking marginally less languid.

'What's an authorized officer?'

'For what?'

'Authorized to deal with stripey buff and purple cards.'

'Oh, that. I am. Hang on to it just now. The procedure is that you sign the back of it in my presence, and I mince it in the official destructor in the presence of an authorized witnessing officer, and then issue a destruct certificate. I'll come down to the bay tomorrow and collect it.'

'Thanks.' Campbell had remembered the sergeant and begun to wonder about fixed penalties and what constituted unlawful possession.

'I'm sure we've met.'

'Hm?'

'I said I'm sure I know you. I'm sure we've met before.'

Campbell looked at the security officer again. No bells rang. He tried to imagine him without his Edwardian facial hair. Still no joy. To flatly disagree would have been antisocial. 'Really?' he said. 'If so, I'm sorry, it escapes me.' It was faintly possible that he had treated the man at some point in the course of his Casualty job, in which case it was more than likely that Campbell would have forgotten him even if the converse did not apply. 'Perhaps.'

'Yes . . . I'm sure,' said Lieutenant Muir. 'Absolutely certain. At a party, I think. Where are you from?'

'Edinburgh,' said Campbell.

'That's it. A party in Edinburgh . . . Marchmont, maybe.'

'Could be,' said Campbell. He had been to dozens of parties in Marchmont, as had thousands of other people of his vintage and innumerable previous generations. They were part of growing up in young professional Edinburgh. At not all of such parties attended had Campbell remained absolutely sober throughout, and it was possible that he had met his questioner, and perhaps even talked to him for quite a long time, without being able to recall specific details with complete clarity at this juncture. 'Maybe,' he conceded.

'That must be it, David. A party in Marchmont. I must have been in a minehunter visiting Rosyth. A nurses' party. Or maybe secretaries.'

Campbell was listening as much to Lieutenant Muir's accent as he was to what he was saying. It was odd, mainly nondescript south-of-England wardroom, with occasional vowels that rang wrong. He tried to recall a sample.

'Anyway, it was a great party.'

'Was it?' The odd vowels sorted themselves out. Lieutenant Muir, like Campbell, was Scottish, but had perhaps been living among the English too long, to the detriment of his diction. In any case, his name should have been enough. Campbell felt a bit stupid. 'You from Edinburgh?'

'Naw,' he said in a comic accent not unlike Able Seaman McGuffy's. 'Ah'm frae Dundee.' He reverted to his previous mode and added, rather primly, 'Of course we haven't lived there for ages.'

'Where are you now?'

'Fareham.'

'Where's that?'

'Just north of Portsmouth. Handy for the Navy.'

'I suppose so . . .' Campbell had no wish to lay himself open to a mortgage, wife and kids monologue. There were things of more immediate interest this chap might know about. 'Any idea when we're off north?'

Lieutenant Muir's face changed suddenly. His jaw set and he came much closer to Campbell and muttered, 'Careless talk. It's a *provisional* deployment. Only about four people on board are meant to know about it and you aren't one of them.'

'Oh. Sorry . . . It's just that my appointer did say . . .'

'Typical. One red stripe and they think they're God. Three and they act like it.' Lieutenant Muir was referring to the marks of rank of a medical officer, which had bands of red between the gold stripes. Campbell thought them rather dashing, but they clearly annoyed this chap. 'Bloody doctors . . . Sorry, doc. But your branch just doesn't seem to take security seriously.'

'I'll do my best,' said Campbell, taking a swig of his beer. Anything for a quiet life.

'Bear it in mind,' said Lieutenant Muir, sounding severe.

'Cheesy hammy eggy topside doctor sah,' said the strange high-pitched voice, very close. Campbell turned round to see a small Chinaman in the uniform of an RN steward lay down on the bar top a plate with a kind of multi-storey grilled open sandwich, topped by a fried egg. It smelled good and he remembered he hadn't eaten much since leaving *Cerberus* the previous evening. He thanked the steward.

'Okay sah. I bring coffee or you like beer.'

'Beer's fine, thank you.' The Chinaman left the wardroom and Campbell idly wondered how Oriental stewards compared to surgeon captains as risks in the security officer's black book. Rather than mention or enquire about the racial origins of the steward he decided to act as if the most natural thing to expect on a British warship in a remote harbour in the Highlands of Scotland was to be served an exotic sandwich by an unexplained Chinaman.

'I suppose you're wondering why we've got Chinese cooks and stewards?' Lieutenant Muir asked. Campbell had started his sandwich. 'It's to do with another provisional deployment. However, having twenty-one of them on board does add a little substance to a persistent rumour that we're going to end up in Hong Kong.'

'Really,' said Campbell through a mouthful. It was hard to tell if this fellow was joking, or simply being excessively serious about his job.

'Still bending the doc's ear, Ken?' Lieutenant Ayres, the navigator, had returned, bringing another officer, a blond sub-lieutenant somewhat the worse for drink. 'Henry, come and meet the doc. David Campbell. Sub-Lieutenant Henry Blake, Royal Navy. Henry's very interested in medicine. Gets the *Gynaecology Illustrated Weekly*. Full colour. Don't you, Henry? He's coming on nicely with the pictures. We've even started him on the words.'

'Fuck off,' said Sub-Lieutenant Blake.

'See what I mean?' said the navigator.

There was a knock on the door and it opened. A very well-dressed petty officer stood outside, with the almost naked leading regulator behind him.

'Officer of the day, please sir,' said the PO.

'What will they think of next?' said Lieutenant Ayres,

putting down his glass and leaving. The young sub-lieutenant focused rather laboriously on Campbell and said, 'D'you normally have your own practice, sir?' The words seemed to be giving him some trouble.

'No,' said Campbell. 'I've been a hospital doctor till now.'

The officer swayed slightly. 'Sorry you missed the mess dinner . . . Great sport. But that's a lot of rubbish about me being interested in . . . gynaecology . . . I mean . . . I'm interested in women . . . Who isn't . . . Oh, sir. I think they might have found you a customer.'

Campbell turned round. Lieutenant Ayres was beckoning him from the door. Campbell went out and joined a group in the passageway consisting of the officer of the day and the duty PO together with the leading regulator in his now customary dress. Ayres said, 'PO, this is Lieutenant Campbell. Doctor just joined. Say all that again.'

'Well, sir. It's Sambo again. I mean Able Seaman McGuffy. I was called to the quarterdeck ten minutes ago. The police launch was alongside and they wanted to speak to the duty senior rate. They said they'd fished somebody out of the hoggin and they thought it was one of ours. And it was. It was Sambo, in his eights, lying in the launch all wet. He'd been swimming when they got him, they said, but he'd gone a bit quiet after they'd pulled him out, and did we want him.'

'Where is he now, PO?'

'Down his mess. We took him off them. He wasn't under arrest or anything. They weren't bringing charges. Thought he'd just fallen in.'

'What's he like now?'

'Cold, sir. Teeth chattering. Dozy.'

'Talking?'

'Yessir.'

'I'd better see him.'

'Would you like to take the doctor down, PO?' said Ayres. 'Which mess?'

'Seven, sir.'

Campbell followed the PO aft, up the ladder, through the room with 'Secret' on the doors, down another ladder and further aft along the main passageway. They stopped at a square hole in the floor with a hand rail round it and a ladder leading down. The PO said, 'I'll go first.'

The mess deck was about the same size as the wardroom. It contained about twenty bunks. There were a few tables and chairs in the spaces between the tiers of bunks. A certain amount of brightening up had been done, mainly with soft porn pin-ups. Some of the sailors had turned in, and a few sat round a table. The PO led Campbell round far from the hatch, to a bunk in a tier against the ship's side. The quartermaster who had attempted to stop Campbell entering the sickbay sat on a lower bunk, shivering. He was well wrapped up in white seaman's jersey, with a towel round his neck and ears, and had on a pair of dry denim trousers of service pattern. His hair was spiky and damp, and his face pale, with red-rimmed eyes. He glowered ahead and did not look up.

'Shall I leave you with him, sir?'

Campbell pondered the delicate problem of ethics, etiquette and naval law the question posed. McGuffy said, 'Away ye go, Jim. Ah'll no kill him or anything.'

'Thanks, PO.' Campbell sat down on the bunk opposite, and couldn't think of anything to say. After a while he asked, 'How do you feel, Able Seaman McGuffy?'

McGuffy looked up and said, 'Cold,' and added, after a distinct pause, 'sir.' The man was conscious and, clinically speaking, alert. Although he had been very much at risk of dying of cold only minutes before, he had been fished out and was dry and warming up. There was no particular medical problem that Campbell could think of, except, of course, why he had done it.

'How did it happen?'

'What, sir?'

'You getting into the water. Did you fall, or what?'

'I jumped, sir.'

'Oh. Were you . . . trying to do away with yourself?'

McGuffy started and looked at Campbell with disbelief. 'Whit me? Ye mean me commit suicide and kill masel'? No' me, sir.'

'Well, I did wonder . . .'

'Oh, no, sir. No' me. Ah've goat everything tae live for. In fact that's why Ah wiz wantin' oot.'

'Out?'

'Yessir. Ah wiz goin' on the trot. Swimmin' for it. And the busies fished me oot.'

'I see.'

'See, sir, the reason I wisnae there tae see ye on board wiz Ah wiz makin' a wee phone call. Tae the wife. Well, she's no' the wife but we've got a couple o' kids and she's good tae me and she's missin' me and so's the weans and Ah dinnae want tae go up there again.'

Campbell wondered if Able Seaman McGuffy were one of the security officer's privileged four with official knowledge. 'Up where?'

'Well, we're goin' up the ice, aren't we, sir?' Campbell let that one pass. 'For at least a month, eh, sir? An' Ah'd had a few down the mess. Between you and me, sir, aboot a dozen cans.' He looked round and lowered his voice. 'Then somebody must have slipped me a Mickey Finn, sir, 'cause Ah wiz no' masel' when I took the gangway.'

'Why did you swim for it, McGuffy? And not just go through . . . the usual way out?'

'Because they took away my purple card when they started on aboot me bein' absent from my place of duty, and drunk because some bastard slipped me a Mickey Finn.' His voice trembled with righteous indignation.

Despite the absence of a nuclear deterrent to worry about, the purple security system seemed to have found a useful, even challenging role in retaining for the Crown the services of Able Seaman McGuffy. It looked like one for the officer of the day.

'I see. So you're feeling all right now, are you?'

'Well, you know what it feels like when someone's slipped you a Mickey Finn, sir. But otherwise no' bad.'

'Fine, McGuffy. I'll ask the LMA to come down later and see you're still all right.'

'Thanks, sir. Sir, everybody says we're goin' up the ice tonight. Is that right?'

Ayres was waiting at the top of the ladder. 'Is he all right, doc?'

'He'll live. Cold but not ill. Drunk from the sound of things.'

'Not anything else?'

'Don't think so. He's fine just now and the LMA'll take another look at him later.'

'The leading hand of the mess will keep an eye on him, too. I'll see him in the morning. He usually pleads guilty and goes to father for weighing off.'

'Usually?'

'Well, almost always. He's perfectly all right when he's at sea. Just goes a bit silly sometimes in port. Starts wanting to swim back to Govan if he's pissed enough. He wasn't too bad tonight. Probably thought he'd head for Greenock and take the train from there. Anyway, it's all covered by leaving the ship without permission.'

'Why's he called Sambo?'

'Not sure. I think he was a little grey behind the ears when he joined. Coming on though.' The navigator sounded like a world-weary but still faintly optimistic scoutmaster.

As they walked back to the wardroom the ship's tannoy crackled into life. 'D'ye hear there?' it said, with a fine old-navy flourish. 'The ship is under sailing orders. All shore leave is cancelled. The captain will address the ship's company at 2330. That is all.'

'Sorry, doc,' said the navigator. 'Should have mentioned it. Quick change of plan. Father rang from *Nemesis*. They've flown him up and we're off tonight. Should have mentioned it. It was only confirmed when you were having your chat with Sambo. Hardly a surprise though. What we needed.'

In the wardroom much had changed. The bar was now closed and blank. The few officers present were now dressed in severe-looking high-necked dark blue pullovers. One was checking through a blue signals folder. The sub-lieutenant was flicking over the pages of *Country Life*. The steward was emptying ashtrays. Campbell's remaining half glass of beer had disappeared, and the last, admittedly now probably cold and charmless, fragment of his sandwich had gone, too.

'You still haven't seen your cabin, have you, doc? Henry, help the doc with his gear from the bay to his cabin. Next to Bob in the cabin flat aft.'

'Aye aye, sir.' Sub-Lieutenant Blake got up, looking much more sober than shortly before. 'Roll on the next box of middies.'

Installed at last in his cabin, Campbell could readily have washed and gone straight to bed (to bunk?). He had been on his feet for most of the previous twenty-four hours; he felt grimy and exhausted but the sudden warlike developments of the past few minutes seemed to indicate, though no one had actually told him so, that he should change into something a little more naval and stay up at least until the captain's proposed revelations at 11.30. He unpacked and put away all his things in a variety of ingenious drawers and lockers.

The cabin was small and irregular in shape, an eccentricity dictated by the ship's side, which formed its outer limit. There was no porthole, and it occurred to Campbell that it might actually be below the waterline. Nonetheless, it was home until he heard to the contrary, and it had its good points. There was a bunk, about four feet off the floor (deck?) with only about two feet of headroom above it. It formed the top layer of a highly individual and naval piece of furniture comprising a locker on the left, with a little shoe cupboard forming its lower quarter, a drop-down desktop arrangement, which opened to reveal a bookshelf, a small internal lockable cupboard and a reading lamp and, below all that, a couple of large drawers.

There was a small steel washbasin folded up against the wall, which dropped down for use and emptied when you folded it up again afterwards. There was a bedlight, or possibly bunklight, a larger light above and beside it a dim red bulb, perhaps for some arcane seamanlike or military purpose. The door was metal, and incorporated in its lower half an inset labelled 'Crash Panel: Do not use for ventilation'.

Campbell changed, into the kind of outfit at present in fashion in the wardroom, and hung up his suit at the far end of the rail in the tall locker because it sounded as if he wouldn't be needing it for some time. He checked in the mirror above the basin and found that he looked quite naval after all and went upstairs to await the commanding officer's address to the ship's company.

There were more people in the wardroom again. Campbell sat down next to a short man in glasses.

'Hallo, doctor,' he said. 'Ronnie Baker. Supply Officer.

Settling in all right?'

'Yes, thanks.'

'You've hardly really had time, what with all this. But can't be helped. Cabin all right?'

'Lovely.'

'Bit on the tight side, those outboard cabins, but quite cosy once you've settled in. Your steward's Leading Steward Ho. A nice steady lad. 'E'll look after you. Especially good with shoes and pressing, is Ho. He'll look after you and see you're all right.'

'Oh. Thanks. He's one of the . . . the . . .'

'LEPs.'

'Oh.'

'Locally Enlisted Personnel. Brackets C. Meaning Chinese. Ho's one of my merry band. I'm their divisional officer. Twenty-one I had, at the last count. Fifteen able rates, four leading hands and two POs. One of whom pretends he doesn't know English, to avoid admin. But he can cook so we don't worry.'

Campbell looked more closely at Lieutenant Baker. Though undoubtedly Anglo-Saxon in origins, he had a chubby round face and slightly high cheekbones. His hair was black and straight and now concentrated mainly at the back of his head. His eyes were dark brown and twinkly. The overall effect was faintly but not absurdly Oriental. Had some exceptionally gifted appointer chosen him from a vast cohort of similarly qualified but more Nordic-looking possibilities for this ship, and hence for his task of looking after the Chinamen? Or was it simply that, by some process of adaptation, he had got like that since he had started in the job?

'Someone was saying *Winchester*'s off to Hong Kong,' said Campbell, to keep the ball rolling.

Lieutenant Baker twinkled. 'You don't want to believe all the buzzes you hear in this steamer, doctor. But that one's true. Aren't you coming with us?'

'I don't know,' said Campbell, who in the course of the previous fortnight had completely got out of the habit of thinking ahead.

'We're certainly billeted for a doctor to join about now and come out with us . . .'

'Could be,' said Campbell, thinking of his appointer's most recent phone call. 'I'd be the last to know.'

'Oho. Have you been mucked about?'

'Not a lot,' said Campbell, in the finest traditions of naval understatement. 'No. That sounds fine.'

'Well, don't take my word for it. But I'm pretty sure it's you. And I'm paying you.'

'Thanks.' Sometimes it slipped Campbell's mind that he was being paid, and quite handsomely, for all this. After about three years' intermittent attachment to his local reserve division, mainly mucking about in minesweepers for the odd weekend, with the occasional fortnight's so-called 'training' thrown in, he had come to look on the Navy more as an amusing if slightly eccentric pastime than as a potential livelihood. But come to think of it, if he were to spend a few months at sea, he would run at a considerable profit. Most things on the ship were free, except drink, and that was cheap. And the pay just went clicking on without your actually doing much, like a taxi meter working in reverse.

'Come up and see me tomorrow. I'm in a funny little office near the starboard oerlikon. We'll enter you in the ship's books. Get your next of kin and where to send your remains and all that. Joining routine. About ten. Finish by stand-easy.'

'I'll be there . . .' They sat and waited and Campbell, to pass the time and get a little background for what was to come, asked the supply officer, 'What's father like?'

'Oh, I'm the last person to ask. Not a bad old stick, I suppose, but very hard on pussers. Really seems to have it in for the supply branch. He'd be down there countin' me dried peas if I let 'im. Fine otherwise. Straight. Fair. The troops like him. Good driver. Good at this sort of thing.'

Right on cue the tannoy crackled and said, 'D'ye here there. Captain speaking. As most of you know, and as some of you know officially, we are about to move up to the line again. Many of you will be disappointed at this, but you shouldn't be. Our place is at sea. The charms of Loch Ewe, as I am sure you have found out, are limited, and it is very doubtful if we could have moved anywhere more salubrious over the festive season. As you know, Christmas leave has been off the menu for many months, so nothing has changed and there is no cause for disappointment now.

'So we're going north again. We sail at midnight and will get up there as fast as the old donks will take us. The situation is this. Gunboats are manoeuvring round the fleet and menacing individual ships. No incident has yet – I repeat – yet taken place. But the temperature has risen, diplomatically if not weatherwise. We're next in line. We're going up.

'Last time up we did well. We prevented much damage to others and we avoided it ourselves. The ship's company as a whole acquitted itself well, and the command knew it, as you saw for yourselves in the signal promulgated on your notice-boards on completion. I have no reason to believe things will be different this time. That is all.'

There was a short silence. Outside, in the passageway, a sailor sang 'Here we are again'.

HMS *Winchester* prepared to leave harbour. Through the long last half-hour alongside, the ship came gradually to readiness. Phones rang and telegraph bells clanged. Gruff voices, distorted by microphones designed to be robust rather than sensitive, checked back and forward, using short automatic phrases. Throughout her length control systems and communications were checked. Mail closed and the last blue bag went down the gangway. The shore power and telephone cables were disconnected, and freshwater hoses thrown back on the quayside. The stout web of hawsers holding the ship to the wall was reduced and simplified, ready for a final casting off.

The rain had stopped and the cloud was breaking up. The water in the basin was calm, except where the police boat circled like a clockwork plastic toy beneath the tall cranes with their lights. A moon, three-quarters full, cleared a cloud bank. Campbell walked on the upper deck, feeling ignorant and somewhat in the way, as sailors rushed around in the semi-darkness, obviously busy and entirely familiar with what they were doing. A light wind came in off the sea, bringing the sound of the waves outside the basin. The tannoy gave forth long incantations about special sea duty-men, screen doors, scuttles and deadlights, which greatly deepened Campbell's sense of being a new boy. Small groups of men on the upper deck fore and aft did things to ropes under the supervision of clean, idle-looking junior officers with small two-way radios. A lone civilian dockyard employee, evidently of pensionable age, cycled up from nowhere, leaned his bike against a shed, and came and stood by a bollard, one of the two which were now the ship's last hold on dry land. Five sailors, cursed by a PO, hauled the gangway inboard.

It was five to twelve. Campbell had been on board for less than three hours, had seen a lot of new faces, and had names for only a few of them: McGuffy, who, however inopportunely, had welcomed him on board, and was now in God knew what sort of trouble; Ayres, the suave navigator, taking it all in his stride; Ronnie, with his grocer manner and his little flock of Chinamen; the regulator who appeared not to own, or at any rate wear, any items of conventional uniform; and the sub-lieutenant who was interested in women but not gynaecology. There were other names, with no faces yet: Leading Steward Ho, good with shoes, and of course the captain, calm and managerial on the tannoy, and the terror of the supply department.

Campbell thought of all this, and much much more, as the dockyard matey hauled HMS *Winchester*'s last hawser off the bollard and sploshed it unceremoniously into the water. With a strange coughing rumble, not the hiss and whir of mighty turbines that the heroes of Campbell's schoolboy reading would have preferred, HMS *Winchester* came under power and slid slowly away from the wall.

The dockyard man turned and shuffled towards his bike without a backward glance. The deck under Campbell's feet vibrated and, in the water round the ship's stern, there appeared evidence of the power of her engines. Great swirling currents, confused and jumbled as the ship responded to wheel and engine orders, glinted in the moonlight. Cranes and lights swept past in rapid arcs, then slowed again as the ship settled on a course for the exit and gathered a little speed. A klaxon on the police launch barked a shrill farewell, perhaps to the ship, perhaps to their erstwhile guest AB McGuffy.

HMS *Winchester* lined herself up on the gap between the two stone piers marking the limit of the purple-area basin, and slid out into the sea loch, taking on a slight roll as she did so. The wind freshened. It was cold. Campbell went below, found somewhere called 'Officers' Washplace', had a shower, swaying slightly to the movement of the ship, and went to bed.

Next morning, despite being adequately forewarned, Campbell was astonished to wake up and find he was four feet from the floor of his cabin, being offered tea by a Chinaman.

'Morning sah, vewy nice day,' said a man who might be Leading Steward Ho. 'You got shoes?'

'Down there somewhere.'

'Okay sah, I find.' He did, and went away. Campbell thought about drinking his tea. The ship was moving steadily over a long gentle swell, just enough to be felt, not enough to put the tea at risk. A phrase of the captain's came to mind. Was the ship going as fast as the old donks would take her? Eventually the steward came back with the shoes, bright beyond recognition, and Campbell drank his tea and got up.

No one talked at breakfast in the Navy. It was a convention Campbell had first come across some years before in a very stuffy wardroom attached to the naval barracks at Portsmouth where, at tables seemingly hundreds of yards long, vast commanders, spaced like moored battleships, had yawned silently over the *Telegraph* and Oxford marmalade. The custom seemed to obtain in small ships at sea too, with less room and commanders very thin on the ground. Only the stewards spoke, and they in hushed and sibilant tones ('Slice o' toas', sah?'). On the whole it seemed a good idea. If men had to live together in groups, it was probably best that mealtime conversation be postponed at least until lunchtime.

At 8.30, remembering the notice on the sickbay door, Campbell made his way along aft to his place of duty. In the 'Secret' room there were now people as well as machines. Sailors moved eerily between patches of orange and purple light, and in one corner the burly red-bearded lieutenant-commander was softly haranguing a worried-looking lieutenant. He broke off, wished Campbell a loud and cheery 'Morning, doc' and resumed his *sotto voce* remonstrance without a pause. The officer under pressure, Campbell realized on the way out, was the pale Lieutenant Muir.

A short queue waited outside the sickbay, two standing, two sitting on the floor. One of the sailors sitting on the floor was so pale as to be almost green. The door was closed but not locked and Campbell went in. The sickbay was empty. Once more naval ingenuity in the use of space impressed him. In an area perhaps only sixteen feet by eight, and with no particular sense of things being crammed in, there was an office, an operating theatre and a ward, admittedly all compact and overlapping, but there in essentials and neatly laid out: desk, filing cabinet and bookshelves forward, then a simple operating table, with theatre lights, sterilizer and washing facilities nearby, then aft of that two white-painted beds, one above the other, not fixed like bunks, but slung in a frame to accommodate the ship's rolling. A portable X-ray machine was lashed to the foot of the operating table, and a series of white-painted cupboards and drawers, all neatly labelled, presumably served as the pharmacy department of this miniature sea-going hospital.

At the far end of the sickbay, beyond the cots, a door opened and a sailor came out. He was doing up his flies. A voice from behind him said, 'That's it then, Snoopy. No booze. No women which is not a problem this week. Keep your hands off it and remember the pills. Next please. Oh. Morning, sir. Leading Seaman Snopes presented with dysuria and a thin early morning discharge on the nineteenth of December, having undergone unprotected exposure with a casual consort ten days before. Direct film negative for GC. A few polymorphs only. Serology carried out.'

Leading Seaman Snopes, who had now finished adjusting his clothing, shifted uneasily from one foot to the other. LMA Smith continued: 'So he's a non-specific urethritis. Now on tetracycline, sir. And doing all right. All right?'

'Aw right, doc,' said Snopes, another Glaswegian.

'Come up again Friday morning. And don't forget not to have a piss first.'

'Right, doc.' Snopes left.

'Morning, sir. Sorry about that.'

'Not at all, LMA. Please carry on,' said Campbell, sounding so naval he surprised himself. 'Is there a lot of this sort of thing about?'

'Here and there, sir. Five since Portland. Three first-timers. Only GCs and NSUs, though. Nothing serious.'

It was all most impressive. The LMA's little case presentation would have done credit to a senior registrar in venereology. Campbell began to wonder if his own best contribution to the health of the ship's company might not simply be to keep out of this chap's way. 'There are one or two outside,' he said, uncertain which way to play it.

'Would you like to see some, sir?' said the LMA. It sounded like the beginning of an 'after-you-no-after-you' game. Fortunately the phone on the desk rang. Smith picked it up. 'Sickbay. LMA.' He put his hand over the mouthpiece and said, 'It's for you, sir. First lieutenant.'

Campbell took the phone. 'Medical officer.'

'Hallo, doc. Number one here. My cabin. Five minutes.'

'Yessir.' The phone went dead. 'I think he wants to see me,' said Campbell to the LMA.

'Well, yes, sir. He would do. After all technically he was the medical officer till you joined us. It might be a sort of handover.'

'What's he like?'

'Well, sir,' said Smith, with some delicacy, 'he's my divisional officer.'

'Oh.'

'I understand he's very experienced, sir.'

'Oh?'

'Old and bold. The rough and tough bit. SD, I think.' Special duty officers had been promoted after service in the lower deck. Not many of them made it as far as lieutenant-commander. 'He has his little ways. For instance, he's not keen on top hamper.'

'What?'

'Anything heavy. Well, more or less anything heavy, above the ship's centre of gravity, sir, that might add to the risk of a capsize.'

'I see.'

'In the sod's opera last time up here, one of the stokers made a beard out of ginger string and put a pillow up his pullover and wandered across the stage between all the acts picking up matchsticks, cigarette ends, sweet wrappers, anything, muttering "top 'amper, top 'amper" and chucking the bits into the audience. Brought the house down.'

'I see.'

'Number one sat in the front, in the middle of the front row beside father, who was wetting himself, muttering into his beard, "Glad they've got the message. Glad they've got the message . . ." Sir, shall I just see these cases while you're up there seeing him?'

'That's fine,' said Campbell, with a faint feeling that events were taking charge and determining the pattern of clinical responsibility already.

'I'll keep anything difficult for your attention later, sir,' the LMA conceded.

'I don't know how long I'll be.'

Campbell left the sickbay, and then returned, even before the first patient had gone in, to find out from the LMA where the first lieutenant lived.

'Me piles, doc. Something chronic this morning. Have a seat.' The first lieutenant was sitting uncomfortably on the edge of a hard chair. Campbell had eventually tracked him down in a cabin of comparative luxury, just below the bridge, with a view forward through portholes looking out over the guns and fo'c'sle. Grey seas stretched endlessly away to the grey sky. Campbell sat down in an armchair.

'Givin' me hell, they are. Thought I'd just got over an attack when wham, this morning, while I was havin' a quiet think in the for'ard trap of the wardroom heads. The bottom fell out of my world.' Campbell, who had been expecting a brisk and seamanlike introduction to naval life generally and the ship's routine in particular, found himself caught in the wrong gear. He adjusted to listen with sympathy. The first lieutenant grinned fiercely. 'Felt more like the world falling out of my bottom, eh? Want a look?'

'Perhaps if I nip back down to sickbay and get some things,

sir,' said Campbell, not dodging the issue but trying to sort things out as quickly as possible and, in view of the seniority of his patient, as far from the gregarious public-ward ambience of the sickbay as was practicable.

'OK, doc. Whatever you think . . . And I'd really rather you kept it to yourself. Smith, that lad of yours, he's all right . . . but he is in my division.'

'Yessir.'

'So it'd be best if he didn't know anything about it.'

'Sir.' That might be difficult, but Campbell resolved to do his best.

Campbell caught Smith between patients and asked for a rectal tray, plastic gloves and appropriate ointments and suppositories, hoping that Smith, presumably as professional in confidentiality as in everything else, would supply them and turn, as it were, a blind eye. The LMA nodded towards the operating table, where everything Campbell mentioned had been neatly laid out already, together with a plastic bag to carry it in.

'Thank you, LMA.'

'Someone I know in the ops room did happen to mention that his nibs had a tooty on this morning, sir, so I put two and two together when he rang, and took the liberty . . .'

'Thank you, LMA.'

'Don't mention it, sir.'

'Thanks, doc. What a relief. Sorry to hit you with a problem on day one.' The first lieutenant was sitting more comfortably. 'Now let's get down to business. D'you play the harmonium?'

'No, sir.'

The first lieutenant looked puzzled. 'Oh . . . We've got an organ, portable, small, on board. But you can't play it.'

'No, sir.'

'Got a . . . guitar or anything?'

'No, sir.'

'You know anything about singing? Choral work. That sort of thing.'

'No, sir.'

The first lieutenant sucked his teeth in despair. 'That's a problem.'

'Sorry, sir.'

'Difficult, with Christmas just round the corner . . . Anyway. That's a side issue. How are you on quizzes, entertainments, things like that generally?'

'I've done very little, sir. In fact, hardly any.'

'I see.' The first lieutenant got up and walked across and looked long and hard out of the porthole, at grey clouds and sea. 'Well, we've certainly got a problem.' After a long pause he said, 'Never mind. Can't be helped,' and walked over to his chair again and sat down. 'Ah. That's much better. Thanks, doc.'

'No trouble, sir.'

'Well then. What else is there? Ah. Father. Wait one.' He picked up a telephone, dialled a number and said, 'Sir. Number one. Have you got a minute for the doctor?' There was a short pause, then he said 'Yessir' and put the phone down. 'Five minutes, doc. You happy about the medical stores?'

'Haven't been through them yet, sir.'

'Tons of stuff. Don't know much about it. Just had to ask for some of everything. D'you know we get a bit of medicine on the XO's course. The three-day brain surgery scheme. Young docs come down from RNH Haslar and teach us how to sew up orange peel. Very handy. Much the same as skin apparently. And bellies. They were very keen on sore bellies. Two kinds of belly at sea. The ones you keep and the ones you get rid of. I forget which is which . . . But I expect you know all that . . . Been to sea before?'

'A little, sir. RNR.'

'Weekends, innit?'

'Mainly, sir.'

'Well, you'll get your sea-time in in this steamer. Starting yesterday. You got a hat?'

'In my cabin, sir.'

'Get it.' Campbell recalled the navigator saying something similar to McGuffy the previous evening, in less auspicious circumstances. 'Always got to carry your hat when you go to see your captain. First time anyway.'

Campbell found his way down to the cabin flat, by a new route he hadn't used before, and back up, within the time allotted.

'Ready, doc? This way.' Campbell followed the first lieutenant ten feet or so along a passageway, to a similar but more luxurious cabin, the door of which was hooked open. Lieutenant-Commander Bowers cleared his throat and tapped very lightly on the door. 'Ahem. Number one and doctor, sir.'

'Ah. Come in, number one. And doctor.' The captain of HMS *Winchester* was seated at a desk writing, as had been most of the exalted officials Campbell had ever been summoned to see, from his primary school headmaster onwards. He stopped writing and got up, which was what they usually did. The two officers went into his day cabin, and the first lieutenant put down his hat, indicating that Campbell should do likewise. They stood until, after the captain and Campbell had shaken hands, they were invited to sit down.

The captain was a man of middle age and middle height, with a sallow complexion and receding hair, some of which was trained loosely across a large bald spot. He looked at Campbell in silence for a moment, with pursed lips and his head tilted slightly to one side, then said, 'Joined yesterday?'

'Yessir.'

'In the evening?'

'Yessir.'

'Did they look after you?'

'Yessir.'

'Settling in?'

'Yessir.'

'First time with the RN?'

'Yessir.'

'Think you'll enjoy it?'

'Yessir.'

'I understand you volunteered for this duty.'

'Yessir.'

'Do you play the harmonium?'

There was an awkward pause. Campbell glanced at the first lieutenant, who had rolled his eyes upward and was gently shaking his head.

'Um. No, sir,' said Campbell. 'I've never . . . learned.'

'Piano or anything like that?'

'No, sir.'

'Oh, well . . . Find the sickbay all right?'

'Yessir.'

'Happy with the LMA?'

'Yessir.'

'I'd like to be kept informed of any major problems in your department.'

'Yessir.'

'And come and see me anyway, once a week . . . on Friday mornings, please.'

'Yessir.'

'Thank you for coming up.'

The first lieutenant was standing up already and had reached for his hat. Campbell did likewise. Moments later they were outside again.

'Fine,doc. All right? Mustn't keep you . . . You'll want to collect your . . . bits and pieces from my cabin.'

'Yessir.'

Campbell went back to the sickbay. The LMA had demolished the queue outside and was cleaning an already gleaming worktop with surgical spirit and a gauze swab. Campbell put down the plastic bag on the operating table.

'The officers' documents are in the bottom drawer of the filing cabinet, sir. If you'd like to keep the key . . .'

Campbell found the first lieutenant's medical records, which were venerable but not especially bulky. He sat down at the desk and leafed through them. Sprained right ankle, HMS *Untoward*, 1948. Tonsillitis, turned in, RNSQ HMS *Jufair*, Bahrain, 1957, etc. The serial notations of weight and blood pressure on the outside of his envelope followed his progress from green youth to his present high responsibilities in HMS *Winchester*. His weight had doubled, his blood pressure not quite. Campbell fished out the most recent card and made a note of the morning's transaction, in the curt, factual, semi-legible style of the service. When he had finished, the table was clear again.

'The master called for you, sir. Said he'd come back.'

'Who?'

'Master at arms, sir. Jossman, jaunty and local head crusher.'

'Oh.'

'About McGuffy,' said the LMA. 'About him being in the rattle.'

'Sorry, LMA. Who called?'

'MAA Flower, sir. He's the chief petty officer in charge of naval discipline on board. Jossman and all that.'

'Oh. The chap in underpants?'

'No, sir. That's his winger, L. Reg. Martindale. Brian, in our mess. The master's his boss. Said he'd come back in ten minutes.'

'Couldn't I go and see him?'

'No, sir . . . I don't think so. He'd prefer to come and see you.' Campbell was happy to be guided by the LMA on the finer points of naval etiquette.

'Was there anything interesting in those four this morning, LMA?'

'Sprained ankle, verruca and two seasicks, sir. No problems. Would you like to see their documents?'

'Not if you're happy.'

'Sir, there's a chap I've asked to come up and see you this morning, if it's convenient. Funny skin thing. Looks like scabies, but no one else in his mess has got it, and it's not getting better on the standard treatments.'

'Who is it?'

'A bunting tosser, sir. Gurnard. Usually quite clean.'

'Got his documents?'

'On the desk, sir.'

'Thank you, LMA.' He read through the recent cards from the envelope, in which Finch had recorded, in clear, squarish handwriting, the development of an itchy rash, affecting elbows, back, buttocks and legs, and the various regimes for scabies which had failed to cure it. Campbell had a feeling he was being tested.

There was a soft knock on the door. 'That'll be the master,' said Finch. 'Since it's a disciplinary matter, I expect you'd prefer to discuss it with him privately, sir. I'll be in six mess opposite.'

He opened the door. Blocking it, and probably the passageway as well, stood an enormous man, perhaps approaching six feet six, but slightly crouched, and far fatter than even the most generous interpretation of the naval rules on obesity would have permitted, had it occurred to anyone to have the temerity to suggest they apply to such a personage. He was dressed not in underpants but in the standard blue woolly pully and vast black trousers. His shoes were a shining example, even to Leading Steward Ho. Campbell stood up, and gathered immediately from the expression on the LMA's face that he should not have done. 'I'll leave you, sir,' he said, ushering the master into sickbay and circumnavigating him, to leave, at the same time.

'Have a seat, please,' said Campbell, fearing for the tubular steel chair beside his desk, which suddenly looked as if it was fashioned out of half-straightened paper clips.

'Thank you, sir.' Both sat down. 'First of all I'd like to say how ashamed I am for the ship at the manner in which you were received on board last night. It's not the first time AB McGuffy's let us down, and I'm sure it won't be the last. However, sir, since it did happen, and since you were a witness if not a victim of an unfortunate occurrence just outside sickbay here, I thought I might hear from you on the point.' A notebook and pencil appeared from somewhere in his clothing. 'He's wisely decided to plead guilty again, but the commanding officer has to have some details to weigh him off with. Can you just tell me what happened, sir.'

Campbell described, in the mildest possible terms, the small misunderstanding which constituted only part of the most recent blemish on the career of AB McGuffy. The master shook his head and sucked in his breath and wrote a few laborious sentences.

'Very nasty case, sir. I think we could probably have him for Disrespectful Conduct too, if we was stuck. But I don't think that'll be necessary. Not when he's dropped himself in it to the extent of jumping over the side. But thank you anyway, sir. The commanding officer will be dealing with the case, probably on an opportunity basis, what with Christmas and the latest incident.'

'Latest incident?'

'Oh, didn't you know, sir. They're coming up with the

rough stuff again. Gunboat in amongst the fleet this morning at 0300. So it's not the line we're heading for. It's designated areas again. Anyway, mustn't keep you, sir. Thank you for your help. I can only say again how sorry I am that, out of all the ratings on this ship, the first you should meet was that 'orrible article from Govan. Good morning, sir.' He got up and went out and when he had gone the sickbay seemed to re-expand to its normal size.

When the LMA came back, Campbell asked him about the latest developments. 'More or less what we'd expected, sir,' he said. 'Didn't you know. They've been messing them about again and it sounds as if it'll be much the same as last time.'

'Really?'

'Yessir. Close quarter stuff, with the ship's company in defence watches. Six hours on, six hours off. We close up first-aid parties, sir, and you don't really get to bed at all. You're allowed to sleep on your bunk with your clothes on, or you could lie on one of the beds in here. My station is for'ard, in two mess with the for'ard first-aid party. But we won't be starting that till midday tomorrow at the earliest.'

'Oh?'

'Yessir. It's amazing how the lads just settle into the routine, sir. And then when we came out of defence watches and started ordinary routine again it was like going on leave. People wandered around singing and . . . Come in!'

Someone had knocked at the door. A little sailor, in blue working dress with crossed flags on the badge on his sleeve, wandered in and looked at Campbell openmouthed.

'Gurnard, sir,' said the LMA. 'Spots. Not scabies.'

'Oh, yes . . . um. Morning, Gurnard.'

'Morning, sir.'

'How long have you had this trouble?'

'Couple of months, sir.'

'Itchy?'

'A bit, sir.'

'Comes and goes? Or there all the time?'

'Sort of comes and goes, sir.'

'May I see it?'

Gurnard looked blank. 'Shirt off, bunts,' said the LMA.

'Oh.'

'And your trousers. Keep your knicks and socks on.' The sailor complied at speed. His skin was mainly normal, but on the outside of his arms, over his knees and on his back there were scattered little red blisters, some older looking, some fresh, and many scratched and scarred. Scabies would have been a very reasonable first guess. Campbell lifted the man's hand and looked between the fingers.

'No interdigital lesions, sir. I checked. Toes as well.'

'Thanks, LMA . . . Ever had this before?'

'No, sir,' said Gurnard.

'Anyone in the family got it?'

The sailor hesitated, then said, 'Not that I know of, sir.'

'Thank you, Gurnard . . . Would you care to wait outside for a moment?'

The sailor made to leave, and the LMA indicated that he should put his clothes on before he did so.

'Interesting case,' said Campbell when he had gone. 'Might be . . . something I've forgotten the name of.'

'Skin book, sir?'

'Yes please, LMA.'

With a flourish of keys he opened a glass-fronted cabinet and produced a slender volume which Campbell recognized as a traditional, concise little book emanating from his own teaching hospital. 'Ah. Forrest, McNair and McCormack.'

'Yessir. Comes free with every frigate.'

'Good little book. Got through the exam by reading its index the night before. Dermatitis herpetiformis.'

'What, sir?'

'That's what he's got. I've remembered. Gets better on dapsone.'

'What's that, sir?'

'What you give them. Might not come free with every frigate. Can't remember its proper name. Works for leprosy, too.'

'Oh. Wait one, sir. In that case I might just have some in my tropical diseases store.'

'You look and I'll check up that that's actually what he's got. Should be. Usually presents as scabies that isn't.'

Campbell checked and found that he was probably right about the diagnosis. The LMA returned, similarly quietly pleased, as his pharmacy had not let him down. The bunting tosser was summoned back, his complaint was explained to him, and the pills issued with suitable instructions. 'May take about a week to work,' said Campbell.

'I can wait,' said the sailor. 'I've had it long enough.'

When he had gone the LMA said, 'Should have warned you about the family history, sir.'

'Oh.'

'Barnardo boy. We've got one or two on board like that. They usually fit in quite well. Queen's their mum and the Andrew's their dad. But it does make the family history a bit difficult.'

'Stand-easy,' said the tannoy. Campbell remembered that he should have gone up to Ronnie's office to tell him, among other things, where his remains should be sent.

At stand-easy in the wardroom Campbell poured himself a cup of coffee and sat down beside the sub-lieutenant. 'I hear you're not musical at all, sir,' he said.

'No,' said Campbell, wondering why everyone thought he should be.

'Pity. With Christmas coming on.'

'What'll happen for Christmas?'

'Don't know. This is my first at sea . . . What happens, Ronnie?'

'Oh, all sorts of things. Father brings round our tea first thing. Then it's Sunday routine relaxed. Then we serve the troops their dinner about four, and my lads serve us our dinner as usual later on. Turkey and all the trimmings. Figgy duff. Crackers, the lot. Gunboats permitting, of course.'

'What about all your Chinamen, Ronnie?'

'What about them?'

'Who looks after them?'

'They do. Same as usual. Don't you worry about them. They'll have their fling when Chinese New Year comes round. It's all in the book. You should see 'em. Makes Christmas seem quite sedate. Oh. Been busy, doctor?'

'Fairly. Sorry, Ronnie. Things kept happening.'

'Come up with me after stand-easy. Just so's we know

where to send the money. And the bits.'

'Fine.'

'Noel, No-sodding-ell. I've had enough. Turn that thing down, Jim.'

'Right away, number one.'

'Passengers enjoying the cruise, doctor? Ching, ching. Fares please. Move right up the frigate please.'

'Lay off, Roddy. He's had a busy morning. Couldn't even fit in his joining routine.'

'Has he?' said Ayres. 'Oh well. That's it for the month then. Over and done with.'

'You're full of beans this morning, navigator. Found us again?'

'We haven't been lost, sir. Not since Henry's stars put us in Saskatoon.'

'It was Lerwick . . . I was out of practice.'

'One's as bad as another. It's all dry land.'

'Hark the fucking herald angels. Just turn it off, Jim.'

'Right, sir.'

'Merry Christmas, doctor.'

'Oh. Morning, sir. Merry Christmas.'

The captain, wearing bell-bottoms and an elaborate silk dressing gown with a sailor's white front underneath, was brandishing a teapot dangerously near.

'Take sugar?'

'No thank you, sir.'

'Okay sah. Velly nice morning sah. Bye sah. No shoes today. Klismas.'

'Bye, sir. Thank you.'

The captain went out, giggling to himself, and Campbell heard him go through a similar routine in the next-door cabin. His tea turned out to be not as good as Leading Steward Ho's, but perfectly drinkable. It was about 8.15. Campbell lay for a while pondering the exact meaning of Ronnie's phrase 'Sunday routine relaxed' and eventually got up around 9.00, when sounds of life could be heard in the adjoining cabins too.

The relaxation element appeared to apply even to the

conventions of breakfast. In the wardroom the table area was not screened off and a few people were breakfasting and evidently conversing as well. A few more were lounging around having coffee. The SRE, the sound relay equipment with loudspeakers in all the living spaces, gave forth yet more Christmas carols interspersed with the voice of a man, possibly already inebriated, enthusing about a children's hospital ward. A patient with a squeaky voice listed about twenty relatives, a dog and a guinea pig he or she wished to have a merry Christmas and asked for 'Jingle Bells'. The first lieutenant looked as if he had been about to say something, and then thought better of it, then said, 'Morning, doc. Merry Christmas. Gunboats permitting.'

'Same to you, sir.'

'I think they will. I mean why the hell should they rot themselves up just for the sake of rotting us up. Christmas innit?'

'I wonder if they take Boxing Day as well,' said the navigator.

'We dunno yet if they're taking Christmas. Who's on watch?'

'Ken, sir.'

'And who's in the ops room?'

'I am, sir. At five minutes' notice.'

'What's the viz like?'

'Same, sir. About ten miles.'

'Sea state?'

'A half going on nothing.'

'They're probably just having a long lie. Boats around?'

'About twenty, number one. Nicely bunched.'

'Any doubtful contacts?'

'No, sir.'

'RAF doing their bit?'

'No, sir. Unsociable hours.'

'Idle buggers. Just as well the Battle of Britain didn't go on till Christmas. We should have kept the Fleet Air Arm . . . I remember in '52. In *Indefatigable*. Before Inchon. Christmas or no Christmas we had a dozen Venoms up, rain or shine. And we . . .'

The navigator and the lieutenant who was probably called

Bob had started to sway slowly in unison, although the ship was steady. Very much as though they had done it several times before, they also made slow soft sloshing and creaking noises, which Campbell recognized after a moment as days-of-sail sound effects. The navigator stopped to flick imaginary specks from his left shoulder, murmuring, 'This parrot shit'll be the ruin of my braid.'

'All right, you pair. Point taken. Anyway, point is, are we expecting our Brylcreem brothers at all today?'

'Perhaps, sir. If they can fit us in between muffins at Lossie and turkey time at Brize Norton. Nimrod. Recce and maildrop.'

'Good of them.'

After a leisurely breakfast Campbell went out for a walk on the upper deck. It was his first time outside the confines of the warm and noisy cocoon of the ship since harbour, apart from the brief excursion up to Ronnie's office. It was not yet full daylight. The sky in the east was greyish pink, in the west greyish blue. The air was still and the ship moving only slowly across endless still water, with no land in sight. To the north, about a mile away, lay a small untidy fleet of trawlers, with an attendant cloud of seagulls swirling over each. The air was cold, perhaps just freezing, but not uncomfortable and certainly no worse than many an ordinary winter day in Edinburgh. Campbell leaned on the guard-rail beside the port oerlikon and decided things could be much worse.

'Doctor!'

Campbell looked up and saw someone beckoning him from the bridge wing. It was Lieutenant Muir, the officer of the watch. Campbell walked forward, past several radio aerials, two searchlights and a series of formidable red boxes marked '3″ R.L. Ready Use'. to join him.

'Hello, doctor. What a way to spend Christmas, eh?'

'No complaints so far.'

'Seen over the bridge?'

'No.'

'Like to see it then? See how us salt-horse officers earn our pay? Better than leaning on a rail worrying about an outbreak of bubonic plague that might not happen. Come in. Been busy?'

'Not too bad.' Lieutenant Muir was just a little too breezy, too forcedly cheerful, in a Butlin's redcoat way, for Campbell's comfort.

'This is it, doc. The nerve centre of sleek greyhound of seaborne destruction. The bridge. Sharp end or bow down there. Stern or blunt end back there. Got it?'

The bridge was untidy and old fashioned compared with those of the two Pluto class frigates of Campbell's recent experience. There were the usual things: gyro compass and traditional magnetic binnacle; a tall chair (sacred to the captain's bottom); a big radar unit with its cathode ray display screen facing aft; a series of indicators showing the ship's course and speed, engine revs, rudder position and wind speed and direction. A sailor stood in a nautical pose, casually twirling a large, traditional and reassuring brass ship's wheel, glancing from time to time at the gyro compass repeater just overhead. The only remarkable feature was a strong smell of Chinese cooking.

'Been to sea before, doc?'

'Once or twice. Mainly RNR.'

'You're with the professionals now, you know. None of this home-for-Sunday-tea stuff. Seriously, are you enjoying yourself?'

Too many people had asked Campbell that lately, often as if the answer might reflect favourably or unfavourably on their own chosen way of life. And it did not seem to occur to them that he might simply be there to pass the time, to earn a salary and to see a little of life outside a teaching hospital (although admittedly his current Christmas-morning circumstances might be construed as taking the latter aim to extremes). Yet on balance, but for the excessively anti-Calvinistic hedonism of the phrase, he could probably be described as enjoying himself. 'No complaints,' he said.

'Good. Well, like I said, this is the nerve centre. Apart from the ops room, which is the other nerve centre.' He turned round to a small chart table and smoothed down a chart, then said, in a falsetto quack which he might conceivably have imagined to be an impersonation of Field

Marshal Montgomery, 'The situation is this. We're here. And they're there . . . or there . . . or possibly there.' He indicated a series of fiord-like inlets. 'Or, of course, back home opening their stockings.'

'How far's that?' Campbell asked, pointing to the coast on the chart.

'About forty miles. The enemy' (in the funny voice he pronounced it 'enema') 'may attack at any time, thus putting at risk the nation's entire supply of fish fingers. Here . . . and here . . . and here. Any questions?'

The sailor on the wheel was not amused. Campbell, perhaps because it was Christmas, pretended to be. 'Someone mentioned air cover. What do they do?'

Lieutenant Muir resumed his impersonation. 'Oh yes. The RAF. Splendid chaps. Fought on our side during the war. Sort of chaps you wouldn't mind going into the jungle with . . . Unfortunately . . . we're at sea.' He went back to his normal wardroom voice. 'Not a lot actually. Have a quick look round in a Nimrod if the viz is good. Three hundred miles isn't much to them, but it's a lot for us down here sloggin' through the hoggin. Last time up they found *Thor* for us. In here.' He picked up a pair of dividers and pointed to a wrinkle in the coast. Campbell noticed his hand was shaking. 'Seen ops?'

'No,' said Campbell.

'Ayres is in there holding court. Be glad to show you round.' Campbell thanked Lieutenant Muir and, without much option, was ushered down a ladder to the room marked 'Secret', where Roddy Ayres gave him a brisk rundown on how, if everything happened to be working all at the same time, HMS *Winchester* could fight off submarines, aircraft and attacking surface ships, under the masterly direction of an officer of vast skill, flair and experience, the Principal Warfare Officer or PWO (pronounced 'peewo'), in this instance himself. When Campbell went back to the bridge, Lieutenant Muir followed him closely for a little while, then cornered him on the bridge wing and, after marking conversational time for a few minutes, said that he must come down sometime and have a chat with him about something.

*

At 5.00 a.m. on Boxing Day, Campbell was hauled from a pleasantly sensual waking dream by the sound of the tannoy.

'D'ye hear there. Officer of the watch speaking. We have been detached from the fleet by command to investigate a doubtful contact moving out from the coast. The ship may have to go to full speed and the weather is deteriorating. Secure for sea. All loose gear to be stowed and heavy articles liable to move are to be lashed down. Stand by to go to defence watches at short notice should a close quarters situation develop. Hands stay clear of the upper deck. That is all.'

Campbell got up and went to breakfast, and was surprised to find that the wardroom table was not in use, but had been secured to the bulkhead with a stout cord, and all its chairs tied leg-to-leg beneath. Breakfast was being served, and various officers sat around the lounge section eating bacon and eggs from plates on their knees. Campbell did not feel especially hungry. The increased movement of the ship at speed, and the previous night's Christmas dinner, limited him to orange juice and cereal. The steward who served him looked more knowing than concerned. Ayres noticed too.

'Bit queasy, doc? Not to worry. Nelson got it. Father gets it. Even Henry here gets it occasionally. Don't you, Henry?'

'Sometimes.'

'If he forgets to take the cure.'

'Only if I forget to take the cure.'

Campbell had a feeling he was being set up for something, but did not rise. Not that it mattered. They carried on anyway.

'D'you think pork fat or mutton fat's better, Henry?'

'Not much in it either way, I suppose . . . Unless you're Jewish. Much more important to see the string's greased properly.'

Campbell got on with his cornflakes. The young lieutenant called Jim put his plate of bacon and eggs to one side.

'And what most people get wrong,' Ayres continued, rather in the manner of a TV cookery expert, 'is trying it too early. You've more or less got to wait until you're pretty ill.'

'Or it has the wrong effect . . .'

'In fact, for the chap who's only a bit queasy it's hardly

worth going to all the trouble. Why not try it, doc?'

'Worked for Nelson. Works for father. Even works for me. When I feel a bit queasy.'

'What?' said Campbell, not to deprive them of their simple pleasure.

'Lump of pork fat on a piece of string. About eighteen inches long. Swallow the pork fat but hang on to the end of the string. And wash it all down with a cupful of warm lard.'

Jim suddenly stood up and walked out of the wardroom. Campbell put his plate of cornflakes to one side and took a deep breath.

'Near miss,' said Ayres. 'Feeling all right, doc?'

In the circumstances the most natural thing would have been to stroll on the upper deck and enjoy the fresh sea air, but the officer of the watch had specifically forbidden that. Instead Campbell went up to the bridge by an indoor route and found, somewhat to his surprise, that it was in darkness. Only a few dim red and orange lights were visible, among the black shapes of the officer of the watch, the quartermaster on the wheel and two lookouts.

'Morning, doctor,' said the voice of Lieutenant Muir.

Slowly Campbell's eyes adjusted. It was not as dark as he had thought. Through the bridge windows the seascape was more interesting than it had been. White crests, dimming rapidly in the distance, marked the wave tops, and the frigate's bow rose and fell much more than Campbell would have guessed from the movement of the ship. Sometimes spray fell heavily back on to the fo'c'sle and sometimes it parted neatly, to fall in the bow wave just aft of the guns. Occasionally the oncoming wave was cut without disturbance, sliced by the rising bow, and sometimes, when the ship slid from one wave and met the next while it was still on the way down, a great double plume shot up, punched into the sky by 2000 tons at speed. The smell of grilled bacon had replaced that of Chinese cooking as the main odour on the bridge. Campbell began to feel hungry again.

'What's up, doc?' said Lieutenant Muir. 'Can't sleep? Sorry. Shouldn't take the piss. Might need you some day.'

Lieutenant Muir had not yet been for his loosely arranged chat with Campbell.

'Is it all right to be on the bridge?'

'Happy to see you. Know what's going on?'

'Well, heard the announcement about a doubtful contact.'

'Pipe.'

'What?'

'Not announcement. You're thinking of British Airways. In this firm we make pipes.'

'Roger. Heard the *pipe* about the doubtful contact.'

'Want to see it?'

'Yes, please.'

They moved to the radar screen. The ship's course showed as a straight line directed westward from the centre of the circle. Another line swept round, painting in flecks of gold against the darkness: the straggling fishing fleet now astern, the jagged land mass ahead and, tracked by a wax-pencil marking on the perspex, the contact, a small firm blip of gold.

'What's doubtful about it?'

'Good question. Short answer: command thinks it's doubtful. Going on a number of things, I suppose. He's on his own for starters. Not like fishermen up here. He's making a bee-line, again not like a fisherman, fussing about with nets. And there's a strong feeling further up that he's coming from somewhere where our feathered friends thought they saw a gunboat on a recce a couple of days ago. Apart from that, nothing. Call it intuition.'

'I see. What happens next?'

'You could ask father when he comes up from ops. But he'll probably be a bit preoccupied. Most likely we'll just check that this fellow's what we think he is, then watch him. We should be there in half an hour . . . Revolutions two five zero. That's us coming up to full speed now.'

Campbell looked round for the nautical equivalent of a speedometer. Its needle crept round towards twenty-four knots, which seemed fairly modest in view of the commotion outside. The ship certainly felt different at speed. If you ignored the speedometer, the old donks, wherever and whatever they were, seemed to manage to move her along quite smartly, and gave everything a tingling, energetic feeling of crudely harnessed power. A few minutes later, with the needle quivering around twenty-five, the ship was really going, smashing from wave to wave, westward into the end of the night, towards the unknown contact.

Sometimes the guns and the fo'c'sle disappeared in spray, sometimes water thrashed on to the bridge windows or landed drumming on the steel overhead. The sensation was one of excitement rather than discomfort. You tensed as the ship slid towards a big one, leaned forward as she slammed into it, then backwards as she drove herself up over it. Sometimes she hung for a second with a strange, sliding weightlessness, as a really big one passed underneath.

'Old girl's doing all right, don't you think?'

'Sir?'

'Winnie . . . Not doing badly for an old girl, um?'

'No, sir.'

'Likes a frolic. A gallop. A touch of the ocean greyhounds. Does her good.'

'Yessir.'

The captain was not in the gathered-brow, quarterdeck-pacing frame of mind Lieutenant Muir had suggested. In fact, he seemed to be rather enjoying himself.

'Fun, isn't it, doctor? This must be what you joined for.'

'Yessir.'

The captain hoisted himself up into his chair and sat looking out, intent and alert, though all there was to see was twenty yards or so of chaotic water.

'About fifteen minutes, Ken.'

'Yessir.'

'Bit of lee. Won't be like this. But won't be a flat calm either. Sixteen-inch light all right?'

'Yessir.'

'Good . . . Health of the ship's company remaining good, doctor?'

'One or two seasick, sir.'

'One or two plum pudding overdoses too, I imagine . . . If the general state of people yesterday was anything to go by.'

'Yessir.'

'Perhaps the PO Cook put rather a lot of rum in it.'

'Could explain one or two things, sir.'

The captain chuckled to himself at this mass absolution. There had been no serious drunkenness in evidence on board, but very few cases of total abstinence. LMA Smith had mentioned that one or two of his shipmates had the odd bottle of sherbet stashed away for special occasions such as Christmas, and sailors had been known to do such things as hoard or trade their official allowance of three cans of beer per man per day (which might have been how AB McGuffy had first trod the primrose path that led, via the Mickey Finn, to his present and as yet unresolved trouble). 'Enjoy Christmas, doctor?'

'Yessir.'

'The singing was all right considering. Pity about the organ, portable, small, though.'

Sometime around 6.00 p.m., after the troops' Christmas dinner but before the wardroom's more sedate celebration, there had been a crowded, untidy, good-natured and perhaps drunken sing-song in the junior rates dining hall, at which the captain had read about three verses of Holy Scripture, after which they had all sung 'Jingle Bells' and 'White Christmas', with the first lieutenant grinning bravely throughout.

The captain had descended from his chair, and moved across to the radar. 'Come round to two eight five, Ken. We want to look at him, not send him in for a paint job.'

'Sir. Starboard ten. Starboard five. Midships. Steer two eight five.'

'Following all this, doctor?'

'More or less, sir.'

'Good . . . Might get a bit busy up here soon.'

'Sir.'

Thus gently dismissed, Campbell went down the little stair to the ops room, which was, if anything, even darker than the bridge. 'Never like this in the old *Indefatigable* before Inchon,' the navigator remarked out of the gloom. 'Boxing Day or no Boxing Day we'd have had fifty Sopwith Camels up there. Right, doctor? Biggles would have sorted out this little lot and been home tucked up in bed with Algy before you could say Richthofen. How's the tummy? All right? Told you. Nothing works for seasickness like the old pork fat.'

The atmosphere in the ops room differed from that of the bridge. Sailors stood or sat over their strange warlike boxes and glowing screens, plotting distances and bearings, chatting among themselves mainly in figures and initials, and communicating more officially with the bridge at regular intervals, via the navigating officer. Apart from the junior rates dining area, the ops room seemed to be the biggest space in the ship, but dark and intricate, without natural light and full of odd corners in which yet another sailor sat engrossed in a radar echo or standing by with a paperback and a bar of chocolate. There was an air of cheerful informality and efficiency, a concern not with appearances but with keeping on top of things. Coming down from the bridge to the ops room was like going backstage in a theatre, or into the kitchen of a restaurant, it seemed to Campbell as he strolled round with his mentor, occasionally reaching out to steady himself on a mysterious box.

'Leading Seaman Pratt here normally runs the submarine department,' said Ayres. 'But while we're up here he's in charge of the coffee. D'you take sugar, doctor?'

'Thanks. No sugar.'

'Biscuit, sir? We've got gipsy creams and half-coated.'

'Oh, half-coated, thanks, leading seaman.'

Ayres cast a proprietorial gesture over the men and the machines. 'As you see, doctor, we keep a general eye on things with our various black boxes. And we tell the front office,' he nodded in the direction of the bridge, 'anything we feel they ought to know. And if they ask us about something in particular we can generally come back with something. How the fleet's spread. Weather. Aircraft about the place. Quickest way home. Favourite for the 2.30 at Sandown Park. Time of the next gunboat. All in a day's work.' They were standing beside a radar screen. 'There we are. That's him. Still pretending he hasn't seen us. Doing the innocent passage bit. Fools nobody.'

The firm gold blip coming out from the coast was much closer now. From the feel of things, HMS *Winchester* was moving around a lot less and had probably slowed down.

'D'ye hear there,' said the tannoy. 'Hands to defence

watches. Hands to defence watches. Starboard watch close up. Hands to remain clear of the upper deck. Assume condition Yankee.' The latter instruction was something complicated to do with watertight compartments. Throughout the ship, heavy rubber-sealed doors and hatches would be closed, to be opened only when someone was actually passing through, and then closed again immediately afterwards. It made getting round the ship a bit inconvenient, but lessened the risk of being sunk.

'And may God bless all who sail in her,' said the navigator. 'Know about this, doctor?'

'The LMA gave me a rough idea.'

'Six hours on, six hours off certainly keeps the mess bills down.' He picked up a telephone. 'Bridge. Plot. Contact now bearing two nine zero. Range one mile. Course and speed steady . . . Don't mention it.'

'What happens now?'

'Oh, father'll probably want to shine a light on him and say good morning, we know you're there and don't pretend it isn't you. Then we'll just keep him company and see what happens. If it's him.'

'Oh?'

'Still just might be something else. You can't say till you've seen him in the light.'

On a twinge of conscience, perhaps only a feeling that the morning so far had been too pleasantly interesting and diverse to justify his pay and uniform, Campbell went back down to sickbay, through an obstacle course of watertight doors, each secured by six heavy metal clips. A stoker in overalls was sitting glumly with his right sleeve rolled up. The X-ray machine had been repositioned, and was now low over the operating table, which was strewn with the yellow envelopes used for unexposed film.

'Hello.'

'Hello, sir.'

'What's wrong?'

'Me wrist.'

'What happened?'

'Slipped, sir. Down below. On an oily step. In the roughers, sir.'

'How did you fall?'

'On me hand, sir. Like that.' He indicated a fall on his outstretched hand.

'Where's the pain?'

He pointed to the base of his thumb.

'That sore?'

He jumped. 'The killick did all that, sir. He took some pictures, too. He's in there doin' them.' He nodded towards the door that Campbell had assumed led to some sort of venereological laboratory.

There was a set of medical documents lying on the desk, pertaining to one D116834C, Trewitt, John Peter, MEM. The LMA had written a card, with an account of the injury and the clinical findings, concurring quite well with Campbell's own quick assessment. Until proved otherwise, the stoker had broken one of the small bones of the wrist, at the base of his right thumb. The X-rays required were tricky postgraduate stuff, with the angles right and good fine detail showing in the bones. If, from his rather basic apparatus, in a frigate galumphing around in a half gale, the LMA had produced the appropriate pictures, he was definitely earning his keep. He emerged from the far end of the sickbay.

'Oh. Morning, sir. I was just going to dry the films then come and find you. MEM Trewitt slipped and fell on his outstretched right hand whilst on watch in the engine room this morning. He has a painful wrist and is tender at the base of the thumb.'

'Yes. I had a quick look at him. What did you think?'

'I'd like you to have a look at the pictures, sir. Could well be. They're hanging up in the dark-room.'

'D'ye hear there. First lieutenant speaking. The doubtful contact has now been positively identified as the gunboat *Freya*. What happens now is up to him. As before, we'll keep him company, marking him close when there are trawlers about and just keeping a friendly eye on him when there aren't. We'll stay at defence watches until daylight, then back to normal sea routine, standing by to go into defence watches again at short notice. That is all.'

Shortly afterwards another voice on the tannoy said, 'The ship is about to alter course and may roll heavily.'

'scuse me, sir. I'll just square up the dark-room before it goes all over.'

The ship slowed down further, then began to wallow horribly. The X-ray machine creaked in its lashings, boxes and bottles rattled in the cupboards and the yellow envelopes scattered on the sickbay deck. The stoker reached out to steady himself, using his right hand, and cursed at the pain. Gradually, as the ship came round, first across the oncoming seas, then away from them, the rolling reached a heaving sickening maximum then subsided to a leisurely corkscrewing motion. The LMA came out into the sickbay again.

'If you'd like to look at the pictures now, sir. They're not dry yet but I think they may be of some help.'

'Thank you.' Campbell followed the LMA down the sickbay and into the little room at the end, which was subdivided into three, with a bathroom complete with shower, a WC and a neat little laboratory *cum* darkroom equipped with steel sinks, red processing lights and an X-ray viewing box. Three small squares of film were draining in a rack. Campbell picked one up.

'That's the lateral, sir. I can't see much on it.'

'No.'

'PA's a bit better. Suspicious. But I think there's something on that one.'

'The oblique?'

'Yessir.'

Campbell held it in front of the viewing box. The scaphoid, the little crescent of bone forming a shallow socket for the base of the thumb, had a tiny crack across the middle. 'Nice pictures.'

'Thank you, sir. A bit underpenetrated, maybe. But I didn't want to repeat them with defence watches being piped.'

'Fair enough. They're pretty good.'

'Quick plaster of Paris, sir?'

'Yes please. Twelve weeks. And he won't be much use in the engine room with it.'

'They'll probably put him on light duty, sir.'

'What's the engineer officer's name please, LMA?'

'Lieutenant Scholes, sir.'

'Big chap?'

'No, sir. Shortish. Thin. Dark hair.'

'I'll see him at stand easy and tell him.' Campbell looked at his watch. It was only eight o'clock. There was still two hours to go before stand easy and coffee.

By dawn the wind had dropped, and the sea had settled to a slow, rolling swell. The first lieutenant decreed a relaxation from defence watches and the troublesome condition Yankee, and people started to go about their usual business of a morning at sea. A little crop of bumps and bruises appeared outside sickbay, and one or two regular consumers of seasickness tablets came to replenish their stores. The restrictions on movement on the upper deck were lifted and Campbell, with many others of the ship's company, went up to look at the gunboat.

She was small in comparison to HMS *Winchester*, perhaps only half as long, and much simpler in outline. The shape of her hull was somewhere between that of a trawler and that of a frigate. She had only a basic navigational radar outfit, and a single, small calibre gun on the fo'c'sle. Her principal offensive weapon was generally known to be not her gun – dismissed by authoritative opinion as a pea-shooter – but her bow, reinforced and sharply raked, designed ostensibly for ice-breaking, but coming in very handy both for cutting the wires ('warps' to the pundits) joining nets to trawlers, and for ramming frigates.

Both ships moved slowly eastwards, about a mile apart, with HMS *Winchester* slightly behind. The sun climbed slowly and the wind subsided to a westerly breeze. That, and the swell, slow and positively gentle by late morning, and coming from astern to impart the easy-gliding, undulating, curiously downhill feeling of a following sea, produced on board a relaxed, almost holiday atmosphere after the tensions of the early morning.

By noon they were within five miles of the trawler fleet. Then, for no apparent reason, the gunboat turned suddenly and headed east again at twelve knots, perhaps twice her previous speed.

'Must have forgot his sandwiches,' said the first lieutenant, as they turned to follow.

In the wardroom at lunchtime it seemed that the proximity of a gunboat representing the opposition added zest to the whole business of being at sea. People larked and jested more than usual, and no one showed any signs of seasickness. The menu, typed by the PO Steward, read: 'Soup of the Day', followed by 'Roast Lamb of Leg' or 'Steak and Kidney Pudding', followed by 'Queen of Puddings'. Apart from the generous spacing and the understandable (from an Oriental) mix-up over lambs and legs, there was something else curious about it that Campbell couldn't quite work out. Then it dawned on him. PO Chan, in an orderly Chinese fashion, had arranged the words so that they were lined up vertically as well as horizontally, with a first column reading, from the top, 'Soup', Roast', 'Steak' and 'Queen', a second reading 'of', 'Lamb', and so on. It was an unexceptionable, even agreeable eccentricity, quite forgivable and adding perhaps to the charm and individuality of life in HMS *Winchester*.

'Go on, doc,' said Ayres. 'Have the babies' heads.'

Campbell must have looked puzzled. He ordered the soup, which turned out to be brown windsor. He was hungry, having eaten nothing since a very early breakfast.

'Now have the babies' heads. With soggy cabbage. Ideal for roughers. Slides down a treat, slides up a treat.'

'Navigator!' The first lieutenant rapped the table with a spoon. As president of the mess, he appeared to be engaged in an endless struggle against forces of playful disruption. He always sat at the head of the table at lunch and dinner, and everyone waited reverently before eating, until he had given the signal by lifting his spoon or whatever, but apart from such basic observances the wardroom, especially its younger members, led by the navigator, seemed to be constantly exploring his tolerance, sometimes imaginatively, sometimes amusingly and sometimes with frank obscenity, like a friendly but high-spirited class pushing a teacher to his limits.

Campbell ordered steak and kidney pudding. His portion consisted of a generous amount of rich, beefy stew, with kidney much in evidence, running out of a mantle of quite tasty dough, apparently extracted from a tin, and still bearing its shape. Most of the rest ordered babies' heads, and got the same.

'Poor little things,' said the navigator. 'Tasty though.'

Ultimate responsibility for wardroom catering lay with Ronnie, the supply officer, and he was never allowed to forget it: any conversation about food, and there was a lot of it, constantly came back to him, ribbing, chiding or (rarely) encouraging him, along the lines of 'Perhaps a bit more salt in the spuds, Ronnie' or 'That's twice this month we've had queen of puddings' (with a subsidiary debate on whether that was too often or not often enough) and 'It's ages since we've had hot-pot' (or roast chicken, or asparagus, or train smash, or pot-mess, or one of a number of other naval delicacies as yet unfamiliar to Campbell). Lieutenant Baker took all this in good part, like someone with a large family to feed. Campbell asked him about what the sailors liked.

'You could give 'em chips and ice-cream, plus some trimmings of course, three times a day and half of them would think they're in heaven. We just ring the changes, though. And the idea with this lot – he indicated his fellow officers – 'is to have different people complaining at different times, 'cause you can't please all of the people all of the time. And I don't mind a bit of stick. You get used to it in my branch.'

'It's ages since we had mushy peas, Ronnie.'

'You'll get 'em, Bob. Don't you worry. All in good time,' he said cheerfully. 'It's when you lot stop complaining I'll worry about you.'

Over coffee Lieutenant Scholes, the engineer, came over and joined Campbell. 'How's my lad then? Any change?'

Campbell had nothing to add to what he had said already at morning coffee, and in any case had not seen Stoker Trewitt since the early morning. The patient was likely to be down in the junior rates mess, mastering the art of eating babies' heads with a scaphoid plaster on.

'I can find something for him to do in the office, I expect,' said Lieutenant Scholes. 'Always little jobs needing doing. Nothing heavy of course, like you said . . . Should I give him a make and mend, to let the plaster dry?'

A make and mend was what Campbell, until a few weeks

before, would have called a half day. Etymologically, it was something to do with a days-of-sail instruction about hands to make and mend clothes, i.e., not to work the ship.

'I think so,' said Campbell, after a moment's reflection. It was the second time that day he had been called upon to make a professional pronouncement.

Shortly after lunch Campbell went for a stroll on the upper deck. The gunboat was nowhere to be seen. To the west, huge snowy cliffs reared out of the sea. The rest of the horizon was empty. The sun had started to go down.

'Saw them off,' said Lieutenant Ayres, now the officer of the watch and presiding over affairs on the bridge. 'Command wants us back with the boats by sunset. So it's back where we came from, unless they've moved without telling us.'

'What happened to the gunboat?'

'Over there somewhere. We don't go inside the ten-mile line. But don't worry, doctor. She'll be back. Quite unfair, really. They can nip home in an hour or so and get into carpet slippers and snooze over the *Reykjavik Evening Despatch*, while we're stuck out here ploughing a lonely furrow in the storm-tossed salty wastes, etc. They could really rot us up in one decent six-hour sortie, if they put their minds to it, or let me plan it for them. They know that we virtually can't start anything, far less use the guns, but just have to stick to the old now-move-along-there-please-just-stand-back-and-let-the-gentlemen-fish routine, and they've seen it all. We did a month up here last time. Got to know them quite well. Stooged along with one lot for days at a time. Once, when we'd been sitting on them for about ten hours, doing nothing, hove to, we were ordered up to another sector. We poked off at about twenty knots, and they came up on the radio, all plaintive, saying, "*Vinchester, Vinchester*. Vere are you going?" '

An hour later HMS *Winchester* was nearing the trawlers again. Another frigate, low, grey and handsome in the setting sun, prowled on the far side of the fleet. Campbell asked about it.

'*Eurydice*. Brand new. Practically wet paint. Don't know what she's doing up here. She might get bent. But there we are. She's command locally. Glamour boat with a four-stripe captain.' A signalling lamp began to twinkle from the bridge wing of the distant frigate. 'Oh, God. There she goes again. Yeoman! I suppose they think using radio's common.' A signaller appeared and clacked the lamp on the starboard bridge wing in acknowledgement. Ayres rang the captain in his cabin and, after a short chat, gave steering orders that brought the ship swinging round to starboard. 'They want us to circle the *other* way,' he explained. 'Slowly.'

While a couple of dozen trawlers, spread over a few square miles of sea, cast and hauled under their eternal wheeling crowds of escorting seagulls, the two frigates ranged round them in a slow pink sunset. Campbell loafed on the bridge and bridge wings, looking around with borrowed binoculars, and generally enjoyed the leisured delights of the seafaring life. Ayres was agreeable company and full of pleasant time-passing yarns. He had been in the Navy for about six years and, as a sub-lieutenant, had been involved in a previous similar confrontation. 'In *Persephone*. Had a marvellous captain. The Navy was his hobby and the ship was his yacht. We used to come up here via a couple of Scottish sea lochs where his friends had shooting lodges. We'd anchor and he'd go ashore and come back a couple of days later pissed as a handcart, with a bloody great dead stag in the boat. The troops loved him. Even the stokers developed a taste for venison. Bit out of touch in some ways, though. Got it into his head that all this business was really about fish fingers, except that he was convinced they were called cod pieces, and no one could bring themselves to go up there and explain to him that they weren't. So he used to come on the tannoy and drawl away for hours about millions of cod pieces for the breakfast tables of the nation. Great sport. And the trawler skippers couldn't make head nor tail of him on the chat net. After he'd done his broadcast to the fleet, with the usual friendly advice about the designated areas and all that, you could hear them chuntering away amongst themselves in pure Grimsby: "Fookin' 'ell, lads . . . D'y'ever hear the loike o' that then? Fookin' 'ell. Sounds as if t'piss'd freeze in 'is toggle . . ."

'Ever heard the chat net, doctor? They can go on for hours

and hours not saying anything except "eeeh" and "aaahaaa' and "fookin" 'ell" . . . We've got one chap in there who keeps saying, "If Ah'd a coople o' great fookin' goons on the front loike fookin' *Winchester*, Ah'd flatten fookin' Reykjavik." And after midnight they generally start drooling away about sex. "Honest. Eeeh. Eeeyah. 'Twere aboot six inches in froont o' me nose and it smelt loovely. And 'twere fookin' winkin' at me." '

That night *Freya* reappeared, in earnest. Once more HMS *Winchester* was detached to intercept her and escort her. This time she headed straight for the fishing fleet at speed. Then began a complex exercise in screening, which would have been dangerous enough in full daylight. The ship came to defence watches, and as *Freya* moved closer and the risk of collision increased, *Winchester*'s ship's company moved to full alert. Everyone, including watchkeepers off duty, who would normally have been allowed to rest, was up and fully dressed, with life jackets and immersion suits to hand. Men gathered in mess decks and passageways, with no one but essential personnel within six feet of the ship's side, and waited.

The gunboat edged round the fishing fleet, always with one frigate or the other in attendance, sliding between her and the threatened trawlers. In HMS *Winchester* the first-aid parties were closed up and, as they were his responsibility, Campbell went round them. In the for'ard POs' mess, the LMA was calmly in charge of three sailors, and was reading a highly technical book on photography. In the junior rates dining hall, three Chinese stewards under Leading Steward Ho were playing a hectic game of mah jong with much giggling and Cantonese chatter. Aft, three grubby stokers, straight from watch, waited under the eye of one of their POs for a test of their clinical skills.

The various huddles of waiting men were quiet, cheerful and unusually colourful, as the rules of uniform had been widely disregarded in the interests of warmth and individuality. People wore favourite items of clothing and there were some very un-naval items of headgear: bush hats smothered in badges, balaclavas and stripey knitted hats. Football scarves were much in evidence, and one man, presumably a

Protestant Glaswegian, had turned out in the full regalia of an ardent Rangers fan prepared for a cold afternoon's combat on the terraces.

A few read or played cards as they waited. One group in the junior rates dining hall played uckers, an arcane, seafaring derivative of ludo, and in the main passageway opposite the galley a man sat reading a fat dictionary, so deliberately that Campbell checked to see if his tongue was actually moving in the corner of his mouth. He appeared to be wading through obscure words beginning with 'T', which sharply reminded Campbell that he was the new boy, and that the vast majority of the ship's company had been through all this before.

At 9.00 lighting was reduced to the red auxiliary system and the ship became quiet but for the noise of engines and ventilation and occasional pipes on the tannoy. The sailors sitting in the passageways fell asleep against each other, or shifted uneasily. Some got up to stretch their legs. Few were now talking. At 11.00 there was a ripple of quiet activity as the cooks came round with mugfuls of pot-mess, another naval concoction, this one a compromise between soup and stew.

From time to time the first lieutenant came up on the tannoy to give the ship's company short summaries of what was going on. These situation reports, later to be much parodied, usually in the context of official cocktaail parties, began, 'Number one speaking. Sitrep,' and went on to give the gunboat's latest position ('*Freya* two cables on starboard beam'), a non-committal view of the possibilities ('She may close or break or try to skip astern'), and some word of instruction to the ship's company, usually about safety ('In the event of finding yourself in the water, do not attempt to swim any distance. Wait quietly to be rescued').

Campbell, bored by inactivity and frustrated by the sensation of being locked up in a steel box while interesting things were going on outside, exercised an officer-like privilege and went for a walk, inasmuch as it was possible to do so through passageways crowded with drowsy sailors in a ship closed up in condition Yankee.

In the ops room, the customary good-humoured calm prevailed. Once more Leading Seaman Pratt conjured up a coffee and once more Lieutenant Ayres was amusingly informative on recent developments. His radar screens showed the trawlers bunched together more closely than formerly. Beyond them, HMS *Eurydice* showed as a larger echo, slightly detached and moving slowly round. The gunboat's gold blip seemed very close indeed, but Ayres was reassuring. 'It won't look so bad from up top. These things always seem more alarming down here. You expect to hear a crunch, look over your shoulder and find yourself having to welcome someone aboard. But he's half a cable away. Or 100 yards to you, doctor. You could probably nip up and take a look when you've finished your coffee.'

Campbell did so, and stood quietly at the back of the bridge, ready to depart at the slightest hint of official displeasure. The trawler fleet on the left was a jumble of lights – deck floodlights, navigation lights, green and white masthead fishing lights – bobbing in the swell. *Freya*, a grey silhouette showing only minimum navigation lights, moved slowly along on the right, sometimes coming ahead, sometimes slowing almost to a halt. Between gunboat and trawlers was HMS *Winchester*, her captain manoeuvring her on wheel and engines to keep her there. When *Freya* surged ahead, *Winchester* followed. When *Freya* slowed, so did *Winchester*. If *Freya* stopped, *Winchester* did likewise.

The bridge was dark and quiet, except for the curt repetition of wheel and engine orders. 'Port five . . . Half ahead both. Midships . . . Slow ahead both . . . Starboard five. Steer one four oh.' The captain sat in his chair, looking right and left, watching gunboat and trawlers and the space between in which he manoeuvred, but mainly his eyes followed *Freya*, watching and guessing, so that to every initiative there would be a response, something that would keep the long bulk of the warship between the gunboat and the fleet.

Half an hour and a couple of first lieutenant's sitreps later, a lot happened very suddenly. First *Freya* speeded up and made as though to squeeze past *Winchester*'s bow, coming much closer at a fine angle on the starboard beam. Then she seemed to stop and spin to port all at once, her bow sweeping aft, just missing *Winchester*'s quarter. The warship, heavier and more unwieldy, slid further before stopping, permitting the gunboat's bow to come across her stern. As *Winchester*'s screws thrashed the water at half astern, and dragged her to a halt, *Freya* slipped behind her into the fleet.

The chase that followed, vivid in impression but afterwards obscure in detail, probably lasted less than five minutes. Having broken the ring, *Freya* darted ahead towards the nearest trawler, on her port bow. The trawler, travelling more slowly, turned tighter, saving her gear from the gunboat's bow. Meanwhile *Winchester* had wrenched herself round in the water to follow on *Freya*'s track. There evolved a *son et lumière*, a whirling pattern of lights to the sound of the captain's voice, rising slightly and rapping out wheel and engine orders more and more quickly. These seemed to succeed in keeping *Winchester*'s bow glued to *Freya*'s stern, usually on the side of the nearest trawler, so that there was some chance of shouldering her off. Boats slid past seemingly at arm's length, so close that Campbell could see the expressions on the faces of the fishermen on their floodlit decks.

Slower, but smaller and more manoeuverable, *Freya* had the advantage inside the fleet, but she could not immediately exploit it. She darted forward, stopped, wheeled and darted forward again, always with *Winchester* on her tail. Suddenly she veered over and headed for a narrow gap between two trawlers, to break free of her pursuer. *Winchester*, too large and unwieldy for her new task and now never less than half a move behind, tried to follow. Nearly 300 feet long, she turned slowly, slewing round and missing the trawlers by yards only, ahead and astern, and took up the pursuit again.

At that moment Campbell realized what was at risk and how close they had been to disaster. For the first time the idea of a collision had translated itself into rending steel and icy water, damage, casualties and possibly deaths. The trawlers nearby looked much larger and more solid than before. Ahead, *Freya* gathered speed down a long opening in the fleet, at the end of which a trawler sat on its own. The distance between pursuer and pursued widened as the smaller ship gained speed more quickly. On *Winchester*'s bridge they watched helplessly as the gunboat bore down on the lone trawler and passed close astern of her at speed, certainly slicing off her gear before clearing the fleet and making off into the darkness beyond.

'Fuck 'im,' said the first lieutenant, composing himself for another short burst on the tannoy. As *Winchester* passed down the lines of ships and beyond the latest victim and out again to resume her slow circling, he said 'Number one speaking. Sitrep. For those of you who might be wondering what all that was about, *Freya* got into the fleet and we followed. On his way out, he cut a warp, and now appears to be making off. We will resume patrolling, marking him again if necessary. Hands to remain at defence watches meantime. That is all.'

Freya kept going and did not return to the fleet that night. *Winchester* continued to patrol, under the fussy supervision of *Eurydice*, keeping a mile or so from the trawlers, and her ship's company was eventually stood down from defence watches at about 1.00. Campbell went to bed; to do so suddenly seemed some sort of privilege or reward, and to be able to undress properly a positive luxury.

Next morning the sea was calm and when the sun rose there were no gunboats around. The two frigates shepherded their charges more loosely and the trawlers spread over the grey glassy sea. Just before lunch the skipper of one came up on the short-wave chat net.

''ullo *Winchester*, 'ullo *Winchester*. *Grimsby Calliope*. 'ow do you 'ear me. Over.'

'*Grimsby Calliope*. Loud and clear. Over,' Lieutenant Muir, officer of the watch for the forenoon watch, replied.

'Want some fish?'

'*Grimsby Calliope*, yes thanks. Over.'

'How many lads 'ave you got on there?'

'*Grimsby Calliope*, about 200. Over.'

'Bloody 'ell. Send a boat anyway.'

'*Grimsby Calliope*, roger. Five minutes. Over.'

'Okay, *Winchester*. We'll have some ready.'

'*Grimsby Calliope*, roger. Over and out.'

Lieutenant Muir rang the captain in his cabin to confirm that there were no over-riding operational objections to the proposal. There weren't. Under the supervision of Sub-Lieutenant Blake, the PO of the watch on deck lowered the

Gemini dinghy into the sea. With a leading seaman and an AB on board, kitted up in foul weather gear and life jackets, it spluttered off towards *Grimsby Calliope*, the nearest trawler.

Ten minutes later it was back, full of writhing cod, some of them four feet long. The seamen clipped the four lifting cables on to the hook from the small derrick on the quarter-deck and scrambled up a rope ladder, then dinghy and fish were hoisted and swung inboard.

At some time during this procedure an incident occurred that was dissected in detail over lunch in the wardroom. The gift of fish was so fresh that one of them had bitten the coxswain of the dinghy, the leading seaman. He was reportedly surprised rather than injured, though it had hurt a little at the time. His injury was not even serious enough for him to have sought specialist help in the sickbay, but the circumstances were discussed at length. The question which proccupied the wardroom lunch table was why the cod should have bitten the leading seaman in the first place. Resentment at being caught would have seemed reason enough, but the engineer officer, who had graduated from the submarine world, had a theory that fish got angry when they were seasick. This drew the scorn of all who spoke on the point, but he was steadfast in his view, and produced evidence to support it. He had supervised the refit of a submarine, and had thought it would be a nice idea to have a fish tank, behind a bulkhead with imitation portholes, to brighten up the wardroom. Somehow he had persuaded the relevant craftsmen to fit it. '. . . A sort of conversation piece, you understand. We thought it'd be nice at parties. People would say, ooh, look, I'm sure I saw a goldfish swim past just now. Or of course if they'd had a few, they might see them and wonder if they should mention it or not . . . Anyway, when she re-commissioned we went out to a fairground and won all these lovely little goldfish, and they were very happy when we were tied up alongside, and they didn't seem to mind dives and being submerged for long periods, but they hated being on the surface. Couldn't stand it, and the rougher it got, the angrier they got. They're just not used to being on the surface. Not built for it, you know. Ended up eating each other on the way home from Malta.' He coughed, then said, 'That was in *Termigant*. In 1961,' as though to clinch the argument.

The first lieutenant was unconvinced. 'Doctor,' he said. 'Fish don't get seasick, do they?'

There was an awkward silence round the table, which deepened when Campbell confessed he did not know.

'I expect he missed that bit of the course,' said Ayres to Henry, in a stage whisper. 'Either that or he's forgotten. I wonder what else he doesn't know. "You've either got asthma or beriberi. I'm not sure which. I must have been off the day we did that." Still, can always look it up, I suppose.'

'Yeah, doc. Go on. Look it up,' said the first lieutenant. 'I got you dozens of books for the sickbay library. You can tell us at tea-time.'

By tea-time there were other concerns. HMS *Winchester* was once again in defence watches, having been despatched by the command to investigate another doubtful contact moving out from the coast. The contact proved to be another gunboat, larger and faster than her predecessor. The two ships proceeded east in failing light towards the fleet. Campbell, equipped with Mae West and immersion suit, both neatly packed but ready for use if required, walked round his first-aid parties again, stepping over sailor's legs in the passageways with a veteran air, and clipping the watertight doors after himself without grazing his fingers. Then he went down to sickbay. He had resolved, like the sailor reading the dictionary, to put the enforced idleness to good use this time. He needed to learn anatomy again for the primary exams for surgical fellowship, and the first lieutenant's sickbay library included a useful primer on the subject.

All anatomy starts in the armpit. Returning there six years on from his first run through as a junior medical student, Campbell found that it had gained nothing in the way of either charm or interest. A few names, mainly in lightly anglicized Latin, floated across the void, and a complex neurological crossroads, in which nerve fibres wandered around in a futile exercise whose only purpose could be to give anatomists something to put in examinations, seemed, if anything, more difficult than before.

The sickbay deadlights, screwed down as part of assuming

condition Yankee, closed off the portholes and cut out any visual distraction. The tannoy system, always kept at low volume to preserve the clinical ambience, carried the first lieutenant's voice, muttering about cables and port quarters, but not loud enough to interfere with study, and the ship seemed to have slowed down, which made reading easier. Campbell was vaguely aware of *Winchester* turning, rapidly then slowly, as he moved on from the nerves to the blood vessels, which were more sensibly arranged.

'Sir.' The LMA stood in the sickbay doorway. 'Sir, you know we've been rammed.'

'No.'

'Yessir. Thought you might have heard the pipe. First lieutenant really did it rather well. Like a football commentator. Anyway, this new bugger just upped and slammed us. Not a trawler within miles.'

Campbell got up. 'Casualties?'

'No, sir.'

'Damage?'

'Only a bit, sir. Split in the ship's side in the POs' sleeping accommodation just aft of my first-aid party. Quite loud from where we were.'

'Any water coming in?'

'No, sir. It's all above the waterline. And the damage control party's putting in a coffer now . . . But I expect we'll be ordered home soon, because of the risk in heavy weather. Be there in a couple of days.'

The next few days turned out much as LMA Smith had predicted. HMS *Winchester* was withdrawn from close patrolling, but held in the area as a reserve until a relief, in the shape of HMS *Cerberus*, became available. Thereafter, in passage south, a number of matters that had been deferred were dealt with, including the troublesome case of R. *v*. McGuffy. He appeared before the commanding officer. Campbell was called as a witness and found himself a participant in a small but imposing pageant of naval justice. The master at arms, a lowering presence who had read out the various charges, stood beside the first lieutenant, who had outlined the case for the prosecution. McGuffy, charged with being drunk on board, being absent from his place of duty while quartermaster and leaving the ship without permission on two occasions, looked neat and penitent. Campbell answered various questions briefly and factually, and was not cross-examined since AB McGuffy, as predicted and as was his custom, had decided to plead guilty and throw himself on the mercy of the court. Henry, as his divisional officer, gave a halting account of circumstances which might be regarded as mitigating the offences, mentioning the sailor's multitudinous domestic difficulties, his injudicious and untidy financial commitments, his unhappy background, his strenuous if intermittent attempts at self-improvement since joining HMS *Winchester*, and his triumph in the field of personal hygiene (described as 'greatly improved turn-out').

The captain, who had said very little, looked pale and extremely serious. With his head slightly to one side, he talked softly and without emotion to the accused.

'Well, McGuffy, I have heard with great disappointment and distress the first lieutenant's account of your latest offences against our mild and reasonable code of discipline, and of your betrayal of our trust by leaving your post as quartermaster. I say disappointment because I had begun to hope that you had turned a corner, McGuffy, and distress because it is clear that you haven't. At least not yet.

'I'm going to give you another chance, McGuffy. I'm not going to deprive you of income and liberty by sending you off to Detention Quarters, though what you have done would be widely regarded as well worth twenty-eight days. Nor am I going to deprive you of a little bit of extra pre-deployment leave that may be coming our way, by awarding any punishment that will confine you to the ship over the next few weeks, because you, perhaps more than any of us, need to spend time with your family, Which leaves me only one choice, McGuffy, and unfortunately it's one that will affect you and the ones you love in the way you can least afford.

'I'm going to fine you, McGuffy, and I'm going to fine you heavily, knowing and of course regretting how much it will affect poor Mrs McGuffy and above all your two little children.'

McGuffy sniffed.

'Fined seventy pounds.' McGuffy sniffed more loudly and Henry blinked. 'To be recovered over three pay days.'

'Fined-seventy-pounds-to-be-recovered-over-three-pay-days,' echoed the master at arms, before closing the proceedings with a brisk recitative of his own. 'On caps. Right turn. Quick march. Report-to-the-regulating-office.'

Shortly after lunch that day, when Campbell was in the sickbay working his way down towards the elbow, there was a soft knock at the door.

'Come in.' A large darkness loomed behind. 'Ah, master. Please take a seat.'

The master at arms hesitated just inside the doorway. There were about him the signs of a good lunch: his normally healthy colour was enhanced, and he had an intensity and deliberation that was new. He was not unsteady on his feet, merely careful. As he sat down at the side of the desk, a dense vapour of rum wafted across.

'Yes, master,' said Campbell. 'What can I do for you?'

He toyed nervously with his hat, now in his lap, and was clearly having some difficulty getting started. Eventually he said, 'Sir . . . Have you ever attended captain's before, sir?'

'Hm?'

'Captain's, sir. The table. Like this morning.'

It was an institution for which the Royal Naval Reserve had little requirement. 'No, master.'

'If you don't mind my saying so, sir . . . I thought as much . . . I know it must be very difficult for you, coming in virtually from . . . civilian street . . . I mean civvy street. But there were one or two little points, sir . . . that I'd be happier if you . . . was to be acquainted with.'

'Oh?'

'Yessir . . . Your hat, for a start . . . although my dad did say that Admiral Beatty wore 'is like that . . . But . . .'

'Like what, master?'

'Like you 'ad it this morning, sir. Slidin' off the back of your 'ead, sir. Like a weekend yachtsman. Sorry, sir.' He had overcome his initial difficulties and was now more himself. 'And when you were giving evidence, sir, you should have spoken to the captain in a loud, clear and distinct voice.

Instead of . . . sort of chattin' to all of us . . .'

'I'm sorry, master.'

'Your shoes were very smart, though, sir.'

'Thank you.'

The master lunged to his feet, and he and Campbell apologized to each other several times more before he left. Afterwards, returning to the flexor muscles of the forearm, Campbell wondered if he, like AB McGuffy, was now marked down to be watched in future for 'improved turnout',

Just before tea, as HMS *Winchester* sped south, the captain addressed the ship's company over the tannoy again: they had nothing to be ashamed of; they had acquitted themselves well; the damage sustained was more of a nuisance than a risk but clearly the ship had to be in tip-top shape for a Far East deployment. Repairs, already arranged and to be carried out in HM Dockyard, Portsmouth, would take between ten days and a fortnight, over which period leave would be granted. The ship would remain in the roster for duty in northern waters for the remainder of the four-week period, after which she would proceed as per the programme.

After that a festive, end-of-term spirit took over. Sailors sang as they worked, and wardroom mealtimes became even more ebullient and playful. No fish had yet appeared on the menu and dark suspicions were aired. When Ronnie, the supply officer, was challenged about this, he said, 'Don't you worry about that fish.' According to reports circulating in the lower deck, and passed on by the LMA, it had been filleted and frozen by the Chinese cooks, and this turned out to be the case. As the ship's company dispersed for leave, each member, if he wished it, was given a cold cube of deep-frozen cod fillet, the gift of *Grimsby Calliope*, and the spoils of war.

PART TWO

'Then we're going to St Helena and Ascension Island. Not sure about the order. Depends which I find first. More coffee, doctor?'

'Thanks . . . How long will we be alongside at St Helena?'

'We won't actually be going alongside. We'll anchor off and use boats. But we'll be there a couple of days. Know someone there?'

'I think I do, actually.'

'Really?'

'Yes . . . A chap in my year. Went out there straight from house jobs. Odd chap. Wants to be a psychiatrist eventually. Interested in birds. You know, ornithology. And Napoleon.'

'A doctor?'

'Yes.'

'Good. That solves one problem.'

'What problem?'

'Well, your problem, really, since you're the SRO. Did no one mention it to you?'

'No.'

'Well, you are, doctor. MO always doubles as SRO. Small ships routine.'

'OK. What's SRO?'

'Thought you'd never ask. Sexual Relations Officer. And you're it. More or less wherever we go the doctor has to rustle up some wardroom crumpet. We do it very nicely of course. You'll have little invitation cards, tastefully embossed, with the ship's crest in gold leaf, saying: "The Captain and Officers of HMS *Winchester* request the pleasure of the company of about a dozen birds including at least one with huge knockers for Jim and a few kind of old ones for Ronnie, number one and the engineer." And the local hospital's usually the best place. So that's why you're SRO. You go ashore with the first boat, with a handful of invites, look up your old chum and say, "Never mind Napoleon and the albatrosses, come to a great thrash on board and bring a dozen women with you. And your wife if you want." '

'This chap isn't married.'

'Great. So he'll know all the local form. Hear that, number one?'

'What?'

'Problem solved. As soon as we get to St Helena the doc's going ashore to the hospital, where his oppo works, and he'll fix up all we need for a couth little party. We've booked you the matron, sir.'

'Oh, d'you know someone there, doc?'

'Yes . . . a doctor.'

'Funny old bloke, isn't he? Had to land a stoker from *Coriander* there in '55. Appendix. Died. Cheery old doctor, though. How come you know him, doc.'

'The chap I know's only just gone out there.'

'Oh. I see . . . Great ship, the *Coriander*.'

Triple expansion reciprocating drinks. Burned FFO. Terrific range. Get you halfway round the world if you didn't mind taking your time. Ideal for South Atlantic patrol work.'

'Was that to stop him escaping, number one?' said the navigator, without smiling.

'Stop who escaping, Vasco?' The first lieutenant's brow furled. 'I'll give you bloody Napoleon. This was 1955. Not 18 bloody 55.'

'You might even have been too late first time, sir,' said the navigator, smiling this time.

'When did he die anyway?'

'Don't know, sir.'

'Anyone know? Ken, when did Napoleon die?'

'1837, sir,' said Lieutenant Muir firmly.

'Yes. That's it, Ken. And there was something funny about him, wasn't there? You know . . . when they cut him up. You must know, doc. Meat and one veg instead of two or something.'

'You're thinking of Hitler, number one.'

'Oh, Maybe I am.'

'Or was he a woman after all, like Tito.'

'Come on, doc. Didn't he have something interesting wrong with him.'

Campbell, whose views had been sought but not yet heard, had a vague memory of having read one or two of the slenderly based and often conflicting items on the topic which appeared from time to time in the medical press. Various endocrine disorders, and a poisoning theory, had been mentioned. One quite possibly mad professor at his teaching hospital was known to have special interest in the subject, but Campbell could recall no short summary of his views. 'I think some people think he was poisoned.'

'That's it, doc,' said Lieutenant Muir. 'Antimony.'

'Was it?'

'Yes. But at the time they thought it was stomach cancer.'

'Did they?'

Lieutenant Ayres, the navigator, stood up to go. 'The doctor's friend's bound to know. Probably got bits of him in bottles all round his surgery.'

'Oh. Has the doctor got a friend in St Helena?' said Ronnie, who had just come in.

'Yes,' said the navigator. 'He's going to find us a dozen dark-eyed beauties for the party and show us Napoleon's whatsit in a bottle. It's all fixed.'

They were three days out of Portsmouth and heading south. Patched up in HM Dockyard, Rosyth, so that all there was to show for the gunboat's efforts was an extra smart bit of paintwork on the starboard side, HMS *Winchester* had then sailed for her home port to make ready for a voyage halfway round the world. In Portsmouth Dockyard, stores parties had laboured to transfer untidy mountains of provisions from the jetty to the orderly intricacies of the ship's stowage spaces. A Wren officer and two men in dark suits had arrived with a series of sealed blue canvas bags and gone into conclave with Lieutenant Muir, the security officer. A sinister grey barge, flying a red flag and towed by a veteran harbour tug, had come alongside and transferred a large number of heavy metal canisters, which had disappeared into magazines below the waterline. Other barges had fuelled her, and a dapper wine salesman, after a tasting session that ran from lunch until tea-time, had topped up the wardroom wine store with a massive order that included everything from light ale to champagne.

Amid such general activity, Campbell found himself enthused to come to grips with his responsibility for the health of the ship's company throughout the forthcoming trip. He went through the sickbay from end to end, vetting the contents of each cupboard in turn, discarding boxfuls of dark bottles of Jutland-vintage remedies, and hardware of a similar age, and returning them in transport organized by LMA Smith to the local naval hospital. Next day, after much thought and nervous speculation about unlikely accidents and diseases, he compiled a shopping list of drugs and instruments he thought he might need and which did not occur in the first lieutenant's generous but random selection of kit. Smith then translated this into a series of very efficient-looking stores demand forms, and together they had gone to a sort of naval medical supermarket and returned with everything they had asked for, including a few things they hadn't thought of till they had seen them on the shelves.

While in Portsmouth, Campbell had also had a chance to remedy some deficiencies in his personal kit. Ronnie had directed him to the Dockyard Clothing Store, which was known for some reason as 'slops', where he handed over his piece of paper and was in return issued with a complete set of tropical uniforms. Thus he acquired a pair of yellowish white buckskin shoes, three pairs of long white socks, six pairs of white shorts and six short-sleeved white shirts (the latter items evidently manufactured by different companies, since the tails of the shirts, when he tried then on in the privacy of his cabin, protruded far beyond the legs of the shorts), a couple of short white mess jackets, with accompanying brass buttons, and two voluminous white suits, high-collared and also brass-buttoned, known officially as Rig 9W and unofficially as ice-cream suits. He had made his way back to the ship with a huge parcel smelling of mothballs, and a feeling that once more life might be taking a turn for the better.

He had also gone ashore into Portsmouth in search of a bookshop which might stock medical textbooks, to supplement the ship's sickbay library and help him prepare for the next year's examination in anatomy, physiology, bacteriology, pathology and biochemistry. For interest, he also bought himself a book on clinical surgery. Though the subject was not included in the primary examination, the book had intriguing pictures and footnotes, and might help to keep his eye on the higher goal.

HMS *Winchester* had finally left Portsmouth on a grey, drizzling Tuesday morning late in January. A few wives and children had come to stand on the ramparts of the castle at the end of the old town as the ship passed through the narrows. A lone bugler on top of the fort opposite acknowledged her shrill respects to the flag of the occupant submariner admiral, and then saluted with his left hand (observers with binoculars later agreeing to exonerate him on the grounds that he had only one arm). The last visual contact they had with the homeland had been the stern of the Isle of Wight ferry, fading nonchalantly into the mist after a near collision.

On leaving harbour, the ship changed from being an appendage of the dockyard and an inconvenient place of work, and became instead an independent naval unit and a closed community. Morale changed more slowly. Through the first day, *en route* down Channel, people got on with their work quietly, perhaps looking backwards in subdued, individual ways. Only a day or two later, they were looking forward again. Somewhere, a committee of selectors met, and a notice appeared detailing a football team for a match against the shore establishment in Gibraltar. Another notice appeared beside it, inviting applicants for lineside seats at the celebrated Gibraltar tram festival which would that year fortunately coincide with the visit of HMS *Winchester*. A few junior rates put their names up, then the first lieutenant's name went up, albeit in someone else's handwriting, and the notice suddenly disappeared.

The details of the ship's medium-term future, the expansive hiatus between Gibraltar and Hong Kong, somehow remained obscure, apart from the intriguing fragment about visits to some South Atlantic islands, including St Helena. Campbell did not pursue his enquiries with the navigator, but settled into the ship's sea routine, occupying himself with a little light study, from which occasional calls to more active medical duties were a welcome distraction. A stoker twisted his ankle running when he should have been walking. A cook cut himself while opening a tin. A few of the younger members of the ship's company came along with vague complaints, the general aim of which seemed to be to verify that medical services were in fact provided on board.

Most of these cases were seen first by the LMA, and later discussed with and seen by Campbell. Thus they shared the work quite amiably, with Campbell's more detailed knowledge of medicine neatly supplemented by his assistant's grasp of naval procedure and his personal acquaintance with the vast majority of the ship's company. When Gurnard, the bunting tosser with dermatitis herpetiformis, reported back for review, with a considerable improvement in his symptoms, Campbell was touched by his gratitude, and felt that he had survived an important evaluation with reasonable credit, but did cause to wonder if the LMA had any more undiagnosed chronic problems poised backstage, to be brought on if necessary, to keep him humble.

Suddenly one morning, as Campbell was strolling on the upper deck thinking vague thoughts about the mildness of the Mediterranean winter climate, Gibraltar appeared out of the mist, not as a postcard cliché of imperial trade routes, but as a sprawling giant of rock, with swirling white cloud spilling over it. On its lower flanks and round its base lay a small town of crowded jumbled streets, which looked as if it had just recently slipped there from further up, and was now contained from further movement only by the fortress walls running along the sea front. Scrub and woods covered the higher slopes, and scattered over it were the impediments of war, ancient and modern: crumbling bastions and huge radar dishes; gun emplacements and groves of radio aerials.

Condition Yankee was piped, together with a complex ritual about entering harbour, and the ship slowed down, then slid between two stone jetties, first followed then nudged by a pair of tugs, until she came to rest, starboard side to, against a wall right opposite an elegant, arcaded, possibly Edwardian building with a clock tower. There were no other warships around, only the tugs, a few tenders and a boom defence vessel, rusty and superannuated. Swarthy labourers, if anything as lethargic as their UK counterparts, took the hawsers and dumped them over bollards. As the gangway was being lowered into place a trio of naval officers, accompanied by a Wren officer and a man in a dark civilian suit, left the block with the tower and came over and stood and waited to come on board. The man in the suit was carrying a blue canvas bag.

Over coffee in the wardroom there was a raucous reunion between Lieutenant-Commander Bowers, *Winchester*'s first lieutenant, and the oldest (but not the most senior) of the three staff officers. Amid the back-slapping and the where-have-you-been-since-whenevers, Campbell detected hints that Ben Bowers was doing rather better in his career than was his presumed ex-messmate, a man of similar age, still a lieutenant, and a lieutenant in a shore job at that. The Wren officer and the man in the dark suit had a quick coffee with Ken Muir, then left the wardroom with him, the canvas bag still making up the party. Another man in a suit appeared, and went into a huddle in the corner with Ronnie, from which words like 'lettuce' and 'bread' occasionally wafted over. Then it was Campbell's turn to make contact with the world outside the ship. Steward Tak informed him that a senior rate from shoreside wanted to talk with him, and he adjourned to the sickbay with a medical branch chief petty officer from something called Naval Health. Together they filled up a form certifying that no one on board had a prolonged or prostrating fever, a persistent rash or erupting glands, and that there had been no excessive mortality among the ship's rats and mice, if any. The chief went on to discuss aspects of preventive medicine. 'Malaria we could have but we haven't, sir. And VD isn't really a problem, 'cause hardly anyone from ships gets a bit. At least not since they closed the border with Spain.'

Campbell returned to the wardroom just as the three staff officers were preparing to leave One of them hesitated in the doorway and scrutinized Campbell's epaulettes, which were somewhat unusual in respectable naval circles. In addition to a lieutenant's two gold stripes flanking the controversial red flash signifying his branch of the service, they contained, in the curl of the upper stripe, a little golden 'R' denoting his reservist status.

'Reservist, doc?'

'Yes.'

'Off to Honky Fid?'

'Yes.'

'Lucky old you.' The staff officer was a young lieutenant-commander, probably still too junior to expect to be called 'sir' by a surgeon lieutenant such as Campbell. 'How did you swing that?'

'Just lucky,' said Campbell, 'Wasn't even trying,'

'We've got one of the unlucky ones here. A two-ring reservist pay bob.'

Campbell looked politely blank and the staff officer elaborated. 'A reservist supply officer. Doing cash in the pay office while our usual Shylock gets his local leave. You might know him.'

Regular officers commonly assumed that the RNR, with several thousand officers scattered over a dozen divisions up and down the country, was a very small club in which everyone knew one anothe1. 'Perhaps,' said Campbell.

'Grossart. Nice lad. From Edinburgh.'

'Oh,' said Campbell. 'Johnny Grossart?'

'That's him. Know him?'

'As a matter of fact I do.'

Johnny Grossart was a wily young lawyer and enthusiastic reservist officer, an agreeable opportunist whom Campbell knew faintly from his occasional visits to their local division, and very much the sort of chap who might turn up in Gibraltar in midwinter, having a working holiday, all found, on the Queen.

'You from Edinburgh, too?'

'Yes . . . How long's he out here for?'

'A fortnight, I suppose. You'll find him in the pay office.'

'I might look him up,' said Campbell, half meaning it. The staff officer left and Campbell went for more coffee. As he did so, the navigator asked, 'Got a friend in Gibraltar too then?'

That afternoon a football team from HMS *Winchester* met a lean, fit, still tanned side from the naval shore establishment. In the ship's team, only Henry represented the wardroom. The rest of the team were in the main unfamiliar to Campbell, but he recognized the leading regulator, now conventionally clad as a goalkeeper. In the course of the game, that official was to let past five shots from a vast selection fired by the contemptuously fit local opposition. In return a stoker from HMS *Winchester* scored one goal, as did Leading Seaman Pratt, the ops room coffee and submarine specialist, to cries of 'Come on, Oily' from the terraces, where a couple of dozen sailors and a good turn-out from the wardroom cheered dutifully. It was the first football match that Campbell had attended for about ten years, and he had forgotten it could sometimes be interesting.

Afterwards most of the wardroom contingent went for a cup of tea in a small, very English café in the square opposite the governor's residence. They sat at a window table and watched two soldiers on guard duty standing stiffly under its porch and occasionally stamping off along the pavement, away from each other and the porch, in perfect synchrony along shallow grooves worn in the flagstones, to stop, stamp and crash round in deeper hollows a dozen paces away, then converge on the porch and each other once more. Over tea and scones, several people remarked independently that they were glad they'd joined the Navy.

The party broke up outside the tea shop and Campbell found a bookshop and bought several paperbacks and a dusty copy of the *New Statesman*, then strolled along the main street, which was narrow, irregular and busy with quite well-dressed people doing nothing in an early-evening Mediterranean fashion. In a dim, crowded shop proclaiming itself to be the Original SPQR Bazaar – Small Profits Quick Returns – he bought from a silent Indian a few monochrone postcards from a boxful in a display falling apologetically between the categories of antiques and junk. One showed captured Crimean field pieces in an ornamental park garden. It was labelled: 'Russian Guns: Alameda Gardens: Gibraltar.' Campbell scribbled on its reverse, 'Will no one take the Red menace seriously?' and dispatched it to Hadden in his surgical unit at the Institute in Edinburgh. On another, portraying a plump, funereal and possibly forty-year-old dancing girl holding a rose between her teeth, clenched as though it were a bullet, he started to write a note to Jean, then abandoned the effort and tore it up into small pieces. Uncertainty about local litter laws, and the forbidding presence on the main street of numerous very British-looking policemen, compelled him to confine the debris to his pocket indefinitely, and he went back to the ship.

'Most people start by asking us how long we've been out here,' said the short, fat girl with false eyelashes. Campbell obliged. 'Fifteen months. And it's about three too long,' she said, taking a large gulp from her drink, an elaborate affair with fruit and ice, that Campbell had somehow found himself paying for. Her friend, who was tall and deeply tanned, nodded in agreement and said, 'And we don't like it.' She was close enough for her contact lenses to be obvious even to an observer of ordinary visual acuity. 'It's very boring.'

'Except for ships,' said the short one.

'Glad to be of service, girls,' said Ayres.

'What sort of ship are you?' the tall one asked.

'Smallish. Grey. Friendly.'

'Are there any others coming?'

Ayres put his finger to his lips. 'Ships' movements. Mustn't discuss. But confidentially, you should make the most of us. And don't tell anyone I told you.' The tall girl looked intrigued,

They were in the bar of the Nuffield Officers' Pavilion, a low bungaloid establishment with a restaurant, bar, dance floor and bowling alley. Someone in *Winchester*'s wardroom had thought there was likely to be a disco later in the evening, and Ayres, on the basis of enthusiastically reported experiences of previous visits, had been confident that swarms of unattached women from the social grades traditionally allotted to the wardroom – nursing sisters, teachers and the like – would roll up between nine and ten.

It was quarter past ten and, besides the pair, probably teachers, talking to Campbell and the navigator, there were only three other females present in the entire premises, excluding servants. One was an expensive-looking blonde having a candle-lit dinner in the restaurant, *tête-à-tête* with Johnny Grossart. The other two were evidently the wife and daughter of a large, crop-haired, deeply tanned man who was sitting at a table belabouring them with a tirade about the senior management of the local branch of Cable and Wireless, delivered in relentless Yorkshire.

'What do you do on the ship?'

'Hm?'

'What are you in the ship?' the short fat girl asked again.

'Oh. I'm the doctor.'

She peered up at him more closely. He noticed that she had contact lenses too. 'Really?'

'Yes.'

'A proper doctor?'

'I think so. I mean yes. You know. The ship's doctor . . . What do you do?'

'Teacher. Didn't you guess?'

'No.'

'Been here before?'

'No.'

'Like it?'

'Hardly seen it.'

'A weekend's about right. Are you really a doctor?'

'Yes . . . Why do you keep asking?'

She lowered her voice and said, 'A friend of mine met a chap from a nuclear submarine. Said he was a gynaecologist. She should have known.' She lowered her voice further. 'He was really a greeny.'

'A what?'

'You know. A greeny.'

'No. I don't.'

'A weapons electrical officer. How long have you been in

the Navy?'

'About eight weeks. Where do you teach?'

'Where we all teach. St Martin's. Service brats.'

'What are they like?'

'Horrible.'

'What age are yours?'

'Seven. And nasty.'

'Really?'

'Yes. From the regiment.'

'Oh.'

'So most of them are half Chinese.'

'Really?'

'Yes. A Liverpool regiment. They were in Singapore. The troops married local . . . What sort of doctor are you?'

'Just an ordinary GD doctor.'

'What's GD?'

'General duties.'

She finished her drink, rather obviously, and looked at her empty glass. The navigator noticed. 'Another of those fruit things, Cheryl?'

'Yes, thanks.'

'That's the stuff. An apple a day and all that. Doc?'

'Oh. Yes, thanks.'

'G and T?'

'G and T.'

'And yours is a brandy and Babycham, Sally.'

The tall girl smiled. The tan on her neck stopped suddenly just behind her ears, which caused Campbell to wonder whether a bottle, or a sunray lamp, or perhaps both, were implicated. As Ayres turned to the bar the two girls had a curious little conversation without words, using only facial expression, with a lot of eyebrow. Ill at ease, Campbell glanced round, and caught the eyes of Jim and Henry, further along the bar. To his surprise, they looked envious. After a while Ayres came back with the drinks.

'Sally . . . Cheryl . . . David . . . There we are. Just what the doctor ordered.'

'Are you really a doctor?' the tanned one asked, in a tone of voice that made Campbell wonder if she were the victim of the submariner gynaecologist *cum* weapons electrical officer.

'He hasn't actually produced his certificates,' said Ayres. 'But he's quite handy with the old Elastoplast.'

They talked. The tall girl seemed to have made up her mind about Ayres, and stood very close to him and laughed at his jokes. The short one continued her ponderous reconnaissance of Campbell, who could find no way out, but recalled with some comfort the words of the chief from Naval Health. The bar began to fill up, and a gaggle of girls, mainly younger and prettier than the contact-lensed duo, arrived, and the rest of the wardroom contingent moved, with despatch but not impolite haste, to close in on them, in a smooth manoeuvre that resulted, within minutes, in a glass in every hand and a man beside every girl. Now Campbell and the navigator conversed without words, unnoticed by the increasingly drunk teachers.

A little drunk himself, Campbell contemplated for the first time the appearance of his wardroom colleagues out of uniform. They looked markedly less impressive, but quite tidy. Most wore sports jackets or blazers, with neat trousers and shiny brown shoes or suede boots, a combination of dress known for some reason as dog robbers. Spread among the girls, they looked like slightly old-fashioned apprentice accountants, or possibly chartered surveyors, on the spree in a pub. Henry was doing well with a little dark girl, pretty and lively-looking.

'How long've you been a doctor,' said the fat girl, sensing his ennui.

'Weeks and weeks. Two years in fact.'

'Where . . . where did you train?'

'Edinburgh.'

'Evening, doctor.'

'Evening, sir.'

On the arrival of his commanding officer, Campbell pulled himself together and did the social bit. 'Sally . . . Cheryl . . . Commander Huxley . . . Our CO.' Cheryl's contact lenses lit up. 'Sally and Cheryl teach here, sir.'

The captain smiled. He was perhaps a little drunk, or vigorously unwinding after the strain of being continually in charge at sea. He focused down on Cheryl. 'I'm actually called Nigel,' he said, 'for the purposes of this exercise.'

Cheryl smiled. The revelation was news to Campbell, who had never thought of captains as having first names.

From the restaurant Grossart emerged, piloting his expensive-looking blonde through the now dangerous shoals of the bar. He nodded a smile of recognition to Campbell. The navigator noticed and said, 'Pal of the doc's.' The tanned girl was obviously not looking at the blonde with Grossart. 'Know her, Sally?' asked Ayres.

'I think she's a Wren, if that's what you call them,' she said distantly. This prompted Campbell to recognize the blonde girl as the Wren officer who had come on board in uniform that morning, with the blue canvas bag for Lieutenant Muir. She had been transfigured by a simple white dress and the traditional expedient of, literally, letting her hair down. The lights had been dimmed and a man was testing sound equipment. A record came on, very loud, and to Campbell's profound relief the captain took Cheryl off to dance. The navigator and Sally followed, and Campbell went off and got thoroughly drunk with the head of the gunnery department, a nice man called Bob, an SD officer who talked a lot about Gibraltar in the old days, in particular about a nursing sister from the Royal Naval Hospital, with whom he had enjoyed what he called a gunner's fuck, 'with a nipple in each ear, listening for the fall of shot'.

The bar became busy and eventually, towards midnight, the Nuffield Officers' Pavilion took on the appearance that optimists in the wardroom had forecast. It was crowded, noisy and cheerful. There were a lot of women about, who, if you were sufficiently drunk, looked all right. A couple of times Campbell found himself talking to girls who turned out to sound much less nice than they looked, and he continued to drink, with a vague feeling that if he drank enough they might begin to sound all right, too. On the dance floor, the navigator and Sally were making the most of a new-found interest in dancing very close together. The captain, in a stiff, old-fashioned way, seemed to be doing quite well with Cheryl. Henry and the lively dark girl were no longer in evidence.

A man with a beard thrust a drink in Campbell's hand and said, 'Doc, I wanna talk to you about something.' It was

Lieutenant Muir, looking very drunk indeed. He was standing in the dim, flickering light, swaying in a way that made Campbell feel relatively sober. He said again, slowly and carefully, 'Doc, I wanna talk to you. About something.' He had a drink for himself in his other hand.

'Let's sit down,' said Campbell.

'Yes, doctor,' said the security officer. 'I've always been . . . the sort of chap . . . who obeys doctor's orders.'

'Fine . . . Here.'

Lieutenant Muir looked as though he was about to buckle at the knees. Campbell slid a chair under him. He collapsed into it, saving his drink by some drunk sleight-of-hand, and putting it down carefully in front of him. Campbell sat opposite. The captain and Cheryl slid past in a clinch.

'Great chap, father.'

'Hm?'

'Our father, which art dancing with that terrible drongo . . . Great bloke.'

'Yes,' said Campbell. 'Seems a nice man. Don't know him very well, of course.'

'I do. Don't I just. Know him bloody well. Never sailed with him before. But know him well from when he came . . . He's a pilot, you know. An intrepid flyer. One of the last of the great naval aviators.'

'Really?'

'Yes, he is. Well, was. Jetsh. I mean jets. Flew from carriers. *Ark* and all that.'

'Did he?'

'Big stuff . . . Sea Vixens. Jets. Kick the tyres, light the fires, last up to fifteen grand's a cissy and all that. Front line squadron.' The last word gave him some difficulty.

Campbell, through his own haze of drink, remembered that Lieutenant Muir had been about to come and talk to him about something since they had first met. 'Is that what you wanted to talk about?'

'What?'

'Father. Is that what you wanted to talk about?'

'Sort of. I'm coming to it. The point is . . . he's a great bloke and wouldn't see you stuck . . .' Lieutenant Muir paused and took some more whisky and said, 'I don't want it

. . . I didn't want this one . . . Or the last one. Why am I drinking it, doc?'

'Is that what you wanted to talk about?'

'Well . . . that sort of comes into it, too. In a sort of way . . .' He peered across at Campbell. His eyelids were drooping.

'Ken,' said Campbell.

'What, doc?'

'You were going to . . .'

'What, doc? . . . Doc.' He paused and refocused.

'What?'

'I'm sure we've met somewhere before . . .' He shook himself suddenly and put his whisky to one side. 'Terrible.'

'What's terrible?'

'Me bending your ear like this . . . How's your glass?'

'Fine. Really. I've had plenty. Thanks, Ken. Plenty.'

'Pair of pissheads,' said a kindly voice behind Campbell.

'Lieutenant Gault,' said the security officer.

'Lieutenant Muir,' said the gunnery officer. 'Lieutenant Campbell?'

'Hm?'

'David, old son,' said Bob, Lieutnant Gault, the gunnery officer, 'we've got a taxi. Or d'you want left for the patrol?'

'Thanks, Bob.'

'Come on, Ken.'

'Thanks.'

They made their way out of the noise into a cool quiet night. A taxi waited. It drove them along the shore road to the dockyard gate, where a policeman who had seen it all before waved them past without looking at their identity cards. At the top of HMS *Winchester*'s gangway the duty quartermaster waited, and saluted smartly as the three officers came back on board. The man was well turned out and stood to attention while they passed on their way to the wardroom, but as they did so Campbell sensed a disapproval, not quite amounting to disrespect, and was chastened to meet the steady gaze of Able Seaman McGuffy.

'Sorry about St Helena, doctor. Pity. Especially with your

oppo being there. And now we'll never get to know about Napoleon's whatsit. But this other place we're going to sounds quite fun. I've just looked it up in the port guide. VD and malaria are rife. That's in your bit. Under "medical". And the water's terrible. Oh. I meant to ask. What's yellow fever?'

'Where are we going?'

'Banjul.'

'Where's that?'

'Where Bathurst was. Until it changed its name.'

'Oh. Gambia?'

'That's it. Know someone there, too?' The navigator asked the question so seriously that Campbell suspected a genial mockery, but was insufficiently sure to respond in kind. He said, 'I don't think so.'

They were standing on the starboard bridge wing. The navigator, sextant in hand, was waiting for sunset and the first stars.

'What's yellow fever anyway?'

'Pretty horrible,' said Campbell. 'But you won't get it.'

'Go on. Tell me. Do things drop off?'

'No. You turn yellow. It's jaundice. A kind of hepatitis. Get it from monkeys. At least you get it from insects who've got it from monkeys. But everyone's had the injection. We checked. So no one'll get the disease.' Campbell and Smith had been through the medical documents of the entire ship's company, checking that all immunizations were up to date. A few defaulters, discovered and sent for, had rolled up their sleeves to catch up with the rest. Since then, and it had been several days previously, Campbell had had no work whatsoever to do.

'How long does it last?'

'Ten years officially. Unofficially, just about for ever.'

'We all got it at Dartmouth . . . Mad old doc. A commander. Thought tight underpants were the root of all evil. "Get rid of those silly knickers and get yourself into boxer shorts, laddie. Let 'em dangle as Nature intended." So I'll live, will I? Or at least not die of yellow fever.'

'No.'

'D'you know anything about Gambia, doctor?'

'Not a lot. It's up a river, I think.'

'Oh, I know how to find it all right. I've checked up on that sort of thing. But I meant what's it like. Not very big or internationally heavy, I gather.'

'No.'

'Can't really be, if father's down to play golf with the prime minister.'

'Is he?'

'Saw it in a signal this morning. They're playing the Brit high commissioner and the French ambassador. Saturday afternoon. Lunching at His Excellency's first.'

The sun sank to the horizon. The sea was calm and HMS *Winchester* swished comfortably along at her cruising speed of sixteen knots, her bow wave foaming out, pink in the sunset. Just ahead, a fish broke the surface, leaping out of the water and staying there, gliding across the sea for five or six seconds. Several others followed. Campbell had never seen flying fish before, and was impressed. They sped horizontally away, a few feet over the water. One or two touched the surface and splashed with their tails, and appeared to take off once more, gliding dozens of yards further before dropping from sight into the water again.

Campbell and the navigator watched. The navigator seemed pleased. 'You only get 'em when the water warms up. That's good . . . Sort of shows I took the right turning after Gibraltar . . . But you can't be too careful,' he added, patting his sextant. 'Just going to check up and see what our stars foretell.'

The news that HMS *Winchester* was not after all going to visit St Helena neither surprised nor disappointed Campbell, who had been sufficiently exposed to the vicissitudes of naval planning in his first few weeks in the service to be permanently imbued with a scepticism about all arrangements until they were actually fulfilled. Gambia sounded interesting. Items of Commonwealth geography, acquired many years before from a dour pedant in a flapping black gown clouded with chalk, surfaced haphazardly. Scramble for Africa. Hot. Wet. Groundnuts. Sleeping sickness. (And how did you stop people getting that?)

'Why was it changed?'

'What?'

'The programme. From going to St Helena.'

'Don't know. Either St H. didn't want us any more. Or Banjul suddenly did. Diplomacy. Anyway, all those funny little places are fun. The ones that don't get many ships. They don't get blasé.'

'Like Gib?'

'That's it. "Any more ships coming after you?" and all that . . . No, we'll be the social event of the season in sunny Banjul. Wait and see.'

The sun went down. The stars came out. Ayres did slick, quick things with his sextant, rattling off readings to one of the three midshipmen who had joined the wardroom at Gibraltar. Then he disappeared into the chartroom for a while, and emerged, smug and smiling, before dinner, obviously having better evidence of their exact location upon the face of the waters than the mere presence of a few flying fish.

The next morning, since it was Friday, Campbell went up to see father, who was not in his cabin, but out on the upper deck, in a sheltered little corner for'ard of the port oerlikon and known, Campbell subsequently discovered, as 'father's garden'. He was sitting in a deck chair, with a cup of coffee at his feet, reading a novel by Angela Thirkell.

'Ah. Caught me, doctor,' he said, when Campbell appeared. 'Just having a little read with my stand-easy. Had coffee? Liu!'

The steward appeared before Campbell had expressed a view, and it would have been impolite to decline at that stage.

'Sugar, sah?'

'No thanks, leading steward.'

'Well, doctor. And how's the health of the ship's company?'

'Remains good, sir.'

'Splendid.'

There was a long silence. Leading Steward Liu brought Campbell a cup of coffee. The captain's coffee service was fine bone china, with fluted cups rimmed in gold and crested with the insignia of Her Britannic Majesty's Board of Admiralty, though that august body had some years previously been processed into something called MOD(N). The captain put a tasselled leather bookmark in his place in *April Chimes* and looked very seriously at Campbell, with his head to one side. 'No . . . um . . . little souvenirs of Gibraltar?'

'No, sir.'

'Good.'

'Not so far, that's to say, sir.'

'Oh?'

'Well, sir . . . Some things may take quite a while to show up, sir.'

'A week?'

'Perhaps longer, sir. Some of them.'

'Really?'

'In extreme cases, sir, up to ninety days.'

'Good lord. D'you think the sailors know that?'

'Shouldn't think so, sir.'

'Shouldn't they?'

'Perhaps, sir.'

'Well. We should tell 'em, shouldn't we. Especially with this Banjul business. D'you know VD and malaria are rife?'

'Just heard, sir.'

'Well. They are. All sorts of ghastly tropical things, I imagine. Know all about them, doctor?'

'A little, sir . . . I'll read up a bit more. We've got a good library.'

'Splendid . . . How about giving us a chat?'

'A chat, sir?'

'Yes. Bone up on 'em, and give us all a chat on the SRE. See LRO Soper. He's the chap. You know. Works the gramophone for the mess decks' record request programme. Runs the SRE compartment, where it's all done from. Just aft of that sponson. Jolly chap. Red hair. No. Dark. Thinning. He'll fit you in, show you how to use the mike and all that.'

Campbell knew LRO Soper's voice, but not what he looked like. His was the relentlessly cheerful banter of 'Down Your Grot', a twice-weekly home-made chat-and-record show inescapably broadcast throughout the ship. It was an unselfconscious parody of the worst of local radio, tailored for shipboard life, rich in innuendo, nicknames and barely suppressed ribaldry, and, after a time, compulsive listening. The idea of Campbell's contributing a solemn exercise in health education, even a limited and immediately useful one on how not to get a dose of Bathurst/Banjul, was not to be acted on without careful thought.

'Good,' said the captain. 'That's fixed. Look forward to hearing it . . . And there's another thing . . . .' He reached under his deck chair and produced a buff manila file (known in naval circles as a 'pack') boldly labelled 'WGO'. He patted it and said to Campbell, 'Did anyone mention that you're WGO?'

'No, sir.'

'Well . . . Doctors always are. Except in ships carrying padres. Nothing to it. Just liaise with the local Brits, usually the consular element in the embassy, or, in the case of Commonwealth countries like this lot we're off to now, the high commission. Find the graveyards and just check 'em off. Grasscutting. General smartness. State of repair. And run up a quick report. General remarks. Particular points. The usual stuff. You write it, and I despatch it. To CWGC.'

'CWGC, sir?'

'The War Graves people. They're awfully good. Really keep tabs. See. We send in something like this. This is a copy of one from Andalsnes. Dismal business in 1940, I think, but well looked after now. All ships looking in, especially in off-beat places, send in the gen and they keep the overall picture up to date. And if you think anything needs attending to, let the local consular chap know, and he'll see to it. You usually find he pays a chap to cut the grass and so on. He'll see to anything. That's notes for action. And the next ship checks up. It's a jolly good system. There you are, doctor. All yours.' He handed Campbell the file. Its title was neatly typed across the top: 'War Graves Officer'.

'Thank you, sir.'

'Interesting little job, WGO . . . Know anything about whales?'

'No, sir.'

'Oh, well. Not to worry. There's a little book on 'em. You'll be whale-spotting officer, too. Ronnie'll give you the pack on that. Not so sure who that one reports to, but it'll be in there somewhere. Something to do with conservation. You just keep a record. Lookouts'll tell you if anything crops up. You simply write down what sort, how many and where. Again they keep an overall picture. We can have a chat about it next Friday . . .'

Campbell finished his coffee rather quickly, partly because he thought the captain was indicating that their interview was drawing to a close, and partly because he had no particular wish to be made responsible for, say, plankton research, keep-fit classes or a study of wildlife in Gambia. After all, he was still trying to get down to a serious shot at re-learning anatomy.

He stood up to leave. The captain smiled goodbye. Campbell walked away. The captain called him back. 'Doctor. Your file.'

To prevent any further such omissions, Campbell went straight across to Ronnie's office on the other side of the upper deck, and collected the file on whales, signing for it in a ledger, then he went down to the sickbay, where, on the operating table, the LMA was making a sort of collage of pin-ups from magazines. Naked, honey-coloured girls, variously pouting and leering, had pasted-on speech bubbles coming out of their mouths, saying things like 'I've taken mine,' 'Have you taken yours?' and 'Regularly is best . . . Regularly,' in the LMA's clear, squarish block capitals.

'It's my anti-malaria campaign, sir,' the LMA explained. 'If it's all right by you, I'll stick this up by the main galley counter, where the top of the queue stands. And we just give a big tin of Paludrine to the PO cook. He lays them out in a saucer, the lads have a gawp at this lot to remind them while they're queuing, and they take a pill and eat it with their dinner. Tins for the senior rates' messes, the LEPs and the wardroom. Normally the stewards put them out in a glass with the cruet, sir.'

'I see . . . Good. I hear VD's rife as well.'

'So I gather, sir. It's in the port guide.'

'Father wants me to talk about it on the SRE. Said to see LRO Soper.'

'Shall I get 'im up, sir?'

'Not sure yet what I'm going to say.' He went over to the

glass-fronted library cabinet. 'Ah. Massie's *Basic Venereology*. And how are we off for . . . um . . . condoms.'

'Tons, sir. Thousands. Bottom cupboard over there. Generally leave a couple of hundred with the quartermaster. You might want to mention that on the SRE.'

Campbell took the little textbook, whose cover was bordered by tastefully arranged spirochaetes alternating with gonococci, in red and purple.

'Shall I ask Soapy to come and see you about the SRE, sir?'

'Yes, please, LMA.'

The SRE compartment was hot and sticky. Even in the short-sleeved, open-necked shirt prescribed for officers' evening wear in the tropics, Campbell felt unpleasantly warm. And the topic of his discourse did nothing to reduce his discomfort. LRO Soper had played records requested by the chiefs' mess, which he referred to as the old folks' home, presumably because most of its inhabitants were over thirty. He cued Campbell in after a Beatles record.

'And now after that rave from the grave for Uncle Nobby "No-you-can't-have-any-more-you-can't-have-worn-out-the-last-lot-yet" Wedgewood, in the part-worn bathchair in the corner, we come to our celebrity guest live artist for tonight, Lieutenant Doc David Campbell, who's going to tell us lots and lots about lovely, lovely Banjul, or – as they call it down the old folks' home – Bathurst. Doctor Campbell.'

Campbell cleared his throat. A needle jumped across a dial, and LRO Soper winced, clutched his brow and put a finger to his lips.

'Ahem,' Campbell began. 'I want to talk to you tonight about an important and difficult subject. As many of you are doubtless aware, Banjul is an interesting place where we can all expect to enjoy ourselves, but it's my duty as doctor to add a note of caution. VD is, um, rife. Venereal disease, that is, disease spread by sexual contact, takes various forms. Among the commonest is one called gonorrhoea. Rarer but more dangerous is syphilis. And in the part of West Africa we are about to visit various other forms exist.

'The organisms which cause these diseases may lurk unseen in the female genital tract, which has been described as, um, a microbiologist's nightmare, and it is unwise to accept assurances that the, er, girl . . . you are talking to is, as she might say . . . clean . . . And symptoms may take as long as ninety days to appear. I would therefore urge you all to take advantage of the facilities afforded to those proceeding ashore, and to use them carefully, to avoid the risk of disease. That is all.'

LRO Soper flicked a switch and took back his programme with a short tape of wild bongo drums. 'So there we are,' he burbled into his microphone. 'Have a wonderful time but play it safe. Lad I knew once went ashore in the Windies, WI and had a wonderful time, safely of course, bein' a good lad. Then fancied another wonderful time, but he'd run out. So whaddiddedo? He turned his welly inside out and carried on firing, and a fortnight later he thought he'd lost the wife's best friend. So there we are, me hearties. Free at the gangway. Wellies from the Queen. Don't be shy, the QM's at it too. And have a lo-o-o-ovely time in won-der-ful Bath-urst or Ban-joo-oo-ool. And so we leave the old folks' home and tonight's edition of Down Your Gorgeous Grot.'

He flicked a switch, which produced a sudden surprising burst of 'Charmaine' and said, 'Thank you very much, sir. Kind of you to come up. I'll mention the question again in my next programme, if I may. They need reminding, I'm sure.'

On his way back down to the wardroom Campbell overheard a sailor address another sailor as 'a microbiologist's nightmare', and reflected on the difficulties of practising good preventive medicine in the Navy.

As the ship moved south, following a distant and unseen African coastline, sun and warmth came to be taken for granted. The first enthusiasts stripped off to a decent minimum and stretched out to sunbathe. The white tropical uniform of shirt and shorts, which made the ship's officers look as if they had dressed up to play a stainless, allegorical troop of Boy Scouts, lost its strangeness and became familiar, cool and convenient. Pale, unhealthy-looking forearms and knees turned reddish-brown then simply brown. Campbell, along with others from the wardroom, started spending time lying in the sunshine on the bridge top, a space reserved for officers' sunbathing and known for some reason as Monkey Island. He read a little, sometimes from the anatomy book, which held a gruesome fascination for his fellow idlers. Once he took up the clinical surgery textbook, with its footnotes and antiquated illustrations, but did not repeat the experiment, as he got little chance to read it himself.

The problem of the shirt tails was the only difficulty Campbell encountered over this otherwise trouble-free period. When, shortly after Gibraltar, a note had appeared on the ship's daily orders stating that tropical uniform (cryptically referred to as 5Ws) would be worn from the following day until further notice, Campbell found himself compelled to attack a shirt with a pair of surgical scissors from the sickbay, hacking off about eight inches all around the bottom, to bring it above the level of the hem of the shorts. Later, he had a quiet chat with Ronnie and learned that the ship's tailor, a Chinese civilian called So-So who worked in a tiny space in the bow, for'ard of the gun bay, would see to the rest quickly, cheaply and professionally. Campbell took a bundle up, and they were delivered back to his cabin within two hours, each shirt neatly reduced to smartness and decency, with a tidy hem that put his own jagged efforts to shame.

The last full day before the Banjul visit saw a breaking of the easy rhythm of sea routine, with people a little restless, looking forward and preparing. Various details were discussed, with much weight being given to the views of the first lieutenant, who had visited Bathurst, as it then was, some fifteen years previously. Stanchions appeared round the quarterdeck and the fo'c'sle, and awnings were rigged on them and then taken down again. In the wardroom there was talk of mail from home, no post having been received on board since Gibraltar. A complex set of duplicated papers was produced and distributed, detailing background on the port to be visited, including health information ('VD and malaria are rife') and a very short list of places of interest. A wardroom social programme was posted. It listed a shipboard cocktail party for the first evening alongside (described as 'CTP 1800–2000. Rig 6Ws' which made it sound like a painful duty), a reception ashore the following night and a cinema guest-night on board immediately prior to departure. Various visits and sporting facilities were outlined. All in all, it sounded like a thoroughly acceptable holiday, combining the exotic with the hedonistic, and Campbell recalled, with a little wonder, that he was being paid to go on it.

Strolling on the upper deck, on the last evening at sea, he reflected, briefly but more generally, on his recent fortunes. No one had died, or even been seriously ill. No major blunder had marred his first weeks in the service (the minor matter of his deportment at McGuffy's assizes would not, he thought, be held against him permanently). His own little empire was running smoothly, mainly thanks to LMA Smith, who could have run it perfectly well without him. Unless someone perforated an ulcer or fell down a hatchway, or a school of whales turned up to be spotted, he had nothing to do before dinner except dress for it, and he was strolling, comfortably warm, on the upper deck of a frigate in passage in the tropics.

There were probably worse ways of spending February, he thought, stopping to watch a couple of men under punishment working off their debt to law-abiding naval society, chatting happily as they touched up the paintwork on the quarterdeck in the dog watches, which was the sort of thing that happened to naughty sailors now that keelhauling had been abolished.

Next morning, after a short passage upriver from the open sea, HMS *Winchester* berthed at Banjul. The port area turned out to be a simple wharf, with nothing bigger than a river boat in sight, beside which the frigate attained the monstrous and warlike aspect of a Dreadnought. The air was still and moist and the heat, after the air-conditioning of the ship's interior, a physical assault. A few ragged palm trees stood in dutiful reminder that this was Africa, and a series of vast yellowish heaps on the dockside, together with a pervasive odour of roast groundnuts, confirmed the schoolroom orthodoxy on the staple export of the country.

Even before the first hawser went ashore, *Winchester*'s visit was, as the navigator had predicted, a big event. A swarm of thin black children grinned and waved. Market mammies, voluminous black matrons swathed in shocking prints, stood with trays of local edibles (an undocumented health hazard?) on their heads, waiting where they thought the gangway was going to be. A little group of Europeans, consisting of two young men in lightweight suits carrying briefcases, and one older man with the now predictable blue canvas bag, also stood waiting, but apart, as though nervous about being confused with the black ladies. At the last minute a large car with a Union flag swept up the quayside and drew to a halt. A man in a linen suit bounced out and waved.

'Looks like the Great White Queen's man in Banjul,' muttered Ronnie out of the corner of his mouth. He and Campbell were standing with the midshipmen by the port oerlikon, in a row scornfully described, by those with more to do when the ship was berthing, as the spare officers' goofing party.

When the ship was secured to the precarious and in places clearly rotting wharf, they went down to the wardroom. Once more Campbell was called upon to certify his ship free from contagious fevers, this time to a uniformed African who introduced himself as the superintendent port health officer-in-chief, and whose teeth were all filed to sharp points. He declined Campbell's offer of a coffee and then, when no alternative was proposed, accepted it. Afterwards Campbell escorted him to the gangway. They shook hands. Just as the official was finally leaving, he pressed a pink card into Campbell's hand and said, 'All very nice clean girls. I check.'

'Ah. Doctor.'

'Ma'am?'

'I thought you must be the doctor . . .' She smiled. 'Red stripes.'

'Oh. Yes . . .' Campbell smiled foolishly, and could not think of anything to say.

'Terribly smart. In fact you all look terribly smart.' The lady had the poise and easy determination of a thoroughly professional cocktail-party-goer.

'Oh?' Not simply from the heat, Campbell sweated. Secretly, he agreed with her. The captain and officers of HMS *Winchester* probably all thought they looked rather dashing in tropical mess undress, of short white jacket with gold-wired epaulettes and brass buttons, dress shirt, bow tie, black trousers and cummerbund and, in most cases, highly polished black shoes. It did things for them that the baggy, dark-blue woolly pullies of a few weeks ago had not. Even the scruffiest of the new midshipmen had succeeded in looking presentable, and was making the most of it with a tall deeply tanned blonde.

'We're all terribly pleased to see you,' said the lady. 'We haven't had a ship for ages . . . At least a year. But the French had one in December. So something had to be done.'

'Really?' The change in the ship's programme was perhaps explained.

'Only a corvette. And one of their chaps caused a spot of bother . . . So we're very pleased to see you.'

Campbell thought of one or two potential diplomatic liabilities among the ship's company, and hoped that they would not betray the simple faith in their good conduct that this pleasant middle-aged lady appeared to sustain. There was an awkward pause, then the lady said, 'Yours is much bigger.'

'We're a frigate,' said Campbell.

'I think that's what Rodney asked for.'

'Hm?'

'Rodney. His Excellency. The High Commissioner. Anyway. Jolly nice to see you.' The lady put her drink down on a step protruding from the Bofors gun and took a packet of cigarettes out of her handbag. She offered one to Campbell, who declined. One of the Chinese stewards appeared from nowhere and lit her cigarette with an expert, almost conjuring flourish. 'I didn't think you would,' she said. 'Sensible doctor . . . Where did you train? You don't mind my being a bit nosy, do you . . . ?' She came a little closer, carefully not blowing smoke in his face, and said, 'I'm a nurse. Or was a nurse, I suppose I should say.'

'In Scotland,' said Campbell. She smiled, possibly because of his accent. 'In Edinburgh.'

'Oh. Not the Institute?'

'Yes.'

'Gosh. You didn't.'

'Yes.'

'Really? How marvellous.'

'You know it?' Campbell asked.

'Gosh, yes. Trained there,' she said. 'Loved it . . . Well, hated some of it. But how marvellous . . . I shan't tell you *when* I was there . . . But who might you know?'

Campbell had not thought about the Institute for weeks, and was now suddenly compelled to imagine which of the grim-faced beldams now treading its corridors as senior nursing staff might once, in another age, have been girls together with this lady of indeterminate years whom he had just met at a cocktail party on a ship in the Gambia.

'Sheila Parsons,' she announced abruptly.

'Oh . . . David Campbell,' said Campbell, when he realized that she had been introducing herself.

'Let's see,' she said. 'One or two of the lads might still be around . . . A surgeon. Bertie. A houseman when I staffed on six.' She paused and sipped her drink again. 'Heard he's a consultant there nowadays. Hard to think of it. McSomething.'

'McElwee?' said Campbell. 'Consultant on nine and ten now.'

'That's him. Lovely chap.' She smiled. 'Imagine my forgetting his name,' she added mysteriously.

Pompous, bullying old fart, thought Campbell to himself. 'Yes,' he said. 'Friend of mine worked for him. Seems an interesting chap. Don't really know him.'

'Does he still wear his silly bow ties?'

'I believe he does,' said Campbell.

'How fascinating . . . Is there still someone called Oliver Croom-Lyon around?'

'I don't think so,' said Campbell, not wishing to sound off-putting, but Edinburgh did produce an awful lot of doctors.

'And how about Henry? I *know* he's still around. Henry Creech?'

'Oh, yes,' said Campbell. 'Very much so. My old medical chief.'

'Never! A chief?' She smiled. 'Shows how old *I* am. But I shall always think of him as a very green houseman getting a ticking off from sister for dipping a biscuit in his tea once.'

They both laughed and Campbell said, 'It didn't make any difference. He still does it.'

'How wonderful!' She looked as if, after a couple of hundred cocktail parties too many, she was beginning to enjoy herself. 'Bertie once . . .' She stopped, looked thoughtful, and smiled, then said, 'Hermione would be simply fascinated to meet you.'

Campbell panicked, suddenly seeing himself spending the rest of the cocktail party haltingly rehearsing the foibles of half-forgotten doctors variously dead, departed or still doing damage, with a couple of silver-haired matrons slowly succumbing to the effects of reminiscence and HMS *Winchester*'s gin. The lady gripped him lightly and expertly by the left elbow and steered him aft.

'It's David, isn't it?'

'Yes.'

'Hermione!'

'Oh . . . Hello.'

'Come and meet the doctor.'

The girl said, 'Excuse me,' and smiled a polite goodbye to the navigator and left him and came over towards Campbell and Mrs Parsons. She was too young, by about thirty years, to have been a staff nurse when Henry Creech was a green houseman and Bertie McElwee a bright young thing. And she was also rather pretty. The navigator took a sip of gin and tonic, eyeing Campbell philosophically over the top of his glass.

'Hello,' said the girl.

'Hermione. David. David's just been telling me the chaps I knew in Edinburgh are all tottering down towards the grave.'

The girl smiled and said, 'Gosh. Do you know all mummy's old boyfriends?'

'Nobody said anything about boyfriends,' said Mrs Parsons, not meaning it. She had finished her drink. The navigator pounced on her empty glass. 'Gin and tonic, ma'am?' He walked over to where one of Ronnie's Chinamen was beginning a trek round with the topping-up jugs, giving a strong impression that he would be back smartly and might not subsequently go away.

The first thing that Campbell noticed about Hermione, apart from the fact that she was very pretty, was that there was a little pink patch on her nose where it had begun to peel. She looked up at him, with her lips still practically touching her glass, and said, 'I overdid it,' and, after a pause, 'only my nose.' Her eyes were big and brown.

Mrs Parsons had turned towards the navigator, who was coming back with her drink. She was standing foursquare, an immovable object in a pink print dress, athwart the direct line between the navigator and her daughter. 'Sheila Parsons,' she said, in a halt-or-I-open-fire tone of voice, and out of the corner of his eye Campbell saw Ayres skid to standstill with two full glasses in his hands, without mishap and smiling bravely throughout.

Hermione giggled and said, 'She's rather awful. And I'm not called Hermione. I'm Emmy.'

'Hello, Emmy.'

'Hello, David.'

Once more Campbell, who was new to this sort of thing, could think of nothing at all to say.

'I'm a nurse, too,' she said, to help him along.

'Oh?'

'At Tommy's. . . St Thomas's.'

'In darkest Tooting?'

She smiled. 'Know it?'

'Not really. Knew a gasman who trained there and then came to work in Edinburgh.'

'Who?' she said, adding 'But I won't know him.'

'Baird-Brown. Anthony Baird-Brown.'

'Never heard of him.' They both laughed. 'How are all your sailors keeping?'

'All right. I think.'

'Don't they all get sunburn?'

'No. It's an offence.'

'Really?'

'Yes.'

'What happens?'

'To what?'

'To sailors who get sunburn.'

'No one has.'

'But they must.'

'Oh. It's only an offence if they can't work because of it. They're mainly very sensible. One fell asleep in the sun and got a bit peely. But he's all right and he wasn't off duty.'

'So he wasn't keelhauled.'

'No. Not even a little. What happened to you?'

'Oh, my nose? Just being greedy. I'm not out here for very long . . . And we were out on a picnic the day before yesterday and I wanted a quick tan . . . and now I feel like a traffic light at stop.'

'It's actually quite fetching,' said Campbell with all the gallantry a glass and a half of gin and tonic bestows.

'Have you been busy?'

'Not very. But I don't mind.'

'That sounds as if you've been in the Navy for years and years.'

'Only since just before Christmas.'

'Like it?'

'It's getting better all the time.'

'Do you actually have to do much doctoring? I mean really?'

'Not a lot. Yet. I think I'm mainly here in case of something.'

'Do you have a hospital?'

'A little one.' He pointed to a spot on the quarterdeck roughly corresponding with the ceiling, possibly known as the deckhead, of his sickbay. She looked intrigued.

'Really? What about nurses?'

''fraid not. But I've got an assistant. A sailor. I think he knows about bedbaths and proper hospital corners. I know he can take temperatures and I suppose he could fluff up pillows if it came to the bit.'

'Hospital corners are rather old hat now,' she said, rising agreeably to his bait. 'Most of our patients are under downies . . . Oh.' She laughed again. She had nice teeth.

'How's your glass?'

As though summoned by telepathy, Leading Steward Ho appeared with a jugful of pleasantly tinkling gin and tonic, which averted the risk of leaving her even briefly with Ayres still around, though Campbell noted that for the moment that hazard seemed to be under control. ('But how do you know where you are, if it's dark and you can't see land *or* the stars?')

Poker-faced, Leading Steward Ho topped up Emmy's glass and Campbell's. They thanked him and he passed on his way to succour others. She looked carefully at him as he walked away.

'Is he Chinese?'

'Mm. All our stewards are. And the cooks. So we get chop suey every second Wednesday.'

'How lovely . . . What else do you get?'

'Everything. All sorts of things. They're very good . . . The crew enjoys a well-balanced diet,' he said in his doctor's voice.

'So no one gets scurvy?'

'Or beriberi.'

'Or pellagra?'

'Or kwashiorkor.'

'Or osteomalacia?'

Campbell had run out of relevant diseases. 'How did you know all these?' he asked by way of conceding defeat.

'We've just done vitamins. And I passed the exam.' She lowered her voice and said, 'You all look terribly smart.'

'It's the feeding,' said Campbell. 'Keeps us bright-eyed and bushy-tailed. Gleaming coats and cold wet noses and all that. And, of course, the sea air helps.' She laughed and spilled some gin and tonic on her wrist, and put her glass in her other hand and licked it off.

'I meant your uniforms.'

'Oh . . . yes.' For some reason he felt like telling her it was the first time he'd worn it. The arrival of Henry, looking slightly drunk, prevented any such disclosure.

'Hello, Emmy. Henry. Emmy.'

'Hello.'

'Hello. Has the doctor explained to you . . . about after? The routine?'

'No,' said Emmy, a little suspiciously, 'I don't think so.'

'Well, I will. If he hasn't. You haven't, doctor, have you?'

'No.'

'Well. 'slike this. This . . .' He indicated the throng on the quarterdeck. '. . . is work. And we generally like to relax a bit after work. Have a little drink and so on. Down where we live . . . The wardroom. Spot of chop suey if you feel like it. But only people who aren't work. No dignitaries . . . of any colour. Just a few friends . . . Do come.'

Emmy looked to Campbell for explanation and guidance. 'Yes,' he said. 'Do come.'

'Are you going, David?' she said. He nodded. 'Will there really be chop suey?'

'Honest,' said Henry. 'Cross my chopsticks.'

She laughed, and said, 'I'll have to tell mummy. And gosh I'd better circulate . . . Later, David?' She went away, and Henry consoled Campbell with a drunken, dirty wink.

By 7.00 Campbell was sufficiently drunk to take on the full social duties of a naval officer. He found himself talking to a big fat black man in a cream-coloured uniform, who regaled him with tales of his two-year secondment to the police in Glasgow, which he explained was in Scotland, not England. He was on whisky, to good effect. Fluent with drink, he described how the people there behaved at football matches, and what they did at New Year, and how many good friends he had there, and how much he had liked their music, and how, when he had left that force, his colleagues had presented him with a box set of records by the City of Glasgow Police Pipe Band. 'Rerr music,' he said, dewy-eyed with the thought of it. 'I listen to it and feel the soft rain and think of the kilts and the happy days we had. And you should have seen the magnificent horses of "B" division.'

Eventually he padded off in search of more whisky and Campbell took the opportunity to slide round between the guard-rail and the throng to see what had happened to Emmy. She was talking to Ronnie and a short black lady wrapped up like a Christmas present in a brilliant red print toga. Over the top of the black lady's head he caught her eye, and got the impression that she would probably come down for some chop suey, then he went on to listen to a complex gynaecological saga from a gaunt English lady with a wizened, almost saurian tan, who had introduced herself as the first secretary's wife, and, between operations, glanced keenly round the company, keeping an undisguised eye on who was doing what and with whom. After the hysterectomy she needed another drink and so did Campbell, and when he went to get them Ayres caught him and said, 'Watch her. She runs the list. Keep her sweet.'

'What list?'

'Who comes to official functions. Well, the women who come. Which is hers?' Campbell pointed to one of the glasses. Ayres thoughtfully unstoppered a gin bottle and livened up her drink quite a bit. 'Her husband's a miserable-looking bugger, too. Do your best. It's for *Winchester*. And the whole Navy. We don't want her crossing people off just for having a little fun. Just keep her sweet.'

Campbell returned to his duties, and listened sympathetically to the wound infection, the deep venous thrombosis and the pulmonary embolus, which were by no means so concisely presented, but had to be divined amid a morass of symptoms, garbled clinical detail and verbatim quotations from the patient, her relatives and the medical and nursing staff. ('I don't know how you put up with all that pain and misery, Mrs Uprichard. I just don't.') Her surveillance of the events of the party slackened considerably as she abandoned herself to her tale and to the effects of the navigator's gin. Then quite suddenly she looked at her watch, thanked Campbell for his sympathetic attention and said, 'Must find Henry,' and strode off muttering, 'Super party . . . super party.'

Other people had left, had begun to leave or appeared to be thinking of it. A motley and unsteady procession of suited, uniformed and robed European and African men, together with their equally variegated wives, trailed over the gangway and stood around, like refugees from a fancy dress party, leaving a curiously selected rearguard on the quarterdeck. There were the ship's officers, and a higher proportion of young women than could have been attributed simply to the operations of chance. A fat Englishman in a lightweight suit and club tie was haranguing the gunnery officer, who was listening in a fashion which suggested there might be something in it for him, and an African police officer, perhaps junior or deputy to the man who had been to Glasgow, was finishing his last drink by crunching and swallowing the ice-cubes, then chewing the slice of lemon and spitting the peel over the guard-rail.

Campbell looked round for Emmy, wondering why her mother insisted on calling her Hermione. She was close behind him, and slightly to the right.

'Hello.'

'Hello.'

'You look as if you've been working quite hard.'

'I was. Mrs First Secretary.'

'Oh. Molly Uprichard?'

'I think so . . . Gynae problems.'

'Yes. That's her. And a breast.'

'Funny. She never got round to that. Just switched off on the dot of eight.'

'She would. She's the boss lady round here. Socially. Made an awful fuss after that business with the Frenchman. So we're all on our best behaviour.'

'Oh,' said Campbell, sounding perhaps disappointed. Emmy smiled.

'But mummy says it's all right . . . to come downstairs . . . Will there really be chop suey?'

'I should think so. If Henry says so.'

'Good. I think I could be a bit peckish soon.'

'Well, they're quite good at Chinese food . . . It's a sort of *specialité de la maison*.'

'Of course. It's quite a big ship, isn't it?'

'About 3000 tons.'

'It's nice.'

'We like it.'

They were leaning on the guard-rail (a practice of which the first lieutenant disapproved) looking down at the water. The swiftness of the tropical dusk was still surprising to Campbell: already it was almost completely dark. Emmy was standing closer than he would have expected from the duration of their acquaintance. She smelled extremely clean and faintly perfumed (a very nursey combination) and a little of gin and tonic.

Small fires, possibly for cooking, twinkled among the huts on the opposite bank of the river. After days at sea, land smells, rich with earth and plants and fresh water and intermingled, in this instance, with the more complex odours of an African town, constituted an unexpected luxury.

'How long are you out here for?' Campbell asked, to break a thoughtful silence.

'Hm? Sorry. I was miles away.'

'Oh. How long are you out here for?'

'Just three weeks,' she said, after another longish pause. 'It's . . . a bit different from Tooting. And the first time I've been here. Before that we were in Muscat.'

'With the embassy?'

'Mm. Daddy does security.'

Campbell was interested, but felt it would be not only unprofitable but unwise to pursue the details, since she was no doubt well-versed in fending off such curiosity, and there was no purpose in alienating her.

'In the embassy here now?'

'Well, it's actually a high commission. Same, but Commonwealth.'

'How was Muscat?'

'Wild. Interesting. I was there for three months between school and starting at Tommy's. Here's nicer. So small it's really quite fun. And terribly British. The policemen and all that. And sort of . . . naïve.'

'Naïve?'

'Mm. Well, the Africans anyway. Sort of straightforward. But the Brits are like Brits anywhere. Maybe worse because there aren't very many of them. Terribly tiny community. Most of them were here.'

'Mrs First Secretary and all that.'

'Yes. A bit crushing. And bitchy sometimes . . . Anyway, we're all glad you've come.' She turned from looking into the river, and smiled at Campbell in a way that was probably just friendly but could have easily led to a misunderstanding.

'Coming down for a bite shortly?' said a voice behind them.

'Oh. Hello, Ronnie.'

'Hello . . . Hello again, Miss Parsons.' The supply officer's face was shiny and pink from the party, and he looked less Chinese than usual. 'Come down and see how the poor live.'

He drew Campbell slightly to one side and said, 'First lieutenant's cabin's the ladies' cloakroom for tonight. Usual routine. Heads and so on. OK?'

'Thanks, Ronnie.'

'Lovely. See you both in the wardroom shortly.'

While Campbell was waiting in the passageway outside the first lieutenant's cabin for Emmy and a rather plain girl, an acquaintance of hers, Ayres came along with the deeply tanned girl last seen early in the evening talking to one of the midshipmen, and the fat Englishman, accompanied by a cheerfully glowing fat blonde, possibly his wife.

'Evening, doctor. The Edinburgh connection strikes again, eh? Nothing to beat the old Scotch Mafia.' Ayres turned to the fat man. 'Wherever we go, the doctor here always knows somebody. Doctor, this is Bert. Unilever. Oh. Sorry. Marnie . . .' The fat blonde smiled. '. . . David Campbell. Our quack.'

'Is this where I can go for a pee?' said Marnie, looking round. The first lieutenant's door opened and about half a dozen girls (how did they manage these things?) emerged smiling, fragrant and generally spruced up after the minor dishevelment of the cocktail party. Emmy was among them. Henry, who had appeared from nowhere, looking distinctly more drunk, and sly and lecherous with it, joined Campbell in escorting the girls down the short companionway joining the first lieutenant's cabin to the wardroom passageway below. Because of some eccentricity of the ship's ventilation system, a gusty updraught of warm air played around the steps as the girls descended, giving rise to much billowing of skirts and girlish laughter. Henry's expression assumed a grotesque, even comic lechery, fortunately observed only by the navigator and the doctor.

Emmy's plain friend was called Olga Uprichard, a revelation sufficiently disturbing to merit passing on to Ayres, once they had all reached the wardroom and begun to mingle again. The navigator thought for a moment then said, 'I'll have a word with Henry. Got to fix up a good time for the queen bee's ugly daughter. Olga, eh? Maybe her dad's Moscow's man in our foreign service in Banjul, and not just another boring old Brit first secretary. Olga. Right.'

Ayres found Henry, and Campbell found Emmy, who was holding a gin and tonic without much relish. 'Honestly, I'm a bit out of practice with this stuff, David. Will you have it and get me just an ordinary tonic . . . And I've hardly eaten anything at all today.'

Campbell went across to the bar and asked Steward Tan for a straight tonic, overhearing as he waited a cryptic conversation between Ayres and Henry, a classical naval exchange, with a senior officer briefing a junior, putting him in the picture, identifying the target, stating the objective and inviting questions before despatching the mission. 'But she's horrible,' Henry protested. 'Probably goes like a ferret,' Ayres countered. 'Only needs asking. You know the sort. Do your stuff.' Campbell watched, half expecting Henry to salute, do a smart about-turn and march off to his fate.

'Stray tonic sah,' said Steward Tak.

'Oh. Thank you, Tak.'

Emmy and Campbell swapped glasses, getting their hands mixed up and touching a lot as they did so.

'Do you all live in here?' she asked, looking round the wardroom.

'Sort of. It's our lounge. And sitting room, and bar, and dining room. And where we have parties. Oh, and it's my operating theatre at action stations too. There's a big light up there.'

'But you all have cabins as well:'

'Yes. Next floor down.'

'What are they like?'

'Small. Neat. Well, mine's a bit untidy. But all right.'

'And what about your sickbay?'

'Oh, it's on this floor, but right at the back. Under the gun at the place where we had the party upstairs, and to the right.'

'What's it like?'

'Smallish. But big enough. A sort of office, with beds and an operating table . . .' Campbell wondered about inviting her along to see for herself, but noticed the first lieutenant standing looking round, much as the first secretary's wife had been doing half an hour previously, and decided that, however tempting the prospect of taking Emmy off for a quiet guided tour of the sickbay, it could perhaps wait a little. She seemed to interpret his hesitancy and said, 'Perhaps you could show me later.' Campbell felt a sudden warm surge of lust. They sipped their drinks.

Everyone seemed to be enjoying themselves, a great deal more informally than at the preceding cocktail party. The loud Englishman was getting very drunk and his wife was deep in conversation with Bob, the gunnery officer. A little cluster of the rather more mature lady guests had gathered in a corner round Ronnie and Lieutenant Scholes, the engineer, and appeared to be just as happy as the two decidedly young, possibly even schoolgirl, sisters who were standing with their backs to a bulkhead, under considerable pressure from all three midshipmen at once. Ayres and the deeply-tanned blonde were talking to the weapons electrical officer, a man notoriously faithful to his wife, and therefore safe to share a blonde with briefly at a party. Henry was talking to Olga.

'At last.'

'What?'

'Smell it?'

'Oh.'

A variety of Chinese cooking odours filled the wardroom and eventually the PO steward emerged from behind the curtained-off section, and spoke briefly to the first lieutenant, who nodded. The curtain was drawn and quite quickly the officers and their guests formed themselves into a queue for a Chinese meal, not just the chop suey canvassed by Henry, but a generous selection covering the dining table, and flanked by a pile of plates at one end and a couple of dozen glasses of white wine at the other. Emmy and Campbell were not at the front, but near it. There was a choice of forks or chopsticks. She took the latter, and so did Campbell, though few others present did.

'Where did you learn to use them?' she asked.

'Sat next to a Chinese chap in French at school. Taught me to pick up paper pellets using two pencils. Quite useful. But I never really understood the subjunctive.'

'I learned from my amah. When I was four. In Hong Kong. Chinese food never tastes right from a fork.' Campbell agreed. The PO steward watched them approvingly.

Afterwards, the buffet was cleared away, the curtain drawn again, the table dismantled and, with a little alteration of the lighting and some attention to the wardroom stereo system, the dining area was converted to a small but adequate dance floor. Two of the midshipmen launched out with the schoolgirls, and were soon followed by Olga and Henry, who seemed now to be doing the thing for its own sake, and not simply in obedience to a direct order from a superior. Ayres and the tanned girl took the floor, too, and it occurred to Campbell, that, pending a visit to view the sickbay, he might as well follow with Emmy, who seemed keen enough, and danced close, so that he could smell her hair, and feel the softness of her body through his 6Ws.

'Sah.'

Campbell opened his eyes and lifted his face out of Emmy's hair and turned round. Steward Tak was standing loosely at attention, solitary amid the grappling couples on the dance floor.

'Oh. Yes.'

'Duty senior rate, sah.'

'Thanks, Tak . . . Excuse me.'

'Business?' Emmy said.

'Probably.'

They went into the lounge part of the wardroom, blinking in the light. Emmy waited while Campbell went to the door. One of the stoker POs, scrubbed and smart beyond recognition in the evening uniform prescribed for his rank in the tropics, was standing outside.

'Sorry to bother you, sir. Small incident ashore. No locals and nothing nasty. Some of our lads drinking. One injured.'

'Oh?'

'Cut eyebrow, sir.'

'Thanks, PO. LMA on board?'

''fraid not, sir. He's marked as gone ashore.'

'Where is the man?'

'Starboard waist, sir. With the patrol.'

'Thanks, PO. Take him to the sickbay flat, please. I'll be along right away.'

Emmy was looking worried. Campbell explained to her

what had happened, and said he thought he might be ten minutes or so sorting it out. She looked around rather anxiously, and saw Olga and Henry, now resting from their labours, and joined them as Campbell left.

The victim, one Ordinary Electrical Mechanician Maudsley, was comfortably drunk and rather vague about how he had acquired his injury. 'Might have walked into something, sir. It's nothing serious. . . Just having a quiet pint ashore with my oppo, and must have walked into something . . .' Campbell told him to lie on the operating table. He climbed unsteadily on to it and, while Campbell was looking around for suture material, swabs, forceps and so on, fell asleep.

The cut was short and clean, in the line of the eyebrow. There was little bruising round it and no dirt in it. Campbell washed it, shaved a tiny area round it and put in three fine black stitches. The Chinese meal in the wardroom had done much to counter the effects of the preliminary gins, and he worked quickly and neatly. His patient, being tough and drunk as well, would probably have dismissed a local anaesthetic as an effeminate self-indulgence, had one indeed been offered. He mumbled gratefully and eventually sat up and was taken away by the duty senior rate. Campbell made a careful note of his injury in the medical documents, as the matter would almost certainly be the subject of deliberation at the captain's table in due course.

On the way back to the wardroom, through the friendly whirring warmth of the ship's interior, Campbell wondered what might have been happening at the party in his absence, in particular whether the navigator might have made a late recovery from Mrs Parsons' triumphantly disabling manoeuvre earlier in the evening. He need not have worried. On the way through the ops room he distinctly heard, from deep in its intricate darkness, an exchange of voices, one being the navigator's, the other not being Emmy's, which set his mind at rest. No harm was done, but that incident and its sequel were afterwards frequently referred to as 'the night the doctor nearly spoiled my blind pilotage night entry'.

The party in the wardroom had thinned out. The first lieutenant and the gunnery officer had gone ashore with the Unilever couple, and the younger officers were beginning to loosen up and enjoy themselves. The lighting in the lounge section had been dimmed, and the music was louder. Steward Tak had gone off duty and the midshipman who had been unlucky in the question of the schoolgirls was now behind the bar. Emmy was still with Olga and Henry.

'How's your victim, doctor?'

'I think he'll live, Henry.'

'Good show, sir. If you don't mind my saying so, you've done pretty well as the anti-death officer.'

'Thanks, Henry.'

'So far.'

The girls laughed, and Olga looked adoringly at Henry. Campbell, who was used to this sort of ribbing, thought about the remark, then said, 'I'll do my best, Henry. Even for you.' Emmy took his hand and squeezed it and they went back to the dance floor.

This time Campbell was in no doubt that she wanted to be shown over the sickbay quite soon. To slow, late evening music she came close to him, soft against his chest and neck, and her thighs seemed to follow his, even to anticipate them, in a way which gave rise in Campbell to palpable lust, which appeared to make her dance even closer. A couple of slow numbers later they left the wardroom.

As they did so, Campbell began to worry about their route aft. There were two possibilities. One was to go for'ard through the senior rates accommodation, and up a steep ladder and through a hatch on to the fo'c'sle, up a further ladder on to the bridge wing, then down and aft on the upper deck, through a screen door and down a further ladder to the sickbay flat. The other was through the ops room. With some trepidation Campbell chose the latter, because it was shorter and far less complicated, and with any luck the navigator would now be elsewhere.

As soon as they had gone through the door marked 'Secret', it was clear that he was not. The ops room was in darkness as before. To its usual noises, the various hums and whirrings of shipboard life, was added a regular rapid sighing noise, steady in rate and intensity. Campbell decided to walk quickly and talk a lot, and hope that Emmy, being unused to the ways of the sea, would, if she heard it, put it down to the workings of some obscure piece of navigational or communications equipment.

They reached the other end of the ops room, with Campbell gabbling brightly about OEM Maudsley's lacerated eyebrow, and appearances more or less preserved, then descended a companionway and walked aft along the ship's main passageway to the sickbay. It was locked, so Campbell twirled a bunch of keys and they went in. He felt around for a particular switch in the array by the door, and succeeded, first time, in getting one which turned on a single light down at the far end, by the bunks, throwing a soft and passably romantic glow over his little empire. Emmy looked round, wide-eyed. 'It's lovely,' she said. 'Everything . . . in such a little space.' Campbell noted with some displeasure that the lower bed was occupied by a series of cardboard boxes including one marked boldly in red, 'Condoms GS: Qty 5000: Property of MOD(N): Not for Resale'.

Emmy had begun to wander round looking at things, fortunately at the office end of the bay. She picked up something from the desk. 'What does "F Med 5" mean?'

'It's just a record card. That chap I sewed up.'

'Why does it say "Rank Rating Pencil"?'

'That means you write that bit in pencil.'

'Why?'

'In case they decide to promote him,' Campbell explained.

'Or reduce him to the ranks?'

'I don't think he's got far enough up for that yet.'

'What's OEM?'

'Ordinary Electrical Mechanician.'

'Imagine being called Ordinary Electrical Mechanician Lancelot Frith Maudsley?'

'I don't think anyone does. I think he's called Oggy.'

'Oggy?'

'Yes.'

'Why?'

'Because he's from Guz.'

'Where's Guz?'

'Plymouth,' Campbell was quite proud of this piece of naval lore, 'which is where they guzzle oggies.'

'What?' Emmy was amused and confused and possibly a

little drunk.

'He's from Plymouth. Which is called Guz. Which is where they eat oggies. Which are sort of Cornish pasties. I think. So he's called Oggy.'

'Stands to reason,' said Emmy, entering into the spirit of the thing. 'I should have thought of that . . . Silly of me.'

She stood with the card in her hand, looking astonishingly lovely in Campbell's usual place of work, where, to his certain knowledge, no women had trod since he had joined the ship eight weeks before (which might partly have explained why she looked so astonishingly lovely).

' "Probable fracas ashore. Two cm laceration left eyebrow. Not KO'd. Three BSS. Review for ATT booster mane," ' she read. 'Poor Oggy.' She handed Campbell the card. Their fingers touched, and stayed touching. She looked up at his face. She was just a little bit drunk, in a sensible, nursey, ladylike sort of way, and there was certainly no question of Campbell, in vintage rakehell fashion, having filled her full of liquor in order to have his evil way with her. In fact he was rather nervous and almost stone cold sober himself, the effect of sewing up OEM Maudsley having been to concentrate the mind wonderfully.

She laid the card back on the desk and took both his hands in hers, and looked down at them. Her brow presented itself within easy kissing distance. 'You've got nice hands,' she said, in a small, soft voice before he had got round to kissing her. 'Nice doctorish hands. Square and sensible.' She turned them over and looked very closely then said, 'Gosh. Your heart line meets your head line.'

'Both hands?'

''course, silly. Look. That.' She traced a line across each of his palms with an index finger.

'Do you read tea-leaves too?'

''course.'

'And have a broomstick and talk to your cat?'

'Naturally.'

'And believe in all that rubbish about stars?'

'Yes.'

'So does our navigator.'

'Roddy? Really? Does he?' She looked surprised and

intrigued.

'Of course . . . How d'you think he got us here?'

She laughed and said, 'Oh, David,' and suddenly kissed him properly. She was warm and smelled of gin and Chinese food and nice perfume. Standing in the sickbay, Campbell put his arms round her, which was even nicer than it had been when they had been dancing in the dark bit of the wardroom. They kissed again, then Campbell leaned down and nuzzled her neck. She made appreciative little noises and held him more closely.

They had been standing that way for perhaps half a minute when Emmy suddenly gasped and squeaked, 'Oh god!' and clutched at Campbell in terror. He stiffened and looked round to see what had frightened her. A sailor, in the blue shirt and shorts of tropical working dress, was emerging from the door at the far end of the sickbay. It was Smith, clearly embarrassed.

'Oh . . . I do beg your pardon, sir,' he said. '. . . I'd no idea . . .'

Emmy looked at the LMA in amazement, as if he were a bug-eyed monster alighting from a flying saucer, and clutched Campbell's hand. 'It's my assistant,' he said. 'LMA Smith.'

'I'm terribly sorry, sir . . . I'll leave you . . . Goodnight, sir . . . Ma'am . . .' He slid rather sheepishly past them and out of the sickbay door. Campbell smiled. Emmy began to laugh, a bit hysterically, then said, 'Is that the chap who does hospital corners?'

'That's the man . . .'

'What's down there?' she asked, pointing down to the door from which Smith had appeared.

'Loo . . . Lab. That sort of thing.'

'And . . . what's he?'

'LMA Smith.'

'What's LMA?'

'Leading Medical Assistant.'

She hugged him again. 'Gosh I got such a fright. He was . . . buttoning up his front.'

Campbell smiled. 'Why not? There's a loo in there. And there aren't usually ladies standing in here . . .'

'. . . groping the medical officer,' she said, giggling. 'Poor chap. Will he be . . .? I mean . . . I shouldn't be here, should I?'

'Strictly speaking not. But he's terribly discreet,' said Campbell, who had already realized that the incident would, if leaked a little – e.g., to more or less anyone except the first lieutenant – do his standing generally in the ship no harm whatsoever. Emmy stood with her back to the desk, looking round as if she were expecting at least a surgeon rear admiral to pop out of every cupboard, and it was clear that they could not simply take up where they left off, at any rate not for the moment. Campbell glanced at his watch. It was ten to eleven. A number of practical details asserted themselves.

'David.'

'What?'

'Mm.' She came closer. 'Is it really that time already?'

'Oh. Is it past your bedtime?'

She smiled. 'Sort of.'

'Shall I take you home?'

'Mm, I think we should . . . They don't worry, but . . .'

'Fine . . . I think I'll have to slip into something comfortable. Can't go ashore like this.'

'Oh. Pity.'

'First lieutenant wouldn't like it. Is it far?'

'About ten minutes.'

'Taxi?'

'No. Walking. This really is a small town.'

'And do . . . people like us walk about at night?'

'Gosh yes. It isn't Tooting.'

They left the sickbay and, while Emmy waited in the wardroom, Campbell went down to his cabin and changed into what the navy called 'plain clothes', clothes other than uniform. When he came back she looked at him carefully, as though to check it was really him in sandals, slacks and an open-necked shirt.

'You look different.'

'You look the same. Lovely.'

As they walked along the quayside holding hands, a few straggling sailors, convivially grouped in twos and threes, were still making their way back to the ship. By the gate a pair whom Campbell recognized as stokers stood embarrassed while a third, in a dark corner behind a hut, had a torrential pee. 'Honest, Wiggy,' said the man in the corner, his voice a slurred mumble over his splashing, 'if it's rife, I've got it.'

The main street was tarmac, with capacious, rather smelly concrete drains on either side. Watchmen snoozed in the doorways of shops. There were tethered goats, and funny old cars that looked as if they were being saved from the scrap-yard only by the devotion and heroic improvisations of their owners. The night was warm, and noisy with insects variously buzzing, clicking and rattling. Emmy and Campbell turned off on to a side road surfaced with crumbling laterite, then into a cul-de-sac, a little estate of astonishingly ordinary-looking suburban houses.

'Welcome to Little England,' said Emmy. 'We're just in here.' They stopped at a house that would not have looked out of place in a quiet street in Corstorphine. 'Come in,' she said. 'For a little while.'

On a table in a sort of lounge place was a thermos flask with two mugs beside it.

'Typical of her.' Emmy did not sound pleased. 'I bet it's cocoa.'

It was, which rather pleased Campbell, but seemed to annoy Emmy, as though her mother were conniving at and even, *in absentia*, presiding over a part of her life for which she might expect to exercise detailed responsibility. She was no longer anything like as close and cuddly as she had been in the sickbay prior to the advent of the LMA. They drank the cocoa. She talked about nursing, and London, and a bit about her mother, and then rather a lot about someone called Tom, a clinical psychologist, evidently a close friend. Campbell's mind turned towards his naval duties and officer-like responsibilities, and, when a suitable opportunity presented itself, he asked, 'What are the consular bods like?'

'Hm?'

'The consular chap. I'm supposed to see him.'

'What for?'

'Well . . . It's a sort of job I've been given.'

'What?'

'I've got to look at some graves. Soldiers' and sailors'. And the consular lot are supposed to help me.'

'I should think that'd be Alec,' Emmy said, sounding suddenly nursey and practical. 'And they're probably all in the British cemetery.'

'Where's that?'

'A mile up the coast. It's nice.'

'I've got to go and check they're being looked after.'

'Can I come, too?'

So it was that, late the following afternoon, Campbell and Emmy made their way by car to a green and pleasant graveyard a mile to the north of the town. A man was waiting for them, a middle-aged African, an ex-soldier, to judge from his tattered khaki garb and the way he stood with his hoe held stiffly to his shoulder. He welcomed them and showed them to the corner Campbell sought. They walked, Campbell and Emmy following their barefooted guide, past ornate Edwardian memorial stones, unmistakable imperial monuments in the English style, with carved weapons, draped flags and proud but sorrowing Britannias. Further on were the simpler tablets of lesser mortals (though still white and still imperial). They recorded the small tragedies of the colonial era, the brief careers ('of a fever, in his twentieth year') and the pathetic multiplicity of infant deaths.

The soldiers' and sailors' graves were kept apart, their tombstones mainly small and drawn up in a neat eternal parade. They bore names, ranks, numbers and dates. A few had phrases of explanation: 'died of wounds', 'died of fever', 'drowned in a river accident'. Some were inscribed 'erected by his messmates' or 'in loving memory of a good comrade'. One of the earlier stones bore two doggerel quatrains, beginning 'We'll never hear your voice again . . .' and ending 'Dead, but remembered still'.

Campbell worked from a list supplied by the consular department, which was conveniently arranged to coincide with the rows of graves. Uniformed, and carrying a clipboard, and followed by his little retinue, Campbell inspected them. As with most military inspections, there was little that invited adverse comment, and the fact that those whom the inspection most concerned were dead added a touch of the surreal. From time to time Campbell imagined at his elbow some fell sergeant muttering such things as "Arbottle! When d'you last 'ave your grass cut then?'

They walked up and down the rows, and stopped only once, at the grave of one Petty Officer Bardwell, late of HM Riverboat *Agile*. Although otherwise not bad for 1917, its kerb surround was cracked and the stone itself was listing to the right. Campbell made a note, the consul would arrange a repair, and some day another naval officer would come along in uniform with a clipboard and PO Bardwell's grave would be inspected once more, and measures taken if it were not up to standard.

In twenty minutes or so he checked off three-and-a-half pages of dead soldiers, sailors and occasional airmen against the rows of tombstones in the stubby grass, then they walked back to the gate where the official car was waiting. At Emmy's whispered suggestion, Campbell gave the African gardener a pound. He sprang to attention, presented arms with his hoe, took the money and then saluted, army fashion, palm forward, with a fine flourish and the stylish tremble practised by smarter soldiers and marines. As he drove back with Emmy to the High Commission building, Campbell felt a curious, quite unexpected satisfaction in his role as HMS *Winchester*'s War Graves Officer. He resolved to write his report as soon as possible.

He did not get a chance to write it until the ship was back at sea. The rest of the Banjul visit passed in an agreeable bustle of formal and informal social occasions, long evenings spent mainly with Emmy, and short, hot afternoons spent resting. There was little work and duties were mainly social. The evening after the trip to the cemetery the wardroom went *en masse* to the official reception ashore. Emmy was there, too, and laughed at their high-necked brass buttoned uniforms, saying that they looked like the chorus from *Madam Butterfly*, but that did not stop her spending the greater part of the occasion with Campbell.

Afterwards, following a quick trip back to the ship to change, Henry and Olga and Campbell and Emmy, and Ayres and the deeply tanned girl, who was called Gail, went to a beach restaurant, one of the town's few gestures to tourism, a few miles to the south. In the taxi out, Emmy snuggled close, in a fashion that made Campbell think that he might hear less about her boyfriend at home than he had heard on the previous evening.

The earlier part of the evening was not a great success. The restaurant consisted of a series of charcoal grills and their attendants in the open air, a small covered area where food was prepared, and an open-air bar staffed by sleepy youths whose sloth in fetching drink was matched only by their insolent reluctance to subsequently return with the change. The party lay around a low table on the beach. They drank local, rather chemical beer and ate kebabs, except for Olga, who recoiled from Ayres' description of them as 'monkey on a stick' and refused to eat anything. Thereafter, from being silent and sullen, she became drunk and remarkably indiscreet, so that even Henry was moved to feelings of fastidiousness and attempted to restrain her, failed, and had to settle for trying to divert or dilute her revelations, all the while making her drunker still. Ayres and Gail, after lying mingling their toes in the sand for half an hour or so, got up and said something about taking a stroll along the beach for a breath of fresh air, then disappeared. Olga went very quiet and had to be taken home, which left Campbell and Emmy lying on the sand, listening to the surf and looking up at the tropical extravaganza of stars. They talked drowsily, happy to be left together, and reluctant to move for fear of breaking a fragile, recent understanding. Then she started to talk about her boyfriend again. Campbell listened to her doubts, and felt he was doing her some good. Emmy explained that Tom was reliable, succeeding thus, perhaps inadvertently, in making him sound boring. Then she explained that her friends found him boring, and that some of the things he thought were a bit funny. She told Campbell again that Tom was a clinical psychologist, as though that explained his sundry disagreeable traits, then she explained about his unfortunate background, which included bereavement and boarding school, then she got very close to stating he wasn't much good in bed. 'But he's reliable,' she concluded, snuggling against Campbell as a land breeze rustled in the palm trees.

Eventually they left the beach restaurant, woke a taxi-driver who was fast asleep in the back seat of his crumbling Peugeot, and were driven back to the place Emmy called Little England. They drank Mrs Parsons' cocoa quite quickly, then, with a minimum of romantic preliminaries, got down to serious business on the sofa. Campbell was surprised by her enthusiasm and expertise, and even more surprised when, at a stage in the evening when it is not customary in polite society to be seen to change one's mind, she informed him that she wished to remain faithful to Tom, but would do her best for someone who had done so much for her. Rather than face the prospect of limping back to the ship suffering from an affliction that had not troubled him since his pre-permissive undergraduate days, Campbell agreed, and the ultimate surprise of the evening came in the manner of her carrying out this favour. He lay watching the top of her head, reflecting that he had never really wanted to visit St Helena.

PART THREE

It was too early to go for breakfast. Campbell stood on the quarterdeck wondering if he ought not to take another turn round the upper deck. This was not the easy stroll that a cruise liner or an aircraft carrier would have afforded, but a complex obstacle course of ladders and companionways up and down, the fo'c'sle, the oerlikon deck and the quarterdeck being on different levels. Eventually he decided to stay where he was and wait, possibly even until colours, then go down and eat. Not that staying on the quarterdeck was unpleasant, simply that, after a long time at sea, it was getting a little tedious. It was twenty-one days (or thereabouts, such details rapidly diminishing in importance as the weeks went by) since Simonstown in South Africa, their last port of call, and there was no certainty about the time or location of their next landfall. Ayres, normally agreeably indiscreet on such matters, was not now giving anything away, and rumours multiplied.

HMS *Winchester* lay in still grey water. The sun had presumably come up, since it was light, but was nowhere to be seen. The sky, grey and hazy, merged imperceptibly into the sea. Visibility was difficult to judge. There was no horizon, and nothing on the water to which one could guess a distance. The air was warm and humid, but not yet oppressively so. Campbell leaned on a guard-rail and imagined various possibilities in the mist: *Winchester* might still be just off Banjul, or anchored at Spithead, or even moored in the Thames, with the Houses of Parliament only a few hundred yards off in a warm London pea-souper. At her masthead a radar aerial swept round, picking bleak empty reality from the surrounding greyness.

They had been on the patrol line for almost a fortnight, and nothing had happened. Nothing had happened on the patrol line for rather more than five years, and Campbell had reason to believe, from reading the *Observer* and *Guardian* and a number of naval files marked 'Top Secret: UK Eyes Only', that not much was likely to happen in the next five years either. Nonetheless, a certain warlike spirit was being maintained. Gun drills were practised, and a boarding party consisting of a junior officer with a pistol and half a dozen sailors with rifles was turned out from time to time. No one really believed that it would ever deploy in earnest to take over, in the name of Her Britannic Majesty's Navy and in fine Victorian style, some rusty blockade-running tanker stopped by a warning shot across the bows from *Winchester*'s 4.5 inch guns, but there was an undemanding duty to continue to pretend that it might.

Sometimes, in the last fortnight, it had occurred to Campbell that warships might be forgotten about, and continue to function independently of command and half the world away, until someone in an office in London said, 'Gosh, it's a while since we've thought about HMS *Whatever*,' and then signals would fly, and normality be restored and everyone would pretend that nothing had gone amiss. The only suggestion that HMS *Winchester* had not simply been overlooked came from the continuing and eloquent silence of the navigator.

The larger question, the future of this remote and tedious patrol, with its diligent maintenence of a presence where nothing was likely to happen, also exercised Campbell's mind. There were alarming precedents, principally that of a detachment of guardsmen under a subaltern which still camped nightly in the basement of the Bank of England, some 200 years after the cessation of the civil disturbances which had led to their help being requested in the first place.

When and how did temporary necessity become unbreakable tradition? Would a British warship, mindlessly patrolling an obscure corner of the Indian Ocean, become one of the world's more exotic tourist attractions in the 1990s?

Already there were touches of tradition breaking into the arrangement. When *Winchester* had relieved HMS *Blundestone*, their captains had met for dinner in the latter, and Commander Huxley had brought back with him in the seaboat the Beira bucket, a galvanized pail with a hole in the bottom, which was inscribed with the names of all the ships that had served there since the inception of the patrol some seven years previously. It was now installed with the mess silver in a glass-fronted cabinet in the passageway by the captain's cabin, and would be handed on, with HMS *Winchester*'s name added to the roll, when they were relieved. Meantime, they took their turn.

The water under the guard-rail was still and clear. A small shoal of garfish, lean powerful creatures with narrow beaks that gave them the unreal appearance of science-fiction pike, emerged from under the stern and swam along the ship's side. They had been circling HMS *Winchester* for several days, disdaining the various baits of the ship's company, and causing much frustration among the organizers of and participants in HMS *Winchester*'s Grand Beira Angling Competition. They swam clockwise round the ship, sometimes disappearing for short periods, and always resuming their circling clockwise when they came back.

'Five minutes to colours,' said the tannoy. 'Ratings detailed close up.' A sailor in whites appeared from the mortar well with a folded and roped white ensign, and clipped it to the halyard of the flagstaff at *Winchester*'s stern, then disappeared again, probably for a quick smoke before the little ceremony popularly known as 'saying good morning to the Queen'. Campbell decided to wait. The sky was brighter, with a suggestion of blue overhead as the mist thinned in the sun.

A disturbance in the water astern caught his eye. The stillness was broken first by a noiseless swirling, created perhaps by a large fish near but not breaking the surface, then by a sudden rush of flying fish, splashing starwise from the centre of the disturbance. Some came towards the stern of the ship, skimming like strange organic missiles, and one, higher than the rest, cleared the counter and flopped into the mortar well aft of the quarterdeck. It lay there on the plating, momentarily still, then thrashed about glinting wetly, until one of the two Chinese laundrymen darted out from his place of work right next to the mortar well, stood on one of its fins to immobilize it, bent down, picked it up, knocked its head smartly against one of the three barrels of the ship's main anti-submarine armament, and disappeared with it into the laundry.

Campbell watched with interest, wondering what would have happened if the arrival of the flying fish had coincided with the ceremony of colours, which was due any minute. No doubt the British serviceman's respect for ritual and the Chinese civilian's opportunism in the matter of food would have permitted the two to proceed simultaneously and independently, though it would have been interesting to see that theory put to the test.

At 7.58 Bob, the gunnery officer, as officer of the day, accompanied by one of the midshipmen and a leading seaman, emerged from a screen door and took up position on the Bofors deck, aft of the gun, looking out over the stern. Below, an ordinary seaman fingered the halyard connected to the folded flag nervously, as though injudicious handling might cause it to give him a mild electric shock. Bob looked at his watch. The leading seaman raised a bosun's call to his lips. Over its high thin note the tannoy said, 'Colours. Hands on the upper deck face aft and salute.' Bob, the midshipman and Campbell did so, Campbell feeling guilty, because he was hatless and should therefore not have been about on the upper deck for that solemn moment which begins the naval day.

The ensign was broken, and lay against its staff, lank and lifeless in the tropical calm. A few seconds passed and the leading hand piped the two falling notes of the 'carry on', then the tannoy, to make the thing absolutely clear, said, 'Carry on.' Feeling vaguely uplifted by this formality, Campbell went down to breakfast with the others, remembering for some reason that it was Saturday.

'What's the matter, doc? Slept in?'

Lieutenant Muir, beside whom Campbell had thoughtlessly sat down, not only talked at breakfast but did horrifying things to his fried eggs. Campbell watched, fascinated and revolted, while he waited for his own. Lieutenant Muir usually had two fried eggs for breakfast, usually on fried bread. It was his custom to anoint the yolks with sauce, a large central daub being applied to each, prior to a singularly repulsive manoeuvre with a fork, which resulted in a loathsome whorl of yellow and red (or yellow and brown or, rarely, yellow and red and brown), which he then proceeded to spread over the whites and the fried bread.

No one in the wardroom particularly approved, and occasionally the practice elicited some gentle ribbing. The first lieutenant, Campbell suspected, did not like it, but could invoke no rule or custom to stamp it out, there being nothing to stop a naval officer doing more or less what he wished with his morning eggs, and the matter being insufficiently serious to justify an absolute veto on the appearance of the relevant condiments at the breakfast table. So nothing was done but, even after two-and-a-half months, Lieutenant Muir's breakfast ritual retained a capacity to shock.

'Got your name down for the sports then, doc?'

'Hm?'

'Can I put you down for the wardroom B team? Volleyball.'

'Sorry, Ken . . .'

'Sports Day, isn't it? Doctor hasn't been reading daily orders, has doctor? Grand Beira Sports Day, including Donkey Derby with sundowners.'

'Oh yes. And a funny hat competition?'

'That's it. Got your funny hat all ready?'

'Thinking about it,' said Campbell.

Lieutenant Muir licked a polychromatic mess from his fork, leaving a few blobs of deep Rembrandtesque orange on his beard. 'Wardroom's got to be seen to be involved,' he added, rather menacingly.

'Hang on. I'm judging. So I can't.' Campbell remembered that not only was it Saturday, but it was Sports Day and Donkey Derby Day and Funny Hats Competition Day as well. Smith, an active member of the entertainments committee, which organized such events, had mentioned it and told him about the various arrangements and asked him if he minded helping by judging the funny hats. He had said he did not, and had subsequently forgotten all about it.

Campbell ate his bacon and eggs quickly and retired to the lounge section with his coffee, hoping that Lieutenant Muir would not follow. He sat looking at a copy of the *Daily Telegraph* that was more than three weeks old, and took refuge in its oddities: the 'In Memoriam' notices; the advertisements for personalized number plates; the strange cryptic little items in the personal column, presumably the upper classes' equivalent of the scrawls that tramps were said to leave for each other on gateposts. He was interrupted by a knock at the door, and had to glare at one of the midshipmen in order to get him to answer it. The middie did so, rather grudgingly, and immediately referred the resulting query back to Campbell.

'It's someone wanting a rifle.'

Campbell did not know under what circumstances rifles were issued, or to whom, or even for that matter by whom, and was pleased to see Ayres taking an interest from the other side of the wardroom. The navigator got up and went over to the door.

'What is it, Williams?'

'They want a rifle, sir. On the Bofors deck.'

'What for?'

'For the angling competition, sir. They think they've won. PO Deuchars and PO Thow. But they want a rifle to kill it.'

'Kill what, Williams?'

'This shark on the Bofors deck, sir. Say they want a rifle.'

'A rifle?' The first lieutenant erupted from behind the curtain, napkin in hand. 'What the bloody hell do they want a rifle for?' The wardroom door was open. Williams was standing in the passageway outside, as he should have been, with the navigator and the midshipman, now joined by the first lieutenant, standing in a little semi-circle within. The first lieutenant was bristling with curiosity and official indignation, mainly the latter. 'Rifles? I'll give 'em bloody rifles. What's the problem?'

'It's this shark, sir. On the Bofors deck,' said Williams, who was obviously not very bright, but bright enough to know that this was getting complicated. 'They want to kill it. The POs, sir. They thought blowin' its brains out would be best . . . It's quite big, sir,' he added.

'Rifle my arse,' said the first lieutenant, throwing his napkin on to a chair. 'Let's have a look. You don't need bloody rifles to sort out sharks.' He bustled out of the wardroom and off down the passageway aft, followed by a rather sheepish-looking AB Williams. For a stout middle-aged man, the first lieutenant could move quickly when he had to.

'Probably worried about his paintwork,' said the navigator. 'Bullets might ruin it. He's really got terribly fussy since that Iceland business. Shall we stroll up and see the show?'

By the time Ayres and Campbell had made their way up to the Bofors deck, about fifty or sixty people, perhaps a quarter of the ship's company, had done so, too. It was half past eight. Most of them should have been elsewhere, at their places of work, with only a handful of off-duty watchkeepers free to spectate at the capture of what was likely to be the prizewinning catch of HMS *Winchester*'s Grand Beira Angling Competition. The audience was ranged in a wide arc, for'ard on the deck. Aft, directly behind the gun, lay a shark possibly ten feet long from the tip of its snout to the end of its tail fin. It was dull brown in colour, with white undersides and looked, so far as Campbell could judge, unwell but not dead. There was a steel hook embedded in its lower jaw, to which no line was now attached. Its eyes were small and dull. The skin around its gills rippled emptily and its fins flicked against the green-painted deck. Although it was quite a long shark, it was not very heavily built, being at its widest extent no larger in girth than a moderately well-fed man.

'I thought I'd best be here, sir. In case of accidents.' Campbell turned round. It was Smith. 'Close thing earlier on. PO Deuchars thought it was dead and tried to take the hook out of its mouth. Got quite fresh with him.' Campbell realized that the LMA was explaining why he was absent from his usual place of duty at this time in the morning.

'How did they get it out of the water?'

'Gemini hoist, sir.' Smith indicated the davit from which the ship's rubber dinghy was launched. 'They got it inboard, then took the line off and started treating it as if it was a nice little trout or something.'

'Someone came asking for a rifle.'

'That was PO Deuchars' idea, sir.'

'First lieutenant wasn't awfully keen.'

'Didn't think he would be, sir. He's not keen on the angling competition as a whole. Thinks it's an excuse for not working.'

If indeed the first lieutenant held such suspicions, they seemed to be perfectly justified. Sailors were supposed to work normally on Saturday mornings at sea, not stand around waiting ghoulishly for petty officers to be maimed by sharks, but after two weeks on Beira patrol any diversion, however trivial, was welcome. The two captors of the beast stood with the first lieutenant. It was not clear from their demeanour how the officer responsible for the day-to-day running of the ship was taking this novel threat to good order and naval discipline: whether as a problem to be solved, a nuisance to be got rid of as quickly as possible, or an unusual challenge to his organizational skills. Of the people on the deck, the trio with most responsibility stood nearest the point of maximum danger, but discreetly so, in the relatively safe zone directly behind the shark and out of reach of its tail.

PO Deuchars, a feckless man from the less technical lower reaches of the electrical world, known to Campbell only because he had been out of date for his cholera immunization, had begun to gesticulate in a fashion that suggested he was trying to show the first lieutenant how close he had been to losing an arm, and therefore how necessary it now was for drastic measures to be taken. The first lieutenant glowered and listened, the short gingery hairs on his lower lip bristling forward independently of the rest of his beard, as they did when he was concentrating.

The shark, perhaps having forgotten it had been caught, flicked its tail lazily from side to side, a manoeuvre that, in happier circumstances, would have resulted in its sliding rapidly away from the trio now discussing its further discomfiture. Nothing happened, so it waved its tail more vigorously, then thrashed wildly about on the deck, arching up and beating down again, its movements taking it several feet nearer the port guard-rail. Then it vomited up a smaller shark and lay still again. The spectators cheered and someone, probably not an officer, said in an officer-like voice, 'First prize and runner up, PO Deuchars.'

It was now more apparent to Campbell why the shark was being treated with such respect. It still had quite a lot of life left in it, and its mouth was very big, perhaps fifteen inches across, and lined with rows of triangular, backward-pointing teeth. The coarser solutions, such as rifle fire, though messy, had at least the merit of being thorough. How long could the shark lie there and still be dangerous? Unfortunately, that sort of knowledge seemed to be expected of doctors in the Navy. Campbell hoped that no one would ask him.

After further deliberations the first lieutenant turned round and summoned to his council of war one of the seamen POs, who listened and then in turn summoned one of his leading hands, who looked suddenly alert and then strode off with purpose in his very tread. A ripple of awed speculation, *corrida*-style, swept round the crowd. The first lieutenant walked towards the shark and, remaining still behind it and outside the arc of its previous tail-thrashing display, inspected it more closely.

'Top 'amper,' said the crowd's wit, to the delight of his audience. The first lieutenant looked round and bristled his beard in the general direction of the remark. A few minutes later the leading hand came back with nothing more dramatic than a coil of throwing line, the light rope used to lead mooring hawsers ashore or transfer small items between ships at sea. The first lieutenant and the petty officers went into session once more, with much gesturing and glancing round to the shark, which lay mainly still now, munching glumly at the lineless hook.

From the trend of events it was clear that the artillery faction had not prevailed in the discussion. The two POs who had caught the shark looked on while the other two sorted out the details, then everyone watched while the first lieutenant had ideas and the seaman PO put them into effect, which, the crowd seemed to agree, was more or less what first lieutenants and seamen POs, respectively, were for.

The tail of the shark, still waving sometimes from side to side, but less hopefully than before, was the first object of their attentions. The PO made a generous running noose from his line, and tossed it over the long uppermost part of the shark's tail. The lower part, still firm against the deck, if scraping sometimes from side to side, prevented the noose from passing completely over the tail to be tightened at its root, the presumed objective of the manoeuvre. At this point the shark showed no signs of lifting its tail clear of the deck to expedite its immobilization, but lay flicking its fins a little, and moving its tail slightly but not enough. The crowd watched.

The first lieutenant, who had been standing back as the PO worked, suddenly intervened personally. 'Right, PO!' he said, darting forward and grasping the shark's tail and lifting it clear of the deck. The PO, if not actually anticipating the move, followed it up smartly, flicking his noose forward, completely over the shark's tail, and pulling it tight, an action which goaded the shark to new paroxysms of fury. With tail and fins it lashed the air and the green-painted metal deck. It arched and convulsed and snapped lethally at nothing, heaving itself up, sometimes almost pirouetting on tail or fin, and flopping back heavily on to the drumming plates of the Bofors deck.

The crowd, briefly awed by the first lieutenant's intervention, soon returned to its previous view of the occasion as a sporting contest, and cheered each new effort from the shark rather as though they had come a long way and paid money to follow its fortunes. And in a way, they had a point. Campbell, having read a book or two, suddenly saw it as pastiche Hemingway: the Middle-Aged Man and the Sea. Whether as top hamper, or as a threat to the paintwork, or as a potentially powerful waste of sailors' time, the first lieutenant was clearly against sharks. And the shark, to judge from the way it had behaved since the arrival of an example of the breed, didn't like first lieutenants. Hence, of course, the vociferous sympathy of the crowd.

Amid all this, the seaman PO was hanging grimly on to his

end of the throwing line, as though participating in some sort of marine rodeo, while, under the supervision of the first lieutenant, the leading seaman was fashioning, from the rest of the rope he had brought, an even bigger running noose. Gradually, the shark's efforts subsided, and while brute force spent itself intelligence was at work.

The next move began with a completely unexpected initiative. To the surprise and delight of the crowd, they lassoed the PO, passing a noose right over his head. The PO, who had had things briefly explained to him, was not in the least alarmed, but stepped, as daintily as is possible when one is holding on to a ten-foot shark, through the noose, so that it travelled, still large and slack, over his arms, down his line, then, with a well-timed flick, over the shark's tail and forward, still loose, on to the widest extent of its body, just behind the fins.

The crowd hated it. Like fans whose champion has taken a count of eight and may not rise, they switched from noisy loyalty to silence and doubt. It was now obvious that good order and naval discipline in HMS *Winchester* was exacted even from sharks, and that ultimate sanctions lay with the first lieutenant. Not that it hadn't been an interesting contest, and one that any sailor who had ever been subject to censure from that officer might have watched with particular fascination, but now that the outcome was no longer in doubt, the peak of its crowd-appeal was past.

The final reckoning was terrible to behold. Shark fans watched silently as the second noose tightened, and the line from the first was made fast to a guard-rail stanchion. Like some awful gallows, the gemini hoist was swung round and the noose, now biting into the shark's body just behind its fins, was attached to it. At the command of the first lieutenant the leading seaman took the controls of the electric winch and the shark was lifted from the deck twitching feebling against its fate, to hang twisting slowly in the sun.

'Right then,' said the first lieutenant, moving round the line of watching sailors, 'Show's over. Got no work to do? PO Fowler? Get your lads sorted out and down on the fo'c'sle. Like I said, starboard fall wants seein' to . . . I'll be down shortly to have a look . . . Good lad, Milton-Thomson. Had your fun. Now work, like the Queen pays you for . . . Well, doc. Got no invalids today? What'd you think of that then? Like I said, no need for rifles. You just hang the buggers up to dry, eh?' He bustled off, perhaps to finish his breakfast.

'. . . is requested to report to the first lieutenant's cabin,' said the tannoy.

'Didn't catch that.'

'I'll turn it up, sir. They'll say it again if it's important.'

'The medical officer is requested to report to the first lieutenant's cabin,' said the tannoy, obligingly, but more loudly and perhaps a little testily.

'That's what it sounded like . . . Will you carry on here, please, LMA?'

'Certainly, sir. There's just him and the sprained ankle for review.'

'Him' was the naked sailor lying curled up on his side on the operating table, having a Eusol wick replaced in the crater of a now extinct abscess on his buttock. 'Not to worry, Podge,' said the LMA, by way of reassurance, patting the sailor's haunch. 'It's comin' on lovely. In fact we're very happy with it . . . Yessir. I'll finish with him and see the ankle and let you get up there. Probably something to do with our little festivities. You're remembering about the funny hats, sir?'

'Yes, thanks, Smith . . . Six o'clock.'

'Or thereabouts, sir. Depends on how the Donkey Derby's going.'

'Fine . . . Excuse me.'

Mysterious summonses were part of the ship's routine. Quite early on, Campbell had got used to them, and had learned that only rarely were they a prelude to anything serious. Excited calls on the tannoy, 'MO to the bridge at the rush,' of which there had been quite a few in recent weeks, usually meant not that the officer of the watch had just perforated his hitherto unsuspected peptic ulcer, but that the port lookout had just caught a glimpse of something (rarely still in evidence by the time Campbell got there) that might have been a whale spouting. To drop everything and turn up fairly quickly wherever requested was a point of honour as well as discipline among officers and men alike, although to an outside observer the ability to do so might have been regarded as evidence of what J. K. Galbraith would have termed 'hidden unemployment' and what lesser men might have thought of as having nothing to do. Campbell went up to the first lieutenant's cabin prepared to be interested rather than surprised by whatever it was, another attack of that officer's old trouble being a strong possibility, if grappling with sharks was one of the things that brought it on.

He was quite unprepared for the group that was sitting waiting in the first lieutenant's day cabin. It consisted of the captain, the navigator, the gunnery officer and the first lieutenant himself, all looking very serious.

'Ah, doctor,' said the captain, reproachfully.

'Sorry to keep you waiting, sir. Had a case on the table.'

'Oh. Will he be all right?'

'Yessir.'

'Good. Sit down, doctor.'

'Read that, please.'

Commander Huxley handed him a sheet of paper bearing a printed heading with the ship's crest and 'HMS *Winchester*', under which was typed 'At Sea', with the day's date, and, in a neat paragraph near the middle of an otherwise empty page, an instruction headed 'Conduct of the Security Organization'. It went on: 'The undernoted officers will make an enquiry into the manner of discharge of his duties by the Security Officer; and make a report to me; and make recommendations.' Underneath was a brief list of names: Lt R. A. K. Ayres, RN (Chairman), Lt R. Gault, RN, Surgeon Lt D. G. Campbell, RNR. The document was signed 'Nigel Huxley, Commander, RN, Commanding Officer.'

Campbell read it twice, because of the ungainly clutter of prepositions in the middle, though it was perfectly clear what was meant, then looked with curiosity at the captain's signature, round and innocent, perhaps unchanged from his days at prep school or his first savings account.

'Understand, doctor?'

'Yessir,' said Campbell.

'Today. And with the utmost discretion.' Commander

Huxley got up, his officers standing with him as he did so. He nodded to the first lieutenant, then addressed the navigator. 'Look forward to reading your report. This evening. Thank you, gentlemen.' He went out.

'There's a can of worms we could have done without,' said the first lieutenant gloomily as soon as the door had closed behind the captain. 'Ever been on a board of enquiry before, doc?'

'No, sir.'

'Not much call for that sort of thing in the RNR, I suppose. Anyway, like I was telling them while we were waiting for you, use this place like it was your own. Helps keep the thing quiet. And there's a typewriter in the bureau. You can use a typewriter, can't you, doc?'

For some reason Campbell found himself thinking about previous inquisitions on the subject of 'organs, portable, small'. 'A bit, sir. Two fingers and a bit rusty.'

'That's one more than either of those two,' said the first lieutenant. 'So you've got yourself a job as secretary. Right, Vasco?' The navigator nodded. 'Play it however you like, within the rules. Keep it quiet and make it quick. Very jumpy about security, is father. Must have had a near miss with something in that line before . . . Any questions?'

The last query was more in the nature of a valediction than anything else. The first lieutenant looked very much as if he'd rather be down on the fo'c'sle, chivvying people about minor details of paintwork. He too left, leaving the three members of the board of enquiry to begin their work.

'How about starting with some coffee,' said the gunnery officer. Neither of the others said anything, so he got up and went over to the telephone and rang the wardroom. 'Tak? There's a good lad. Three nice cups of coffee and some spare in a pot. And maybe some biscuits. First lieutenant's cabin . . . OK?' Tak's voice, squeakier over the ship's telephone system, said 'Sah,' and the gunnery officer returned to his seat.

The navigator turned to Campbell. 'Well, doctor, I suppose you're wondering why you're here.' Campbell agreed that he was. 'It's because, in the absence of any evidence to the contrary, we think you're honest. Which is a good thing.

And because you know nothing at all about the security business. Which is even better. You've never been on a board before.' Campbell agreed again. 'Don't know what the civilian equivalent would be. And it'd be different in Jockland anyway. Probably purely a service thing. Fuck-up control. Three wise men. That sort of thing. A balls-up is suspected, a board is convened. Nothing heavy. A ship matter. No one from outside.'

The practical problems of running the thing as anything other than a purely ship matter did not appear to have occurred to the navigator. 'The idea is that the three of us have a quick saunter through Ken's patch, particularly the books side, and hand something up to father between tea-time and the Donkey Derby. Then it's up to him.'

'I see. But just us meantime.'

'That's it. And like he said. Discreetly. We don't want every little LRO running round saying "ho ho, sir's in the rattle". Time enough for all that when he is. If he is. And we've got to be quick. Command,' he pointed through towards the CO's accommodation, 'can't bear hanging about in any form. If we aim for tea-time we'll probably be all right for dinner.'

'On a Saturday, of course,' said the gunnery officer. 'Gault's Law of Maximum Imbuggerance. I hate these bloody things. I've sat on two . . . and two have sat on me, so to speak. This one makes it three–two, if you see what I mean. Gives me a nasty feeling . . . Still and all, we might as well get on with it. After coffee . . . Could be worse, I suppose. Did a terrible one in *Sycorax* about six years ago. We all had hangovers. Silly bloody HCO lost the helo. Lost in the soup for twenty minutes. Dead Ants Davies was driving it up the wrong side of Arran, looking for Prestwick. They both got logged in the end.'

The chairman of the board of enquiry, who had not spoken for some time, showed sudden interest. 'Was Dead Ants in *Sycorax*?'

'He was, the mad bugger,' said Bob.

The navigator brightened up. 'I was in DTS with him . . . I was actually on the famous original Dead Ants run. At Wilhelmshaven in third year. Typical DTS show. Best-bib-

and-tucker sort of place. Fortunately it didn't go far. You should have seen us, doc. A disgrace to the nation . . . We had this silly game where, when someone shouted "Dead Ants!" in the bar, the last chap to get down on his back on the deck with his legs in the air had to buy the next round. Anyway, we were ashore, on the beer, in the best part of town with little ornamental gardens but not a pissoir in sight for love or money, and old Davies felt the need, so we all stood round in a circle, nonchalantly, and he was in the middle getting on with it when somebody yelled "Dead Ants!" '

Bob, who had no doubt heard the story several times before, was shaking with amusement anyway. Campbell, who hadn't, was glad to be diverted from the grim and puzzling business of the board. 'And just left him standing there?' he asked.

'Well,' said Ayres, 'that's probably what the chap who yelled "Dead Ants!" thought would happen. But old Ants was so well trained, or drunk or something, that he was on his back with the rest of them, kicking his legs in the air in the middle of this ornamental garden in the south part of Wilhelmshaven, and . . . not exactly covering himself with glory. Still, Nato survived.'

There was a knock on the door. 'Sah.'

'Good lad, Tak. Just bring it in . . . Oh, Roddy. What about lunch? Have it here and work straight through?'

'Might as well,' said the navigator. 'Might spare us a few problems . . . Tak.'

'Sah.'

'We'll have lunch up here. Will you ask the PO Steward?'

'Sah.'

Tak left. There was now no excuse for not beginning. A silence fell. Bob stirred his coffee. Campbell turned over in his mind numerous vague questions, but felt that they could probably wait. Ayres put his clipboard on his knee and wrote '(1)' at the top left-hand corner of his notepad. The sun, shining obliquely through a porthole behind Campbell, picked out a brilliant ellipse on the fabric covering of the navigator's armchair.

'It's a total fuck-up, isn't it,' said Bob after a long pause.

'Probably,' said Ayres. 'But we need details.'

'Like . . . how long it's been a total fuck-up,' said Bob.

'That sort of thing. How long. How bad. How much. No. How widespread. Father's a details man.' The navigator added a '(2)' and a '(3)' at points one-third and two-thirds down the margin of his notepaper, and wrote in his stylish, chartwork hand, 'How long?' 'How bad?' 'How widespread?'

'That's a good start,' said Bob, taking out a packet of cigarettes. 'Got a match?'

'Sorry, Bob.'

'I'll have some of number one's.' He got up and looked round the cabin. 'He said to make ourselves at home . . . Let's see . . .' He found a box of matches on the first lieutenant's bureau. 'There's other things you have to sort out. Oh, yes . . . Who else . . . And who should have spotted it. That should be enough to be going on with. That's what we did in the first of these things I was on. Wardroom mess account in *Leviathan*. First commission. Busted the doc, poor old drunk bugger. Five questions. How long? How bad? How much? Who else? And what went wrong that it wasn't spotted earlier?'

'Risk,' said Ayres.

'Christ yes,' said the gunnery officer. 'It's not just the wardroom crisps and nutty fund.'

'That should come first,' said Ayres. 'Looks good. "In our opinion the risk of compromise of classified material of possible value to a hostile power" and all that. Then the rest. Like we said. And recommendations.'

'Court-martial the bugger.'

'That's up to father. I think he wants views from us on necessary action about compromised material, if any. Changes in routine. Accelerated destructs. Maybe a fleet warning or cancellation. That sort of stuff. Technical side. Then he'll wield the boot. How and where is up to him.'

'What d'you think he'll get, Roddy?'

'Minimum a logging. Maximum an admiral's displeasure. If it's what I think it is. But we'll have to do the digging . . . You lost, doctor?'

'Pretty thoroughly.'

'Ideal. Like a jury. But you'll get the hang of it . . .'

There was another pause, in which Campbell felt himself

expected to say something. 'How did it surface?'

'What d'you mean, doc?'

'What made people . . . think things? You know. How did father . . .'

'Oh. You mean why are we here?'

'Roughly. Yes.'

'Good question. Quite a small thing, actually. In an SB. A tactical signals book, known to its friends as ta-fuck.'

'What?'

'Big T big A big F brackets UK. Tactical and administrative frequencies, United Kingdom. Codes, roughly speaking, though it's not called that. It's actually a series. The problem cropped up in TAF(UK) Seven Alpha. One of the LROs drew it for a routine signal, and wasn't getting it right, and took it to Jim. Found a paging error . . . It's here somewhere.' Ayres reached behind him and took from the first lieutenant's bureau a pale blue book, and handed it to Campbell. On the front was a fierce black block-capital SECRET.

'Can I look?'

'Well, we wondered about blindfolding you for the duration of the enquiry, doctor, but decided against it . . . You're cleared for this sort of thing. Page seven alpha one dash one four.'

The pages of the book, which were actually looseleaf, and held in the pale blue card cover by two brass screws, were not conventionally numbered, but grouped in sections and numbered again within the sections. Page 1 – 14 (of volume 7A) was an orderly mass of five-digit numbers. Clearly SECRET did not necessarily mean interesting.

'See the top left-hand corner,' said Ayres. 'Small numbers in the margin.'

'1172?'

'Yes.'

'That means November last year. Now turn to page 11 – 4.' Campbell did so. At first glance it appeared that there were two such pages, but a closer look revealed that one was actually another page 1 – 14. Campbell turned back to the first page 1 – 14 to check. The main difference, unless one started to compare the serried masses of five-digit numbers, was in the top left-hand corner, where the second page 1 – 14 was marked '0573'. Campbell checked the two pages against each other and asked, 'Is that what we're investigating? A filing error?'

'Exactly, doctor,' said the navigator. 'It's only a filing error. Take two aspirins and it should go away.' He sounded a little scornful.

'Steady on, Roddy,' said the gunnery officer. 'Some of us are just beginning.'

'Sorry, doctor. It's not . . . only a filing error. But also what my old mate and colleague from the straightforward world of gunnery would call a total fuck-up. The number in the margin, a date really, shows when the page was superseded and should have been replaced. About four months ago. And instead of that, the page is still there, when it should have been removed, ceremonially shredded in the official mincer and then tastefully commemorated with a destruct certificate signed by two officers holding at least the ranks of sub-lieutenant and lieutenant in the Queen's Royal Navy. So it's a filing error plus.'

'And father thinks there might be more of those?'

'That's what we're going to spend our Saturday finding out. The LRO took the book to Jim, who noticed that the page should have been superseded, and told number one. He looked for the obvious misfile, and found the page that should have been there, in with page 11 – 4. Then he had what he calls a feeling in his water, and took a quick look in some of the SB safes. He and Jim together, which they're entitled to do, as first lieutenant and communicator.'

'And?'

'The feeling in his water was right. All a bit suspicious of a total fuck-up. They didn't even go through all the safes. The first two were bad enough.'

The phone rang and Bob got up to answer it. 'First lieutenant's cabin. GO speaking. Sir . . . Sir . . . Right, sir.' He came back to his chair. 'Lunch is off. At least not up here. He wants us all in the wardroom, acting normal.'

'Who does?' said Ayres.

'That wasn't the PO steward on the blower,' said Bob. He sat down again. 'Number one. Says father wants a *very* discreet enquiry. So no private lunch parties. Just act normal. No point in arousing unnecessary jitters . . . On the off-chance it all blows over.'

'Might be difficult,' said Ayres.

'Acting normal?'

'No. Being *very* discreet. Best we could do is make it look like a routine check, I suppose, with no more than two of us at a safe at any one time. And just get round all the safes in turn, empty them, bring the stuff up here, and page by page it.'

'Bloody hell,' said the gunnery officer. 'It was all page by paged about a fortnight ago . . . Still . . .'

'If ta-fuck seven alpha slipped through like that . . .'

'. . . anything might have.'

'Who page by paged it last?' said Campbell.

'That's one of the embarrassing things. And why Jim's not on the board, even though as comms officer he'd be a natural.'

'Oh. I see.'

'Look.' Ayres turned to the back of the book. In a well-thumbed last page, TAF(UK)7A, a secret code book, bore the initials of the various officers who had checked its contents down the months of its much-amended existence. The most recent were Jim's. 'I can imagine number one having a bit of a sense of humour failure about that.'

'At least that gives you something to put into that last bit,' said the gunnery officer. 'The bit about what slipped up to let it happen.'

'Right,' said the navigator, starting a new sheet of notepaper. 'That's the trouble with small ships. Every time you have one of these, you end up with everybody in the rattle. Probably signed up some duff ones myself. I was on the last SB muster but one. It was in Falmouth. I think I had a hangover.'

Campbell felt he had not contributed much, and that the board of enquiry could probably have done very well without him. The world of the security books, the SBs round which their activities revolved, was one which had concerned him very little. He had heard people moaning in the wardroom about the tedium of SB musters, when disinterested officers made detailed checks, perhaps in the manner of accountants doing an audit, balancing accessions against destruct certificates, and checking what was there against what should have been there. It sounded tedious and exacting work, which he considered himself fortunate to have avoided so far. A sudden thought occurred. Where was Lieutenant Muir, the officer now under suspicion, who had been about to have a serious conversation with him since their first meeting?

Ayres stood up. 'Well . . . I suppose we'd better get on with it. Bob, if you stay here and do a systematic check through ta-fuck seven alpha doctor and I can fetch up the rest of the stuff from the safe in the RDR and whizz through it . . . It's easily the biggest chunk, and I'd feel better if we get it out of the way first.'

The RDR, the radar direction room, was a relic of *Winchester*'s original function as part of a carrier escort group. It was a space rather like the ops room, if a little less impressive, filled with equipment concerned with the detection and tracking of friendly and hostile aircraft. Now that the days of carriers were numbered, and naval aviation shrinking to a covey of helicopters, the RDR was an anachronism, persisting without a role, except for the duration of fanciful exercises with the RAF. On the Beira patrol it was supremely useless, a dark irregular room half filled with silent obsolete-looking grey machinery and blank lifeless display screens.

Campbell and Ayres stood in front of its SB safe.

'Sing 'em out, doctor.'

'Twenty-seven. Four turns left.'

'Roger. Two seven. Left two three four.'

'Sixty-one. Seven turns right.'

'Roger. Six one. Right two three four . . .'

The slip of paper from which Campbell was reading the combination to the radar direction room SB safe had been obtained from an envelope, sealed and signed along the join of the flap by no less a person than the first lieutenant, which they had obtained in turn from the communications office safe, after due consultation with Jim, who knew its combination off by heart.

'That's it. A last sweet click and open sesame . . . God, it even *looks* untidy.'

To the non-expert eye it did not. The safe, little more than a heavy steel cupboard welded to the after bulkhead of the RDR, opened to reveal two shelves of books and folders of various sizes, numbering perhaps twenty-five in all, with unassuming covers and titles like JSB 1895 NATO Supp 2. Only one title made sense to the general reader. It was a book called *Eastern Bloc Ship Identification. Vol. I: Tankers and Bulk Carriers*, and had a picture on the cover. It would not have looked out of place in a Princes Street bookshop. The rest were plain, with their uninformative titles and CONFIDENTIAL or SECRET in bold type above.

Between them, Ayres and Campbell managed to take the entire contents of the safe. With a stack of books steadied under his chin, Ayres reached out and closed the now-empty safe, twirling the combination lock to an unassailably random number. Together they went back up to the first lieutenant's cabin.

'The bugger's really been slacking.' Bob was standing impatiently by a porthole, smoking another cigarette. 'Ta-fuck seven alpha's in shit order. That thing Jim picked up and a couple more pages duplicated. The old ones not taken out. Just left there. You'd think he'd forgotten all about destructs. That's them.' He thrust an opened-out cigarette packet at the navigator. On it were scribbled the page numbers of the lapses hitherto uncovered. Ayres took it and started a new page on his notepad, titling it 'Misfiles and late destructs', and subheading it 'TAF(UK)7A'.

'Thanks, Bob.'

'You know, when I was checking through this stuff while you were away, and finding all these, I could practically hear the bugger sayin' to himself, "At least they're safe in here . . . I'll see 'em off tomorrow . . . Hardly worth starting the destructor and digging out the chit book just for a few little pages . . ." All that sort of crap.'

Campbell was interested. Bob's impatience with the security officer sounded like impatience with himself. 'Have you ever done an SB job, Bob?' he asked.

'Once was enough. Ten months and no disasters, thank God. It's the sort of job where you're either right on top of it or hopelessly behind. I was usually on top of it.' Campbell and Ayres had put down the heaps of books and Ayres was sorting them out, referring sometimes to a list of contents from the RDR safe. 'It was in *Aconite*,' Bob went on. 'Just after I'd been promoted. So I was super-keen and got stuck into the old blue bags as soon as the shore blokes handed them over. My little destructor machine was always chomping away, and the rest of the wardroom used to get really pissed off with me always bein' at them for signatures. But it's the only way. Either you're on top of the SBs or they're on top of you. Hit them every minute you get the chance to. Otherwise you end up with a shithouse like this on your hands.'

'Were there any pages missing?'

'What, Roddy?'

'Anything unaccounted for? He's got double entries, and overdue destructs, and one misfile. Was that all?' Ayres, standing at the other side of the cabin, and still sorting out the books from the RDR safe, sounded very professional.

'Nothing so far,' said Bob. 'There isn't anything in here that doesn't have the superseding page beside it . . . So maybe he's just slack in his destructs.'

'That would keep life fairly simple,' said Ayres, sounding as if it were too much to hope for. 'Doctor. You know roughly what we're looking for. Check page numbers and supersession dates where they appear . . .' The navigator paused and looked thoughtful then said, 'No . . . Sort out that lot. Most of it is straightforward stuff with no changes and no destructs. You don't have to read it or anything. Just check it over to see that all the books and pamphlets are there, and that no obvious chunks are missing. It's all confidential at least, but nothing frightfully James Bond. You don't mind?'

'Not in the least.' Campbell, who had not joined the Navy to dabble in ciphers and intelligence, did not feel slighted. He took his allotted heap and settled down. Most of the items in it were proper books with words and sometimes pictures, rather than the endless pages of figure and letter groups which seemed, to judge from the attention being devoted to them by the other two, to form the most important part of the work. He sat comfortably in an armchair, with a page of the safe's contents list, checking a series of books and pamphlets mainly concerned with the maintenance of the ship's electronic equipment. After them came the book about Eastern Bloc shipping, then there were a few interesting things about the weaponry of the potential enemy, which went beyond the degree of detail usually available to the public in Sunday newspapers. All the books and pamphlets which should have been there were there, so he went on to check that each was intact, learning as he did so some interesting things about missiles called Scud, Skipper, Scullion and the like, all of which sounded as if they would do terrible things to HMS *Winchester*, if ever the potential enemy became an actual one.

Ayres and Bob riffled through the code books, Bob's exasperation becoming a little more obvious each time he discovered some new atrocity and scribbled a note about it. Ayres sat like a schoolmaster correcting a heap of exercise books, going through each with unhurried efficiency, occasionally shaking his head, and writing what were undoubtedly damning comments on his notepad. Watching him, Campbell decided to get himself a clipboard at the next possible opportunity, just for the aura of efficiency and authority the possession of one implied. The three sat working quietly for forty minutes or so.

Eventually Ayres put the last of his blue looseleaf books aside. 'Doctor?'

'I think it's all here.'

'So it should be. If he's made a cock-up of that stuff it could only be by positively trying to. Bob?'

'Another eight. Mainly in the LTPs. All except one like those first three.'

'But one not.'

'In LTP Bravo Zulu Six. A page out of date and nothing new beside it.'

'When? When was the supersession due?'

'Last month.'

'And just one?'

'Definitely.'

'I've found three more in this lot. Three of those. A couple of dozen of the others. All in the last month. Looks nasty.'

Bob lit another cigarette. 'Crypto room safe next?'

'I suppose so,' said Ayres. 'Doctor. How about organizing

some more coffee while Bob and I take a walk?'

The gunnery officer and the navigator gathered up the books from the RDR safe and left. Campbell rang the wardroom for coffee. Tak said, 'Okay sah. I bring. And fresh cups.' Campbell stretched his legs by walking round the first lieutenant's day cabin, which was perhaps three times as big as his own little box downstairs. It was curiously devoid of personal items. Most naval officers had family photographs, or team groups, or pictures of girlfriends, or posters, or even simply beermats from exotic places to soften the rigours of naval interior design. The first lieutenant had his brass telescope, leather-cased and purely a ceremonial instrument, hanging by his bunk, and that was about all. Apart from some cufflinks on the bureau top, everything else in sight seemed to be official and impersonal: bits of uniform, service publications and documents, the standard cup and saucer by the bedside, awaiting the next morning's cup of tea.

From the feel of things, HMS *Winchester* was on the move again. Campbell looked out of a scuttle and saw glassy sea moving past at about five knots. Such was Beira routine: a long do-nothing pause, lying at one end or other of the patrol line, then a few hours steaming, usually along the line, or sometimes off to a rendezvous with a tanker, then back to lying in wait for the blockade runner that would never come. Campbell opened the scuttle. A soft breeze generated by the movement of the ship stirred the stale air in the first lieutenant's cabin. It was warmer now, but not yet really hot. He looked at his watch. It was half past ten.

'Sah.'

'Come in.'

Tak, looking a bit undernourished, as many of the LEPs did in tropical whites, came in with a tray, some more cups and fresh coffee.

'You like limers also sah?'

'Oh. Yes, thanks, Tak.'

'I think gunnery officer will like.'

'Yes . . . Ideal.'

Before the other two came back Tak had returned with a tall iced jug containing the bitter fizzy reconstituted fruit drink which the Navy issued free in tropical latitudes. It was an acquired taste, which Campbell had been working on for some time. He poured three glasses, and started on his own. He still did not quite like it.

'Great stuff, doc. Just what I needed. A big glass of Harry Limers.' Tak had been right. Bob drained a glass and poured himself another. 'The boys in the crypto room must think something's up . . . Looking kind of interested when we wandered in and cleared the safe. You could see them thinking, "Hm. *Might* be a routine check." Mind you, if they don't pick up the odd hiccup in this stuff, who's going to?'

Behind him, Ayres was carrying a dozen or so blue books. 'Right, doctor. No comics among this lot, so you'll be doing your bit along with us . . . Queen pays you plenty,' he added in a perhaps unconscious imitation of the first lieutenant. He divided the books into three, and gave Campbell some notepaper. They sat quietly, drinking coffee or limers, checking the code books page by page. Campbell's four books had typically unforthcoming titles – BRAX18 Bravo, etc. – and took a long time to get through. The expectation of finding errors sustained his attention, but it was easy to imagine how, in a routine check, the assumption that nothing would be amiss could lead to boredom, inattention and the sort of failure demonstrated by Jim in his last check through TAF(UK)7A.

Ayres finished his share first, and took the last book from Campbell's heap. The gunnery officer, writing on a piece of the navigator's notepaper rather than the cigarette packet on which he had begun his investigations, laid down his last book with a sigh. 'Like I said, it's a total fuck-up. Half a dozen more in this lot. You'd wonder how he could come in to breakfast every day and face number one and the rest of us. And he seems to have got worse over the last month.'

'Same here,' said the navigator. 'A bit slack till about four weeks ago. Then bloody idle.'

Two smaller collections of SBs, from the communications office and the ops room, followed quickly. By 11.30 Ayres was working at the first lieutenant's desk collating the errors detected on to one columned sheet of paper. He had none of the haste or excited untidiness of a man who, after hours of tedious investigation, thinks he is on to something, but sat writing neatly in the columns, drawing together the various discrepancies the three had found, under different headings signifying, from left to right, errors of increasing gravity. There was no breakthrough, no leap of intuition. The main finding was as obvious, logical and unexciting as the answer to a primary school arithmetic problem. Twelve pages all due for replacement within the previous month were not where they should have been. Ayres wrote down the date after which errors had become more than mere procrastination, then, in his neat square handwriting, added: 'Banjul'.

'Banjul?'

'Yes. From there on he's let the end go. That's obvious just from the books, and it's about as far as we can go without involving him. We've got to look at his accessions list, and his book of destruct certificates, and we need him, to get into his own cabin safe.'

'What about those twelve pages? D'you think they'll be in there, too?' Campbell asked.

'Shouldn't be, but I hope they are, if you see what I mean.'

'They'll be in there,' said Bob.

'What if they are?'

'He'll be in biggish trouble. But probably even worse if they aren't. When we find them, the panic's over. And they're probably in there. But they shouldn't be, because cabin safes are not, repeat not, for the storage of classified material. They don't have combination locks. Just close with a key, and half the tiffs in the Navy could run one up for you in less than ten minutes. No, if he's got twelve pages of this stuff in his cabin safe along with his destruct certificates, his pocket money and his hotty mags, he's in trouble. And if he's lost them, he's finished.'

'So what do we do?' said Bob. 'I mean right now.'

'Adjourn,' said Ayres, shaking his papers together and attaching them neatly to his clipboard. 'Have lunch. That sort of thing. I'll write this bit up and we'll meet again at two.'

Campbell worried once more about the officer whose affairs they were so damningly investigating. 'What about Ken? Where is he?'

'In the recreation space,' said Ayres, 'organizing the Donkey Derby.'

'I hope he makes a better job of it than he has of the SBs,' said the gunnery officer.

'Does he know?'

'I don't know,' said Ayres, sounding rather casual. 'It's need to know. And he doesn't need to know till two o'clock. Say half past. Give us time to tidy up this lot. Then we can have him up here and read him his horoscope and find out what he thinks he's been up to. Then we locate the missing pages, dash off a quick report and let the doctor get down to some serious typing, with the top copy to go up to father by tea-time.'

'They'll be in his cabin safe,' said the gunnery officer, less certainly.

'I think so,' said the navigator. 'Stupid bugger.' He glanced at his watch. It was five to twelve. 'Ideal. Just in time for my merpass. Then a quick bronze before lunch. See you all at two, boys. And remember we're a very discreet enquiry.'

Of all the officers on board, only the navigator had skills of which Campbell was in awe. The power of command, whereby you made people want to do what you wanted them to do, an attribute demonstrated *par excellence* by the captain and to a lesser degree by the first lieutenant, the navigator and, surprisingly, also by Henry, did not interest him much. It was a useful and sometimes impressive trick, as much part of their job as the ability to put a patient at his ease was part of his own. And the other various technical and organizational skills of the gunnery, supply and weapons electrical officers were again simply what one would expect: the strengths of specialists. But Ayres, with his disarming self-mockery ('Let me see now, if we've turned the corner this must be the Indian Ocean.') and his silent haven-finding art, embodied a discipline special to the sea. Before dawn he went up with the midshipmen and took them through the routine of morning stars. At noon, the meridian passage, the merpass he had just excused himself for, saw the sun across its zenith in a similar routine. At dusk, after the stars had come out but before the horizon had vanished in darkness, he was up again.

The midshipmen, the officers under training, went with

him, and fumbled with their sextants while he coached them, then watched in awe, like awkward music students at a master class, while he wielded his own. The midshipmen's subsequent calculations, laborious and untidy, resulted in a palm-sized scatter of points on the chart, while his, clustered like a winning group at Bisley, fixed the ship firmly on the face of the waters, with an accuracy that the various bits of electronic kit ranged round the masthead could rarely match. If he had any pride in his skill, it was secret. When he went off to do a fix, he left as though in pursuit of some eccentric habit, of no general interest or importance. 'Yes,' he said, looking at his watch again. 'Merpass.'

He wandered off with his clipboard. In turn Bob gathered up his papers. 'I'll take yours too, doc. Roddy's got all we need in his notes, and we don't want rough work sculling around. I'll lock it in my cabin safe, and see to it when this is all over. Put it through the destructor when we've got ourselves a new security officer.'

'Is it as bad as that?'

'That's about the least bad it could be, old son,' said Bob, lighting another cigarette. He was clearly in no hurry to start anything else in the half-hour or so before lunch. He sat down again. It occurred to Campbell that he might, simply to pass the time, be on the point of becoming a little indiscreet. After all, he had had more experience of boards of enquiry than most, and from the receiving end, too.

'What d'you think'll happen, Bob?'

'Automatic job change for starters. Then, like we said, minimum a logging, maximum an admiral's displeasure.'

'What's that?'

'The admiral writes to you, saying he's not pleased.'

'And you have the letter framed, and hung round your neck?'

Bob smiled. 'Never thought of that. I didn't with mine. Maybe I should have done. No . . . Most important thing about it is that it goes in your documents. Something in the nature of a firm tap on the wrist. Two might sink you. But it's really up to father, and whoever sees to it if he decides to pass it on.'

'So it might remain purely a ship matter?'

'Since it's SBs, father's at least got to tell somebody. But it might go no further than just that . . .' Bob paused. 'It depends on how much fuss they want to make about one particular page.'

'Something in particular?'

'Well . . . It's sort of need to know. But you're on the board. A page of gossip.'

'Gossip?'

'Yes.'

'Oh.' Campbell was left speculating. 'Was it you that found it was missing? Or Roddy.'

'No. Roddy did.'

Campbell remained curious. 'What sort of gossip?'

The gunnery officer smiled and laughed. 'No . . . GOSSIP. Golf Oscar Sierra Sierra India Papa. GOSSIP. It's a kind of . . . system, for talking to subs. Global-Oceanic Surface-Submarine something. Information Propagation, I think.'

'Is that . . .?'

'Yes. Very. It's hot property. Nobody talks about it much.'

'I see.'

'That's why we're sweating. That's what father's really worried about. Ta-fuck's nothing.'

'And if this stuff's compromised, say by spending a couple of weeks in Ken's cabin safe . . .?'

'People might get very annoyed . . . If it's been compromised. And the thing about compromising this sort of stuff is that, if you're not sure whether it's been compromised or not, it's best to assume it has been.'

'Someone in the ship?'

'Well. We're all decent chaps. But we're not all awful careful. And we're not all cleared for handling GOSSIP. So it might be nasty. Depends on father . . .' Bob, perhaps realizing he had talked carelessly, suddenly changed the subject. 'Ever been to a Donkey Derby before, doc?'

'No.'

'Well, when we've sorted out this shithouse we'll go down there and buy ourselves a horse and win a fortune. Cleared ninety pounds in half an hour in *Stygian*, when I was a killick. Three of us really cleaned up a race. Saw off a syndicate from the chief's mess. So we all got hell for the rest of the commission. That's the sport of kings for you.'

'Bugger Beira,' said the first lieutenant. 'I'll have the babies' heads. Then the figgy duff. Gotta have calories in the tropics, don't you, doc? Besides, it helps me get my head down in the afternoon . . . I don't know how you can face those avocados again, doc . . . Ronnie, this must be about the twentieth time we've had these bloody things since Simonstown.'

'I'll check the menu if you like, number one. I'm pretty sure it's only the twelfth.'

'Something like that,' said the first lieutenant over a spoonful of brown windsor soup. 'Twelfth at least.' For some reason surgeon lieutenants were regarded as among the better sort of lieutenant, so frequently Campbell found himself sitting near or even next to the first lieutenant at lunch. It was a dubious privilege, occasionally giving access to inside information or hints of higher thinking on important matters, but more often affording only fairly limited discourse on the menu, for and against, more commonly the latter.

'Maybe he gets them cheap,' said Ayres with great gravity. 'From his cousin in Cape Town.' The navigator hunched his shoulders and rocked to and fro a little over his salad. ' "Not fifty rand a box I'm asking," ' he said in a high wheedling voice. ' "Not even thirty rand a box. For you . . . I give them to you. Twenty-nine rand. Twenty-eight if you take a dozen boxes . . . Oy oy oy. For my cousin I risk the poorhouse. And these are the finest avocados you ever saw. Kosher. Every one." '

Ronnie continued with his soup. The midshipmen were half amused, half mystified by the navigator's lunchtime cabaret. Ken Muir, sitting next to the supply officer, laughed out loud. 'Only another ten cases to go, eh? But it's nice to keep business in the family, isn't it, Abey?'

'The things I do to stop all you lot getting scurvy,' said Ronnie eventually. 'And it's not for any thanks I get.'

'Have you got cousins in Hong Kong, too, Ronnie?' Ayres asked. ' "Ha, Lonny. Boxa lychees. For you velly cheap. One hundred cases, twenty pound O.K." ' The jest did not take off as well as its predecessor, perhaps because of the inhibiting return of one of the LEP stewards bearing babies' heads for the first lieutenant.

'What about the mailies then?' said Ken out of the blue.

'What mailies?' said Ronnie. 'Something else being kept from the workers?'

'Security officer!' The first lieutenant bristled his beard in Ken's direction. 'It's not gone firm, so as far as I'm concerned it's not happening, until it does, that is. So there's no point in sittin' nattering about it.'

'Another mailies buzz? Third this week. Makes you wonder what the crabs are up to,' Ayres mused aloud on why the RAF had not produced a long-rumoured maildrop. 'Probably stuck at Nairobi . . . Wildebeests on the runway, I expect. Or maybe they've run into some people in a bar and forgotten about us.'

'Bloody well better hadn't,' said the gunnery officer. 'All my Open University stuff's blobbing up in the post. History of Ideas has come to a dead stop thanks to them. I was really looking forward to getting stuck into logical positivism.' The gunnery officer, who had joined the Navy as a boy seaman twenty years before, having worked for two weeks behind the counter of Woolworth's in Armagh ('Throwin' up a good white-collar job, me mum said'), was now catching up with his education. From time to time he came down to Campbell's cabin with an essay for the doctor's comments, or a bit of sociologese for deciphering. He was doing postal courses in the History of Ideas, the Urban Environment and something called Aesthetics One ('Take Botticelli now. There's a man that could paint').

Other people had other reasons for looking forward to a maildrop. One of the midshipmen at the other end of the table paused over his soup and appeared momentarily thoughtful. Ayres noticed and pounced. 'Reckon it'll be a hotts, Adrian?' Hauled from his reverie by the sound of his name, the midshipman started. Ayres donned an expression of comic lechery, leered and whispered breathily, ' "Oh, Adrian . . . My love for you is running down my right leg." ' The lad blushed scarlet. There was an appreciative pause, then Ayres got going again. 'Or maybe one from home . . . "The guinea pig is all right but missing you of course. Try not to worry. Hope the postal order helps. Don't spend it all in the tuck shop . . . Your loving mum. PS. Do you want a beach ball for Hong Kong?" '

'Navigator!' The afflicted midshipman was embarrassed but probably not altogether miserable at the navigator's sallies, and everyone else was enjoying the show immensely, but the first lieutenant felt nonetheless obliged to make some gesture in the name of good order and naval discipline.

'Just a bit of sport,' said Ayres mildly. 'Middies need ragging. Stops 'em getting homesick.'

'I'm only homesick when I'm at home,' said the first lieutenant darkly. 'Not a lot of salt in the spuds today, Ronnie.'

Campbell knocked at the door of the security officer's cabin. 'Ken . . . D'you have a minute?'

'Wait one.'

It was half past two. The security officer was required in the first lieutenant's cabin to assist the board with its enquiries.

'Hello, Ken.'

'Oh. Hello. Come in, doctor.'

The security officer looked a little discomfited. There was no means of knowing whether he knew of the board's existence or not. There were officers who heard things, and officers who did not. From what he knew of life on the ship, Campbell thought that Ken was not the sort of officer who had close informal links with the petty officers or the lower deck generally, or the curiously political awareness of feeling that some members of the wardroom seemed to demonstrate. Perhaps the sort of officer who got himself into this kind of trouble would, by definition, be the last to hear about the consequences of it. Most likely he would not know, and in any case it appeared that his embarrassment might have other, more immediate causes. He was standing in a dressing gown, with his back to the door. A tired-looking copy of *Penthouse* lay on his bunk.

'Just having a quiet snooze before the Donkey D.,' he said brightly. 'But glad you dropped in . . . Been meaning to have a quiet chat with you.' From Campbell's expression he must have gathered that the call was not a casual one, of the sort that officers make on each other's cabins, to swap paperbacks, or borrow cufflinks, or whatever; and that the time for quiet chats was perhaps past. 'Is there some problem?'

'Sort of,' said Campbell. 'Sorry, Ken . . . We'd like to have a sort of word with you . . .'

'We?'

'Roddy, Bob and I.'

The front of the security officer's dressing gown was hanging very straight now. 'An enquiry?'

'Yes.'

He had been pink. He was now pale. He put his hand up to his mouth. Bearded, shifty and sallow, in striped dressing gown and sandals, he stirred in Campbell an absurd recollection of a Sunday school wall poster, a reproduction of a Victorian painting called 'Judas Rebuked'. He put both hands up to his face and leaned against his bunk. 'It's all there,' he mumbled through his fingers. 'It's just . . . '

Campbell waited. He did not finish his sentence. 'Good, Ken.'

'That's fine, Ken,' said Bob, from outside the door. 'That's what we'd hoped.' Ken turned round to face him. Bob stood in the door. 'Come on, Ken.'

'D'you want the rest now . . . ? It's all here. Like I said.'

'That would be fine,' said Bob. 'If it's no trouble.'

'Of course.' He reached into his bureau for a bunch of keys, fumbled with them and opened a small safe on the bulkhead beside the cabin door. The three officers, two in uniform, one not, stood round it and looked in. It contained a small jewellery box, a handful of loose five- and ten-pound notes, a cheque book, a small but vividly pictorial book of a sort Campbell had last seen in the quartermaster's desk in *Cerberus*, and a large manila envelope, folded double.

'It's all here,' Ken said, taking out the manila envelope. The little magazine fell on the floor as he did so. Bob picked it up, glanced at it and threw it lightly on to the bunk beside *Penthouse*, then took the envelope from Ken.

'It's been opened.'

'Yes . . . I checked it . . . It's all right.'

'Good . . . That's grand. Well. I'll just take it up and check it again with John. You follow on in a couple of minutes with the doc . . . When you're dressed. We're in number one's cabin . . .'

The gunnery officer left with the envelope. Campbell reflected that he would have made a more than adequate branch manager for Woolworth's in Armagh, had he abided by his mother's wishes and stuck at it.

Somewhat improved by uniform, Ken duly appeared in the first lieutenant's cabin, and was at once sent off again to bring up his accessions documents and destruct certificates. While he was away the members of the board discussed what the captain's written order had described as 'the manner of discharge of his duties by the security officer'.

'Silly bugger,' said Bob.

'Certainly doesn't look like much more than that,' said Ayres. 'If his accessions stuff's all right, and his destructs no worse than we think they are already, we just put father fully in the picture and leave it to him how much further he wants to take it. And there's probably not a lot he wants to do. Minimize the fallout, that's the idea with these things. No nasty smells hanging about over our trim greyhound of the sea and all that.'

'And he'll be relieved as security officer?' Campbell asked.

'Replaced. Relieved is when nothing's gone wrong. He'll be replaced.'

'Who by?'

'Don't know. It's up to father. Any of us could do it, really. Not a big job if you stay on top of it. Ken'll get by as a watchkeeper, and get a lot more of the shitty-little-jobs-officer things to do. Port liaison, NBCD, public relations and all that. Won't do any of us any harm, except him. Reshuffle the minor portfolios. Good thing from time to time. Makes you think about things again.'

'How d'you think he'll take it?'

'Ken?'

'Yes.'

'Quietly, if he's any sense. Hasn't got much option. But he

should be grateful. Father'll want to keep it a ship matter, with info only to command. No court-martial. No 'Officer dismissed his ship' stuff in the *Telegraph*. Just a quick job-change and no bones broken. He'll get off lightly and if he's got any sense he'll know that, and know that the sooner he forgets about it the sooner everyone else will too. And he'll have a small black mark in his documents, of course, but the Navy's very forgiving.'

'Won't stop his promotion?'

'God, no. Might slow it up a bit, and he won't get to be head of naval intelligence, but as an average joe watchkeeper he's got the same future as everyone else.' The navigator paused and smiled. 'For all that's worth.'

'That's right enough,' said Bob. 'They're good at not holding things against you. Did twenty-eight days myself once. When I was a lad.'

'Did you?' said Campbell. 'Where?'

'Stonecutters,' said Bob. Ayres seemed to know already about the wilder flights of the gunnery officer's youth.

'Where's that?' Campbell asked.

'It's a sort of tourist trap in Hong Kong harbour. Not many boats, and a lot of sharks about. Just did me time, then everyone forgot about it.'

Campbell was interested. Perhaps thoughtlessly, he asked 'What was it for?'

'To teach me a lesson,' the gunnery officer said quickly, as though he had said it often before. 'And it worked. And when it came to my board for a commission one old commander noticed it and muttered something about the spirit of aggression being a fine thing in its place, and seemed to be quite keen on gettin' me through . . . Anyway . . . Ken'll be all right. Whole thing'll be gone and forgotten in a year or two.'

Eventually Lieutenant Muir came back with an untidy envelope file of documents, a ring-backed file of completed destruct certificates and two books of destruct certificate counterfoils, like cheque stubs. Ayres took the envelope file, Bob the rest. The former contained details of the classified material received on board HMS *Winchester* during her present commission. The collection of destruct certificates detailed the various secret documents that had been shredded in the destructor, each item being described then certified as destroyed, with the appended signatures of two officers.

Bob flicked through the counterfoils. 'Where's your current book? Both these are used up.'

Ken looked shifty. 'Might take me a minute or two to track it down,' he said. 'It's in my office somewhere. Probably in the combination safe. A new book. Haven't actually started it yet. It's just the blank book. Can I go and have another look?'

Bob and Ayres glanced at each other. 'If you want,' said Bob. 'Sure there's nothin' in it?'

'Sure,' said Ken. 'In fact that's what's been holding things up. A few destructs overdue. I just couldn't lay my hands on the book of blank chits . . . I expect it'll turn up in no time now. And perhaps we could just tidy things up right away when it does . . .'

'Yes,' said Bob. 'Maybe. Anyway, just see if you can find it.' Ken went out.

'Silly bugger,' said Bob again. 'That's probably what's behind it all. Gets through a book of destruct certificates, can't find a new one, gets behind with the destructs and finishes up letting the end go on the whole SB organization.'

'Sounds like it,' said Ayres.

'Like I said, either you're on top of it, or it's on top of you. Bet the silly bugger just didn't get enough when we were storing ship in Pompey. What if I did that? "Sorry, sir. We're fresh out o' bullets." '

The navigator pursed his lips. 'I'll check that one out . . . And if he hadn't been too bloody stupid to tell someone before it all got to this stage, somebody at home could have stuck another book in a blue bag or even on a Herky and got it out to us in a day-and-a-half.'

It had previously occurred to Campbell that *Winchester*'s trip halfway round the world was a picnic on such a grand scale that someone was bound to have forgotten something, as commonly happened on picnics. The ship had avocados, a harmonium, anti-leprosy drugs, champagne, even the traditional red envelopes for the LEPs' Chinese New Year presents; everything you could think of and many things you couldn't, and one officer had omitted to embark enough of a certain sort of pieces of paper, and now his career was suffering. A minor lapse, followed by a silly, panicky cover-up, seemed to be the short diagnosis of the disorder that afflicted the SB world, though as junior member of the board Campbell was probably not the best person to point this out.

Ayres had started to write again. On a blank sheet on his clipboard he jotted a number of headings, with spider lines spreading out to patterns of sub-headings, the whole forming a skeleton draft of the report the captain expected to be reading at tea-time. As discussed, the first heading after the introduction was 'Risk', and there was no doubt that, technically at least, a risk of compromise existed, in that high-grade classified material had been stored in a low-security safe for a period of weeks. The risk to the material was its accessibility in a mortice-lock safe in an ordinary cabin. For the great majority of the time under consideration the ship had been at sea, with RN personnel only on board. The remaining few days had been spent partly in Banjul, where a number of civilians, presumably roughly vetted by the local Brits, had been on board, and partly in a heavily guarded South African naval base, probably not a hotbed of Eastern Bloc espionage activity.

While the security officer was looking for a book of blank certificates he probably would not find, the board went through the files then discussed this problem. Bob was cheerfully obscene, and Campbell still a little bemused. The navigator got down to his writing again, and shaped up official-sounding phrases for his second draft ('a small but definite risk of compromise must be deemed to have been present for a period of about thirty-one days . . .').

Twenty minutes later Campbell found himself wondering how Ken was feeling, and voiced his thoughts. 'Let 'im stew,' said Ayres. 'And let's get on with this.' He and Bob worked on through their files, and Campbell felt spare. When they had finished, the three got together to fill out Ayres' skeleton draft into an orderly report beginning '1.1. General', in fine naval fashion. They were interrupted by a soft knock on the door. Ken came back.

'Sorry about that, chaps,' he said, as though apologizing in a cricket pavilion for a dropped catch. 'Sorry. I can't find it, for the life of me.'

'It's not as bad as that,' said Ayres, almost smiling. 'Not quite. How about checking through the accessions? Find out how many books of blank chits you started with. There you are.' He handed Ken the envelope file. 'They're classified, so they'll be entered in that as they came on board.'

Campbell was first puzzled then impressed by what Ayres had just done. Handing the file to Ken was a way of saying they still trusted him. By offering the accused a seat on the bench, so to speak, a courtesy had been observed which would have been most unusual in civilian life, but could be seen as useful or even necessary in a small ship, where people had to live together after these things. Moreover, it was likely that the navigator, who had checked the file himself only minutes before, knew pretty well what the security officer would find.

Ken sat down and began to leaf through the file. 'Good God,' he said, after an interval, with all the astonishment of an actor doing the stupid policeman in a radio play. 'Well, that explains everything. There *never was* a third book . . . Ha, ha, ha . . .' His merriment, never convincing, withered under a glance from the gunnery officer.

'Really?' said Ayres. 'Well, I suppose it explains a lot. Thanks, Ken . . .' He took the file back and went on, with a promptitude verging on the impolite, to say, 'Fine . . . If you'll excuse us, we'd better just churn out a couple of pages about the whole business for father. Wants it by tea-time. Probably want to see you himself later.'

Dismissed, Ken stood up and left. As soon as he had closed the door, perhaps even before, Bob was mimicking his mirthless 'ha, ha, ha', adding, ' "Sorry chaps . . . dearie me . . . What a lot of fuss about next to nothing . . ." ' in what he might have imagined to be an imitation of Ken's wardroom accent. Ayres and Campbell were amused. Bob's hostility waned. 'Come on, doc. Make yourself useful on this board. Ring down and get Tak to bring us up the same again. Coffee and limers. Let's hack this bastard and then go to the races.'

The board set to and drew up its report, describing the overall state of the ship's security books, their safety, the relative disorder of their stowage, the laxity with which recent changes had been implemented and the risk to the twelve unfiled pages. The various discrepancies were recorded, with their references, in detail in a supplementary page boldly titled 'Annex Alpha', and the remainder of the body of the text described how, in the opinion of the board, the present state of things had come to develop. In addition to expressing its serious reservations about the zeal and diligence of the officer most concerned, the board went on to note that routine checking procedures, though observed, had been insufficiently rigorous, citing Jim's cavalier check on the contents of TAF(UK) 7A, though forbearing to mention him by name. The board made three recommendations: that its report be discussed with the security officer at the next naval port visited; that blank destruct certificates be obtained as soon as practicable in order to regularize material held; and that serious consideration be given to the possibility of handing the responsibility for the SBs on to another officer.

By 3.30 the heat of the day was over. The first lieutenant's cabin seemed smaller than it had been in the morning at the start of their deliberations. Bob had finished his packet of cigarettes. The report was complete. Campbell was left alone with a jug of coffee to type it out on the first lieutenant's rickety portable. It ran to two-and-a-half pages, double-spaced, with the tabulated page of errors tacked on. With a little help from a bottle of correcting fluid, he managed a sufficiently presentable version within the time allotted, and took it, with the handwritten original, through to the navigator's cabin only a few minutes before the time at which the captain normally took his tea. Ayres read it carefully, said, 'Thanks doctor,' reached for his hat and disappeared in the direction of father's garden.

'For a start, it's got nothing to do with donkeys. More like snakes and ladders. Except there's money on it. Like I said, I cleared ninety quid when I was a lad. Three of us. They roll out a canvas strip on the Bofors deck, round the gun, with all sorts of things painted on it, in the squares. Water-jump, back five places, that sort of thing. You'll see it. And somebody rolls a big dice, and your horse, a wee plywood cutout thing on a stand, needs a six to start, then it's off, and the first past the post, takin' account of all the nonsense about jumps and falls and back so many places, is the winner. Owner gets so much, and who owns it, I should've said, is decided by an auction before the start, the prize money comin' from the price of the horses sold, and everybody who's interested in that sort of thing bets like mad. Just like a meeting, with a proper bookie and odds. And of course everybody's a bit pissed, and usually wearing a funny hat.'

'I see . . . I actually heard about that . . . Got roped in for judging, along with father and an LRO.'

'Christ knows what the Russians might think, lookin' at us,' said Bob. 'Anyway, how about joining in a syndicate. With me and Roddy. We could sort of spread it about we're takin' it kind of seriously and spent the whole day in number one's cabin, discussin' tactics.'

'How much?'

'Oh. We should get a horse for about forty quid. Say forty-five maximum. Thing is to go for one of the middle races. Before that nobody's interested and the kitty's just washers. Hardly worth it. And by the end they all think they're the Aga Khan, and you can't get a horse for under a hundred.'

'A hundred? Who's got that sort of money?'

'Syndicates,' said Bob. 'And the chokeys save their breath for the last race. A bunch of laundry boys in a cruiser I was in once came out with a win worth nearly a thousand quid. No fix, despite all what Jack thought.'

'Have you talked to Roddy?' Campbell, who had not even attended a flesh-and-blood horse race, was a little hesitant to commit a day's pay to such a venture, but was rather drawn by the company. Bob seemed to know his way around and, if the navigator came in on it, the thing was probably not only respectable but stylish.

'Right, doc?'

'Fine.'

'I wonder what's keeping father? Not usually one for hanging about.'

They were standing in the passageway outside the captain's cabin, having been summoned in a somewhat unusual, almost Nelsonian fashion, by means of a messenger midshipman, presumably to avoid the use of the tannoy in the somewhat delicate, and no doubt by now rumour-charged, circumstances.

'Why does he want us anyway?'

'Dunno,' said Bob. 'He knows what we think . . . If we do all right in the second race, would you be in for a bid for a horse in the third?'

'Maybe,' said Campbell. 'If Roddy agrees and the money's right.'

'Ah, doctor.' Behind them the captain had opened his door. 'And Guns. Kind of you to come up . . . I hope you were talking about the Donkey Derby.'

'Yessir,' they both said, very quickly. The captain smiled. 'Come in.'

'Thank you, sir.' They went in and laid their hats on the top of the captain's bureau, beside the navigator's. Roddy was sitting on the bench seat against the outboard bulkhead. The other two sat down where the captain indicated, in armchairs. He himself sat down last, on a higher, hard chair, completing an irregular square.

'A sorry business, gentlemen.'

'Sir,' they all mumbled at once.

'But not, I hope, a disaster.' He turned to Campbell and the gunnery officer. 'Roddy and I have been through your report in detail . . . I've already thanked him for his part in it and would like to thank you now for yours. It's . . . short and to the point. And on time, as I expected it would be. You have been both, um, prompt and, I take it, discreet, and I need hardly remind you that . . . discretion is a continuing virtue. The matter remains . . . not one for discussion. Any questions?'

There were no questions.

'I note your recommendations, and for a number of reasons have passed the charge of the SBs on to Roddy, with effect from now. I'll be speaking to Ken in a moment about that. For public consumption, and because it's probably time we did something of the kind anyway, there'll be a general shuffle of a lot of jobs.' The captain paused and smiled faintly. 'I thought you'd like to stay in the gunnery world, Bob, and I expect you'll want to hang on to your whales, doctor. But there are a variety of non-specialist things due for a swap around. I'll be seeing number one about that tomorrow.'

He stood up. 'Thank you, Bob . . . Thank you, Roddy.'

The thanked officers made to leave, and Campbell was uncertain what to do. Leave unthanked? Or respond to this curiously negative probable invitation to stay in the Presence.

'Doctor . . .' The captain had noticed his hesitation, '. . . a word.'

Campbell put down his hat. 'Sir?'

'Your first board?'

'Yessir.'

'Not a lot of call for that sort of thing in the RNR.'

'No, sir.'

'What did you think?'

'Sir?'

'Of the board. The whole idea.'

'Oh . . . Interesting, sir.'

'Interesting?' The captain sounded as though Campbell had declared himself to be idly curious, or perhaps unduly intrigued by the world of secrets.

'Yessir . . . I mean . . . quite unlike anything I've had to do with before. And very quick.'

'Yes. That's the ticket. No messing about. Not in this firm. As you've probably noticed.' The captain paused. Campbell wondered if he ought to be trying to make conversation. The captain, who seemed to divide his life between the bridge, his cabin and his little upper-deck 'garden', ate alone, and seldom saw any of his officers for anything other than a brief and businesslike meeting, and communicated with his ship's company mostly via a first lieutenant with whom he appeared to have little in common. He could easily be seen as a lonely man, whose loneliness might currently be greatly exacerbated by the sheer boredom of Beira. 'Doctor . . .'

'Sir?'

'I'd like you to go and ask Ken to come up and see me.'

'Sir.'

'Don't normally use my doctor as a runner . . . But if you wouldn't mind . . .'

'Not at all, sir.'

'No need to discuss things. But you know what it's all about.'

'Yessir.'

'Fewer people in the know meantime, the better.'

'Yessir.'

'Need to know.'

'Yessir.' Campbell picked up his hat again.

'Doctor . . .'

'Sir?'

'We've got another little board today, haven't we?'

'Sir?'

'Something to do with hats, I understand.'

'Oh. Yessir.'

'I must say I am rather looking forward to that. Aren't you?'

'Yessir.'

'About six?'

'So I understand.'

'Splendid . . . Now, if you'd kindly . . .'

'Yessir.'

'And it's Admiral Gorschkov! Admiral Gorschkov just in the lead as they come out of Bofors Bend and into the home straight . . . Can anyone stop the Admiral now? He's cleared that last water-jump like a horse who really hates getting his feet wet . . . A truly magnificent leap and now he's out there at least two lengths ahead of his nearest rival . . . who's Drake's Drum. And now it's Drake's Drum who's challenging. Drake's Drum looking stronger . . . What will he pull out of the bag . . . ? Oh. Oh dear. It's a three and a big disappointing splash for Drake's Drum. Right into that water-jump and back into the mob with Aggie Weston, Eskimo Nell and Northwood still trailing there. Eskimo Nell. And now it's Eskimo Nell's turn to challenge. Can she pull the big surprise? Will she live up to her reputation as an in-de-fatigable stayer and a fine finisher and show us all something special at this late stage in the race . . . ? And the stewards are just inspecting the dice now . . . It's a one! Well, that's certainly not what we expect of Nell of the North, is it? And now it's . . . Thanks, Nobby, old son. Thirsty work for your commentator here at the Beira course, with the sun beating down, the visibility perfect and the going officially described as firm. Yes . . . Yes. Now it's Aggy with a truly magnificent challenge. A six! A six that puts her *right* up with Admiral Gorschkov. How does she do it? They say she trains on tea and rockbuns, reads her Bible regularly and never touches hard liquor. An example to us all. And that's how she does on it . . . A truly magnificent challenge to the Admiral, whose jockey must now be really sweating . . . What a finish it's going to be. I don't remember one like it since Moshe Dayan beat Farouk's Fancy by a nose in the Mediterranean Stakes in '56, and there aren't many of us around who can remember that . . . Do I see number one smiling? He must have had his money on Moshe.'

The commentator was perched in the aimer's seat of the Bofors gun, looking down at the toy horses on the curved canvas track beneath. He had a green eyeshade, binoculars about a foot-and-a-half long slung round his neck, a can of beer in one hand and a microphone in the other. Officers are never drunk on board, but a casual observer might have wondered if he had been drinking at least enough to quench his thirst. He barked into his microphone with a frenetic wet-lipped commitment indistinguishable from its Aintree model. It had taken Campbell some minutes to recognize him as Len, the weapons electrical officer, normally a quiet and undemonstrative member of the wardroom, promoted there, like the first lieutenant and the gunnery officer, only after years of service on the lower deck.

Around the gun and on both sides of the track were crowded perhaps 150 people, well over half the ship's company, who had turned out for an afternoon of semi-official frolic and disorder, a necessary suspension of the rigours of the naval seagoing routine, for which custom dictated a riotous departure from the usual rules of dress. Sailors wore caftans or swimming trunks, tee-shirts or denim waistcoats, burnouses or kilts, evidently more or less as they pleased.

There was even a little discreet transvestism in evidence, some of it from people about whom Campbell might have hazarded a guess, some completely surprising, as in the case of a stout and hairy north of England stoker now sporting a tutu.

Their hats were something else again. For the competition there were top hats and bowlers, deerstalkers (one adorned with five-inch surrealist salmon-flies), panamas, toques, cloches and (already on a short list for Campbell's eventual participation in judging the competition) a cartwheel straw hat embellished with several hundred paper and tinsel flowers, worn by a lissom electrical mechanic also sporting a string vest, black fishnet tights and high heels.

For the moment, however, attention was focused on the race in progress. Admiral Gorschkov had not maintained his promise and remained three squares away from the finish, having had successive ones from the last two throws of the dice. The rest of the field bunched behind him. Even Eskimo Nell and the still less fortunate Northwood looked as if they might be in with a chance again, as all five horses were crowded within six squares of the line. The spectators, already loud with beer and excitement, shouted in crescendo as the dice rolled for Aggy Weston. Len, frantic at his microphone, roared the outcome over their noise. 'It's a three . . . A three it is . . . And that's put Aggie ahead, yes ahead of Admiral Gorschkov in this most exciting finish here at Beira . . . There's nothing in it now. Everything still at stake. Any horse could still win . . . I think . . . No. It's Northwood. Yes, it's Northwood. A steady unexciting race he's had so far but he's up there now with the rest of them and that's where he's got to be. Can he do it? Can he still do it? He could. Truly he could in this tre-men-dously exciting finish . . .'

The owners and backers of Northwood clutched white-knuckled at their beer cans as Leading Regulator Martindale, in blue underpants and a tail coat, shook his bucket. The dice tumbled out, uninfluenced by the combined voices and drunkenly focused collective will-power of the Northwood faction. 'Four!' They groaned, and everyone else cheered like mad, sudden disaster for them having been at least temporarily averted.

'And now it's the Admiral again. Admiral Gorschkov. His luck has simply got to turn. If he can make even four he's home and the race is his . . . What a finish! What a truly magnificent finish! And it's . . . it's . . .' The crowd howled delight and disappointment. 'A three it is. A nose from the line. But can he last out now? Can he fight off the terrific pressure from the back? Has he a chance? Can he still do it? I doubt it, but stranger things have happened on the turf . . . And now it's Drake's Drum. Never a horse to give up. And can he break through now and get clear and over the line?' The crowd bayed round Martindale and his bucket. It gave forth a three. They cheered and swore. A course steward, more sober than the vast majority of his shipmates, passed between the seething rows lining the home straight and lifted Drake's Drum forward to share the square just short of the finish with a distinctly threatened Admiral Gorschkov.

'And now it's Nell! The Pride of the North . . . And it's a . . . Yes . . . YES! It's Eskimo Nell . . . By a length. And what a finish . . .' Sailors cheered, shouted, hurled overboard empty beer cans, and probably some full ones, too, clutched each other and fell about laughing and weeping. Their din was huge and joyous. They milled around on the Bofors deck, Beira forgotten.

A little apart, the three owners of the winning horse were jubilant, in an appropriately wardroom way. Campbell found himself shaking hands with both the navigator and the gunnery officer at once, in a complicated three-way manoeuvre like an initiation rite.

'Thank fuck for that,' said the gunnery officer.

'Close-run thing,' said Ayres, quoting Wellington, perhaps unconsciously.

'Maybe fifty each, Vasco?' Bob was glowing with beer and joy.

'Fifty-two forty,' said Ayres. 'They round it down to the nearest ten, with the bits to the Welfare Fund . . . Enjoy the race, doctor?'

'Yes, thanks,' said Campbell. Fifty-two pounds was getting on for four days' pay, and the first unearned income of his life. 'Very interesting.'

'Great finish.'

'Great finish.'

'Like a beer?'

'Thanks.' Campbell had made himself a rule about drinking at sea, but the circumstances were rather special. 'Thanks, Bob.'

'Champagne if you want . . . Later. We should put on a few bottles for the wardroom. Saturday night at sea and all that.'

'Fine,' said Ayres. 'Beer now. Champagne later.'

'Justice must not only be done, it must be seen to be done.'

'Sir.'

'Of course we're all agreed that Flenley's effort, in its own way, was good.'

'The feathery thing, sir?'

'Yes. That's the one. Good in its way, but nothing like the effort put into it. Compared with our eventual choice. No . . . Ellis had my vote from the start. As soon as I walked on to the Bofors deck I thought, that's it.'

'It was rather striking. And of course, in its own way, Pratt's hat had its points.'

'Yes. But again, no real *effort*. It was a clever hat, but not a great hat.'

'I thought it was funny.'

'Funny, doctor?'

'Yessir. You know. Funny.'

'Oh. Yes. I see what you mean.'

Leading Seaman Pratt had turned up in a Mad Hatterish topper of enormous size, constructed from white cartridge paper and inscribed, in alternating spirals 'BeiraBeiraBeiraBeira' and 'We're-here-because-we're-here-because-we're-here-because-we're-here', with twin streamers trailing behind, bearing the same legend.

'And it was a funny hat competition.'

'Yes. I see . . . I suppose it really depends on what you mean by funny. Oily's was definitely the most amusing hat. Did you know he was called Oily?'

'Yessir. I believe I did. No idea why though.'

'The drink.'

'The drink, sir?'

'Come on, doctor. Surely you've heard of it. Of course if you people up there spend all your time drinking Glen-somebody's whisky you've probably never heard of Noilly Prat.'

Campbell was puzzled. The captain's pronunciation of the words was so precisely French that the connection with the leading seaman's nickname was not at all obvious until he had thought about it for an embarrassing interval. 'Oh. I see.'

The captain was smiling. 'No . . . I think we discharged our duties this afternoon quite adequately. Quite adequately. The best hat won. And the sailors do take these things seriously.'

'So I gather, sir.'

Tak arrived with more champagne, and topped up the captain's glass then Campbell's.

'This really is awfully kind of you.'

'Bob's idea, sir.'

'Terribly kind. All the real racehorse owners I've met have been most frightfully stingy. Cheers, Guns.'

'Cheers, sir.' Bob, whom Campbell suddenly suspected of having already celebrated their good fortune in the chiefs's mess, had joined them. 'Our pleasure.'

'Of course you're an old hand at this sort of thing, I gather.'

'Had my luck in the past too, sir.'

'Splendid. Splendid. Must just have a word with the other lucky owner . . . Where's Vasco?' Bob pointed Roddy out to the captain, who left them.

'Right, doc?'

'Fine, Bob.'

'Heard the buzz? We're off tomorrow.'

'Off Beira?'

'So they say. For'ard POs. Just looked in on my way to dinner, to keep in touch. Got in from the top. PO Tel.'

'Where to?'

'Maybe Mombasa.'

'What's it like?'

'Sailors' run. Cheap and rough. Lots of laughs. But it might not be there. Might be Mauritius.'

'What's that like?'

'Fantastic. Broke my ankle in a frigate and spent two months there in '59. If I'd known it was going to be like that I'd have done it deliberately. Anyway. It's need to know. Officially CO and Vasco only.'

'That's interesting . . . He's been holding out.'

'Anyway, that's it, old son. No more buggering about on Beira. Fun in the sun, what we all joined for. Tak!'

The wardroom was celebrating. Officially it was simply a Saturday night at sea; a more formal dinner, with some of the mess silver out, a special menu, a little extra fuss from the stewards, and all officers in mess undress. Unofficially, there was rather more to celebrate, principally their imminent departure from the patrol line, though it was uncertain how many of those present knew about that. A day at the races, and the passing off, without too much blood or trouble, of the board of enquiry would also have served as pretexts had no other been to hand. Champagne, courtesy of Eskimo Nell, was at least getting the occasion off to a good start. By the bar one of the midshipmen, possibly the one called Nigel, was drinking it at a rate more appropriate to lager, and talking to his fellow middies rather loudly. Campbell thought he heard him saying something about his uncle who was a member of the Mombasa Club. Tak came round again, unasked, and topped up Bob's glass and Campbell's.

'Good lad, Tak . . . Doc, you don't mind me telling you something . . .'

'What, Bob?'

'You should stay in the Mob. Join properly.'

'D'you think so?'

'You like it . . . You've just about swallowed the hook. What've you got to leave for?'

'Well . . . Got a job lined up.'

'What sort of job?'

'A surgery job. In my teaching hospital. Good unit.'

'We'd better talk about it again. After Mauritius.'

'Or Mombers.'

'Or whatever. Cheers again.'

'Careless talk, doctor. Ha ha.' Bob and Campbell looked round. They had been joined by Ken, who had just come quietly into the wardroom. He looked uneasy, but not,

Campbell thought, as uneasy as Campbell would have done had their positions been reversed. Bob ushered him in and explained about the champagne. 'We had a wee bit of luck. And got out while we were winning.' The truth was that Ayres and Campbell had had to restrain Bob physically when the bidding for horses in the last race had gone, as expected, to three figures. 'Tak!' The steward brought a glass for Lieutenant Muir, who took it, smiling without warmth.

He was dressed, as everyone else was, in tropical mess undress, but there was something indefinably wrong about it, even to Campbell's inexpert eye. His jacket was brilliantly white and well-pressed, his tie neat and straight. He had non-standard, rather flashy gold buttons in his shirt-front, but that was allowed. Eventually it dawned on Campbell that there was something gravely wrong about the shoulder boards, the black, cloth-covered epaulettes bearing the two gold-lace stripes signifying Ken's rank. The little loop on the upper stripe, which in Campbell's epaulettes enclosed the protective reservist 'R', was the wrong way round, not looping under from ahead – 'like a bow wave' as someone had once helpfully pointed out at an early stage in Campbell's naval career – but curling awkwardly forward. Once defined, the error gained hideous proportions. He had put his shoulder boards on the wrong sides of his mess-jacket.

As a solecism of dress in the dress-conscious world of the Navy, it was by no means unknown, and usually pounced upon with general hilarity, the offender being fined a round of port. For Ken on that particular evening it might not be so easily laughed off. Campbell wondered how to tell him. Bob, having seen to it that Ken's glass was full, had conveniently left them. Campbell resolved upon the direct approach.

'Ken.'

'What, doc?'

'You're going astern.'

'Christ!' Ken glanced in panic at each shoulder in turn. 'So I am!' He went as pale as he had done earlier that day, in his cabin. 'Excuse me . . . Hang on to my drink . . .' He left.

'I thought you'd never notice, doc.' Bob had come back. 'I left you to it, hoping you'd pick it up eventually. If I'd told him, he'd probably have burst out crying, poor bugger.'

'Poor bugger.'

'And he didn't get one bloody letter in the maildrop.'

'I noticed that.'

'Did you? Did you now? Ah, well. Slowly we're making a proper pusser's doctor of you. How's your glass?'

'Fine, Bob.'

'I think Ronnie wants us to sit down quite soon. Somethin' about a *consommé*.' His handling of the term was breezily approximate. 'Hope the ex-security officer gets himself sorted out quickly and doesn't come back with his flies open or anything.'

Ken returned, in good order, and the wardroom sat down to dinner. As usual, the first lieutenant presided from the head of the table, with the captain, by tradition a guest of his officers, on his right. The rest of the seating plan, presumably concocted by Ronnie and the first lieutenant, had one or two points of interest. Ken was next to the captain, and Bob was as far from Ken as their ranks permitted. Campbell found himself near Bob, a little below the salt, opposite Henry, at that point in the table where the commissioned officers gave way to the midshipmen, one of whom, Nigel, presumably the most junior, sat at the foot of the table. As 'Mr Vice' he was opposite number one, and charged with the duty of toasting the Queen.

Ronnie's Chinamen had excelled themselves. The silver gleamed. Each napkin was a work of art, a crisp abstract swan of white linen, sacrilege to unfold. After the first lieutenant's gruff atheist '*Benedictus benedicat*', they were unfolded, and dinner began. *Consommé*, prawn cocktail, brochette of ham and veal, and brandy scrolls succeeded one another in an atmosphere of leisured ceremony. A good Chablis gave way to a perfectly drinkable claret, in somewhat more generous quantities. People behaved as if they were eating out, and took their time, and did not complain about the saltiness or otherwise of the potatoes. They talked in turn to their neighbours on either side. Voices were not raised. There was no *bêtise* or hilarity which might have provoked the first lieutenant to bristle his beard at anyone, or call a subordinate to order with his soup-spoon. The stewards floated silently above and around the diners, equally participant in this agreeable, slightly make-believe event.

Len, on Campbell's left, was still hoarse from his stint in the aimer's seat of the Bofors gun. Campbell asked him about his interest in the turf, a question which seemed suited to the slightly formal circumstances. Len, six foot two and possibly fourteen stone, had once wanted to be a jockey, 'but gave up at five foot nine and joined the Mob.' He still went to race meetings at home when he could, he said, sounding perhaps rather grander than he meant to. A moment later he confessed that his interest in racing had first been kindled when, as a boy, he had helped with his father's illegal bookmaking business in Runcorn.

The midshipman on the right, whom Campbell eventually remembered was called Adrian, seemed rather subdued, or perhaps at that thoughtful stage of drunkenness which preceeds nausea. He made dutiful small-talk, saying 'sir' a lot. It transpired that he had heard some bad news in the maildrop: the so-called 'Dear John'. The girl in question, evidently a stunning seventeen-year-old he had known for five years and loved for four-and-a-half, who was at present waiting to improve her A levels to read Human Ecology at Sussex, had given him up in favour of an unsuspected rival whose main advantage was being there, a scion of a local car-hire firm, who was a roadie (what ever that was) to some kind of travelling musical group. The midshipman recounted all this morosely through the prawn cocktail and might have gone on well into the brochette had not Henry interrupted and silenced him by saying languidly, 'Well, hard luck and all that . . . How's the guinea pig?'

After the brandy scrolls, the first lieutenant said, 'Mr Vice,' and Nigel stood and said, 'Gentlemen, the Queen.' Then there was that magical naval moment, when all remain seated, in a negative event of magnificent simplicity, separating the Navy from the whole of British society. The 'trusty and well-beloved friends', as their commissions described them, saluted their monarch by mumbling over glasses of port. Bob snatched a cigar from Tak, who was standing so close he must have been briefed.

The port was passed round again. The midshipman on the right became totally silent. Len confided in Campbell that he hoped to be able to buy his daughter a pony soon. Henry, hitherto suspiciously sober, at least in appearance, was talking to the midshipman on his left about Dartmouth. 'Not what it was. No sport left. Practically gone comprehensive. Full of earnest little snotties with A level sociology and no idea how to behave.' Henry sounded as if he had left the place thirty years ago when in fact two was a more likely estimate. He cited instances of the sort of thing that no longer happened 'now they're all learning politics and which knife not to eat their peas off.'

The port came round again. The first lieutenant called for the toast of the evening from Adrian, who stood up, blinking, and said, 'Wives and sweethearts.' Conventionally upright, the wardroom mumbled the time-worn 'May they never meet.' Then they all sat down. Adrian stifled a sob. Henry, Len and Campbell all noticed, and said nothing.

Eventually the first lieutenant and the captain got up and went through to the lounge section, and the others straggled after them. Campbell found Ronnie and congratulated his department on the dinner.

'All in a day's work. And my lads get more fun out of that than they do scramblin' eggs.'

'I thought it went very well,' Campbell ventured.

'Bit of a problem deciding what's room temperature for claret in this part of the world,' Ronnie mused. 'But jolly pleased to hear customers happy.'

'Brandy snaps a bit on the crisp side, Ronnie,' said Ayres. 'Got winged by a high-velocity fragment of number one's. Otherwise probably the best caff in the immediate vicinity.'

'We do our best,' said Ronnie. 'Who's havin' a liqueur? Remy Martin, men? Doc?'

'Let me,' said Ayres. 'You sure about the Remy Martin, Len? I thought you ran perfectly well on two-star.'

'Thanks, Roddy.'

'Thanks, Vasco.'

'Ronnie?'

'Thanks, Roddy.'

'Tak!'

'Sah!'

If a sixty-thousand-ton tanker, laden with precious oil for

the illegal regime in Salisbury, had chosen that moment to dart from nowhere towards the port of Beira, no doubt HMS *Winchester* would have risen to the occasion. Jim was on watch, radar sets were manned, and gun crew and boarding party could be mustered within five minutes, the impact of the latter no doubt greatly enhanced by the immaculate tropical mess undress of the officer in charge. But nothing had happened so far to suggest that their services might be required that evening, and the planned departure of HMS *Winchester*, just revealed, suggested that they might in fact not be required for months or even years. The officers relaxed.

'Doctor . . .'

'Sir?'

'A word, if we may . . .'

'Sir.'

The captain stood slightly stooped. There was an empty brandy glass in his hand. He was, Campbell realized, physically a rather slight man, much shorter than Len, and more lightly built than the engineer. Apparently untouched by the day's festivities, he was cool and courteous in his summons of Campbell. There was nothing about him at that moment more than the unemphatic authority of an old-fashioned family doctor.

'Could we have a little word . . .?'

'Certainly, sir.' Campbell had not felt drunk until the captain had called him over. He now recalled that he had put away quite a bit since Eskimo Nell's final dash for the line.

'A small thing, but I thought it best to . . . You've noticed Ken's turned in?'

'I hadn't, sir.'

'He's got the morning.'

'I see, sir.' The morning watch was four hours, starting at 4 a.m.

'. . . It struck me that you might want to have a quiet word with him.'

'Sir?'

'I think he probably wants to talk to somebody . . .

Difficult for me . . . especially at dinner. Though, of course, it was perfectly right for number one to put us together . . . And . . . I don't know . . . perhaps you might want to give him some sort of light sedative.'

'Even if he's going on watch, sir?'

'Oh, well . . . Very much up to you . . . up to you to decide . . . Very light sedative might do more good than harm. But I think the main thing is to go and have some sort of chat.'

'I see, sir . . . I'll go down right away.'

'No . . . I didn't mean that . . . Give it ten minutes or so, then just drop in . . . if you feel like it. It'd come well from you. From what he was saying at dinner . . . he seems to think you're an approachable sort of chap. In the know, but not too close for comfort, if you see what I mean.'

Campbell tried to count the number of times Ken had proposed that the two of them have a quiet word. 'I'll pop down shortly, sir.'

'Finish your drink. Gosh, yes. Finish your drink first. You might find he wants to tell you one or two things . . . This and that. Up to him, of course . . . I must say I thought the prawns were first-rate . . . I still wonder how Ronnie and his Chinamen do it . . . Ronnie!'

Ken's cabin was in darkness, and smelled of warm socks and aftershave, Campbell knocked softly again at the half-open door.

'Who is it?'

'Doctor.'

'Oh, doc . . . Come right in . . .' There was a rustling in the dark, and a light clicked on. Ken, lean and evidently naked under a single sheet, blinked at Campbell. 'Come on in. Have a seat. Kick that stuff out of the way.'

Campbell complied. The resulting jumble of uniform under the drop-down sink might have been a harsh symbol of the day's proceedings. He stooped to tidy it up. 'Leave it,' said Ken. 'The steward'll sort it out in the morning. How's the party?'

'All right,' said Campbell. 'How are you?'

Ken half sat up in his bunk, his knees drawn up to his

chest, his face in shadow from the little lamp behind him. Campbell settled into the folding armchair from which he had just removed Ken's crumpled mess-kit.

'I've got the morning.'

'Oh . . . look . . . I shan't stay long . . . I just wondered . . . you know . . . how things were. But if you'd . . .'

'No . . . don't worry about my beauty sleep. I've really been wanting to have a sort of quiet chat with you for quite a while.'

'You mentioned it once or twice.'

'Wish now I'd come earlier.'

'Oh. Was it about . . . all this business?'

'Basically yes. And one or two other things that've been worrying me.'

'For a long time?'

'Long enough.'

'Oh . . . I see.'

In the shadow Ken might have been attempting a smile. 'The Navy's not all gung-ho recruiting-poster stuff, you know,' he said. 'Gunboat-bashing, showing the flag and all that.'

'I suppose not.'

'In fact, there are times when it's all too idiotic even to laugh at . . . Even the lads cotton on to that now and again.'

What Ken was saying had little of the power to shock. Campbell was aware that not everyone in the Navy was happy all of the time. Every week since joining he had seen a handful of sailors whose presenting medical complaint was quickly redefined, usually by the patient himself, as a greater or lesser degree of unhappiness with his lot. Most of them felt better after talking about it, and many developed a curious amnesia for 'the day they went and told the doc the lot'. Campbell regarded this gentle psychotherapeutic function as one of the easier and more interesting parts of his job. But Ken's problems, however much he cared to blur them into the larger category of lesser discontents among sailors, seemed more serious. 'I know,' Campbell said. 'People tell me.'

Ken became more animated. 'You know that one of my lads came to me a couple of days ago and sat in my cabin, right where you're sitting, and cried. He kept saying, "What's it for? What's it for? It's just silly. The whole thing. Dressing up in silly clothes to do silly things by silly rules for silly people. It's all silly." '

'Was that Benstead?'

Ken looked surprised. 'Yes.'

'The red-haired RO?'

'That's him. You know him, doc?'

'Came and said more or less the same thing to me on Tuesday. Girlfriend trouble, I think. But he seemed to be quite enjoying the Donkey Derby.' There was a long pause, then Campbell said, 'Ken . . . You've had a bad day. Is there anything I can do to help . . . ? Give you something to relax you a bit?'

'Doctor Campbell's little pills for unhappy sailors?'

'No magic, Ken. And I'm certainly not pressing anything on you. You're the one . . .'

'. . . who's got to sort it all out?'

'If you want.'

'What do you mean?'

'Well . . . That wasn't what I was going to say. I meant, if you can get your head down all right, and get up and go on watch at four, good for you. Seriously.'

'Splendid show, what? Bloody but unbowed. The boy stood on the burning deck and all that?'

'If you want. I just meant it's good that you can just carry on doing your job . . .'

'As if nothing had happened?'

'Sort of.'

'As if I hadn't been knocked down, jumped on and torn up for arse-paper? Career-wise. And believe me, there wouldn't exactly be a queue of chaps falling over each other to do the morning after a Saturday night at sea.'

'Probably not.'

'So it's just as well they didn't take my fucking watch-keeping ticket while they were at it. No. Business as usual. Muggins in the chair at oh four double oh, standing by to take the blame for mutinies, collisions, accidents, disasters, acts of God or other unnamed foreign powers. Just like the Queen pays me for. With a bacon sandwich at six and Ayres drifting up at eight saying, "Now let me see, can anyone remember where we were yesterday?" Silly sod.' Ken drew his knees tighter towards his chest. Campbell, comfortable in the little armchair, nonetheless felt that not much was to be gained from continuing the conversation. He leaned forward and began to get up.

'Doc . . .'

'What?'

'Why is it all so fucking awful?'

'What?'

'The whole silly sodding system. Pieces of paper that suddenly get so important you can't sleep for thinking about them. Captains who treat you as if you've lost the keys to Fort Knox, and then go awfully decent on you to keep you in the system . . . I suppose he told you to come down and have a quiet word . . .'

Campbell said nothing.

'He would. I bet he bloody did. Tea-time I've let him down, and by God he's made sure I know about it. Dinner-time I'm saveable, so he sits next to me and talks about Angela fucking Thirkell and rock-gardens to show me he thinks I'm basically a decent chap. Dammit, I must be. Otherwise they wouldn't have let me in. And now it's bed-time and he sends you down with the Horlicks and Elastoplast. To show the Navy cares.'

'Maybe it does.' Campbell got up to go.

'Doc. Sit down. I want to talk to you.' Campbell complied.

'You know I didn't get a letter today, Not one miserable fucking letter.'

Campbell said nothing.

'Not even from her friendly bloody solicitor.'

There was another silence. Campbell said, 'I don't think I know about this.'

'She's upped and offed.'

'Suddenly?'

'Sort of. Thought about it for a while. Then did it. Suddenly.'

'When?'

'Got the news in sunny Banjul.'

'Who else knows?'

'Father.'

'When did you tell him?'

'He shuffled up in his slippers at five o'clock one morning, when I was on watch. We had a chat on the bridge wing.'

'How long ago was that?'

'What?'

'Telling Father.'

'In passage from Banjul to Simonstown. Say four weeks ago.'

'And when did she go?'

'Probably when we were in passage from Gib.'

'Complete surprise?'

'Not looking back on it.'

'What do you mean?'

'Well . . . She went cool and dutiful. No rows. Should've thought of it, I suppose. "Why's she stopped picking shit out of me?" A question every faithful husband should ask himself in the circumstances . . . Feel like a drink?'

Campbell was shocked. To keep a private supply of alcohol in one's cabin was a very serious offence. 'No thanks, Ken. Had quite a lot today already. More than usual.'

'Mind if I have one?' He did not wait for an answer, but reached down into a drawer and poured himself a large whisky into the cup more usually associated with an officer's morning tea. 'You shouldn't.'

'What?'

'Mind. Save you a pill.' Campbell smiled. 'I know what you're thinking, doc.'

'What?'

'What a fucking mess. Job problems. Drinks. And dahling-palavah.'

'What?'

'Wife trouble.'

'Never heard the expression.'

'Pidgin. Picked it up from a lady I knew in Banjul.'

'Really?' Campbell found it hard not to sound a little more interested in this.

'Yes. "Dahling-palavah be hard-oh" was what she said. Native talk. Oh, don't worry, doc. I haven't been at the black ham. White lady. Well, nicely tanned. And pink inside like

Queen Victoria. Marnie.'

'The Unilever bird?'

'That's her.'

'I thought . . .'

'Guns?'

'Yes.'

'So did he. Well anyway, she fancied something younger so Guns has got it in for me. As you may have noticed . . . You haven't asked me about *him*.'

'Who?'

'The chap the wife fucked off with. A crab. And not even a flying crab. A flight lieutenant who intrepidly pilots a desk to do with squadron training schedules.'

'Know him?'

'Sort of. Met him. At what must have been the beginning. Then not, of course . . . But I expect he understands her.' Ken had almost finished his half cup of whisky. Campbell had the feeling that, especially after a mess dinner, he'd had rather a lot of information to assimilate, and had contributed little to the case, apart from the obvious function of plain man's psychotherapy, i.e., listening. He floundered on a bit.

'Did she think that . . . you didn't?'

'That's what they usually say. Marnie did. It's a ritual. Like crossing your fingers. Before you open your legs. But I was actually quite fond of her. Whether I understood her or not. And of course there's the mortgage and all that.' Naked but for a sheet, and clutching a large official teacup now empty of whisky, Ken looked not far short of pathetic.

'Are you drinking a lot?'

'Yes and no, doctor. A definite maybe on that one.'

'Every night . . . ?' Campbell indicated the teacup.

'Except when I'm on watch.'

'D'you drink in the mornings?'

'Once or twice. Worried me. At first.'

'Sleeping all right?'

'If I get the dose right.'

'What?'

'Maybe a quarter of a bottle.'

'How long?'

'What?'

'How long does that make you sleep?'

'Till maybe half past three . . . Ideal for mornings. Get up then and do something. Even if it's just listening to the lookouts discussing their last shag. Plus, of course, being responsible for the safety of a million pounds' worth of gear and all you lot's precious lives.'

'What if you're not on watch?'

'What do you mean?'

'What do you do at half past three in the morning?'

'Drink, maybe. Just a small one to tip me over. Or have a quiet worry about something. Ta-fuck alpha and all that.'

'Job getting on top of you?'

'Until this afternoon.'

'Sorry.'

'It's all right. You've had a busy day, you're entitled to forget little details.'

'Are you eating all right?'

'What?'

'Your appetite. Is it all right?'

'You can go off avocados.'

'But generally . . . ?'

'I could leave out two meals a day, I suppose. I think I just go to the wardroom for the company.'

'And how d'you feel . . . generally?'

'What do you mean . . . generally? How would you feel if you were me . . . ?' He hunched forward and muttered, 'You'd feel twitched. You'd feel you weren't making much of a job of anything. And you'd be right. And you might be wondering a bit about your future.'

'What sort of thing?'

'The Mob. Everything. What, if anything, is worth the trouble.'

'Trouble of what?'

Ken reached down for his bottle again. 'Oh, I'm not going to embarrass everybody by walking off the back and playing silly buggers with the Beira sharks . . .'

'But it did cross your mind?'

'Once or twice.'

'Ken . . .'

'Don't worry, doc. Promise I won't. I'll do my duty by

God and the Queen, help other people at all times and obey the Scout Law.'

'When did you start to feel like this?'

'Like what?'

'That things might not be worth the trouble and all that.'

'Recently, a lot. A little, a long time ago.'

'How long ago?'

'Months. Autumn. Then it got worse with the job. Fucking SBs. Then, of course, a spot of the old wife trouble hardly helped. Goes for a chap, what? Gets him down, don't you know?'

'Ever felt like this before, Ken?'

Ken snorted. 'Well I've never lost a wife and a career within a month. No, not that I can remember, now you come to mention it.'

'I mean . . . bad patches maybe not as bad as this. But bad patches. In the past.'

'D'you think I'm nuts, doc? Mental? Unstable? Straw in the hair? Barking mad and all that . . . ? Sorry.'

Campbell stood up. 'You've got a lot to cope with.' He could think of nothing to say that would neither patronize Ken nor rouse him to further scorn and thus perhaps make things more difficult later. 'Can we talk about it again?'

'A quiet chat?' Ken grinned over his cup.

'That's an idea. You all right for the morning?'

'Don't worry, doc.'

'Goodnight, Ken.'

'Doc . . .'

'What?'

'Thanks.'

'It's all right.'

'And . . . thanks for mentioning . . . the little matter of . . .'

'What?'

'Going astern.'

'Oh. That.'

'Gave me another chance. So did father. Must be policy for me.'

'See you tomorrow, Ken.'

'See you tomorrow.'

*

Campbell made his way from the cabin flat back to the wardroom. From an open hatch leading to the fridge flat below came a steady stream of warm, humid air. A sailor in a boiler suit, probably an MEM on his way round the four-hourly checks on continuously running machinery, waited at the top of the companionway for him to pass, rather exaggerating the necessary space between officer and man, perhaps out of regard for Campbell's mess undress, perhaps (and less likely) as a mute and unassailable criticism of the midnight roistering of the officer class.

Was Ken simply depressed? As far as Campbell could remember, there were two kinds of depression: one that happened in response to adverse circumstances, and one that could happen to anyone, anytime. And (psychiatry being a notoriously imprecise subject) there might be a third, in-between group of people with problems, who might have been heading for a depression anyway. A lot of the symptoms Campbell had asked about – the disturbance of sleep, the loss of appetite, the 'diminished enjoyment of life', as the psychiatrists called it – would have fitted the diagnosis, though to have pressed on and asked Ken about his bowel habits (depressives get constipated) and any family suicides and so on would have been going rather beyond the remit of the 'quiet chat' agreed by all to be the thing for the time being. Such details could be elicited in the morning.

Depression affected efficiency and relationships. Had Ken developed a mild depressive illness in the autumn, prior to the onset of his difficulties with the SBs and the problems with his wife, and suffered the professional and marital consequences of the illness? Or was it the other way round? Had life gone bad on him, for other, external reasons, with the subsequent onset of a 'reactive' depression? Or, psychiatry being psychiatry, was it a chicken-and-eggish mixture of the two extreme theories: the 'interaction of previous personality, psychopathology and life-situation' stuff that Campbell as a student had never really come to grips with?

The drinking was the most alarming feature, and the one that could get Ken into trouble quickest. The first priority was to get him off alcohol and on to something that would get him to sleep without the risk of a court-martial, and then reassess the problem after that. Perhaps a few weeks on one of the anti-depressants neatly stored in Finch's pharmacy would help. All part of the rich tapestry of life, thought Campbell as he reached the wardroom flat, and a change from sprained ankles and the clap.

'There's a formula for this but I'm buggered if I can remember it. You can work it out if you know the height of the beer can, the distance from the bar top to the deckhead, and this formula that I can't remember for working out pyramids. Something to do with the sum of an arithmetic series. In fact it's dead simple if you can remember it. Ah. Doc.'

Campbell had not meant to linger in the wardroom, as only Bob and one of the mids remained, but having looked in, and been consulted, so to speak, he realized he might now find it difficult to leave. And one more beer might not go amiss. 'Sorry, Bob. Pyramids?'

'Pyramids, doc. It's a sort of formula. See. We put one can on top of two others. Easy. Doubles the height. But to get one more can up, you need three, and so on. And say we needed seven high to get the deckhead . . . I'm sure there's a formula. So is Nigel.'

'Yessir,' said the midshipman, with great concentration.

'Beer, doc? For the pyramid . . . Nigel, if you're passing the fridge . . .' The fridge was in the opposite corner of the lounge section of the wardroom. Nigel had not looked as if he were about to pass it, or go anywhere near it, but none the less he walked unsteadily over towards it, having sensed the wishes of a superior officer in a way that might take him far in the service. 'And get one for me. And have one yourself. For the pyramid. Doc, give the chits a fair wind.'

Campbell slid the book of bar chits along towards Bob, who wrote "Cans x 3. GO" in an unswerving hand then suddenly said, 'How's Ken?'

'All right, it seems.'

'Poor sod . . . Father's not amused. The bad smell might bring his name to notice, in a bad-smell way.'

'Beyond the ship?'

Bob fell silent as Nigel came back with three cans. 'I can't remember it, Guns.'

'What, Nigel?'

'The formula, sir.'

'Never mind, son. They might still make you an admiral. Thanks.'

'Cheers.'

Bob gazed at the row of cans on the bar. 'There must be millions here. Jillions.' Campbell and the midshipman listened. Bob gestured outboard to the mighty deep. 'Here. In the hoggin. Zillions. Think about it. Three cans per man per day. And they had carriers with squadrons borne when this thing started. Plus escorts. That's easy ten thousand cans a day. In bloody great heaps and banks and shoals.'

'We could go back for them,' said Nigel, 'when the world's mineral resources run out.' He had some trouble with 'mineral resources'.

'They could become a hazard to navigation,' said Bob. ' "Super tanker grounded on beercans. Beira closed." Serve the buggers right . . . That's it, lads. A few million more and we could easy close the port. Then you wouldn't need a patrol or even a bloody guard ship. Why did nobody else think of that? . . . More beer.'

Campbell was barely halfway down his can, but did not resist another. The medical officer, the gunnery officer and the midshipman, who improved a little with acquaintance, discussed naval affairs generally and the problem of Beira in particular far into the night. The pyramid of empty beercans eventually reached the deckhead, but when it did no one bothered. No further theoretical work on the formula was attempted, and they did not even count the cans.

At about half past one the gunnery officer opened a scuttle and stationed Campbell under it. Then he went back to the bar and tossed the beercans one by one, using both hands as if they were shells and he were a boy seaman once more, serving a gun. At first Campbell kept up, catching the cans and throwing them out into the warm night to join the millions on the ocean floor, then he slowed down, or Bob speeded up, and he was bombarded by half a dozen final tins, rapid fire.

The midshipman had gone to sleep in a chair. They woke him and Bob locked the bar. Campbell, indulging in an odd drunken fancy to visit his department, went unsteadily aft to the sickbay. To his surprise he found Smith at work, cleaning out the little laboratory place at the far end. The LMA was tolerant of Campbell's mild disarray, and wished him good evening, and explained that most of his mess were on night working party, and it was in any case cooler for cleaning and heavy work. They chatted for a while, though afterwards Campbell could remember little of what they had discussed.

He returned to the wardroom cabin flat, at peace with the world. The ship, enclosing and alive, was as quiet as ever it was, but still whirring and humming, and sometimes creaking slightly as it moved over the water. The night working party was scrubbing out the Burma Way, and made space for Campbell as he walked for'ard. In a dark corner a sailor sang softly to himself as he scoured under a companionway. His voice was light and pleasant, and to the tune of 'What a Friend We have in Jesus' he crooned:

'Me no likee Bleetish sailor,
Yankee pay five dollar more.
Yankee call me honey darling,
Bleetish call me fucking whore.'

PART FOUR

'No, Vasco. You've got the wrong end of the stick. Lesley Ann wasn't Mauritius. Lesley Ann was Simonstown. You're getting her mixed up with . . .'

'Lesley,' said Ayres.

'Plain Lesley,' said Henry.

'Well, plain enough. Bigger, too.'

'That's right. Lesley was Mauritius. Big girl. Bondage, wasn't it, Len?'

Len put down his coffee, picked up *Country Life* and perused the over-£200,000 properties.

'Yes. Lesley Ann was something else,' said Ayres.

'Spiky shoes?' Henry suggested. 'Bit of fladge?'

'Yes. That's her. Violence. The Simonstown sjambok queen.'

'No . . . You're thinking of . . .'

'Right. Not her. That was . . . Carolyne. Ah. Yes. Lesley Ann was into *sex*. In a big way.'

Len got up and went over for more coffee, looking a little worried.

'Anyway, with a filing system like Len's got, these things are no problem . . . Cross-indexed. Name, port and perversion . . . All stowed away. Shipshape and Bristol-fashion.'

'In case he goes back . . .'

'Or in case one of his fellow greenies in some other steamer wants a phone number. You know. The old boy network. "Hallo, Len. I'm off to Banjul and looking for a bit of the other. Got anything?" So he says, "Can you hang on, Bert? I'll just check . . . Was it something special . . . ? Now in Freetown, just down the road . . ." '

Len was no longer browsing through the lush acres and seven public, thirteen private mansions of the Home Counties. He had risen from his chair and was looking nervously out of the scuttle at the islands, now larger and more frequent. *Winchester* was due alongside at HMS *Tenebris*, the Hong Kong shore establishment, in an hour and a half.

'Right then. That's enough of that.' The first lieutenant, who had been listening to but not participating in the conversation of his junior officers over coffee, got up and paused, addressing the empty centre of the wardroom. 'A joke's a joke. In its place. But no more of that stuff from twelve-hundred hours. End of story.' He bristled his beard vaguely in the direction of Henry and the navigator, and bustled out.

'I expect with him it's a bad conscience,' said Ayres, as soon as the door had closed. Len looked relieved. 'I saw him. At the Galle Face Hotel. He thought I didn't but I did. Quite a torrid little knees-up with that widow in Colombo.'

'With the wart on her nose?'

'Yes. Wasn't it . . . Irma, or something?'

'That's her.'

'Irma La Douche. Something like that . . . And do you know . . . Even our Ronnie . . .' He leaned closer to Henry and whispered, for everyone to hear, 'Banjul.' He winked ponderously. Ronnie, undoubtedly the most devoted and punctiliously well-behaved married man in the wardroom, went a little pink. 'D'you know he talked to the same woman for *eight minutes* at the cocktail party?'

'Really?' said Harry. 'Eight minutes! Might I ask who?'

'Doc's pal. The lady from Edinburgh.'

'Ooh. Not *Mrs Parsons*. The siren of the Banjul bridge set? Eight minutes! Unchaperoned?'

''fraid so.'

'Wonder what Jenny'll think?'

'I expect he's told her already. "My dear wife . . . I have a confession to make. Tonight I talked to another woman for eight minutes. I hope you can find it somewhere in your heart to forgive me . . . Dearest one . . ." '

At the mention of his wife's name Ronnie had gone pinker still, and was bright red by the end of Ayres' little turn. 'You rotten lot,' he said. 'Just you wait till you've got some class bint lined up in here. Len and I'll bring out the scrap book, won't we, Len? "Seen with a friend relaxing in Mauritius." Just you wait, navigator.'

'Anything but that,' said Ayres placidly. 'Tak!'

'Sah.'

'Tak, could we have more coffee? Oh . . . while you're here, Tak. D'you think we're anywhere near Hong Kong? Look right to you?'

'Dunno sah.' It was clear that Tak held firm views on specialization and division of responsibility within the Navy. 'More coffee sah?' He may have been more puzzled than amused. He filled up Ayres' cup, then said 'Fink so sah.'

'There you are, men. Expert corroboration. I think we'll be all right.' Tak went off laughing with the officers, or possibly at them.

It was hard to make much of what the LEPs thought about anything. Only in the past week or so, as they neared home, had their official faces begun to relax a little. Prior to that, it seemed a matter of complete indifference to them whether *Winchester* was nudging gunboats off Iceland, beating off mock attacks by training aircraft in the Channel, refuelling from a tanker off Ceylon, or simply sitting amusing the sharks at Beira. They worked their routines, talked to each other in half-swallowed monosyllables, said 'sah' a lot and looked after the wardroom very well. They lived in a little mess deck which was always the cleanest and tidiest encountered in the course of captain's rounds, and, perhaps their chiefest virtue, they never discussed wardroom affairs with the other ratings.

Campbell had had little to do with them professionally. One or two of the younger ones got seasick and asked for medication. One leading cook, a man who spoke, or admitted to speaking, only minimal English, had succumbed, shortly after Campbell had joined the ship, to a febrile illness accompanied by a rash. With one of the LEP petty officers, Campbell had gone down to the mess deck to see him, and decided to put him into one of the beds in the sickbay because he was ill and it was not clear what was wrong with him. This involved a routine form which included a question about next of kin. When Campbell asked him about this he could not make himself clear so he pointed to a framed picture of a chubby Oriental family group. The PO elaborated in Cantonese. The sick man looked as though Campbell had told him all hope was gone, but eventually gave a Hong Kong address, consisting mainly of numbers, with all the enthusiasm of a man making a dying deposition. Several days later, when the patient was back in his mess deck convalescing, his illness still undiagnosed but rapidly receding, Campbell noticed that the framed family group had given way to a pneumatically nude Anglo-Saxon blonde. Straying perhaps from a truly Hippocratic detachment, he had commented on this. The man had laughed nervously, reached out and turned the pin-up over to reveal the family group on the other side.

LEPs never, to Campbell's knowledge, got drunk. They gambled sometimes, playing mah-jong at lightning speed, chattering like sparrows. They had an extra holiday, all their own, for Chinese New Year, and they had celebrated it, according to Ronnie, who had attended as their guest and divisional officer, with the slightly circumspect formal gaiety of an old-fashioned family Christmas.

Once, after a discussion with Ronnie about his 'merry men', as he called them, Campbell had borrowed the relevant official handbook and had been amazed by its tone: at once solicitous, simplistic and respectful. The 'pusser's guide to the inscrutable' described in crisp naval prose how there were 'basically two sorts of Chinese', went on a lot about 'face' and how to preserve it in the context of naval discipline, outlined ethnic virtues with a breezy Victorian lack of embarrassment ('Cantonese are clean, thrifty and industrious', 'heavy drinking is unknown', etc.) and hinted at less admirable qualities ('gambling on games of chance may create problems', 'signs of opium smoking may sometimes require to be sought'). It went on to describe in detail the arrangements for the New Year festival ('monetary gifts, presented in the morning in red envelopes, amounts corresponding to naval rank – see Table 1'). After reading it and handing it back to Ronnie, Campbell had often toyed with the idea of drafting, for his own amusement, a similar official handbook on the management of Scotsmen in the Navy, and suggesting that others, on Welshmen, Liverpudlians, etc., should be considered, if suitable authors could be found.

The spare officers' goofing party, which, after a series of ceremonial entries to various ports *en route* to the Far East, had begun to acquire an *esprit de corps* all of its own, assembled for'ard on the Bofors deck, port side, near father's garden, with a few minutes in hand before the time appointed for falling into line. Campbell usually stood beside Ronnie, who talked out of the side of his mouth and was amusing company, and tended to avoid Ken, who insisted on taking things very seriously, with strict observance of silence and standing properly to attention. Ahead, the peak of Victoria Island, a low irregular cone rising from a stubble of waterfront skyscrapers, marked Hong Kong, their destination. Four months out of Portsmouth, a weary catalogue of diversions and delays behind her, HMS *Winchester* approached harbour. The slow boat to China had almost made it.

'Hands fall in for entering harbour. Procedure Alpha,' said the tannoy, following with the usual rigmarole about screen doors, scuttles, hatches, etc.

'Smartly there, doc. Chin up.' Ken had appeared on Campbell's left. On his right, Ronnie grunted disapproval of such formalities. 'Psst . . .' he murmured. Campbell inclined slightly to the right.

'Very smart turn-out, doc.'

'Thanks, Ronnie.'

'For a medical man.'

They were in the usual tropical uniform of white shorts and shirts, but instead of being casually bare-legged and sandalled, as at sea, they wore white buckskin shoes with long socks. Sunday-best caps, with glossy peaks, were much in evidence. From a suitable distance they probably looked quite smart.

'Little woman said she'd be in blue.'

'Oh?'

'Sort of cornflower, she said. And near the end of the jetty . . . I bet they're all in blue.'

Campbell's mind went back to the rain-swept gaggle of wives standing under Portsmouth castle earlier in the year. Regularly throughout *Winchester*'s voyage, letters had arrived with news of the wives' charter flight, arranged to meet the ship in Hong Kong. Len's wife was secretary of their little organization, and the captain's wife, naturally, president. Wives of all ranks had subscribed, and a few fiancées and other varieties of close friend (the lady known to the captain as 'poor Mrs McGuffy' among them) were also expected to turn up at HMS *Tenebris*, many with accompanying children. It seemed to Campbell that the prospect of their presence somehow diminished *Winchester*'s adventure, as though a rather dashing Boy Scout troop had marched for days through a wilderness, to be met in the middle of it by a party of mums with flasks of soup. And there was the further problem of the impact of wardroom wives on the wardroom. As the first lieutenant had already indicated, many subjects could no longer be talked of.

'Here we are,' said Ronnie. 'The lads out to meet us.'

'Minesweepers?' Campbell squinted ahead at the little grey ships. Over the months he had been working sporadically on warship recognition.

'No, doc. Near miss. Patrol boats. Same hull. Bofors aft, instead of all the mineswiping gear. But basically the same apart from that.' The four patrol boats waited ahead, two on each side, and dipped their ensigns and exchanged with *Winchester*'s bridge the thin pipings of bosun's call, as the frigate passed between them, then they fell in behind, still two on either side, to escort *Winchester* on the last few miles of her voyage halfway round the world.

There was lots for the goofing party to look at. Every sort of native craft, from tiny shells that could, but for their matchstick-men crews, have been mistaken for floating dustbins, to huge tourist-brochure ocean-going junks with hulls castled like medieval warships and vast eccentric sails. Conventional shipping, from tramps to supertankers, bustled around, seemingly in all directions, and, as they neared the narrows between Victoria Island and Kowloon on the mainland opposite, Campbell's mind, ever alert to the possibility of disaster, turned to the rich prospects of a last-minute shambles: a junk cut in half by the frigate or, for that matter, a frigate cut in half by a supertanker. He muttered something to that effect out of the side of his mouth towards Ronnie.

'Not to worry, old son. Father isn't going to risk his promotion by dropping us in it now. It's only traffic. Like this all the time round here. Perpetual rush hour.'

The analogy of a busy crossroads was comforting. These things generally looked more alarming than they were. *Winchester*, fresh from the country, so to speak, from wide oceans where they might not see another ship for days or even weeks on end, could expect to feel herself a little overwhelmed, at least to begin with. As though to make the point, a medium-sized junk slid down the port side, only yards away, jinking between the frigate and her escorts.

'Cheeky sod,' said Ronnie.

'Take 'is name,' said Ken.

They forged on through late morning heat and haze, then, as the Hong Kong waterfront drew nearer, slowed down to a stately six knots or so. On a cream-coloured building overlooking a jetty, a tiny white ensign fluttered. Around and above it clustered the commercial might of Hong Kong, huge office blocks bright with neon signs in English and Chinese, and above them again rose the Peak, dark green and scarred with roads and scattered buildings and outcrops of rock. Campbell had not meant to be impressed, but was. A shot rang out, very close and loud. To his embarrassment, Campbell started.

'Not to worry,' said Ken. 'One of ours. Salute.'

'Do we?' said Campbell. 'Now?'

'No, doctor. Bob's gunners do.'

Blank after blank slammed its echoes round the harbour, then a saluting battery ashore began its reply, a twinkle of light and a spurt of smoke from the jetty under the white ensign preceding each report, as HMS *Tenebris* acknowledged the thunderous respects of HMS *Winchester*.

'Cloth-eared bloody gunners,' said Ronnie. 'Have us all

deaf. Just as well the yellow millions enjoy fireworks.' For some reason Campbell remembered a fragment of song to the effect that in Hong Kong they beat a gong and fired off a noonday gun.

As the last echoes faded, *Winchester* drew level with the buildings of the shore establishment, now very near, and slowed down further. The escorts, with a modesty befitting their small size, wooden construction and lowly status, hung back as the frigate prepared to make her entrance, on a tight turn round the jetty, into the sheltered basin of HMS *Tenebris*.

'Told you,' said Ronnie. 'Cornflower is the colour of the week . . . There they are. And all at the end of the jetty . . .' Ronnie was excited, and had almost ceased to pretend to be standing to attention. On Campbell's other side, Ken was still and silent. 'Oh yes. Yes,' said Ronnie. 'The son and heir's in grey shorts. And that's the little woman . . . cornflower, like half of 'em. And a big white hat.' Campbell got the impression that eight minutes spent talking with Mrs Parsons in Banjul did not constitute a serious threat to Ronnie's marriage.

Winchester swung slowly to port and nosed into the gap, preparing to come alongside the landward side of the jetty. There was an onshore wind that made the manoeuvre a little more interesting than it might otherwise have been. The ship slowed and for an awkward moment felt as if she might heel away from the jetty before a line could be got ashore. Two little tugs hovered nearby, like lady companions keeping an eye on a tipsy dowager. Their services were not required. A stream of wheel and engine orders brought the ship's head round. A leading seaman on the fo'c'sle swung and heaved, and a throwing line arched into the wind, fell and landed a comfortable six feet in from the edge of the jetty. A shore-based LEP in working blues pounced on it and hauled it in. HMS *Winchester* had arrived.

A band on the jetty struck up. Its members were small and neat, in pale khaki with black boots, hats and belts, and thin brown knobbly knees. Their instruments were for the most part those to be expected of a uniformed band, except that the euphonium and the drums looked, in comparison with their players, extraordinarily large, and, in addition to the usual drums, brass and woodwind, there was a variety of unusual percussion. Through the gong-noises, tinkles and half-musical crashes floated a melody eventually recognizable as 'Over the Sea to Skye', possibly the only remotely maritime item in the repertoire of the band of the Royal Hong Kong Police.

'How on earth did you manage without milk and papers and so on?'

'D'you know it rained for practically the whole of February and the garden was a sea of . . .'

'And, of course, you won't know about Boofy's puppies . . . well, how could you? But I didn't want to say it in a letter. Anyway, it must have been that awful . . .'

'You must be completely out of touch with things like the price of tomatoes.'

'Did you have to do lots of operations?'

'We saw a bit in the paper about you. "A British warship is in the area." We thought that must be you.'

'Darling, *please* stop doing that . . .'

'What was February like where you were?'

'I honestly couldn't have put up with her for a day longer . . . I know she *means* well . . .'

'They're actually very good at British food.'

'No thanks . . . Darling, please *stop* doing that or Mummy'll get cross.'

'No. We all have cabins downstairs.'

'I know you're most awfully brave about being seasick, but I did wonder . . .'

'It's just she always thinks something awful's happened if you forget her birthday.'

'I wouldn't have mentioned it unless I thought you'd all heard about it already, from Len's wife, but it *was* a bit difficult.'

'Kevin and Anthea weren't sick once. Well, except a little bit. Somewhere over India. Mainly Anthea.'

'*Darling*!'

'How're you doing, son . . . ? Get pissed. There's bound to

be another doc ashore. All your worries are over.'

'Thanks, Bob. Steady on.'

'Squeeze over here and meet the wife . . . Marion. Our doc. Young David. He's going to join properly.'

'Are you, David?'

'I . . .'

'Give Hong Kong a couple of months to work on you, doc.'

'Darling, if I've told you once I've told you a thousand times.'

'But what was that Banjul place actually like?'

'Tak!'

'Sah.'

The wardroom was extremely crowded. Children were few but, in the main, troublesome. There was room to stand but little room to move. Marion, Bob's wife, was tall, and had to stand half-stooped under a ventilation trunk slanting down from the deckhead. She was a teacher, and in her own words 'quite approved of Bob playing sailors'. This was her third trip to join him abroad, and she seemed very organized about it. She asked Campbell some of the more sensible of the usual questions, and he found himself trying to explain what he did in his copious free time. Somehow, preparing for the first part of the Fellowship examination had not figured as large in his programme as had been originally intended, but he told her about it anyway, then about the surgical job to which he was returning in a few more months. She asked about his contract and he explained to her how these things, in Edinburgh at least, were fixed up in the old-fashioned, gentlemanly tradition of 'my word is my bond', though confirmation in writing from Mr Gillon would no doubt arrive in due course. Then she asked him how he had enjoyed the trip out, and, having begun to talk about it, he realized that he must sound like someone who had just come back from an unexpectedly delightful holiday.

Not all the women in the wardroom were UK-based wives. There were four or five girls in white uniforms, two at least wearing the epaulettes of Wren officers. Without being visibly impolite (he hoped) to Bob's wife, Campbell had noticed that Henry and Ayres seemed to have succeeded in avoiding the details of British weather and the price of tomatoes by cornering a pair of them near the bar. He emptied his glass, then noticed it was empty. There was no steward in the vicinity. Bob was no longer around. Marion, perhaps sympathetic, suddenly said, 'Must have a word with Jane Huxley,' and picked her way into the crowd to the left. Campbell headed for the bar with his empty glass.

Ayres, looking out over the shoulder of the taller of the two uniformed girls, saw him coming. On the basis of what was visible from directly behind, Campbell decided that the taller girl was prettier, and took aim through the crowd accordingly. Her hair was short, wavy and very clean. Her neck was tanned and, as far as necks can be, pretty, and there were little curls growing forward under her ears. She wore the complicated black, gold and red shoulder insignia denoting a sister in Queen Alexandra's Royal Naval Nursing Service. As he got nearer, Campbell developed an odd feeling about her, with more to it, he thought, than a fair amount of gin on an empty stomach.

Ayres introduced them. 'Meet our sawbones. You might as well. Probably have to work with him. Sister . . . Um. This is . . .'

'David,' said Joan.

'Joan,' said David.

'Christ,' said the navigator. He was genuinely awestruck. While Joan and Campbell grinned inanely at each other, he shook his head and rolled his eyes upward. Harry, too, was most impressed, and had momentarily stopped talking to Joan's colleague. 'The Institute?' said Ayres.

Perhaps because they were both in uniform, Joan and Campbell did not kiss, hold hands or even touch each other. Joan looked older, or possibly just more grown up, and, if anything, prettier, probably because of her tan. She spoke first. 'I knew you were coming. In *Winchester*. You were on a list.'

'I didn't even know . . . How long've you been in the Mob?'

'Six months . . . You're nice and brown.'

'So are you. And you've had a hair cut.'

'I swim a lot.'

'What's it like?'

'Swimming?'

'No. Here.'

'Really super, David . . .' She paused. 'You'll like it. Gosh.'

'Lovely to see you.'

'Lovely to see *you*.'

There was a moronic and embarrassing pause, coinciding with a general silence in the wardroom at large. The navigator said, 'What are you drinking, doctor?'

'Hm?'

'Drink. A wet. Drinky-poos. What you came over for.' He was smiling and Henry was laughing.

'Oh . . . G and T, please.'

'Joan?'

'Tonic.'

'Henry?'

When their drinks arrived, Campbell and Joan somehow detached themselves from the rest and found themselves in the nearest thing the wardroom had at that time to a quiet corner. Briefly they held hands, with Campbell keeping a look out for the censorious beard of the first lieutenant, and feeling disturbingly randy at Joan's touch.

'You're looking really lovely.'

'You only say that when you want to . . .'

'Sssh,' said Campbell, glimpsing his commanding officer talking to a stern-looking woman, presumably his wife. 'This is a wardroom.'

'It's true though, isn't it?'

'And I do.'

'So do I.'

Their hands touched again, and Joan said, 'It's absurd.'

'What is?'

'Everyone in here must feel like that.'

'It's still a wardroom.'

Joan glanced round. Campbell found himself looking at her ears and wondering if they still tasted the same. Henry joined them, drunker than before, with a full glass in his hand.

'Doctor . . .'

'Henry?'

'Doctor, sir . . . and ma'am.'

'Yes, Henry.'

'Pray enlighten me . . . If I may presume to enquire . . .'

'What, Henry?'

'Was it childhood sweethearts?'

'Hm?'

'No,' said Joan.

'Oh. I see what you mean,' said Campbell.

'So it was a proper hospital romance.' Henry looked at them, took a long sip of his gin and tonic and said, ' "Nurse Masson tripped along the corridor of the surgical block, her usually pale cheeks aglow with anticipation . . . Dr Campbell, she knew for certain, was on duty in Scutari, the busiest ward in the hospital, that night." ' He was swaying a little.

'Something like that,' said Joan. 'Are you all right?'

'Fine,' said Henry. ' "Dr Campbell, the dashing young house intern who only a week previously had said to her 'Pass the forceps, nurse. This man will die if we do not act quickly.' " '

'That's more or less exactly what happened,' said Campbell.

'And it was the Institute?' said Henry, being his ordinary drunk self again.

'Yes,' said Joan and Campbell together.

'And you really know each other?'

'Yes,' they said.

'Lovely,' said Henry. 'Doctor, sir, you've fallen with your arse in the butter again. Sir.' He went away, shaking his head.

'Again?' said Joan. Campbell watched Henry's retreat, and across the wardroom noticed the first lieutenant bristling with interest. Over the top of a small thin lady's head, he too was watching Henry.

'Are you living on board?' said Campbell, refocusing on Joan.

'What?' she said, sounding lost.

'Oh. Sorry. You know what I mean. In the shore establishment here. On board ashore. In *Tenebris*.'

'Oh. I see what you mean. No. Gosh. Six months and I'm still learning the language. No. I'm RA.'

'What?'

'Resident Ashore.' They both smiled. 'In a flat with Robin.'

Campbell's heart sank. 'What does he do?'

'She. She's a Wren O. PA to A Sec.'

'Sometimes you speak it like a native.'

'She's nice. Madly in love with the CO of *Penningham*.'

'What's that?'

'Inshore sweeper. Small patrol boat, really. He's rather dashing.'

Campbell noticed her glass was empty. 'Drink?'

'No more thanks, David. Duty.'

'Today?'

'Yes. At *Tenebris* pool. There's a sort of swimming afternoon for any *Winchester* kids . . . whose parents want a bit of peace and quiet.'

'Really?' said Campbell. The Navy seemed to think of everything. 'Parents wanting a little time together . . .'

'Yes,' said Joan.

'To look round their married quarters, I suppose. Or just chat about the price of tomatoes.'

'That sort of thing.'

'Good for the Navy.' Campbell glanced round the wardroom. There was Ronnie and his Jenny. Would the son and heir be sent swimming whether he liked it or not? And there was the CO and his stern-looking hockey girl, Jane, and Bob and Marion, who were beginning to show unwardroomlike signs of wanting to be elsewhere, and the first lieutenant and his thin anxious-looking little wife who might be worth checking for thyrotoxicosis. Perhaps, in Joan's phrase, everyone *did* feel like that, and the Navy in its wisdom had decreed an appropriate half-holiday, with baby-sitting facilities as required. Campbell reached to take Joan's empty glass. Their hands touched.

'I'm on duty this afternoon,' said Joan, sounding rather casual about it, 'but we could meet later in *Tenebris* wardroom. There's usually tea at five.'

'I can hardly wait.'

'You better. Must go.'

*

Campbell collected another small gin and tonic to celebrate, in a cautious and preliminary way, what looked like an extraordinarily happy stroke of luck. Then he went across to join Jim and the navigator. As he did so it occurred to him that, after three months, there was now a sharp distinction in the wardroom between those who would live ashore, in married bliss or whatever, and those who, like Jim, Ayres, Henry and himself, would remain on board. They talked, but not about that.

Slowly the wardroom emptied. Shore-based guests, like Joan and her friends, had already for the most part left. Of the *habitués*, Ronnie and Bob had disappeared with their wives. The little woman who was presumed to be the first lieutenant's wife was standing on her own, waiting. Campbell wondered aloud to Ayres if someone ought not to go across and make light conversation.

'He won't be a minute,' said the navigator. 'He'll just be stopping Henry's leave then leaping ashore with the rest of them. Fast black taxi up the hill to the old married patch, then down to business and let the little woman have a proper look at the bedroom ceiling.' He spoke softly, his lips scarcely moving. No one laughed. The presumed Mrs Bowers turned towards them and smiled. The wardroom door opened and she was beckoned from outside. She left, smiling goodbye.

'Drink, doctor?' said Ayres.

Campbell's glass was half empty. 'No thanks. Had enough. What about lunch?'

'When the last of this lot goes, the duty stewards, boot-faced as hell at not getting up homers first day in, will throw us some bully beef and beans . . . Always the same. When half the wardroom's resident ashore, catering goes to rat-shit. They just let the end go. Have a drink, doc.'

'No thanks.'

Henry reappeared in the wardroom and joined them. 'Guess who's duty this weekend? And next.'

'Been a naughty boy?'

'Apparently so. Got bristled at. "Bit o' duty, keep you off the sherbet." But I'm not bloody duty today. Thanks, Jim. G and T. What about you, doc?'

'No thanks.'

'Sickbay ashore's got the weight.'
'I know.'
'So have another. A sharpener before lunch.'
'No thanks.'
'Why not.'
'I'm meeting someone . . . for tea.' It sounded lame, then a suspicion dawned that they might have guessed he was meeting someone for tea, and be conspiring, in a convivial expression of envy, to render him drunk and incapable.
'So?' said Ayres. 'Have a little drink before lunch.'
'Oh, all right.'
Ayres' face livened. 'What'll it be?'
'A tomato juice, thanks.'
'Fine . . . Tak! Bloody Mary for the doctor. Double vodka as usual.'
Campbell drank it anyway, with a what-the-hell feeling, but drank no more before lunch, which turned out to be sub-standard but not nearly as dire as predicted.

Afterwards he went down to the sickbay to see what had cone in the mail. As usual, the LMA had laid things out for him on the desk, with the *British Medical Journal* (four weeks' worth) on the left, the things that looked like routine drug-advertising bumph on the right, and items of possible interest or importance in the middle. There was only one letter in the middle. The envelope bore the crest of his teaching hospital, but was likely to be nothing more intriguing than yet another demand for settlement of a laundry bill from his residency days a year before. He opened it anyway.
It was not a laundry bill. The envelope contained a small sheet of notepaper headed 'The Royal Charitable Institute for the Care of the Indigent Sick' with 'Casualty Department' in slightly smaller letters below. Underneath that on the heading was 'Mr J. M. M. Gillon, Consultant in Charge'. It would be about his surgical job for November.
It was. It began 'Dear David' in J.G.'s handwriting and continued in typescript: 'As you read on you will doubtless be disappointed, but it is my difficult and painful duty to inform you that our provisional verbal agreement that you

should spend a year with us on the unit can no longer be regarded as extant.' It went on for a couple of paragraphs which Campbell did not read immediately. He left the desk and sat down in the little folding armchair Smith had secured to the operating table, and thought about Edinburgh and the Institute and then in some detail about Mr Gillon and his job. Two things stood out: one, that J.G. had a reputation, consciously cultivated and hitherto, so far as Campbell knew, entirely unblemished, for being a man of his word; and two, that the 'provisional verbal agreement' now discarded had been the outcome not of any specific effort or petition on Campbell's part, but had arisen from an initiative by Mr Gillon himself. Campbell had gone at the end of his six months in casualty to see him, to bow the knee, to make polite farewell noises and generally enact the vaguely tribal rituals that were an integral part of the Edinburgh medical scene, and had been surprised to find himself leaving the interview with an unsought but welcome offer of employment a year thence. His time with the Navy had been arranged accordingly, and his token efforts at relearning anatomy and clinical surgery had been undertaken as much with a view to impressing J.G. in November as to passing the primary surgical fellowship exam.

Now it had all gone for what the first lieutenant would have called 'a ball o' chalk'. Campbell sat glumly in the sickbay. The pre-lunch vodka began to bite, making him feel tired and a bit flat. The ship was still and quiet, with only the whir of the ventilation system, which, after three months mainly at sea, sounded like silence. It was darker than usual too, because *Winchester* lay starboard side to the jetty so that the sickbay scuttles looked out only to a moist, oily wall covered with black seaweed and barnacles.

Campbell's considered reactions were less simple than his immediate sense of disappointment. For a start, he had never felt entirely sure about a career in surgery. You spent a couple of years assisting with breasts, piles, hernias and varicose veins, then up to five years doing them on your own, and then, if you were lucky, an appointment committee agreed that you could do them for the rest of your life, with occasional light relief in an acute abdomen. He did not feel bereft of an avocation. It was more a sense of being left without a marker on the way ahead. J.G.'s job, the much-coveted senior house officer post in general surgery, had served Campbell as the only fixed point in his professional future, and now it had gone and was as if it had never been.

He got up and went back to the desk to read the letter to the end. 'Unfortunately my offer of the post to you was made when I was under a misapprehension. As you are doubtless aware, that SHO job is normally keenly contested and the year in question proved to be no exception. I had interviewed many highly qualified and motivated young men' – was that an oblique but perhaps valid criticism of the addressee? – 'and had come to a decision and made a firm offer to a candidate who will now after all be taking up the appointment. The misunderstanding which resulted in my provisional offer to you resulted from a failure of communication between myself and this candidate . . .' etc., etc. The letter ended with a lame, curiously haughty and contorted apology, and a conventional assurance that Campbell could always rely on his old casualty chief for a good reference should he ever need one.

Campbell screwed the letter up and threw it in the waste paper bin then, on second thoughts, fished it out and smoothed it flat again. It had a certain curiosity value, as the record of a painful and conspicuous lapse by a man of honour, and might serve as a useful reminder of the uncertainties of life on the greasy pole of hospital medicine. He locked it away in a desk drawer to which only he had the key. LMA Smith, though a close and trustworthy colleague, had no cause to know of his disappointment.

Returning to the armchair, Campbell sat down. It was all rather complex, but at least Joan would understand. She knew him, the Institute and Mr Gillon. She would say sensible things, such as 'You never wanted to be a surgeon anyway,' and 'You'd get bored listening to his war stories again and again over the hernias.' He would tell her about it as casually as possible, and see how she responded. And he was going to see her at five o'clock.

*

Now that she had popped up so unexpectedly halfway round the world from where he had last seen her, Campbell was only a little surprised to find himself taking her for granted already. Over the eighteen or twenty months of its edxistence, their relationship did not reflect very creditably on him. She had treated him better than he had generally treated her, but she did not seem to hold that against him. They had met when she was a first-year staff nurse on the ward where he was a houseman, at comparable stages in their careers, except that Joan knew her way around the ward and its workings much better than Campbell did, at least to begin with. He had found himself depending on her, because she was uncomplainingly and unconspicuously helpful, and had never succumbed to the temptation, irresistible to many of her frailer sisters in the second oldest profession, to make herself look clever by making the houseman look foolish. Then he had noticed she was quite pretty, as well as being efficient and good-humoured, and they had played odd little games on the ward to make time together. Then, after one drink in a pub somewhere, which had probably been Campbell's idea, she had invited him up to her flat for a coffee he still hadn't had, and seduced him with that same cheerful tact and competence that characterized all her clinical work.

For several months they had been together, comfortable and habitual. When he was off duty he slept at her flat, when he was on she slept in the Residency. If she had to get up at seven to go on an early duty, she phoned him at eight to make sure he didn't sleep in. Sometimes, in contravention of a tiresome Institute rule, she even did his morning bloods for him. On the ward they never touched each other, except as though by accident, and always addressed each other by their correct professional titles. Between them, and despite a dotty and incompetent ward sister, they ran things to everyone's satisfaction. Even old Creech seemed a little less sepulchral when he went round his patients with Campbell and Joan.

When she got appendicitis and was admitted to a surgical ward, he had proved negligent and unfaithful, and there had been a long gap. By contrast, when he was recovering from hepatitis she was around, agreeably involved, even active in his convalescence, but not oppressively so. Then they had somehow come adrift again. He could not recall having said goodbye to her, but had heard that she had left the Institute. How kind and how typical of her to turn up here just when he needed her. It occurred to him that, when he went ashore to meet her for tea, he should probably take his toothbrush.

He got up from the armchair. It was quarter past two. On the spur of the moment he decided to change into plain clothes and go for a walk through the naval base and out into the town, to take a first look at the place, buy some postcards and have a quiet civilian coffee on his own somewhere. He tidied the desk by dumping the still unopened BMJs and drug adverts in the waste paper bin, and walked up to the far end of the sickbay, reflecting again on the professional responsibilities of the voyage out.

No one had died. No one had been seriously ill. He had been furthest extended by some tricky suturing on variously lacerated sailors (the most memorable of whom was an obscene Glaswegian, the ship's butcher, who had split open all four fingers of his left hand while hacking pork chops in a gale and a half off Ceylon; afterwards, when Campbell asked him if it hurt, he had grimaced and said, 'Honest tae Christ, sir, it's throbbin' like a nun's cunt'). None of the nightmares of medicine afloat – head injuries, contagious fevers or serious abdominal problems – had occurred. He had been called to advise on the chlorination of fresh water (and got it wrong); he had identified creepy crawlies from a condemned batch of flour; he had signed innumerable immunization certificates; he had pronounced on sprained ankles and the clap. And he had continued to maintain a good working relationship with Smith the LMA, who, on the further evidence afforded by three months at sea, could almost certainly have managed the whole thing by himself. What the rather florid phrasing of his commission termed 'especial trust and confidence' remained more or less intact, as much by luck as by skill or judgement.

He was looking at himself in the mirror above the wash-basin, and deciding that uniform quite suited him, when there was a knock at the door. Jim opened it slightly and said, 'Visitor, doc.'

'Come in.'

Jim stayed outside, simply holding the door open for another officer in uniform, and disappeared. The visitor was a short tubby man wearing the badges of rank of a surgeon commander.

'Sir,' said Campbell, half standing to attention.

'Dr Campbell?' said the surgeon commander. 'I'm Dr Watson, from *Tenebris* . . . Sorry to . . . um . . . ambush you like this, but what I've come about . . . has to be handled with . . . tact and some despatch.'

'Please sit down, sir.'

'Thank you, Dr Campbell.'

In his hand the man held a file marked HIGHLY CONFIDENTIAL, a phrase which did not appear in the officially sanctioned spectrum of vocabulary for degrees of naval secrecy, but a surgeon commander who introduced himself as 'Dr' might be capable of any enormity. He sat down in the armchair, and Campbell sat at the desk.

'I'm afraid there's been a . . . most unholy balls-up . . .' He sat with his knees pressed together, his file clasped to his chest and his lips slightly pursed. 'About you.'

'Me, sir?'

'Yes, Dr Campbell . . . Unfortunately for you. Or perhaps fortunately. Depends on how you look at these things.'

'A . . . balls-up, sir?'

'Yes, Dr Campbell. Affecting you. But in no way attributable to you. Or anyone in *Winchester*, I hasten to stress.' Dr Watson was agitated and a little pink. He paused and shifted his file on to his knees. Campbell started to ask a question just as his visitor was about to continue his explanation. That confusion was followed by a longer pause, then Campbell said, 'What's happened?'

'Well,' said the surgeon commander, shifting in his seat, 'nothing's *happened*. But there's been a most ghastly muddle . . . Well, perhaps I should say a considerable muddle. Considerable, shall we say, but not uncontainable. Which is why I've come to see you myself.'

'I see,' said Campbell, to make him feel more comfortable. 'Some sort of naval muddle?'

'Well, no. Not exactly. If it were a *naval* muddle it wouldn't be such a problem. It's more of a *branch* muddle.'

'Branch muddle?'

'Yes, Dr Campbell. Medical branch. Definitely a branch muddle. And I'd like, if possible, to keep it that way. That's why we didn't do this by signal three weeks ago.'

Campbell was now in no doubt that fate had another large gesture in store. Having found Joan in Hong Kong and lost a job in Edinburgh within the space of two hours, he should, he reflected, have been prepared for a little more. He sat not knowing whether he wished this man would get on with it and tell him or not. There was another long pause. The visitor was, by the standards of the naval medical service, a very odd fish. He seemed excessively sensitive to bureaucracy in disarray. Most naval doctors had a breezily piratical approach to administration and its frequent lapses. This chap was more like the sort of obsessional civil servant who would worry about losing a paperclip. While the bearer of the bad (or good) news fumbled for a form of words, Campbell reminded himself that people who can't take a joke shouldn't join the Navy.

'It started with a signal about you,' he said very quickly, as though having determined to make a clean breast of things. 'Six weeks after the unfortunate business of Surgeon Rear Admiral Wallwark-Waring.'

On Campbell's first day in Portsmouth Barracks as a green surgeon subby, a chief petty officer called Brown had told the class that if you wanted to be an admiral you had to have a funny name, and had cited several examples to illustrate the point. He had not, so far as Campbell could remember, mentioned a Surgeon Rear Admiral Wallwark-Waring, who certainly added strength to his case. Dr Watson had stopped again. Campbell prompted him gently. The business had become as difficult as getting a proper story out of a shy sailor with his first dose.

'Admiral Wallwark-Waring?' he murmured.

'Yes . . . Just before Christmas.'

'Just before Christmas?'

'Most unfortunate. Almost certainly an accident. Jolly old chap. But if someone falls over the bannister of the eighth floor at the Ministry of Defence people always talk . . . However, in his case it was almost certainly an accident. His

A Sec said he was *sliding* down the bannister on his way home after the office party . . .'

'Sliding down the eighth-floor bannister?'

'Yes. Most unfortunate.'

'I see . . . But . . .'

'Well, old Wobbly – he was called that because of his initials, obviously – old Wobbly . . . Wobbly was not . . . what one could call . . . methodical.'

'Was he the appointer?'

'Yes. Yes, of course. Didn't I say so?'

'Um. Not yet, sir.'

'Gosh yes. He was the appointer. Desk in an awful muddle. Taken months to sort out. And in the middle of it all I got this signal. Branch only. About you.' He had opened his file and extracted the uppermost piece of paper from a sheaf held in a spring clip. 'You might as well read it.'

The signal, a standard layout of smudgy purple type, began with the customary Martian paragraph of address groups and teleprinter hiccups. The first comprehensible line read 'Medical staff in strict confidence'. It went on in proper naval signalese, laconic and enumerated, '(1) Campbell DG Surg Lt RNR. (2) This offr expected Chatham Sickbay end Jan. (3) No record of current posting. (4) Any information welcome.'

'I see,' said Campbell.

'That's it,' said his visitor, taking back the signal. 'You . . . um . . . shouldn't be here. It's all most awfully embarrassing. But so far a strictly branch matter. No reason why it shouldn't remain so. I think we'd all be . . . most grateful if you'd refrain from discussing the detailed background to your draft with non-medical colleagues.'

'My draft?'

'Chatham. Wednesday . . . I'm most awfully sorry . . . Or perhaps you have some friends or relatives there?'

'I don't think I do,' said Campbell.

'Poor old Wobbly,' said Dr Watson. 'Everyone's been most awfully decent and loyal about tidying things up.' He rose to leave. 'You're the last, I gather . . . I am sorry.'

'Flight details? That sort of thing?' said Campbell.

'All fixed, you'll be glad to hear. Come and see me

tomorrow in *Tenebris*. Then you'll have a day to sort things out and hand over to the chap who should have come out in *Winchester*. He'll be terribly pleased. Been kicking his heels here for nearly a month. Well . . . Sorry about all this, Dr Campbell . . . Inevitably, in a complex organization . . .'

Without appearing to be hastening his visitor's departure, Campbell opened the door for Dr Watson, ushered him out, and saw him to the gangway. Then he went down to the wardroom. Henry and Ayres, who had split a bottle of hock over lunch, were now at the brandy stage. Campbell joined them for a large Remy Martin.

'How awful for you.'

'I was a bit surprised.'

'The day after tomorrow?'

'If that's Wednesday.'

'Oh, David.'

Joan sounded quite upset, which made it worse. They were sitting in the lounge of the *Tenebris* wardroom, a cool first-floor room looking out on to the waterfront and the view across the harbour to Kowloon. Campbell had changed into civilian clothes. Joan was still in uniform. 'Did they tell you why?'

'Some sort of nonsense in the Madhouse,' said Campbell gloomily. All self-respecting seagoing naval officers referred to the Ministry of Defence as the Madhouse. 'I should have gone straight to Chatham after Iceland. But no one told me, and no one knew where I was.'

'We've had a spare doctor here for a couple of weeks. No one would really say why.'

'He's getting *Winchester*,' said Campbell, feeling suddenly possessive. 'And I'm getting bloody Chatham.'

'There were rumours . . .' Joan came a little closer over the tea things, pausing as an LEP steward floated silently past. 'A chap in the appointer's office?'

'The appointer,' said Campbell, glancing at a stout commander evidently asleep under the *Telegraph*. 'I thought I'd be here for a couple of weeks at least. More if I was lucky.'

'We've got a couple of days,' said Joan. She finished her

cup of tea. 'So come on. I'll take you on a quick whiz round. A condensed version of the standard tour . . . But I want to get out of this lot first.' She patted the large unflattering white skirt of her uniform. 'I'm fed up with the Navy this afternoon.'

'Me too. Can I come and watch?' The slumbering *Telegraph* stirred a little and Joan giggled. 'Come on. I've got Robin's car. She's off somewhere in a Lancia.' They got up. Their faces passed close together. 'David. Have you been drinking?'

'The condemned man had a stiff brandy. He needed it.'

They walked out of the wardroom block into blinding sunshine. Robin's car was a traffic-scarred Beetle, mainly red. It wouldn't start. Joan talked to it. 'Come on. Come on, Lily.'

'Lily?'

'Lillimarlene, actually. And she does better if we talk to her.' Campbell remembered that most Wren O's had cars with silly names. It started second time and they chugged from the wardroom inland along the wall of the basin in which *Winchester* had at last found rest. The ship looked small but smart, with awnings rigged and a few seamen, presumably men under punishment, working on the upper scupper. Again Campbell felt the pang of impending homelessness.

At *Tenebris* gate the sentry was checking the ID card of an incoming driver. Though not anything like as formidable as that of HMS *Nemesis*, the guardroom, wall and gate had a purposeful air, probably enough to stop a half-hearted Hong Kong riot, even if they did not look like ever amounting to much against the might of mainland China. Through the outer office Campbell could see a long corridor of cells. A sailor in shabby detention blues was mopping the floor.

The sentry turned his attention to the VW, smiled at Joan, saluted and beckoned them on. Outside the gate was Hong Kong which, to the casual observer, looked like Manhattan with Chinamen. Campbell rubber-necked unashamedly.

'It's great, David,' said Joan. 'I wish you were here for ages.' He reached out and squeezed her hand, and they almost ran over an old lady in black pyjamas. 'We're up in

Mid-Level. Where the poor whites live. Five minutes. Maybe a bit longer. And if this heap dies, we'll take a taxi.'

'Is it all like this?' Campbell asked over the engine noise as they started up the hill.

'A bit here, and a bit more on the other side. Kowloon's something else. But bits of it are quite country. And the tourist traps are fun.' They passed a department store a block long whose windows would have put Princes Street to shame, and probably would have been good in London. In the next block was a bank with a turbaned Sikh holding a long, Khyberish rifle sitting in the doorway. Then at some traffic lights a tiny man pushed a vanload of vegetables, somehow suspended on a bicycle, slowly past them.

The road curved up out of the business section, and on to the beginnings of the Peak. On their right, downhill from the road, about a thousand labourers, rushing around like spiders on a web of bamboo scaffolding at least twenty storeys high, kept up the onward march of progress with another addition to the skyline. Across the water was another city, in places as high but stretching much further, and between them the ferries passed, shuttling across the busy narrows that had so alarmed Campbell that morning. The gradient got steeper and the car's original gurgle had risen to an anguished, despairing roar. 'Don't worry,' said Joan. 'Nearly there. That's us.'

'That?'

'Yes. Fifteen storeys. Quite cosy by local standards. And we've got the top. Nice roof too. We're very brown.'

'I noticed.' He reached out for her hand again. She ignored it, slowing down and manoeuvring off the road on to a spiral ramp leading to an underground parking space. There were only a few cars in it, and no people. Joan switched the engine off. Campbell took her hand again. This time she did not ignore him. They kissed. Campbell nuzzled her neck, scratching his ear on the braid of her shoulder board. Joan made a happy little noise, then said, 'We're too old for necking in cars,' and straightened up, reached over into the back seat for her regulation QARNNS handbag – tropical version, white kid leather – and opened the door.

*

As Campbell had suspected, from what she had said about the roof, Joan was brown all over. He told her it suited her.

'Why don't you sunbathe properly in ships,' she asked, fingering his white bit.

'Because we don't,' said Campbell, trying to imagine what the first lieutenant would have had to say about her suggestion. Probably something crude and vivid, along the lines of 'because we don't want a lot of so-called officers and gentlemen forgettin' themselves and endin' up playin' daisy chains with the midshipmen'.

They had made love unceremoniously, as soon as they had entered the flat. With a post-coital gin and tonic in his hand, Campbell sat on the sofa looking out at yet another Hong Kong view.

'Gosh.'

'What, David?'

'The ship. You can see it.' *Winchester*, a toy in the distance, lay snug in the toy harbour of the *Tenebris* basin.

'Are you getting gloomy?'

'No.'

'Really, David?'

'Well . . . Seeing you . . . and . . . seeing you is amazing and tremendous and almost makes up for the rest of it.'

'Thank you kindly, sir.'

'But, if I couldn't take a joke, I'd think the rest was pretty bloody awful.'

'Come on. You shouldn't even *be* here. And you've had three months of fun that was meant for someone else. I mean coming out here.'

'I suppose so. And who wants to be a surgeon anyway?'

'Listening to all those boring old war stories . . .'

'. . . cobbling up hernia after hernia . . .'

'. . . day in day out . . .'

'. . . for years and years and years . . .'

'And of course Chatham might be bliss.'

'Might be.'

'And Hong Kong's super.'

'Worth at least twenty-four hours. If not thirty-six.'

'Which is about all we've got,' said Joan, sittinr up from where she had been lying with her head in his lap. 'So what do you want to do?'

'Right now?'

'Yes.'

'Finish my drink and go to bed.'

'David . . .'

'It's a carefully thought out decision about the quality of life. In fact why don't we just stay in bed for thirty-six hours?'

'Because it seems rather a long time.'

'I don't think so. You don't know how bad my quality of life's been recently . . .'

'Poor David.' She put her head in his lap again. 'But . . .'

'Come on.'

'Perhaps we should discuss it again . . . in about ten minutes.'

'Maybe fifteen,' said Campbell, distinctly cheered.

Joan twisted round to look up at him. 'Then we could have a quick coffee here and a whiz round the island when it's cooler but before it's dark . . .'

'Ideal.'

Campbell was beginning to find the sofa a bit prickly. Joan lay against him, warm and perspiring despite the air-conditioning. Their clothes were scattered around on the floor, beginning, just inside the door, with Joan's uniform and Campbell's tie. A detective, working from the pattern of distribution of the male and female articles of apparel, would have correctly deduced that they had more or less raped each other.

'Come on then.'

'Oh, all right . . . Gosh, sex and the single bed?'

''fraid so. Come on, David. You know what the Navy's like.'

'Oh, I'm not complaining.'

'Good.'

'That's nice . . .'

'That?'

'Yes . . . That . . . Mm . . . Keep doing it.'

Joan kept doing it, until some further progression seemed in order, then they lay down, with Campbell on the outside, just as they had done in his single bed in the Residency at the Institute. He put his arms round her, astonished again at her nearness and the easiness of everything they did together. She kissed him on the mouth, firmly, almost innocently to begin with, then gradually changed to wet, tonguing movements that drew Campbell into a friendly vortex of lust, an eyes-closed world of touch and thrill and moist smooth lips. Thirty-six hours would be a good start, thought Campbell, snugly encompassed, with Joan's hands roaming over his spine and ribs, and her tongue still rippling against his. She softened somehow in his arms, lay uncertainly under him as though waiting for a sneeze, then thrust up against him again and again, gasping half-words, then lying still. He waited, then whispered in her ear, 'Feeling better now?'

'Yes, thank you, doctor . . . Let me go on top.'

Later they were looking at a wine list.

'The Australian hock's supposed to be all right,' said Joan in her helpful voice.

'. . . comparing favourably with a Welsh claret,' Campbell quoted from a classic TV sketch. Joan laughed. They were in a floating restaurant, moored off a village at the back of the island called, for some reason, Aberdeen. Joan's condensed tour had consisted of a noisy, sometimes frightening gallop round the colony in her flatmate's crumbling VW: a two-hour spectacular of East and West, of affluence and busy poverty, of colonial fragments and the brave new business world of Hong Kong. They had roared through the tunnel under the harbour and popped up in Kowloon. They had ventured cautiously past the last knobbly-kneed policeman in the free world to look through a fence at three Communist ducks swimming in a rice paddy. They had returned to Victoria Island and done Wanchai in the early evening, sampling two of its dozens of nightspots. In one, a plastic Bavarian bierkeller, a jazz band composed of off-duty British sergeants played passable fifties big band numbers for half a dozen customers. In the other, a classic dim and sultry den called the Seventh Sea, accompanied gentlemen such as Campbell were the exception. Spotty, lonely-looking US conscripts sat in dim corners with dangerous-looking hostesses, perhaps trying to forget Vietnam.

The floating restaurant had been another of Joan's ideas. It looked like the product of miscegenation between a pagoda and a Mississippi showboat, and was anchored with half a dozen others off the curiously-named fishing village. They had parked their car, walked across a vast wobbling raft of jam-packed sampans, hiring one of the outermost to take them the last few hundred yards over the sea to dine.

The menu offered several hundred variations on fish and rice with local sauces, and a children's corner of steak and ice-cream, presumably added with the Americans in mind. In the middle of the dining deck was a large glass tank crowded with sluggish, world-weary fish. A waiter with a net, directed by a customer, was groping in its cloudy water. They watched.

'You can choose fish from the tank if you want,' said Joan.

'Hm. Perhaps not.'

'Seems cruel, somehow.'

'I know what you mean. Silly, isn't it. Yes. Let's have pre-killed fish instead.' They ate and talked. There was a lot to talk about. The hock was much better than Campbell expected. They left the restaurant at about ten o'clock and went back to Joan's flat.

In the middle of the night Campbell was wakened by someone knocking loudly and insistently on a door. Joan did not stir. Campbell lay for a moment wondering if he should get up and answer it, then he heard other doors opening, footsteps within the flat and a curt conversation between a male and a female voice. The bedroom door opened and a little blonde girl in a kimono came in. Campbell sat up. Joan woke slowly.

'Are you Doc Campbell?' said the blonde girl.

'Sir.' A tall youth pushed past her. 'Sir, it's hellish urgent.' It was Henry. He switched on the light. Campbell blinked. Joan sat up, rubbing her eyes. Henry gaped at her.

'What's up, Henry? What's happening?'

'From number one, sir. To the ship. At the rush. I've got a *Tenebris* mini . . . Really at the rush.'

Campbell got up and started to pull on some clothes, not

bothering about socks and underpants. The blonde left. 'You know medical guard is from *Tenebris* tonight, Henry?'

'Yessir. So does number one. He wants you.'

Joan had pulled a sheet round herself. 'Oh, David . . . Please phone me whenever it's over. Or at *Tenebris*, if it's tomorrow.' Henry and Campbell rushed out of the flat across the landing to the lift.

'Thank Christ for that.'

'What?'

'The lift . . . Not closing up and going away. I've got a mini with a hell of a driver.'

For the first few seconds after Henry's summons Campbell had felt guilty. Somehow, he thought, he had broken some rule and the first lieutenant, like the all-seeing, all-knowing all-disapproving god of Campbell's childhood, had sussed him out and sent a messenger of his wrath with a summons to judgement. In the lift Campbell asked again what was going on. Henry mumbled something about urgent, but sort of need to know for now. He looked a bit shifty, and tired, and worried. To Campbell's surprise, his hair was wet. Campbell still felt slightly guilty, but still was unable to find any rational grounds for doing so. He was off duty, *Tenebris* had the weight of being medical guard, and he had punctiliously rung the quartermaster to let the ship know where he was, even leaving a phone number for his brief period of residence ashore. That too was odd. Why hadn't they just rung him? (The answer to that was probably something to do with transport: he would get to the ship most quickly in the manner proposed.) And if it was medical, why hadn't they simply roused the *Tenebris* duty doctor? Campbell decided it was probably a medical problem, perhaps not as urgent as the summons suggested (things very rarely were) and that, for reasons not yet determined, someone in authority wanted to keep it 'purely a ship matter'.

The lift stopped and Henry propelled Campbell out into the street, where a Royal Navy minicar was waiting with its engine revving. An LEP driver threw open the passenger door, Henry dived into the back and the car had started to move even before Campbell was properly inside. He groped for the seat belt as a matter of urgency. The driver, thin and silent, slouched back and drove like a maniac down the hill. They careered through four or five red lights in town, swept past the *Tenebris* sentry, who was waiting with his barrier open, then screeched round the edge of the basin, tyres howling in the night at each turn, and gathered frightening speed for the home straight, the jetty where *Winchester* lay. Helplessly, Campbell wondered if he were going to spoil it all now by drowning them. He didn't, but skidded to a halt neatly opposite the quarterdeck. Jim and the bosun's mate stood waiting at the top of the gangway. The clock on the front of the desk showed half past two.

Campbell ran up on to the ship, not sure where he was heading for, and forgot to salute. The bosun's mate saluted him anyway. For a moment Campbell stood, feeling stupid, then looked to Jim, who was still officer of the day, for guidance.

'Sickbay, doc. At the rush.'

He ran to the screen door and stumbled down the companionway, then aft to his place of duty. The door was closed. He opened it to enter and get on with whatever it was, but it stuck firmly after two inches. The first lieutenant's face appeared in the opening. 'Oh. You, doc. Come on in.' The sickbay seemed busy, but it was not immediately clear what was going on. The first lieutenant, dressed in an unlikely orange silk dressing gown with purple dragons, explained. He looked more upset than Henry. 'I think he's a goner, doc.'

'Who?'

'Your killick. The LMA.'

'Christ. Let me . . .'

Martindale, the leading regulator, stood back from the operating table. On it a pale naked supine figure lay outstretched. A man in uniform, the duty PO, a stoker, bent closely over the head. He was doing the right thing, breathing expired air into the lungs of the victim at a steady rate of twelve per minute. No doubt Martindale, equally well versed in first aid, had been compressing the lower third of the sternum at sixty a minute to maintain circulation. Campbell had no idea how long they had been at it.

'May I see, PO?'

The duty senior rate straightened up. LMA Smith was

dead. His pupils were wide and unresponsive, his face and body deathly pale under the tan. As a formality, Campbell felt for his carotid pulse, then reached out for the stethoscope and listened for heart sounds. There was nothing, but he kept listening, not so much because some faint chance remained, but rather more to set a final seal on things and to convince the first-aiders that all was indeed lost. As he listened, stooped over the corpse, Campbell's eyes passed with a curious disbelief over Smith's face, now setting in death. There were a number of oddities about the corpse, even from this limited inspection. There was a contused laceration just under the left ear, and an abrasion on the chin. The corpse was definitely damp, not just cold, and the dark curly hair was wet.

'Goner, doc?'said the first lieutenant.

'Yessir,' said Campbell. The man who had been breathing into Smith's mouth turned and vomited into the washbasin. Henry, too, went pale. 'What happened, sir?'

'Need to know for now, doc. And I want 'im on ice. That OK by you, doc?'

'I . . .'

'We got plenty of ice. Specially kept for this sort of thing.'

'Couldn't we . . .'

The first lieutenant interrupted Campbell again. 'Right then. Like doc said, party's over. Thanks, Reggy. Thanks, Stokes. Points for trying. And keep your traps shut. Right?'

'Sir,' said the regulator, who was in his usual shipboard dress of blue underpants only. The PO stoker turned from the washbasin, still wiping his mouth with a paper towel. 'Stokes?' said the first lieutenant.

'Sir.' He followed the regulator out. The first lieutenant locked the door from the inside. The three officers stood round the corpse on the operating table. There was another short silence, during which Campbell noticed something else. There was a black rubber wet-suit lying on the sickbay deck, half under the cot bed aft of the operating table. Certain hypotheses began to arrange themselves around the circumstances of Smith's death.

'Same goes for you two,' said the first lieutenant. 'There's goin' to be the mother and father of all official fusses in due course, and then you can chuck in your tuppenceworths, but for now you can carry on sittin' on your tongues.' He looked particularly closely at Henry as he spoke, then turned to Campbell. 'Right, doc?'

'Yessir . . . I'm sorry I wasn't on board . . . Might have been more use if I'd got here earlier.'

'Don't think so. Looked like a stiff when I set eyes on 'im . . . How d'you fix one of those post-mortem jobs, doctor? Quietly.'

To Campbell's knowledge there was no such thing as a black-market in post-mortems. If the first lieutenant wanted that sort of information without too many people getting to know too much, arrangements could be made for the sort of post-mortem that normally followed death in suspicious circumstances. They were discreet but not obtrusively so. 'There's a British Military Hospital here, isn't there?'

'Kowloon side,' said number one.

'I should think they'd do it. Army pathologists.'

'Then they'd have to keep their traps shut. Sounds ideal. Will 'e keep?'

'Sorry, sir. Will he . . . ?'

'Till tomorrow. Will he be all right in here? Or should we break out the medical ice and keep him in it?'

'Be all right in here till tomorrow, sir. Perhaps we should turn the air-conditioning on full, to be on the safe side. Only a few hours.'

The first lieutenant glanced at Campbell as though he were complaining about working after midnight, then said, 'And you're sure 'e's dead.'

Campbell hesitated. 'Dead. Yes. Dead enough to give up trying to resuscitate him, sir.' In that company and that hour it would not have been politic to go into the subtleties of brain-damaged survival, so Campbell left it at that. The first lieutenant bristled his beard slightly. 'D'you want to check, doc? Don't want the bugger creating even more embarrassment than he already has.'

Campbell went over to the desk and picked up the ophthalmoscope and looked into Smith's eyes. The blood in the little arteries in the retina had begun to coagulate, which was the most certain clinical sign of death, short of rigor mortis.

As he looked he also ran a finger over the wound behind the corpse's ear. It was not simply a contused laceration. Under it there was a small but definite depressed skull fracture.

'All right, doc?'

'Yessir.' Campbell straightened up. The first lieutenant was looking at him closely, almost suspiciously. 'I just want to know he's dead,' he said. 'Cause of death and all that can wait till morning.' Henry glanced from the corpse, to the first lieutenant, to Campbell.

'What about his next of kin, sir?' said Campbell.

'Good question, doc. Doc, d'you mind hanging on for a bit? Father's on his way in. If that chokey hasn't landed them both in the hoggin. You can wait in the wardroom. I'm goin' to get meself dressed.' He unlocked the door and ushered them out. As he locked the door again from the outside he muttered, 'This is no time to be lookin' like Madam Butterfly.'

There was a pot of coffee in the wardroom pantry, left over from dinner. Campbell warmed some up while Henry sat subdued, sometimes biting his lower lip. Presumably the first lieutenant's injunction to silence about the death of Smith included a prohibition on talking to each other, and there was little else to talk about. From Henry's manner, from the suspicion that both he and the LMA had been diving, and from the marks of violence on the corpse, a very nasty set of possibilities opened out. Campbell began to wonder if he were in some sense keeping watch on Henry, and thought about it, and decided he wasn't. If the first lieutenant had meant that, he would not only have said so but almost certainly he would have got someone else to do the job. And he would not have sent Henry out into the city to fetch him. Henry sat drinking his coffee, looking as if he wanted to talk but felt he shouldn't. Eventually he said, 'Sorry to spoil your first night ashore, doc.'

'It's all right. Queen pays you twenty-four hours a day and all that.'

Henry smiled. 'Nice girl, Sister Whatsit.' It was a statement, not a question. Campbell agreed, and began to wonder how soon he could get back to Joan. It depended on how long the CO kept him on board, and there was also a transport problem. No official mini would be available for the return journey. Then he realized there was yet another problem. He did not even know Joan's address. Then he had an idea. 'Henry . . .'

'What, doc?'

'Where does she live?'

'What?'

'What's her address . . . ? Have you got her address?'

Henry looked at him and laughed wanly. 'Hang on. It's here somewhere . . .' He fished out a scrawled piece of paper. 'That's supposed to be Havelock Heights,' he said. 'Havelock Heights. Mid-Level. You going to get a taxi back?'

'Thought I might . . . Soon as I can.'

'I bloody would if I were you,' said Henry, with sudden liveliness. Campbell smiled, then remembered the LMA. 'Ghastly business . . . with Smith.'

'Yes.' There was a long silence. Campbell got up and poured himself another cup of coffee. 'Want some, Henry?'

'No thanks, doc. No. Yes, I will. Must say I wouldn't mind a drink.'

'Might not be a good idea if we're waiting for father.'

'Sure.' Henry sat up. 'Bar's closed anyway . . . D'you feel cold, doc? Or is it just me?'

'Not particularly.'

'Right, men?' The first lieutenant, in uniform now, summoned them from the wardroom door. 'Father's got 'ere. Wants to talk to both of you. Henry first. And nothing in writing at this stage.'

Campbell followed Henry and the first lieutenant up the two companionways from the wardroom to the CO's cabin, and stood outside on his own for quite a long time, while Henry's voice, irritatingly inaudible, answered equally inaudible questions from the CO, with occasional noises from number one. After a while he stopped trying to listen and began to wonder again how Smith had died. The various bits of information – that he had met with violence, that both he and Henry (and perhaps others) had been underwater and that number one was giving it all a very high security classification – did not fit together at all well. The phrase 'diving accident' sprang to mind, but it obscured things rather than explained them.

Smith had, to Campbell's certain knowledge, done quite a lot of sport diving, but was not one of the ship's officially recognized divers. Henry was the diving officer, and in that capacity had overall responsibility for all official underwater activities. If any authorized diving had been going on earlier in the night, medical cover should have been available on board. Only two people could have provided this and, of them, Campbell had been snug ashore with Joan, and Smith was dead. It was possible that Smith had dived with the team for which he should have been providing sickbay cover on board, and met with some accident while unofficially under water. If he had, that was awkward, but hardly a reason for a major clamp-down of the sort the first lieutenant was now demanding. These things did not hang together. Campbell stood looking at the ship's trophies and the wardroom mess silver in their cabinet outside the CO's door. He now felt cold and wished that nothing out of the ordinary had happened, that Smith were still alive and that he himself were comfortably back in bed with Joan.

The captain's door opened and Henry slouched out, shaking his head. As he passed Campbell he muttered a lower-deck oath that also served, in happier times, as a wardroom joke. Campbell stood alone again, waiting.

'Doctor!'

'Sir.'

The captain and the first lieutenant were standing side by side in uniform, facing the door. Campbell felt out of place. Uniform and a hat would have been useful, and even socks and underpants would have helped. The captain looked at him with some surprise, and he realized he still had the stethoscope hanging round his neck. He took it off and stuffed it into his pocket.

'Please sit down, doctor,' said the captain, passing behind Campbell to the door, and looking out into the little passageway to check for eavesdroppers. Campbell chose a high uncomfortable chair beside the CO's desk.

'Why not have an armchair?'

'Thank you, sir.' Campbell got up and sat down in one that was both lower and softer than expected, a chair which made it impossible to sit loosely to attention as he had intended. The first lieutenant waited, still standing, until the captain said 'Number one,' at which he sat smartly and stiffly on a bench seat under the after porthole. The captain sat down last. Seated, both were still well above Campbell in his armchair. Both were facing him again.

'Well, doctor . . .' The captain paused and put his head slightly to one side, like a dog hearing a strange noise. 'A very odd, sad business . . . I gather there was no real chance . . .'

'Evidently not, sir. First-aiders did the right things, but unfortunately . . .'

'Quite . . . And you're certain he's dead.'

'Completely, sir. I mean completely certain.'

'One hears of people waking up in mortuaries . . .'

'I'm sure he's dead, sir.'

The captain pursed his lips. 'That . . . sort of simplifies things . . . Probably. But it's still a terrible business . . .' He went quiet again and looked quizzically at Campbell.

'He was very good, sir. I mean at his job. And everybody liked him.' Campbell wasn't sure if the captain's silence was meant as an invitation to provide some sort of obituary for his assistant. The captain remained silent. 'I don't know much about his next of kin.'

'Interestin' question,' said the first lieutenant.

'Quite,' said the captain. 'Doctor . . . I wonder if you'd . . . um . . . noticed anything about Smith.'

'What sort of thing, sir?'

'Over the last few months . . .'

'Not particularly, sir. But I'm not sure what you mean.'

'Oh, anything out of character . . .' The captain sat watching, and might have noticed a flicker of worry. It had occurred to Campbell that people who acted out of character and were subsequently found dead sometimes turned out to have killed themselves. Had he missed a suicidal depression under his nose, within his own miniscule department? He thought about this, then remembered something else: it was hard to kill yourself by fracturing your skull.

'Well, doctor?'

'I was wondering . . . if he'd had any particular reason for . . . killing himself, sir. If that's what happened.'

'Did he seem . . . worried . . . to you, doctor?'
'No, sir. Not really. Not particularly.'
'Not under any particular stress . . .'
'Shouldn't have thought so, sir.'
'And nothing odd about his work . . .'
'No, sir.'
'Nothing at all?'
'No, sir. Very good LMA in all respects.'
'Nothing odd, doctor.'
'No, sir.'
'Hobbies?'
'Sorry, sir. Hobbies?'
'Did he have any odd hobbies?'
'Not particularly, sir. Just the usual sailors' things. Read a bit. Didn't drink much. A bit of photography. I think he played the guitar in the mess deck, too.'
'Photography?'
'Yessir.'
'What sort of things?'
'Places we'd been. People on the ship . . . He's quite good, I think. He . . . used to do his own developing sometimes.'
'Much recently?'
It was clear that the captain was not thinking simply in terms of suicide. Campbell tried to remember the last time Smith had talked about his photography, or used the little darkroom *cum* laboratory other than for X-rays.
'Well,' said the captain. 'You can be thinking about that, doctor. If you remember anything that strikes you as important, just get in touch with me or number one. No one else. And I think number one's already told you that there'll be a full official enquiry in due course. People will come round and take statements. But meantime . . . um . . . discretion. All right, doctor?'
'Sir.' It sounded like the end of the interview. Campbell started to get up out of his armchair. The captain and first lieutenant got up, too. The captain opened the door, smiled the smile of weary politeness, and nodded Campbell out.
Halfway down the first companionway, Campbell remembered that, according to plans just divulged, he was due to leave the colony in less than forty-eight hours, and had not

yet told the commanding officer, the first lieutenant or the supply officer, all of whom, for a variety of reasons, needed to know. The proposed enquiry was an added complication. If it were to take place in Hong Kong and Campbell's presence were required he would either have to stay on or come back to attend it. Both possibilities translated readily into a mitigation of the fate delivered that afternoon, and the prospect of more time with Joan.

In his cabin he washed and cleaned his teeth. There was no obvious reason for not going back to Joan, except that it was four o'clock in the morning. Permission was not required, though Campbell had a feeling that if he requested it it would be refused. He decided that he'd definitely like to see Joan. He put on some socks and left the stethoscope lying on his bunk then went up to the quarterdeck. Able Seaman McGuffy now presided at the desk. Campbell asked him if he had the number of a taxi rank.

'One-just-outside-the-main-gate-sir,' said McGuffy in an unaccustomed spurt of military efficiency, dialling the number as he spoke. 'Be-roon-here-in-just-a-minute.'

'Thank you very much, Able Seaman McGuffy.'

'Don't-mention-it-sir . . . Oh . . . um. Taxi-for-the-medical-officer-of-*Winchester*. Chop chop. Attaboy.' He put the phone down. Campbell waited with McGuffy under the canvas awning. On the water outside the basin the black shadow of a junk passed on its way, its engine spluttering in the night. It was cooler now. A rich, mixed sea-and-city smell, laced with fuel oil, filled the air.

'Nice, innit, sir?'

'A change from Pompey . . . Quiet?'

'Mainly, sir . . . Apart from . . .'

'Of course . . . and . . .'

'Yessir.'

'Bit of bad luck, you getting duty first night in.'

'No' worried, sir. Got the weekend ashore. So Ah'm no' bothered. And the wife's come oot.'

'Oh, good . . . How is she?'

McGuffy's face brightened. 'Smashin', sir. Got a nice wee flat. Wean's doin' fine an' a'.'

'I'm pleased to hear it.' Campbell, who was still a little

uneasy with the Navy's expectation of officer–man conversations, sounded more pompous than he had meant to, but McGuffy did not appear to mind.

'Hear you're leavin', sir.'

Campbell looked around for the approaching taxi. McGuffy did not press him for a response, but explained, 'Mate o' mine's a killick in the *Tenebris* Sickbay, sir. Tells me we were lucky to have you as long as we did, sir.'

'Really?'

'Be sorry tae see ye go, sir.'

'Oh . . . Thank you, McGuffy. Kind of you to say so.'

A red Mercedes taxi drew up, and Campbell went ashore, saluting the quarterdeck and saluted, with particular smartness, by AB McGuffy.

Joan came sleepily to the door in her dressing gown and put her arms round Campbell as soon as he stepped inside.

'I was beginning to think things, David.'

'What sort of things?'

'Awful things . . . But you're here. Gosh. Your ears are cold. What was it?'

'Ghastly . . . and sort of hush-hush. Number one jumping up and down saying "need to know, need to know". And with luck it might keep me here a bit longer.'

'That's nice.'

'Just might. And it was pretty ghastly.'

She looked at him as though she expected him to tell her. He did not, and she did not press him.

'What about a drink?'

'It's practically breakfast time.'

'You look shattered.'

'I am a bit. Yes please. Small-small G and T.'

Joan smiled and said, 'Okay sah,' in LEP English, then, in her own voice, 'I'll bring it to you in bed.'

'Can I have a quick shower first?'

'Yes. If you're quiet.'

'I'll try not to sing.'

'You know what I mean . . .'

'I think so. Is young *Penningham* here?'

'He usually is. So don't wake them. I'll get you a towel.'

After his shower Campbell dried himself thoroughly, especially his hair. Joan sat watching him, holding his drink. 'I hope they keep you here,' she said, sipping it.

'So do I . . . I like it here. And I fancy you something rotten.'

She smiled at him over the top of the glass. 'If I let myself go . . . I could just about fancy you. Hurry up.'

They went back to bed. From the tangle of preliminaries Joan detached herself momentarily to adjust an alarm clock. 'I'm giving us an extra twenty minutes, seeing it's you and you're tired.'

Next morning at 8.15 Campbell, in a fresh white uniform that made him look much better than he felt, knocked at the first lieutenant's cabin door.

'Come in!'

'Doctor, sir.'

'Ah, doc. Take a pew. Wanted a word with you . . .' He was brisk and almost jolly, his normal better self. He sat at his desk, in his bright, tidy cabin. The events of the night blurred momentarily on the edge of unreality, more nightmare than fact. It was morning and the medical officer was visiting the first lieutenant, as he frequently did, and all was as though nothing untoward had happened, except that there was a dead LMA lying in the sickbay awaiting a post-mortem. That was the first item on Campbell's agenda. The second was the matter of his posting, and how it might be delayed. Campbell sat down.

'Thanks for comin' up, doc. Where did my lad find you?'

'He . . . didn't, sir . . . I didn't know you'd sent someone to look for me, sir.'

'Ah, of course. Resident ashore, weren't you?'

'Yessir.'

'I'd forgotten about that. Not to worry. Anyway, point is, gotta lot more questions for you this morning . . . I think father'd like to see you, too, so I'll just give 'im a buzz.' He cranked an old-fashioned telephone above his desk. 'Sir . . .

Number one speaking. Got the doc. He'd gone back ashore, sir . . . Sir.' He put the phone down. 'Right, doc. We'll just pop next door . . .'

The captain's door was open. He was sitting at his bureau with a pen in his hand. There was a half-empty cup of coffee among his papers. He looked as if he had not been to bed since Campbell had last seen him. He stood up and ushered them in, then, with a minimum of ceremony, all three sat down, in the same seats as for their previous interview. There was now no question of it all having been simply a bad dream.

'Doctor . . . I suppose you've heard by now . . .' The captain was looking closely at Campbell, perhaps as though by doing so he could make his meaning more obvious and spare himself the painful effort of explicitly stating something unpleasant. Campbell could think of nothing that fitted the bill except his posting to Chatham. It was possible, indeed likely, that, with appropriate omissions, Surgeon Commander Watson had passed on a version to the command of *Winchester*.

'Yessir.'

'And how did it strike you?'

'Bit of a surprise, sir. But I suppose really only to be expected.'

'Expected, doctor?' The captain's face changed, as though he had just found something he had been looking for for some time. Campbell glanced at the first lieutenant, whose facial expression was in the general area of I-told-you-so, though somewhat slower off the mark than the captain's. Campbell watched with some surprise while number one got up, opened the door and checked the passageway for eavesdroppers.

'Well, yes, sir. I gather it was on the cards.' Campbell was now quite unsure as to how safe it was to assume that they were talking about the same thing.

'So it wasn't a surprise,' said the captain slowly.

'I suppose not, sir. These things happen. Of course, I'm sorry to be leaving *Winchester*.'

'The captain shot a glance to the first lieutenant, who now looked puzzled.

'Sorry, sir,' said Campbell. 'I'm not sure what . . .'

'Leaving, doctor?'

'Yessir. The PMO from *Tenebris* came down yesterday . . . I've got a UK posting, sir. Fairly soon.'

The captain looked utterly defeated. He then said, 'Not quite what I was thinking of . . . But leaving, are you?'

'It seems so, sir. Although I did wonder about . . . the enquiry into the business last night . . .' Campbell saw no harm in making his point early, given that an opportunity offered itself. 'They've got me down for a flight tomorrow, sir. Then Chatham Sickbay.'

'Chatham,' said the captain faintly, as though Campbell had said, 'Ulan Bator.'

'I heard only yesterday, sir. And I thought that was what you were asking about.'

'Let's start again,' said the captain. 'Um . . . Number one . . . Perhaps . . .'

'Sir,' said the first lieutenant, leaving. The captain stood up and walked across to a porthole. Morning sun lit his face in profile. When he turned round again he looked pale and tired. 'Feel like some coffee, doctor?'

'Thank you, sir.'

He rang a bell and a steward appeared. 'Coffee, please, leading steward. Two cups.' The leading steward swooped on the cup among the papers and carried it off. The captain went for a little walk among his furniture while Campbell sat waiting, briefly permitting himself the luxury of thinking of nothing but the moist tingling afterglow of Joan that lingered pleasantly still, inside his starched white shorts.

The captain sat down, in an armchair this time, not facing Campbell but slightly to one side. There was a pause until the steward returned with two cups of coffee, then both sipped silently until the captain spoke. 'Doctor, you could be forgiven for thinking you'd got mixed up with a pretty odd bunch . . .'

'I don't think I quite understand, sir,' said Campbell with all the tact he could muster.

'Well, doctor, we haul you out of . . . your bed, to come and confirm that your assistant's dead, then ask you a lot of questions and don't tell you anything. Then we haul you back and ask you a lot more questions . . .'

'I'll do my best, sir.'

'And all the time you must be wondering . . .'

'. . . what's going on, sir.'

'Exactly,' said the captain. 'And to an extent so are we. So . . . if we might start by just thinking about Smith again for a moment . . . Any more?'

'More, sir?'

'Anything more about Smith? Did you remember anything that struck you as odd that you didn't remember last night? . . . For instance, there was his interest in photography. How did that first come to your notice?'

'Things he read, sir, when I joined. He usually had a book about photography on the go. And he took camera magazines.'

'Did you ever see his stuff?'

'Yessir.'

'How did it strike you?'

'Well, sir . . . Amateurish, really. Not very good. Grainy. Too light or too dark. But all right considering.'

'Considering what?'

'The darkroom, I suppose.'

'Did he spend a lot of time in there?'

'It's the lab as well, sir. So he was in and out all the time. And that's where the X-ray films were done.'

'Yes, yes. I see.'

'Was there some suggestion of something . . . fishy, sir?' Campbell's mind worked on the possibilities of camera-related naughtiness, and got no further than pornography, which was in any case freely available on board, ready made and in glowing colour. The captain looked troubled but remained silent. 'Doctor,' he said eventually. 'on quite another matter . . .'

'Sir?'

'And this is where you'll really start to wonder about what sort of people we are . . .'

'Sir?'

'I've been talking to a good number of people this morning, trying to get a little more background information about . . . a member of the wardroom. The people I've talked to so far haven't been able to tell me much . . . but someone did say that you might be able to help a bit. Trouble is, you see . . . Ken's disappeared . . . Yes. Bit of a surprise.'

Campbell put his coffee down in case there were any more surprises coming. 'When, sir? When did he . . . disappear?'

'Well. Shall we say he . . . wasn't around yesterday. And was absent from place of duty today . . . And the reason that I've asked you to come up . . . for a chat . . . is simply that we really don't seem to be very clear about Ken at all. And someone said he kept having . . . chats with you, doctor.'

Campbell tried to think how many times Ken had talked to him about coming along for a chat, and how few were the occasions on which he had actually managed it. 'For instance,' said the captain, 'I know you had a session with him after the little dinner on Beira. And no doubt on many other occasions . . . from what I gather.'

'Well, sir . . .'

'Funny old business,' said the captain. 'Think you know someone and when it really matters you find out you don't. Seen it before. Middie blew his brains out in DTS when I was a cadet. Everyone thought he was a normal sort of chap, in with some other crowd. You know the way it happens.'

'Yessir.'

'So . . . we were rather wondering . . . if you'd noticed anything odd about Ken lately.' The captain sounded apologetic.

Gruesome images of another acquaintance cold, wet and dead slowed Campbell's answer.

'Well, doctor?'

'Has . . . something happened?'

'We don't know, doctor. He wasn't around yesterday, and he isn't around this morning. It's a bit worrying.'

'Especially after Smith, sir,' said Campbell.

'Quite. So . . . is there anything you can think of . . . that might help, doctor?'

'A bit difficult, sir . . .'

'Confidentiality, doctor? I think in the circumstances . . .'

'I wasn't thinking of that, sir. It's just that . . . I don't really know him, sir. I don't know who thought I did . . . But it was probably only because he kept talking about coming to see me. Rather than actually doing it, I mean. I've hardly ever talked to him for any length of time, and when I did he was a bit . . . guarded . . . bitter, even, sir. The rest of the time he just made conversation. Chatted about this and that. In fact he thought we'd met somewhere before I joined, but I don't remember that. We just talked about . . . nothing, usually. Usual wardroom stuff . . .'

'Did you notice anything odd about him, doctor?'

'Only what you know already, sir. That he kept everyone at a bit of a distance. And the business on Beira . . . made it a bit difficult for everybody.'

'So I gather. How did he take it? So far as you know.'

'He seemed . . . Well, sir, it was difficult because as you probably remember I was on the board that . . . was convened. So he was touchy . . . a bit bitter, really, when I went to see him.' The captain sat listening, so determinedly blank that Campbell had to go on. 'And I wondered for a while if he were . . . a bit depressed. As a cause rather than as a result of that business with the SBs . . . so I saw him a couple of times after that, and since he was all very business-as-usual, and seemed to be getting over it, I didn't . . . do anything about it. In the way of treatment. He seemed all right.' The captain continued to sit silently. 'And as you probably know, sir, he'd had one or two problems on the home front . . . I'm not sure what happened, but things looked poor for his marriage . . . I think his wife actually left.'

'More coffee, doctor?' said the captain, after another studied pause.

'Thank you, sir.'

They waited while the steward came in, filled their cups and left. Campbell wondered if he had said too much on a subject about which he knew little, and wondered also if what he had said wasn't already for the most part familiar to the CO. If half the wardroom had been interrogated this morning (starting at what hour?) on the subject of Ken's problems, it was unlikely that Campbell was adding much to the picture.

The captain looked thoughtfully at his coffee spoon. 'I'd be most reluctant to . . . put you in a difficult position *vis à vis* confidential information, doctor, but it would be perhaps very helpful to know . . . if, to your knowledge, Ken had been . . . possibly drinking . . . a little more than the rest of you down there . . . Any ideas?'

'Very difficult to say, sir . . . Perhaps when he was . . . most worried about things, he might have been having a drink to help get to sleep . . . But I doubt if that was for any length of time, sir.'

'I see . . . I see . . .' There was another compelling silence. This time, having gone too far already, Campbell said nothing. The captain shook his head and put down his cup. 'You know, the crazy thing is that Ken could just roll up the gangway with a bit of a sore head and some story about meeting a friendly native and we could forget about all the nastier possibilities and try to be a bit more . . . helpful in future.'

'I hope so, sir.'

'So do I, doctor. D'you know if he had any worries about money?'

'No, sir.'

'His wife had a job, I believe,' said the captain distantly. 'Big mortgage. Might have been tough going on one salary. But he never mentioned that to you . . . in one of your little chats, did he?'

'No, sir.'

'Ah, well. Let's just hope he turns up.'

'Yessir.'

'And you're leaving us, doctor.'

'Yessir.' Campbell would have found the autocratic vagaries of his captain's conversational style fairly taxing even after a good night's sleep. 'Yessir. The PMO from *Tenebris* told me yesterday.'

'There was something about it among the signals this morning. Bit sudden, but I'm afraid your branch is like that.' The captain smiled. 'We're most grateful to you for all you've done . . . When's your flight?'

'Tomorrow afternoon, sir.'

'Well, why not come up and see me tomorrow morning. We can have a chat. And I hope all these ghastly events will have sorted themselves out. D'you know anyone in Chatham?'

'I don't think so, sir.'

'Lot of pussers in Chatham . . . You might enjoy it. Anyway, we can talk about that tomorrow . . . Oh. Just one other thing, doctor. Very useful suggestion of yours about the British Military Hospital. They came almost at once. Thank you.'

'Sir. Officer of the day, HMS *Winchester*, speaking.'

'Henry?'

''sright, doc. You must think I've got into the habit of rotting you up.'

'Could be, Henry.'

'No panic this time. And it's only just gone ten o'clock. So not to be cross. And I know routine medical stuff goes to *Tenebris* . . .'

'What is it, Henry?'

'Request for the medical officer to see someone in detention, sir.'

'Isn't that one for *Tenebris*?'

'A bit special, sir.'

'Who is it, Henry?'

'Ken.'

'A prisoner?'

''sright, doc.'

'When did he turn up?'

'Ages ago. Ten this morning, I suppose.'

'And why's he a prisoner?'

'Well, he's sort of under guard . . . Officers and gentlemen and all that. Might spend the night in the slammer, though. We don't know yet.'

'Why's he under guard, Henry?'

'Because the patrol found him.'

'What was he doing?'

'Trying to look inconspicuous in a cinema queue of five hundred little Chinamen.'

'But . . .'

'Might be easier to discuss when you get back on board. Number one says take a taxi and charge it to Andrew. I think he meant quite soon, sir.'

'Right, Henry.'

'Sorry, doc. Again.'

Campbell put the phone down and went back to the bedroom. 'What was all that about?' Joan asked.

Campbell burst out laughing. 'They're all mad. And they're determined we're not going to get all night in. Shouldn't take long, though . . . Sounds a bit odd. Officer in the rattle.'

'One of yours? *Winchester*?'

''fraid so. And Henry thinks the first lieutenant meant quite soon.'

'Oh, David.' Campbell sat down on the bed. Joan's hand tiptoed up his spine on two fingers. 'I want a proper cuddle now, and promise you'll come back as soon as you can.'

'All right.'

'That doesn't sound very keen.'

'Sorry. It's really odd. Ken's in the rattle. And Henry's not saying much on the phone. And he's been there since ten this morning, so it's not just dead-drunk-and-will-he-live-doc, like most calls to cells.'

'Well,' said Joan, 'get dressed, go and sort it out and come straight back to me.' She smiled. 'We can start again where we left off.'

Campbell laughed, kissed her and stood up. 'I'll try to remember where we'd got to. And wait for me.'

Joan said primly, 'I'll read a book.'

'Official Secrets Act, generally speakin', doc. Not to worry about the details. That's someone else's job. And he decided quite early on today to do what he could to make it easy for everybody. So he spent most of the afternoon makin' a statement to the *Tenebris* security blokes. And he's going home tomorrow on the same plane as you. Plead guilty. Quiet little trial. Might get ten years. Time off for bein' good, 'e'll be out before 'e's thirty. Silly bugger. Anyway, wants to see you, doc, and I don't mind. Only one thing though . . . the Smith business is still need to know. Right?'

'Sir.'

'So you can go down now . . . MAA Flower's with 'im. I've told 'im you're on your way, and 'e'll just poke off and leave you to it. Our friend 'll probably natter on a bit. Been very talkative all day. Take your time if you think it's doin' him any good . . . Friendly visit'll steady 'im for the next bit. When London gets 'im.'

'Sir.'

'And you're all right for tomorrow, doc?'

'Just about, sir. Seeing the CO at eleven. Details all fixed for the flight. Reporting to Kaitak at 1500.'

'That's three of you goin' from Winnie. His nibs, Reggie as escort, and you. Bit of company, if you don't mind convicts.'

'I . . . wondered about the enquiry into . . . Smith's accident, sir.'

'Shouldn't worry about that if I were you, doc.'

'I gather BMH took over . . .'

'That's right . . . What's this about your draft? Some nonsense in the Madhouse?'

'Something like that, sir.'

'Mainly mad Irishmen, the medical admirals, aren't they?'

'I really wouldn't know, sir.'

'Anyway, quicker you see 'im the quicker you can get back ashore.'

'Sir.'

'And by the way, doctor, for the purposes of this exercise, Smith's alive and well and livin' in the guardroom. Right?'

'Yessir.'

Campbell went down to the wardroom cabin flat and knocked on Ken's door. 'Come in.' Ken's voice was normal, perhaps even cheerful. The door opened a foot or so and stuck. There were shuffling noises inside and the door opened further. The master at arms, in white shirt, black trousers and a huge gleaming cummerbund, loomed large in the cabin. He stood loosely to attention as Campbell squeezed in. There was a half-finished game of cribbage on the bureau.

'Ah, doc,' said Ken.

'I'll leave you, sir,' said MAA Flower. 'I'll not be far off . . .'

'Thank you, master,' said Campbell, sensing somehow

that, as the senior undisgraced officer, he was in charge.

'If you just let me know when you've finished, sir,' said the MAA, still hovering. Campbell nodded, then the master did an 'eyes front', with his chin up, his thumbs pointing down the seams of his trousers and his feet at the prescribed angle of ninety degrees. He eased sideways through the doorway, leaving Campbell alone with Ken.

'Have a seat, doc.'

The little cabin was warm and humid, and the proffered seat hot from its previous occupant.

'Was it a drag to come down?' Ken sounded cheerful still, but more precariously so.

'Not at all.'

'Thanks,' said Ken. 'I appreciate it . . . I . . .' He hesitated. 'I wanted a chat with you.'

'So number one said.'

'I expect you've talked to one or two people since . . . I rejoined the ship.'

'Been kind of busy today . . . But had a brief word with number one.'

'Is he still upset?'

'Sort of, I gather.'

'Father was the worst. "Such a disappointment for all of us, and a betrayal of yourself as much as of your country." Blush-making stuff.' He stopped, leaving Campbell speculating.

'Number one mentioned the Official Secrets Act . . .'

'You don't know, doctor?' Ken brightened. 'You haven't heard? How I ignored the warning signs, put self before country . . . and will pay the full penalty of the law?'

'No, Ken. Not really.'

'Oh . . . I thought everyone would know.'

'It's probably being kept need to know.'

'Oh. Perhaps. But I can tell you, doc, can't I?'

'If you want, I suppose.'

'Shock secrets probe? How a betrayed husband betrayed his country? Plight of lovelorn naval officer? You haven't heard?'

'No, Ken.'

'Soviet sailor-spy trapped as officer flees?'

'Oh.'

There were rivulets of sweat on Ken's brow, and on his cheeks, running into his beard and moustache. He grinned across the cribbage set at Campbell. 'Thought you'd be interested, doc.'

'Of course. I see.'

'But you didn't spot him, doc, did you? And of course I never came for our little chat. If I had done, I suppose I'd be going home anyway, to help put him in the slammer.'

'How did it happen, Ken?'

Ken became more, but not entirely, serious. 'Doc, would you believe, it's just like those heavy cautionary films they show us. It could happen to anyone. Well, anyone with worries to spare and a money problem. And your lad's bloody clever.' He grinned and giggled. 'Shouldn't say your lad, doc. He's Ivan's, through and through. But he worked for you as part of working for Ivan, if you see what I mean. Clever lad. He'd be a colonel in the KGB if it weren't for me . . . Drink, doctor?'

'No thanks, Ken.'

'You look a bit seedy.'

'You still keep it in your cabin?'

'Still have my private sherbet cupboard. Haven't had one today though. Mind you I haven't got a lot to behave myself for now . . . You sure?'

'Oh . . . Yes thanks. Small one, Ken.'

Ken got up and knelt to rummage in his shoe locker. 'Toothglass or teacup?'

'Just a small one. In the glass would be fine.'

Ken's hand shook as he poured the whisky.

'Cheers.'

'Cheers.'

'Here's to the mercy of the court I'm going to throw myself on . . . Might not be too much of this stuff where I'm going,' he added thoughtfully, 'but number one reckons it'll only be for a couple of years, seeing they got Smith.'

A silent alarm rang in Campbell's head. Ken looked down at his whisky. 'Nice of you to drop by, doc. I still feel I can talk to you. You . . . did your best before.'

'On Beira?'

'Unfortunately, it was too late by then.'

'Too late?'

'I'd helped a little too much.'

'With . . . Smith's other work?'

'That sort of thing . . . He's very clever, you know. Knows just when and how hard to push. And he was even quite nice when things fell apart and we had to shut the shop.'

'Shut the shop?'

'Close down the business. Documents for photography. Terms strictly cash. You may recall doctor, that on the day of the Donkey Derby I lost much of my value to those whom, in my folly, I had elected to help. So he shut the shop. Went clean. Nothing on him after Mauritius. Carried on playing in the darkroom with smudgy snaps of jolly jack to keep up appearances, but we really did close down the business. If I hadn't . . . re-awakened interest . . . he'd have been good for another twenty years. On two paypackets. One in roubles.'

'Bloody hell,' said Campbell, shaking his head.

'And majors get quite a lot of roubles, I believe.'

'He was a good LMA.'

'Take my word for it, doc, he was even better at the rest. And very cool when things went wrong on Beira.'

Perhaps because of the whisky, Campbell remembered the mess dinner, then he remembered Smith's nocturnal cleaning spree in the laboratory. 'I see.'

'So I was a bit surprised when he was . . . as indiscreet as he appears to have been.'

A few more alarm bells urged caution on Campbell's part. He listened. Ken went on 'Legging it and getting caught, I mean. But I suppose I forced it on him. "Ask not what your country can do for you, but what you can do for your country." Doc, the worse for him the better for me, right?'

'How do you mean?'

'Well, big trial. Master spy nabbed by watchful Navy. He gets twenty years, I get five or so for being silly. Won't I, doc?' Ken's whisky cup was shaking. 'I mean to say, he's a professional. Big league. And they got him because of me.'

If the first lieutenant wanted to pretend that Smith was alive, and Ken believed that, Campbell was not going to be the one to contradict either of them. 'I don't know, Ken,' he said.

'Any idea where they've got him, doc?'

'Don't know . . . I suppose that's need to know as well.'

Campbell felt very uncomfortable, but sat while Ken loosened up on the whisky and talked about his aberration and its consequences. 'Lay low in Wanchai last night . . . Nice girl, actually. Then wondered about looking in on the Russian trade mission. Wasn't sure which way to jump. Was going off to have a think about it in a kung fu movie when the lads saw me. "Sir," they said. "Sir." '

Through the whisky Campbell tried to work things out. If Ken thought Smith were alive and in custody, he had every reason to tell people the whole story, and conversely, if he had found out soon enough that Smith was dead, he could have bluffed his way through any number of questionings, knowing that his accomplice or mentor or whatever had cleaned up after himself and was now silent forever. And anyone can go on a binge first night in and go adrift.

Ken rambled on, and Campbell sat and tried to work out a few more of the connections and possibilities: what Ken had been told about Smith, by whom and when; what evidence, if any, had linked the ex-security officer to the dead LMA (other than the fact that they had both caused problems within one day of arriving in Hong Kong); and what more would be elicited from Ken when 'London' got him.

'The money was what clinched it,' said Ken. 'Silly, isn't it? Usual reason, they say. Blackmail's old hat and no one's a communist these days. But which of us could really say no to a spot of the ready if we really needed it. And I did. Because of her. And a nice house I wanted to hang on to.' He grinned. 'Pathetic, isn't it, doc?' Campbell said nothing. Ken talked about his mortgage.

Shortly after half past eleven Campbell got up to leave. Ken clutched his arm and fell to drunken weeping. Campbell listened to his sobbing, chilled with the pointless nastiness of it all: loneliness, betrayal, imprisonment, death. He sat a little longer, calming Ken by listening to him, then made him wash his face, and handed him back to MAA Flower, who, before rejoining his cribbage opponent in the hot little cabin, mouthed to Campbell the word 'cells'. As Campbell sat in an air-conditioned taxi purring up the hill to Mid-Level, it was as if he was escaping to a rational world from a nightmare of weakness, cruelty and deception. He undressed and crept gratefully into bed beside Joan.

'David,' she said, 'you've been drinking.'

At one minute to eleven the next morning, Campbell, in uniform, with his better hat in his hand, stood outside the captain's door. He had cleared his cabin, and most of his things were packed already. He had to see father for farewell noises, make a few more duty visits round the ship, finish packing, attend something called a *vin d'honneur* laid on by the wardroom to mark his departure and remain sober enough to be taken by Joan to the airport for three o'clock. Of these tasks, the last might prove the most difficult, he thought as he waited. At eleven precisely he knocked.

'Come in.'

'Sir.'

'Good of you to come up, doctor. You know about these things?' He handed Campbell a small envelope with his name and rank on the front. 'Your 206. That's actually just the flimsy.'

'I beg your pardon, sir?'

'Oh. Sort of report on you. Says you're a decent chap. Get one of these each time you're posted. And annually, of course.'

'Oh. Thank you, sir.'

'Please have a seat, doctor.'

'Thank you, sir.'

'Enjoyed *Winchester*?'

'Yessir.'

'Apart from the last couple of days, I suppose.'

'Yessir.'

'Looking forward to getting home.'

'Yessir.'

'All packed up and ready to go?'

'Yessir.'

'Piece of luck running into your . . . girlfriend here.'

'Yessir.'

'And you're enjoying naval life?'

'Yessir.'

'Jolly interesting, isn't it?'

'Yessir.'

'That was . . . all very unfortunate about Smith.'

Campbell fought down a brisk 'Yessir' and said instead, 'I'm still not exactly clear what happened, sir.' The captain looked a little surprised, the easy rhythm of their conversation having been disrupted. He paused, then said, 'A viper, shall we say, in the bosom of the Navy . . . One or two have turned up over the last twenty years. Even since modified vetting procedure . . . It makes one wonder how many . . . haven't turned up'.

'I gather he was some sort of spy, sir.'

'To put it mildly,' said the captain.

'I know it's not really . . . my part of ship, sir,' said Campbell, using a thoroughly naval expression to help his question along, 'but I did wonder . . . how it broke, sir.'

'What broke, doctor?'

'What happened, sir, to spark off recent events.'

'No harm in telling you a bit, I suppose, doctor. Might even stop you thinking we're entirely stupid. You've already had a chat with Ken?'

'Yessir.'

'And he told you roughly what they'd been up to?'

'Yessir.'

'And he still thinks Smith is . . . helping with our enquiries?'

'Yessir.'

'That was number one's idea. Downy old bird, number one. Had Ken on his own for ten minutes as soon as he came on board. Ken never looked back. Remarkable . . .'

'And Smith, sir?'

'Ah, yes. Smith.' The captain sounded as if he were trying to recall one of his father's under-gamekeepers. 'Still slightly up in the air.' It was a turn of phrase which Campbell would not have used in the circumstances. The captain resumed, rather distantly, 'We might have been under slightly more obligation to have an enquiry if he'd been . . . one of our own chaps. Now it rather looks as if there isn't going to be one. But there's no particular reason for your not knowing what we think happened to . . . your assistant. There was a diving accident.'

'Oh.'

'He was leaving the ship, and Henry's divers were waiting to arrest him. And there was a diving accident.'

'I see.'

'Number one's idea. Again. "Might try a McGuffy," he said. "Dives, doesn't 'e?" ' The captain sounded slightly self-conscious in his mimicry of the first lieutenant. 'He must have been worried when Ken disappeared. But we didn't really have anything to hang on him. So we panicked him.' The captain smiled modestly. 'That was my idea. We sort of faked an urgent draft to Portsmouth for him. Number one gave it to him last night. Told him he'd get the plane home today. Make him think we had something on him even though we didn't really. Quite pleased at how it turned out. Reading spy novels on Beira wasn't such a waste of time.' The captain, rather enjoying himself, stopped suddenly. 'But it's fairly serious. Some quite sensitive stuff probably went over the side in Mauritius. So Ken might have a tough time with the courts. Miserable business, really. And as usual the fleet security chaps'll make us all sweat, now it's too late. Lots of lessons for all of us, they'll say. But it's always just the same lesson over and over again. The other lot are very good. Unfortunately . . . Well, doctor, been a pleasure having you on board with us.'

'Thank you, sir. I've really enjoyed . . . most of it . . . Sir?'

'Yes, doctor.'

'Sir, might I ask . . . what was it that made you think of Smith at all when Ken disappeared?'

The captain smiled. 'I thought we'd finished with that . . . But since you ask, it was quite a small thing. Ronnie's chinamen. One of the wardroom stewards noticed Smith in the wardroom cabin flat several times in the week we left Beira. Once coming out of Ken's cabin. A bit funny, he thought, with a commissioned MO on board. And when Ken bolted the LEP mentioned it to Ronnie . . . Doctor, I'm afraid you'll have to accept my apologies . . . Shan't make it to your *vin d'honneur*. Got a security meeting in *Tenebris*.' The captain smiled, this time sheepishly. Campbell left.

After lunch, as sober as could reasonably be expected, Campbell went down to the sickbay to tidy up a few last things. He filed some loose medical documents so that his successor would find everything in order, and cleared out the locked drawer in the desk. Most of the items in it merited no better fate than the waste paper basket, and he wondered why he'd not ditched them right away instead of storing them. One or two things proved more interesting. There was the letter from Mr Gillon, and, right at the back of the drawer, a buff-and-purple striped card marked 'Purple-Area Temporary Pass'. Looking at it and remembering the security check at *Nemesis*, Campbell remembered also the threat of some dire penalty for the unlawful possession of such a card. He was standing wondering what to do about it when there was a knock at the door.

'Come in.'

'Sir.' The master at arms eased himself into the sickbay.

'Master.'

'Glad I caught you, sir.' The most senior non-commissioned member of the ship's company had had his usual generous lunch, and was comfortably aglow with rum. 'I just wanted to say, from the senior rates, sir, that you've done a fine job.'

'Thank you, master,' said Campbell, slipping the buff and purple card into his pocket.

'It's just a pity you're not taking the two of them home with you, sir.' Campbell must have looked thoughtful, even puzzled, because he did not immediately grasp what the master was talking about. 'I realize, sir,' MAA Flower went on, 'that there are obviously certain aspects of your work that you can't talk about . . .'

'Quite,' said Campbell, thinking among other things of the first lieutenant's medical problem.

'But we think you did a first rate job . . .' The master was swaying slightly. 'You know, sir,' he said with sudden animation, 'I knew as soon as I set eyes on you you wasn't a proper doctor . . . But when I realized the security aspect . . .'

Campbell looked with surprise at the master, who reacted as though reproached. 'Sorry, sir. All that's need to know, I appreciate, and you won't want to talk about it . . . Anyway, sir. Best of luck with your next assignment . . .'

'Thank you very much, master.'

'Goodbye, sir, and good luck.'

'Goodbye, master.'

The master lurched out. Campbell took the security pass from his pocket, tore it into tiny pieces and flushed them down the loo. Joan was due to pick him up in ten minutes to take him to the airport.